THE FIVE-CENT GANG

John I Leggett

※ ※ ※ ※ ※

www.johnleggettbooks.com

ISBN-13: 978-1502468994
ISBN-10: 1502468999

A DeWitt Studio Publication

Printed in the U.S.A.

For K—

The woman I love, and my most tactful critic!

Regardless of where you are—
if you wait long enough—
and listen hard enough—
sooner or later you'll hear a train.
— J. I Leggett

CONTENTS

THE
FIVE-CENT
GANG

The Bridge

The nightmares are less frequent now, but occasionally I still see the face of the fat man. An unforgettable face marred by the purplish hue of a birthmark that covered half his forehead and continued downward to surround his left eye and spilled onto a portion of his cheek.

The first time he questioned me, his voice held the tone of mean gravel. He was fat and he demonstrated to me that all fat people are not good-natured.

He breathed heavily—breathing accompanied by wheezes and coughs. When he came into The Pit that day, I saw his revolver. It was holstered on the rear of his belt and against his enormous backside, it looked like a little kid's gun.

I held it once. We all did, when it came into the possession of The Five-Cent Gang. We passed it among us with reverence.

But the fat man, the gun, all of it brings back memories of the bridge. And now, seeing a bridge...any bridge...brings forth images of the satchel, the rope, and the hunting knife—reminders of that terrible day when things went wrong and mistakes were made that we never expected. After all, our crime was planned with, what we thought, great attention to detail. It was certainly planned as well as a gang of twelve-year-olds could plan such a thing.

And now the occasional nightmares start in the dead hours of early morning with me clinging to a rope and the fat man pulling me upward...toward him. He stands in his sweat-soaked shirt with short sleeves that only cover the top of his stubby arms. I can still see his short little fingers. The joints are fat, and connected, and look like miniature marshmallows. I hear his curses and feel the huge drops of his August sweat drip and fall on my hands and the back of my neck and the top of my head.

After the bridge thing, men died, one from a stroke—the stroke of a baseball bat—and another from lead poisoning or, to be more precise, two .22 caliber bullets to the back of his skull.

After the killings The Five-Cent Gang kept the secret of the bridge and the events that followed. They're incidents we rarely discuss among ourselves and *never* with anyone outside the gang...until now. I think it's been long enough, although, as Dusty once reminded Al, "There ain't no statute of limitations on what we did, man."

But someone has to tell the story and hopefully, telling it will end my nightmares. Something has to help because since that day on the bridge, the memory continues to bring sweat to my brow, drain the blood from my head, and strike fear in my heart. It was the incident on the bridge that pulled all our worlds into years of chaos and confusion. Before I get to that, however, it is important that you know how we came to be on the bridge that day and how the Five-Cent Gang evolved. That's where my story begins.

Chapter One

As kids who were brought up in the early '50s, there were many disadvantages, or perhaps advantages, that we were oblivious to in our sheltered lives. Our black and white televisions were limited to three channels with erratic offerings, the internet had yet to be discovered, and without the technology of cell phones, we were forced to rely on battery-powered walkie-talkies with a range of ten to twenty feet.

I won't try to justify any of our misdeeds by claiming we were disadvantaged youths raised by alcoholic parents. Nor did we claw our way through life in a dirty inner city environment while we played in crime-ridden streets. It was quite the opposite. The city of Waterton was comprised of small neighborhoods that were nestled into a semi- rural area of upstate New York. Unlike Troy and Albany, which bordered us at the north and south ends, Waterton was a smaller, friendlier place. Avenues had presidential names, like Lincoln and Grant, or environmental names, like Mulberry and Riverside, to address the local color or serve as a proud reminder that Waterton bordered the Hudson River.

The avenues ran in one direction while logically numbered streets were their perpendicular counterparts. Only the locals saw these streets because anyone driving through Waterton would be forced to take US Route 32, the major thoroughfare that ran through our town. Travelers would not only get a scenic view of the Hudson but, in the heat of a summer day, would be made aware of its presence in a more aromatic sense that usually caused car windows to be rolled up until the completion of traversing the Congress Street bridge into Troy.

I lived in a section of Waterton known as Port Schuyler. The neighborhood was built into a hill that ran upward from Route 32 and my house was a two-story dwelling that my father and grandfather purchased together. Our family occupied the first floor and my grandparents lived above us. The house sat at the top of the hill and, even now, I can tell you the names of every family on both sides of the street. That's the way Waterton was. Everyone knew their neighbors and hollered friendly greetings across backyard fences. The families were so entwined that when I got home from school on days my mother worked, I could always grab an after-school snack from Mrs. Cavanaugh, our next-door neighbor.

The hill that led down to the main highway was steep and referred to by the locals as the front hill. The street that ran down the back side was not nearly as steep and adhering to form, was called the back hill.

Following winter snowfalls, families gathered on both hills for sledding. Kids and adults would band together as allies and throw snowballs at the sand truck when it eventually came around and interrupted our fun. Little kids and most of the parents used the back hill. The front side had been deemed too dangerous for sledding because once at the bottom, failure to turn onto the lawn of Mr. Murliss's house would send you onto the main highway into a steady stream of traffic. For my friends and me, the longer, faster ride of the steeper slope made it well worth the risk of possible death.

At the foot of the back hill, a left turn took you onto a rarely traveled side street to an area known as The Heights. The Heights was a nice way of saying "a bunch of apartments for old people."

Names like Port Schulyer and The Heights may be indicative to some of areas of affluence, but they were far from it. Ours was a lower-middle-class neighborhood that housed blue-collar workers. It was primarily because of the close family structures that none of us realized we were poor or that our parents often went without. Simply put, we were loved and because we were loved, we were happy in life and oblivious to our poverty.

I had three friends in the neighborhood and we all wore the ritualistic short-sleeved shirts with multicolored stripes dictated by the fashion of the '50s. When school let out for summer vacation, the four of us made the trip to Nunzi's Barber Shop to get crew cuts.

Our heroes were cowboys like Hopalong Cassidy, Roy Rogers, and the Cisco Kid. These were guys who would never draw first or shoot anyone in the back. Likewise, they would never fight dirty or throw the first punch. We were taught to hold doors for girls and to say "sir" and "ma'am" when responding to adults. In our cocoons of naivety, we never had an inkling that life would be anything more than going to school, playing with friends on weekends, and tramping through the nearby woods during our long-awaited school vacations. Within this carefree life, I sometimes wonder how we became involved in a crime that changed our lives and our pattern of day-to-day living.

Chapter Two

My name is August. Strange as that may sound, it could've been much worse. My mother always had an affinity for the stars and planets but preferred astrology over astronomy. My name, as well as the names of future siblings, was preordained in the time my mother referred to as B.C., which I later learned meant before conception. Each child in my family was to be named for the month in which he or she was born. So as odd as my name might seem to some, I realized, as I grew older, it far outweighed the other eleven possibilities.

"You should be thankful," my mother responded to my complaints. "If your father and I had made a connection on New Year's Eve instead of Thanksgiving, everyone would be calling you September. How would you like that? It seems to me you would prefer August. It's a fine name."

When friends and relatives visited, they also suffered from her interest in the stars by her persuasion to have their astrological charts done. She sat them at the kitchen table and, clad in a kerchief that sported stars and crescent moons, she informed them of the coming pitfalls in their lives and how to avoid them. My father never seemed to appreciate her love of the stars and made mention on more than one occasion that perhaps painting or some other hobby might be more enjoyable. On days her craft suffered any willing clientele, she lured my father into the bedroom to play chess.

"I think it's time for a game of chess," she would say. "I need to be checkmated." And then they retired to the bedroom.

It was during my fifth year of life when my Uncle Bob revealed to me that the whole chess thing was a hint for a connection, but neither of the words made any sense to me.

"They're kind of code words," Uncle Bob told me.

That made some sense as I often heard my mother's side of phone conversations. If I happened to be in the room, she would glance my way and then whisper to her phone friend that she and my father had had a connection the night before. Of course, I knew they had been playing chess that night and drew the obvious conclusion that the two were synonymous.

The older I got, however, the less chess they played. It was my Uncle Bob who phrased the coded explanation in a style of delicate terminology only he could conjure. We were sitting on the front porch at the time. He had just finished off his fourth or fifth swig from a small brown bottle he kept wrapped in a paper bag. After each swig, he took a few swallows from his soda can. He told me it was his favorite because it won the award for best soda in all the land. I knew he was telling me the truth because the can had the picture of the blue ribbon on it. He let me try it once but I didn't like it and wondered how it ever won any kind of a prize. Anyway, after several swigs from his paper bag bottle and the blue ribbon soda, he evidently felt a five-year-old was stable enough to accept any truth in life.

"Yep," he continued with his information regarding the secret code words. "Those first few years of marriage, oh boy, your mom and dad were fuckin' like rabbits!'"

Of course not knowing what *that* word meant, I simply thought my parents ate a lot of lettuce and carrots, which had nothing to do with playing chess. Until Uncle Bob's explanation, I always thought it was a game of fun and merriment. Once the game got underway, the sounds emitted from behind the bedroom door were those of laughter and silly giggling. I was anxious to learn the game but my mother told me I would have to wait until I got older. From Uncle Bob's description, it seemed acting like a rabbit and eating carrots behind closed doors was what chess was all about. I was more than willing to wait for the designated age. On the other hand, carrots were still strewn upon my dinner plate with regularity, which added more confusion to the rules.

Uncle Bob tried to clarify my confusion by pointing out that as married people got older they often tired of playing chess. Being so young, I failed to understand it was the reason I never got my long-awaited brother. This was upsetting because I wanted one in the worst way, an ally so to speak, and was even willing to tolerate a February or October if such was the timed result.

With no siblings, I took it upon myself to adopt kids from the neighborhood and spent my days with the Daly brothers, Alphonse and Julian, who lived in the house across the street, along with Dusty Barnes who lived down the back hill and was just a short bike ride away.

We all entered school together and my kindergarten teacher, obviously a woman more responsive than my parents to the needs of a five-year-old, changed August to Auggie, which was much more acceptable to me, and the name everyone continued to use. Everyone except Mr. Murdur, the school principal, who always called me Augustus. I wasn't sure if he didn't know my name or he thought it was sophisticated to have a student in his school with a more cosmopolitan title. Whenever he saw me in the hall, he always found someone to introduce me to—people who already knew me—like the janitor or the school nurse.

"Hey, Mr. Shannon, do you know my friend Augustus here?" he would ask. Of course Mr. Shannon then felt obligated to play along and shake my hand and for the rest of the day it smelled like fuel oil because he was always in the boiler room working on the furnace.

Like me, Alfonse and Julian had been given uncommon names by their parents and suffered a similar problem. I mean who would want to be named Alfonse or Julian? Hearing them announced like, "Hey, here comes Alfonse and Julian" left people to think they were either a sophisticated law firm or a clown act in the circus. Once again, our teacher came to the rescue and Alfonse was shortened to Al. Julian, on the other hand, didn't need any help from his teacher. He was two years older and had a tremendous physique. That alone gave him the authority to dictate to his peers that they were to call him Jules, and any other name would result in a punch to the arm.

Dusty Barnes, obviously had his nickname. He was always sitting in the dirt playing with his cars or soldiers. Anytime someone hit him in the fanny, dust flew everywhere.

The four of us were usually together and Dusty and I were often mistaken for brothers. We had the same hair, same eyes, and the same look of innocence. Once we discovered that look had many advantages, we practiced it and eventually developed a substantial repertoire of angelic expressions. On the other hand, Al and Jules didn't look at all like siblings.

Waterton was divided into two major sections—Port Schuyler and uptown. There was only one elementary school in our end of the city, and that was Public School Number One. Uptown housed Schools Three, Five, Seven, and Nine. We never knew what happened to the even numbers and Al was the only one who asked about them. So in School One, Al and Dusty and I were an inseparable trio and spent all day in the same classroom. As we progressed through each grade level, our daily antics further cemented the bonds of our three-kid camaraderie. Jules, being two grades ahead of us, joined us in the schoolyard during recess. Other than yard time, the four of us were together during our walks to and from school, which allowed for planning our after-school and weekend activities—things like baseball and fort building and bike riding.

Our classroom antics, while sometimes annoying, were certainly within the normal range of youthful behavior but, with each passing year, our teachers, having only one classroom per grade level, had no recourse other than to sit Al and Dusty and me as far from each other as possible.

Our class was a family that, once we entered kindergarten, traveled together on an educational journey. Other than an occasional transient, the same group of kids moved together like a cluster of germs on a microscope slide until graduation. At that point, we would don our homemade mortarboards, adorned with tassels of yarn, and march to the podium. Mr. Murdur would give each of us our diploma signifying our mastery of skills in preparation for the world that lay ahead.

Knowing our lives were planned for us until that day, we were a carefree and content, happy-go-lucky foursome, nestled in our quiet environment. We displayed the normal amount of mischievousness around the neighborhood and, like most kids, kept secrets from our parents.

We knew we had potential for greater things, but to realize our potential, one of us would be required to step forward and become a 'take-charge guy.' It seemed logical that a leader would elevate us to greater deeds of troublesome and annoying behavior, but being that leader was an unlikely hurdle for each of us.

Al was far from assuming any role of leadership. He was the unintentional comedian in the group and it was hard for us to take him seriously. He also spent too much time with fact-finding and seeking knowledge regarding trivial events to be a good leader. His appearance didn't help. His gawky frame gave him a giraffe-like walk, which accentuated a bobbing head and provided the look of a rooster pecking at food in the barnyard. His face was filled with an abundance of freckles and his dark head of hair always sported an oversized cowlick that sprouted up from the back of his head as if he were wearing a weed. Adding to his comedic appearance were his two slightly overlapping front teeth. The combination of all these things just didn't seem to be the characteristics of a serious leader.

To our classmates, Al was a likeable annoyance. Likeable because of his thought-provoking humor, but annoying because of his incessant questions. He always asked the teacher things at the most inopportune times. In our earlier grades, he interrupted readings of good stories to ask the dumb questions about the characters.

"If the riverbank was too far for the frog to jump from the log, why didn't he just swim to shore?" he asked in the middle of *Gaylord Learns to Leap* and,

"When Hansel and Gretel stuck the bone out of their cage to trick the witch, couldn't she tell there wasn't any skin on it?"

His questions continued, and when we advanced to grade four, they often had nothing to do with what was being read or discussed. He constantly interrupted the class as he blurted out whatever he was daydreaming about; questions like, "What would happen if two stars bumped into each other?" or "Do worms go to Heaven?"

He would ask these questions in the middle of a spelling test or during music class in the midst of a song. Annoying as they were, it sometimes seemed as if he was actually stumping the teacher. None of us had his genuine insight into such things and it became a daily ponderance as to what question would next emerge from his attention to detail or his distant thoughts. It was quite obvious that there was just no way Al could lead anyone anywhere.

Jules didn't have much to offer in the way of leadership, either. His two-grade-level advantage over the rest of us was reduced to one when an unfortunate event—primarily a lack of diligence in his schoolwork—caused him to be held back in grade three. This was no doubt a dilemma for the teacher and Mr. Murdur, who were involved in the decision making process. Although I was never privy to his academic capabilities, physically he was already the tallest boy in the class.

After breaking the disappointing news to his mother, his teacher sat him down at the end of the school year. "Jules," she began. "Each year I always ask one student to stay another year and help me out with the new class," she explained.

Jules was delighted and told her he would be happy to help her out and spend another year in the third grade. I'm not sure whether the other students in the class believed the story or, knowing Jules was bigger and tougher than they were, just pretended it was normal to keep a student back to assist the new kids.

The contrast in appearance between Al and Jules might leave a person to conclude that one of them was adopted. Jules was not only above average in size, but unlike Al, he was quiet in the confines of the classroom. He wasn't fat big, he was more muscle big, like a lumberjack. In addition to being quiet, he was easy going and left his desk to wander around the classroom offering help to other students, making sure they had everything they needed. He assumed it was that characteristic that got him the job offer to spend that second year in the third grade.

His clear, square-jawed face held a rugged look that was enhanced by a set of perfectly even, white teeth. His hair was the same dark color as Al's, but unlike his brother's, it held no cowlick and sat on his head in tight ringlets. His gentle nature was only interrupted when there was any sign of danger to his brother. As overprotective as he was, he never took advantage of his muscular physique to hurt or intimidate classmates. At times, he often sprang to the defense of younger kids if the bullies tried anything in the schoolyard. Being raised by a single mother had taught Jules to fend for himself, and she often reminded him that he was the man of the family.

His entire appearance, coupled with the personality of a friendly puppy, made him a popular contemporary in and out of the classroom. Being an ambassador of good will along with being Al's brother, he was welcomed by proxy into our small entourage. Looking back, he was probably as much an amused observer of our group as he was our protector. If he had any shortcomings in his academic abilities, we never noticed, but his proven lack of motivation in schoolwork ruled him out as a potential leader.

The last member of our group was my best friend, Dusty Barnes. Dusty was the smartest. He was the best speller in the class and always managed to decipher the code in word problems, which told us whether we should add or subtract, multiply or divide. He was especially good at the problems that had us figure out what times train A and train B would get where they were going when they traveled at different speeds and went in different directions. It was this type of problem that caused Al to ask, "Why didn't the station master just look at the schedule?"

Dusty lived in a house behind The Heights. It was built years before the apartments for the old people and became hidden after their construction. It was like he had a secret house because anyone who was unfamiliar with the area had no idea it existed. His parents had a private access road behind the apartments, but on my bike I could coast down the back hill, make the turn into The Heights and, with just a few pedal strokes, cut between two of the apartment buildings and be in his back yard. It was a good place to play. It sat on the fringe of several acres of woods where we built forts and made our own adventures.

The two of us were inseparable and being inseparable, had no secrets. In grade two we vowed that whatever happened, we would put our life on the line for the other. It was agreed that even if someone was torturing us, we would never reveal the other's whereabouts if, in fact, the other's whereabouts was the information the torturer was trying to obtain. The discussion was then expanded to include any other information that a captor would try to extract.

In the fourth grade, we used our Campking jackknives to cut small slits in our wrists and joined them together to make us blood brothers. They were not quite the deep wounds produced by the hunting knives Indians used in movies to ensure that lifelong bond of brotherhood, but we felt they were sufficient enough to get our blood mixed together. I would be hard pressed today to find any scar from the ritual.

Dusty and I were so relaxed with our friendship that neither one of us had any thoughts of leadership or, as Dusty once said, "bossing people around." While we all knew we needed a mentor, or "someone to organize things," as Al put it, our predicament left the four of us to aimlessly wander through our deeds of misconduct without any means of certainty or specific direction.

Chapter Three

It was in December of our fourth grade year that we were introduced to the fifth and final member of our group—Jamie McGuire. I was sitting on the floor of the classroom wearing an old robe and a poorly made silk turban that was precariously perched on my head. Linda Delaney had been put in charge of playing Christmas music and students were talking in competition with the overwhelming volume of "Hark The Herald Angels Sing." Other kids were putting on costumes for the first time and Miss Hannigan was trying to distribute necessary props to cast members. She had recently changed Al's role in the play from the third Wise Man to Joseph and he and the Virgin Mary had commandeered two of the shepherds' staffs and were sword fighting in the back of the room. Billie Monahan, who was always getting into trouble, had put on the Frosty the Snowman suit he had found in the closet adjacent to the coatroom. He was chasing people around the room trying to goose them with the huge orange plastic carrot nose he had torn off Frosty's face. Catching people was no easy task as he had neglected to properly secure the clips that attached Frosty's large head to the body section and the additional weight of the top hat made the head bob forward and back, which caused Billie vision problems. It was inevitable that he would eventually trip. When the Styrofoam stomach collided with one of the desks, it was the metal wastebasket that took the brunt of the fall and made a loud clanging sound as it hit the floor. The collision left a permanent indent in Frosty's midsection and the toppled wastebasket spewed discarded math quizzes along with an assortment of wadded papers across the floor. Gobs of pink bubblegum remained attached to the inside. At that point, Miss Hannigan had had enough and called for quiet. The needle scraped across the record giving an abrupt end to the angels singing heralded harks to the newborn King and the chaos of the room turned to silence.

Miss Hannigan then informed us that we were giving her a migraine. By this juncture of the school year, we had made the correlation that a migraine was a headache. It was baffling to me why teachers felt they had to use words that made things difficult for themselves. A perfect example of this was in the third grade when Mrs. Coney stood up one day and informed us that she could smell 'odors' and then asked if we knew where the odors were coming from. Everyone looked around the room giving each other blank stares. No one could answer her question because no one knew what an odor was. If she had simply asked "Who farted?" anyone could've told her it was Andrew Darnecki. Andrew was well known for his silent but deadly emissions that left his body and drifted upward to hang like unwanted clouds over a sizable area around his desk. Mrs. Coney's desk was certainly within his target range.

It wasn't until she had asked three or four times about odors that we associated her question with a simultaneous cloud from Darnecki. At that point, Andrea Shoemaker asked Mrs. Coney if odors were the same thing as farts. This led to a private discussion between Andrea and Mrs. Coney during which Andrea tattled on Andrew and his frequent fart attacks. A second discussion then occurred between Mrs. Coney and Andrew. She instructed him that in the future, he was to stroll into the hallway if he felt such an urge to release odors. As the main reason behind Andrew's gaseous expulsions was to disturb his classmates, the newly mandated stroll to the hallway eliminated that achievement and he saw no further use in cutting wind. Our classroom had been cleansed of odors.

This year, when the word migraine surfaced, it seemed to be a challenge to interpret the coded vocabulary. As it always followed a great deal of noise and commotion in the room, we determined that migraine meant headache. So when Miss Hannigan told us we were giving her a migraine, we now knew it wasn't a gift of any kind.

Now that she had our attention, her lecture followed regarding the importance of the annual Christmas play and how we needed to work together and help each other. We all liked Miss Hannigan, so we settled down. In any case, playing with costumes and props was a much better deal than doing schoolwork.

With order restored, Linda was told she could resume the music—with a little less volume—and the rest of us should continue to find our props and make a list of things we needed. The noise level, which always started at a low murmur, began to the tune of Linda's appropriate choice of "Silent Night." It was then that a pair of red P. F. Flyers appeared in front of me. They were the sneakers of Jamie McGuire. Jamie had been expelled from the only parochial school in the neighborhood and had been in our class for just a few days. We hadn't really met, but I knew he'd been kicked out of Catholic school and that invoked elements of intrigue and perhaps a slight touch of fear. No one knew why he had been expelled but the fact remained that he had been kicked out of school and that was good enough for us. Because of the friendship that ensued, and the fact they were the first words he ever said to me I will never forget that first question of great importance:

"Do you want the frankincense or the myrrh?" he asked me.

When I looked up from my position on the floor to answer, I remembered that Miss Hannigan had moved Al to the role of Joseph to make the new kid one of the other two Wise Men. Like me, he was wearing a poorly made turban. But unlike my stylish robe, his costume was made up of a bed sheet that was draped around him and attached at the shoulder with an oversized safety pin. I could only assume Miss Hannigan had run out of robes and would get him proper attire for the play. For now, he was stuck with wearing a sheet covered with big red and yellow flowers. It was certainly a poor attempt at making what Dusty referred to as "swaddling clothes for kids."

Jamie held a small box wrapped in gold-foiled paper in each of his outstretched hands and, realizing the absurdity of the question coming from a Wise Man draped in a flowered sheet started me laughing. My laugh got him laughing, and he sat down and we continued to laugh together as we stared at the two boxes.

"The other Wise Man already took the gold," he informed me, motioning to Dusty. He was across the room trying to figure out how the ox's head was supposed to attach to Jeremy. It was actually an old ski cap onto which Margaret Thompson had sewn ears, which now caused some confusion. Margaret had mistakenly sewn the two ears facing in opposite directions and Dusty and Jeremy were trying to decipher the front from the back. Before I could answer Jamie's question, he told me if I didn't care, he'd just as soon have the myrrh.

He later confessed that the reason he had asked for the myrrh was in case Miss Hannigan had us do a report on our part in the pageant. It seemed that at St. Basil's, they were always assigned reports for anything they were involved in. Jamie figured myrrh would be easier to spell while frankincense would require a second trip to the dictionary. He had already pawed through it once only to discover that myrrh wasn't in there and chalked it up to it being an ancient word that the dictionary people didn't know about. His only question was whether myrrh had one 'r' or two and he had solved his dilemma by asking Miss Hannigan. She confirmed it had two. Fortunately, we never had to write a report. If we had, he would have discovered that more in-depth questioning of Miss Hannigan would've been a good idea. After being told that myrrh had two rs he made a mental note that it was spelled 'm-u-r-r' and not 'm-u-r' as he'd first thought.

He handed me the small box in his left hand, which had a rubber band around it, presumably to keep the rattling pieces of frankincense from falling out during rehearsals. A few days earlier, because Al had asked me what frankincense looked like, I removed the band to find out. I knew Al wouldn't let the question go unanswered and I was also curious. To my surprise, the box was filled with a few old buttons. Jamie opened his box and found that myrrh didn't look any different than frankincense and so we both laughed again.

"You're Auggie right?" he asked.

"Yeah, and you're Jamie, from St. Basil's." I confirmed. I knew then that finding out why he'd been kicked out of school would give me some leverage with Al and Dusty, but I figured that question should wait.

"What is frankincense anyway?" he asked me.

"I'm not sure. I think it's like incest."

Sandy Murphy, who had been eavesdropping from her nearby desk, expressed her disdain at my response. "You're disgusting, Auggie!" She yelled. "And that's a dirty word!"

I looked at my new friend for help. "What, what'd I say?"

"I think she's talkin' about incest," which, as he continued to explain, "it's like feeling up your sister or somethin'." He then added that it might be incest if it was your cousin although he wasn't quite sure about that.

"Maybe you were thinkin' of incense. You know that stuff you burn that smells like different flavors? That's probably what frankincense is. They even sound kinda the same."

To save time, we agreed on that as a final definition. That first meeting proved to me that, unlike the biblical story, it was because of a conversation involving frankincense and incest that two of the three Wise Men met to begin a long journey.

With Jamie's arrival to our classroom and Al being—as Miss Hannigan put it—'promoted' to the role of Joseph, the parts, as well as the die had been cast. Miss Hannigan had more than likely jumped at the opportunity to separate Al and Dusty and me. Al was upset, but took his new role in stride as he stood in silence with the Virgin Mary at his side. As directed, the two stood and gazed reverently at the newborn babe. Everyone in the class had wondered about the appropriateness of Denise being the Virgin Mary. She was known for chasing unwilling boys around the yard at recess and trying to kiss them. Al had complained about being stuck in the part of Joseph and how he had serious misgivings about standing next to Denise. During one of the rehearsals Jamie surprised Dusty and me with a comment that "Al better be careful. She might try and grab his staff!" Not being as advanced with girls as Jamie, neither of us got the joke until later in the day.

Within our class of eighteen, Jamie had brought the needed increase in the male population to eight. Our class had very little talent, but Miss Hannigan had the foresight to make Sandy Murphy the narrator, leaving the rest of us to simply parade around the cardboard scenery without having to learn any lines. Sandy was one of those girls that no one liked but according to Miss Hannigan, she read with great expression. The few remaining boys were assigned parts as animals in the manger. The ox had been the most popular as it was the only animal in the stable that got to wear a headpiece, regardless of which direction the ears faced. The remainder of the girls were either scenery holders or angels, identified by halos made out of coat hangers covered with aluminum foil.

After many laborious rehearsals, parents came to school and watched Jamie and Dusty and me make that long and tenuous journey to Bethlehem to visit Al and his virgin bride. So it came to pass that as we three kings followed that sacred star in heaven, carrying our gift of buttons, the first of many good memories for the five of us was created. Jamie had been sent to us from St. Basil's by, as we found out later, the misconstrued view of Father O'Brien who had expelled him. But it wasn't just being expelled from St. Basil's, Jamie was a Catholic and we all knew that Catholics were much more religious than Protestants. They went to confession, they did stuff to forgive their sins, and they didn't eat meat on Friday. Father O'Brien, in essence, was a guy who worked for God. It didn't take long for us to realize that our group had not only grown to five in number but, as we soon discovered, Jamie was the leader we needed—a leader sent by God.

Chapter Four

Shortly after the success of our acting debut, the two-week Christmas vacation was upon us. Jamie joined us in building snow forts near home or ventured with us on our occasional winter trips to the woods.

When school resumed in January, he learned that in Public School Number One, the teachers were old fashioned and treated us more like their children or grandchildren. By joining us in the middle of grade four, he became one of our immediate family. As lost souls in search of that mutual sense of understanding that chemistry between people seems to provide, we adopted him. We were so happy to include him in our group that even Al had no questions regarding his entry. With that adoption, our group took on a new personality, which provided Miss Hannigan with an additional challenge. Until that time, she had struggled to keep three of us separated in our limited sized classroom. She now had the additional task of keeping four of us at appropriate distances and found herself continuously rearranging her seating chart. Jamie had a knack for taking command of the classroom. His outspoken comments and wisecracks brought laughter from the class. He was often denied recess for behavior problems and during those days when he was kept inside, our group never seemed quite complete.

Another quality of leadership was his vast knowledge of criminal activity. He was an astute scholar of crime movies and he talked at length of the old time gangsters. Guys like Frank Nitty and Al Capone. Of special interest were robberies of banks and armored cars. He brought a book to school one day, which detailed the intricacies of major crimes and their carefully planned details, their split second timing, and the rehearsed roles of each gang member as they strived for the perfect crime.

"If you want to have a successful bank holdup," he informed us, "you have to cut the wires to the alarm system and know what times the guards come around to check on the doors and windows."

It was obvious he knew what he was talking about and we listened to every word.

"Edward G. Robinson says jobs like that are referred to as capers. We should think about pulling a caper," he suggested.

This information gave credence to all future things we did together becoming capers and they were given code names. All of us except Dusty, whose father was Waterton's Chief of Police, took great interest in Jamie's information.

"Those guys may have done all that stuff," he rebutted. "But they all got caught too. My father said there's no such thing as the perfect crime."

Despite Dusty's proclamation about the perfect crime, it wasn't long after Jamie's arrival that our first caper took shape. We were sitting in an alcove of the school yard during our recess break. It was an area we weren't supposed to be in but Jamie said it was our school and we should be allowed to go anywhere we wanted. When he laid out his plan it seemed harmless enough. He had figured out a way to get a free candy bar from Miss Beezel's corner store. It was one of three stores we passed going to and from school each day.

Al liked to stop at the store because Miss Beezel had a big gumball machine, which contained 'magic' gumballs. Before filling the machine, she wrapped several of the balls in a silver foil paper and put them in with the others. When anyone got a silver clad gumball, she would give the lucky kid a free candy bar.

It didn't take long for Jamie to figure an angle to capitalize on her generosity. He had a flair for presentation and, as we sat in the alcove, he made a big deal about putting his hand in his pocket and withdrawing a closed fist. He then opened it slowly to reveal a gumball wrapped in the familiar silver paper.

"Yeah, so? You got a silver gumball from Miss Beezel's." Dusty's comment was made in a nonchalant manner and I believe all of us silently felt the same way.

"I mean, what's the big deal?" Dusty continued.

"The big deal my friends is I made this one myself...at my house last night." He handed it to me for inspection.

"Looks like one of hers." I admitted. "Where'd you get the foil?"

"From my father's cigarette pack. Last night he takes out his cigarettes and I notice inside they're packed in this foil paper. It looked like the same stuff Miss Beezel uses in the store so I asked him if I could have it."

As strange as this revelation may seem to the average person, we had all thought about wrapping our own gumballs prior to this but we knew Miss Beezel used something other than aluminum foil. We just couldn't find the right paper. Knowing she was a heavy smoker gave credence to Jamie's discovery of the foil inside the cigarette pack.

"Okay, you've got a gumball, now what?" Dusty asked him.

Excitement filled Jamie's voice as he took a folded piece of paper from his back pocket and spread it out on the cement walkway. He smoothed out the creases as we all looked at a drawing of a large square with smaller squares and rectangles inside it. He then explained it was a drawing of an overhead view. "You know, like looking down from the ceiling," as he put it, "of the inside of Miss Beezel's store."

He continued to explain that the big square represented the main counter of the store. The other squares and rectangles depicted the second counter to the side and the back room. Miss Beezel had a television set back there where she usually sat and watched her soap operas. The drawing also contained a circle, which Jamie pointed out was the location of the gumball machine. In addition to the boxes, he had marked five Xs, one to represent each of us.

"Look!" He shouted and pointed to the top of the wrinkled paper where he had written the label: 'The Candy Bar Caper'. "We can use this gumball I wrapped to get a free candy bar anytime we want! I mean I can wrap more of 'em." Without waiting for a response, his finger moved around the paper and he explained his plan in detail.

"Jules, you and Dusty will stand at the main counter," he told us. "That's where Miss Beezel will be—Jules, being the biggest will block any view of the gumball machine. Dusty will just be added protection," he continued.

"Auggie and me will stand at the comic book rack and I'll ask Miss Beezel some questions about when the new comics are comin' in. It'll keep her busy talkin' to us. Al, you'll be at the gumball machine and pretend to put a penny in and then make some noise with the lever like you're turning it. You'll already have the fake gumball in your hand and you'll yell to us that you got a silver gumball. You cash it in and we all leave and split the candy bar!"

Al contemplated the scheme and I could sense one of his questions coming. "Wouldn't it be easier to just steal a nickel from somebody?"

"That's not the point," Jamie said displaying some irritation. "Besides who would we steal from? Our friends? With this caper we can get a candy bar anytime we want. I mean a store is like a big company. A candy bar's nothin' to them."

The comment seemed to be directed toward Dusty to avoid any resistance about it being dishonest.

"With insurance and stuff, it makes the plan perfectly legal," he added.

"What if there's somebody else in the store gettin' a gumball?" Al wanted to know.

"Then you just wait until he's done and walks away. Don't make a big deal out of this. I only picked you to get the gumball because you get one every day anyway. Look, if you can't handle it, I'll get the gumball and you can stand with Auggie."

"No, that's okay. I can do it," Al assured him.

I thought about his statement and the fact that I was actually going to be in on a caper. How did I get involved? I wasn't quite sure if this was stealing or not. Jamie continued explaining his plan and, as crazy as the scheme seemed to be, we all bought into it. No matter what any of us thought, a free candy bar was a free candy bar.

On the walk back to school after lunch, we entered the store to the familiar ring of the bell that signaled our arrival. I heard Miss Beezel's chair scrape the floor in the back room as her TV blasted the dramatic short phrases delivered with precision by the soap stars. I had learned by watching them at my grandmother's house that a haunting chord from an organ always emphasized the drama of each statement. Miss Beezel, a woman in her sixties, appeared in the doorway of the back room. An old shower curtain sometimes covered the opening, but on the day of the caper iit was pushed all the way to one side. As was her habit, she slid her feet along the floor and shuffled to the counter instead of walking. I couldn't see her terrycloth slippers, but I'd seen them on other occasions. One of the two had a rabbit's head on it. Her dog had eaten most of the head off the other. She always wore them, along with the same housecoat that displayed a pattern of huge blue flowers. The sash was untied allowing it to hang open and revealed a flannel nightgown. I was never known for my boyhood cleanliness, but even I could see that both the nightgown and the housecoat needed a good washing. Bits and pieces of anything she had eaten in the past few days were displayed like splatters of paint on an artist's palette.

Jules and Dusty took their assigned positions at the large glass counter and pretended to ponder what penny candy they would be purchasing. Jamie and I stationed ourselves at the comic book rack as planned. I began to get nervous. I figured Miss Beezel probably knew we had already bought all the regular comics for that month. As nervous as I was, I hadn't noticed the comic I'd grabbed was the latest copy of *Little Lulu* and Miss Beezel knew we were only interested in superheroes.

"What can I get you boys today?" she addressed her question to Jules, realizing by this time of the school year that Dusty never bought anything.

I became more nervous as I thought that she must have been wondering why Dusty was even standing at the counter. She was still waiting for an answer from

Jules who responded with a few ummms and uhs as he studied the candies and stalled for time. Jamie hollered over and asked when the new Superman comic was coming in. "First of the month, same as always. You should know that by now," she told him. She then turned her head, straining to keep abreast of the soap opera in the back room. When she turned, the back of her head revealed a bald spot in her thinning hair, which was a mix of white and gray. She looked older than I'd ever seen her. I wondered if she might look younger if she combed her hair and dressed in regular clothes or maybe it would help if she shaved off the gray hairs that stuck out over her upper lip.

She drummed her fingers on the glass countertop and Jules continued to ponder his choices. Al, who was playing the starring role in the caper, was already at the gumball machine and finally pretended to put in his penny. Actually he overplayed his role as he jumped up and down with the excitement of getting a silver clad gumball. I could see that this was probably the reason Miss Hannigan had not given any of us speaking parts in the Christmas play.

Al was full of fake excitement when he brought the winning gumball to the counter and Miss Beezel gave him his choice of candy bar. He selected a Sky Bar. We had voted on a Sky Bar because it had four different flavors and they were easy to break apart. Al was content to keep the gumball. With the caper having been executed to perfection, we all made a quick exit from the store. No one said a word for about a block and then we all burst out laughing. At that point, Al began to unwrap it and, as he slowly peeled off the wrapper, sang the Sky Bar song from the TV commercial. He coordinated the lyrics as each separate piece of the candy bar was slowly revealed. He had a flair for this sort of thing so we all stopped to watch his song and dance routine. When he began singing, and removed the wrapper, it was as if we were all watching a stripper taking off her clothes.

His song began..."You get one——English toffee! You get two—fudge parfait! You get three—honey nougat! You get foooooooooour—peanut whip! You get all four in a Sky Bar!" As he sang the jingle, he broke off each piece and handed it to one of us. His inclusion of an impromptu dance with the song caused a wild round of applause at its completion.

The caper had been so successful that after waiting a few days, we pulled it again. This time around, we bypassed the Sky Bar and opted for a roll of Necco wafers. We had decided to stick with candy that would be easier to divide. On our first run, there had been some dispute over who got what section of the Sky Bar as the pieces weren't labeled and it was more or less potluck. The peanut-butter-filled section was the most popular, but we never knew which end it was on.

"Why don't they label them?" Al wanted to know until Dusty explained that if the company hired someone to label all the Sky Bars in the world, it would cost a fortune and they'd probably raise the price. Being the mathematical member of our group, this was the type of problem on which Dusty spent a great amount of time. To him, it was fun to calculate how much it would cost the company and how much the price of the Sky Bar would escalate. He'd probably work on it and give us a full report.

As it turned out, the Necco wafers proved to be as much of a problem when we divided the bounty. Everyone wanted the brown ones. To settle the matter, Dusty suggested giving each color a point value allowing a more equitable division. He calculated that by counting how many of each color were in the pack and what flavors we each liked, we could come up with an appropriate system. While he tried to explain the process, the rest of us argued about how many points each color should get. By the time the point system was figured out, we had arrived at school and voted to postpone splitting them up until afternoon recess. When we reconvened to get the fruits of our labor we discovered that Al had eaten the whole roll during the spelling test, explaining that spelling made him nervous.

In the weeks that followed, several miraculous turns of an invisible penny in the gumball machine yielded a foil-covered ball. If Miss Beezel was at all suspicious, her concern was brought to a halt during Al's third week of good fortune. As usual, Dusty and Jules stood by the counter to block any view of the machine and waited for Al's gleeful cheer signifying success. He showed Miss Beezel the gumball as he unwrapped it and tossed the silver paper in her trash barrel.

"I'll take a box of Good and Plenty," he told her which was the preselected candy of the day.

Miss Beezel got the box from the glass case beneath the counter. "You must have got one of the leftovers," she told him.

"Leftovers?"

"Yes, I ran out of my silver paper and wrapped all the magic gumballs in nice blue foil. I guess you didn't notice," she continued. "I musta missed one."

Al seemed to be a bit flustered as he took the box of Good and Plenty's. "Y-yeah, " he said, "guess I got the last silver one." By now, all of us were staring at the gumball machine.

"I think Miss Beezel's on to us." Jamie whispered to me and then broke the awkward silence. "Hey guys, we gotta get goin' or we'll be late." With the excuse we needed to get out of the store, we made our exit.

We walked in silence until we were a safe distance from the store. "She knows! " Dusty yelled.

"Didn't you see she changed the colors?" Jamie asked Al. "Christ! You should've noticed."

"How was I supposed to know she was gonna change the color of the paper? She's probably gonna call the cops. Do you think she'll call the cops?" He was addressing me but I had no answer. A lively discussion followed among all of us except Jules who had taken the gumball from Al and was calmly chewing it. None of us realized that Al, in his worry, was eating the Good and Plentys as we walked, and he wound up eating the entire box before we arrived at school.

Dusty and I said we shouldn't go there anymore, but Jamie thought that if we stayed away for a while it would look even more suspicious.

"We need to keep going," he told us. "We'll just buy stuff like we used to."

We voted against Jamie's advice and decided not to go to Miss Beezel's store for a while. The rest of us figured that if we went back right away, she would have cops in the back room waiting to catch us. Only a few months remained until summer vacation so for the rest of the year we purchased candy at two other stores and limited our misbehaviors to the classroom.

None of us realized that this caper was just the beginning of much bigger things to come. We didn't know Jamie was simply a guy who liked to take risks— a guy who would elevate the risk factor with each caper that followed. To us, the elevation of the risk factor went unnoticed and capers   felt quite normal. As far as we were concerned, we were simply well on our way to imitating our gangster role models of Hollywood.

At the time, we had no knowledge of addictions nor did we see any difference between a little old lady running a corner store and a 'company,' as Jamie described it. Not even Jamie recognized his addictions but, looking back, he had them. He was addicted to danger and the adrenalin rush of getting away with something. When Al had asked that obvious question regarding the easier task of stealing a nickel from somebody rather than beat the gumball machine, Jamie had dismissed it. Wrapping a gumball in silver foil had nothing to do with getting a free candy bar. It was the planning and the diagrams combined with the risk and the "split-second timing" as he put it that motivated him.

It was this unseen addiction that would bring all of us to follow along on his capers and eventually expand into areas in which we had no business going. Like lambs to slaughter, he would take us down a path that would lead us far beyond gumballs and candy bars. A very dangerous path that would inevitably lead us onto a collision course with a man we had no business knowing—the guy we would soon refer to as the fat man.

Chapter Five

Although spring was always a nice time of year, it was more of an imposed inconvenience while we waited for the true warmth of summer. This year a visit to the train yard, a pleasure I usually kept for myself, allowed for a cooling-off period following the incident with Miss Beezel. Although there was an ongoing disagreement about her having cops watching us, we decided we should lay low for a while.

The train yard was home to the Delaware and Hudson railroad, which was owned and operated by a conglomerate of companies, but, to me, it was under the sole jurisdiction of the yardmaster that happened to be my grandfather. His right hand man, Mr. Faulk, ran the train operations and, with him in the yard, it was like having a second grandfather around. Actually, Mr. Faulk's work was much more interesting than what Gramps did, and spending time riding around the yard on a big diesel with him was the remedy I needed.

Considering the relationship my grandfather and I had, I was as comfortable around the trains as I was in my own back yard. Whether I was sitting at his huge oak desk in the office or wandering the entangled mass of tracks, I had the run of the place. So when trees began to blossom and the scent of spring filled the air, I often scrambled home from school, changed into my play clothes, and ran to the railroad yard. The biggest event of the afternoon was to watch the 4:37 rumble in. My grandfather never tolerated a breach in the schedule without good reason and the 4:37 was always on time. When the large wall clock in the office struck the singular chime for 4:30 I would join my grandfather on the platform outside his office.

"Your grandmother tells me you got your love of trains from me," he told me one day while we were waiting. "Said you were born on a freight car and then shipped in on a renegade. I think it came from up the tracks that away."

As he made the statement, he pointed to a set of rails that headed toward Albany. The long sweep of their parallel lines made an expansive curve out of the yard until the horizon shaped them into a point.

I knew from experience that a renegade was a train that pulled into the yard with a myriad of cars from yards around the countryside. Once they reached the Waterton yard they would be sorted and redirected to their final destinations. Many were unhitched and moved around the tracks to be connected to other locos scheduled to continue eastbound to Albany. Other cars were moved to the westbound spur bound toward Utica and Buffalo. Some made the run to the southern tier into Pennsylvania while others continued to West Virginia where companies traded lumber for coal cars.

Most of the trains ran right through Waterton and never stopped in the yard. They carried two or three passenger cars and continued down the line to the Albany terminal. The only task for passenger trains was the placement of the mail sack on the throw post which allowed it to be swooped up by the train's mechanical arm and pulled into the mail car.

The 4:37, however, carried no passengers and warranted a multitude of tasks, which kept the crew

busy until supper. Having just punched the time clock
for the four to midnight shift, the men were full of
energy and always calling out friendly jibes to one
another. For a ten-year-old the shift change was an
exciting time to be in the office...the beehive as the
men called it.

On days I stood waiting with my grandfather a
sweeping glance allowed us to survey the entire yard
and, on that particular day, it cleared my head of any
thoughts about Miss Beezel or the fear of possibly
being arrested.

Railroad cars sprawled themselves over acres of
land as if it was their private meeting place. The D&H
hauled a variety of boxcars, flat cars, tankers, and
refrigerator cars—reefers gramps called them. They
were first to make a quick exit to get perishables to
their destinations.

The yard held no bias toward any freight line.
Many cars were owned by the Erie–Lackawanna, others
by the Baltimore & Ohio or Boston & Maine. The cars
of the Delaware and Hudson, however, outnumbered
all the other lines. Those were easily identified by the
huge D&H logo emblazoned on their sides and on the
face of the giant diesels that pulled them. The logo was
bright yellow, in the shape of a knight's shield; the
letters D&H, were in bold blue script. The deep blue
color of the diesels accentuated the yellow shield along
with a bright yellow stripe that ran the length of the
engine and then shot upward to outline the engineer's
cab.

My grandfather always looked very stately when he
appeared and stood on the platform to survey his
empire. He was an older version of my father.
Although both stood a few inches over six feet, the
many years of sitting behind a desk had given Gramps
an expanded waistline. Aside from the extra weight he

carried, the only other differences between the two were my grandfather's double chin and some graying around the temples of his otherwise thick black hair. He had also taken to wearing a pair of wire-rimmed spectacles for office work.

As habit dictated, he reached into his vest pocket and withdrew his watch. Every train coming or going during my grandfather's shift did so under the dictate of his Hamilton. It kept perfect time and he took careful note to ensure that the 4:37 was, in fact, arriving at 4:37. The familiar but deafening blast sounded its strange mixture of a horn and whistle just prior to entering the yard. As it thundered its way in and began to slow, he glanced at the timepiece and gave a friendly wave to the engineer. Today it was Mr. Rosemont—Rosey the men called him—and he tipped his engineer's cap in acknowledgement of the wave.

Satisfied the 4:37 was on time, the Hamilton was returned to its resting place in his vest pocket. When originally purchased, the watch had included a silver chain, which was meant to run from the crown and fall in a loop and continue to a buttonhole in his vest. A silver teardrop-shaped fob accented the chain, an ornament intended to dangle as a decorative accent piece. My grandfather had deemed both the chain and the fob unnecessary and replaced them with a loop of black rawhide.

I heard my grandmother question him once regarding the chain's replacement. In her opinion, the silver chain was a sign of elegance. In his consistently calm voice he explained, "I use it for work, mother. I'm not going to a dinner party."

Unlike most of his jewelry that he had received over the years as gifts of appreciation for reaching various milestones in his career, the watch and chain had been a special gift from my grandmother upon his promotion to yardmaster. Hamilton watches were well known for their perpetual accuracy and his new position warranted only the best. Once the chain was removed, it was thrown into the cigar box that sat on his bedroom dresser to join the jumbled collection of tie clips and cuff links shaped like locomotives.

Although he found no use for the chain, he did see the need for a convenient resting place for his watch and he was known for the wearing of either a dark brown or navy blue pinstriped vest within which the Hamilton sat in easy reach. His vests always covered a white shirt with his top button loosened and sleeves rolled to the elbows. When occasions arose that required a more formal appearance, he added a bow tie to his attire. I don't ever recall seeing him wear a necktie.

He seemed satisfied with the arrival that day. As always, the 4:37 had left the whistle stop at Nineteenth Street at 4:30. This was the train's last stop before Waterton and it sat at Nineteenth Street for three minutes to allow the daily loading of mailbags and parcel post packages. Exactly seven minutes later, the beehive and the outer complex began the daily routine of organized chaos.

I watched Mr. Faulk as he replaced Mr. Rosemont and took over the responsibility of the huge diesel. He and Gramps had grown up together but, unlike Gramps, Mr. Faulk's responsibilities kept him thin and wiry. Clad in his railroad coveralls, he jumped on and off the moving diesels with the grace and ease of a trapeze artist. I watched him swing from one grab bar to another. It seemed so natural for him to take hold of a handle and pull himself up onto a loco. Without any break in movement, he grabbed a second rail and was inside the cab in an instant.

When the train was stopped, I tried to mimic his moves and could manage the first grab bar but my shorter reach wouldn't allow me to swing up and grip the second. He spied me practicing one day and realizing my dilemma, showed me how to use one of the yard hooks to give me that few additional inches I needed. If we were together, he always went first and then turned and extended his hand and pulled me up and into the cab in one smooth motion. His wiry frame was hardly indicative of his strength. Once he gripped my wrist he would swing me with the ease of a carnival strong man. He never mentioned the shortcoming of my inability to reach the second grip. That was the way Mr. Faulk was. Always friendly, always helpful, and he always had a good story to tell. Like Gramps, he was over six feet tall, but on the rare occasion when he removed his engineer's cap, his remaining gray hair was in a horseshoe-shaped band that covered his temples and continued around the back of his head. His lack of hair was one of the many topics of good-natured ribbing between him and my grandfather.

With the arrival of the 4:37, the shift change allowed the big loco to get a four-hour respite from its freight-hauling duty. As routine dictated, Mr. Faulk climbed on board and ran her to an empty spur. If my timing was right, I sometimes climbed on for the short ride to its temporary resting place.

I left the platform and caught up to him when he finished moving the diesel. We then walked to the yard goat, a miniature loco that was used for rearranging cars on the inner tracks. On the goat, I sat in the engineer's seat and rode with him while men hustled around the waiting freight cars. They were already identifying and labeling cars of all sizes, shapes, and colors. The cars were to be moved from one area of the yard to another, and large yellow tags were tied to the ends designating specific types of placements.

Prior to the train's arrival, clipboards were put in place in the office and hung like skewed pictures in an art gallery. They took up a good part of a wall and held transfer slips that had been filled in with a number to identify a rail car. The slip listed the car's contents, its final destination, and to which spur in the yard it would be moved. Sometimes a slip would hold a circled number indicating a switch that would be thrown during the movement. These numbers were sometimes omitted when yardmasters on other shifts filled out the forms, with the assumption that the men were experienced and knew the location and number of every switch. Gramps, on the other hand, always listed the numbers and frowned upon the practice of others who omitted the task.

On afternoons I happened to be in the beehive, I positioned myself behind my grandfather's oak desk. The clipboards on the wall were part of an important ritual as the crew entered and grabbed a work order. They were always boisterous and cheerful as they came through the door, usually in the middle of a conversation. Some would be telling jokes and their use of off-color language would be cut short once they saw me sitting at the desk. They were an extended family and they all had a favorite comment for me. I could wear a blindfold and tell who entered by their good-natured greetings. Binky always called me "Chief" and Harold would give me a "hey buddy...how's it goin' today?" Donnie would remind whomever he was with to "look sharp now, the supervisor's here!" and then give me a wink.

Seeing only their congenial sides I never realized what rugged men they were. I was not around on days when they worked in slickers covered with sleeting rain or on winter days when ungloved hands became numb as they took a sledge hammer to a frozen coupling to loosen a stubborn connection or days when shovels were used to clear heavy snow to prevent delays in schedules.

Waterton had been settled by the Dutch and with the exception of a few, the Dutchmen ran the yard like a fraternity...a brotherhood of men held together with muscle and grit. These were men who put personal differences aside and backed one another in the presence of any foe. It was hard and often dangerous work done by men with callused hands and strong backs. I saw these men rested and relaxed when they grabbed their clipboards. I never saw those work orders when they were completed and tossed into the night man's box at the end of the shift. They were returned rumpled, with stains of grease and oil or sometimes a smear of blood from a cut hand, usually with a corner missing or torn from pocket abuse, each completed task identified by scrawled initials.

I never had any awareness regarding the cocoon of protection the men in the yard offered. I only saw the friendliness the men showed to me and Hogger, the stray cat Harold discovered sleeping in the engineer's compartment of a loco one night. He seemed to be very comfortable when he was found in the cab so the name Hogger, a slang term for an engineer, was the natural choice. One thing led to another, and Hogger became a permanent fixture around the office and the two of us shared the affection of the men.

My grandfather, a man who held a soft spot for any kind of stray, was willing to let Hogger hang around as he put it, but was adamant regarding a litter box. "There'll be no litter box in here smellin' up the place," he told Harold, who was seeking a permanent residence for the cat. "He can stay as long as he can do his business outside." As Harold left the office, Gramps hollered after him adding "and I'm not responsible for any feeding either!" (Although I knew he kept a bag of dry food in his desk drawer for occasions when the men forgot to collect scraps from their evening meals.)

On one occasion Hogger went missing for two days until a worried crew member discovered he had wandered into the yard and hitched a ride on the run to West Virginia and back. Other than that note-worthy adventure, he could usually be found sleeping in his favorite napping place, a small counter beneath the hanging clipboards. Each day as the men entered and took a board from a nail, salutations were given to me and a ruffling of the fur to the office mascot. This was with the exception of Winks who always pretended that he didn't like cats. Each day he cupped Hogger's head in his oversized hands, looked him in the eyes and threatened him.

"One of these days I'm gonna tie your tail to a departing train and send you down the line," he'd say. Then living up to his nickname, he would look over and give me a wink and a smile before he grabbed a clipboard.

My grandfather's notes were known for their legibility. He had started with the D&H as a brass-pounder and because of the hundreds of required writings in translating messages, most telegraphers were known for their penmanship and he took great pride in his handwriting. The men appreciated his calligraphy-like strokes and easy-to-read notes. When picking up their boards and checking the comments on the slips, they were relieved to see them written in my grandfather's hand. When Jeffries, the night foreman, wrote the slips, the men always complained that half their time was lost trying to decipher his hen scratching.

During the first half of the shift, cars were uncoupled and rearranged. Cars continuing on to Albany were placed onto the southbound spur. If nothing had been running to Montreal earlier in the week, cars awaiting that route were pulled onto the track. Mr. Faulk used the yard goat to maneuver cars into position on the spurs, with routine precision. I never would've understood any of the daily routine if he hadn't explained it to me. Walking to the yard goat one day, he handed me a small square puzzle with even smaller squares inside it. The smaller white squares reminded me of Chicklet gum except they had little numbers on them and one square was missing.

"You see all those numbers on here?" he asked me.

"Yeah."

"What do you notice about them?"

I looked at the little squares. "They're all out of order?" I questioned.

"Right! And your job is to put them in order. You see that empty space there where one of them is missing? That's so you can slide them around and rearrange them. So I want you to slide those babies around and put the numbers in order for me. Can you do that? I'll give you the choice of either goin' across the top or you can go top to bottom, although I think goin' across is easier."

By then we were in the engine compartment of the goat and while Mr. Faulk made his routine maintenance and safety checks, I moved the squares around and put the numbers in order.

"There!" I said, pleased with my accomplishment. It was then that he brought me to the window of the locomotive and pointed into the yard and taught me about the renegade.

"You see all those locos and cars out there in the yard?"

"Yeah."

"Well all those cars ya see are all mixed up just like the numbers on that puzzle you just did. And every day, they've got to be shuffled around and put in the right order and reconnected so they can be pulled outta here in one direction or another." He continued to point as he spoke. "Ya got those spurs over there that just dead end themselves only their real purpose is like that empty space on your puzzle where you can push a car into it and later bring it back in the right order. Does that make sense to you, Auggie?"

"Yeah, I mean, I see you movin' cars around all the time, but I guess I never thought about the order or anything."

"Well sir, that's what your grandfather has to figure out every day. And we don't wanna be pushin' any more cars than we have to so we count on him to get it done with the least amount of moves. Now I've seen you on the platform. Figure some day you might wanna be a yardmaster like your granddad. If that's right, I can tell by the way you handled that puzzle, you could get those cars done just the way they're supposed to be, just like your grampa."

It was that kind of lesson that Mr. Faulk always gave me when he taught me things about the yard. Combined with lessons from my grandfather, I gained railroad knowledge that would never be found in a library. I watched the men work, listened to their stories, and learned about trains and switches and schedules. In all that learning, I never realized the knowledge would one day save my life.

Chapter Six

Visits to the train yard eventually became routine excursions and so once again I turned to my contemporaries. Jamie's leadership continued and our escapades took us to the end of the fourth grade. With the Candy Bar Caper behind us, we had learned to cope with the fear of being criminals on the run. At first, each ringing of the telephone brought a quick jolt to the heart. Seeing policemen in squad cars raised thoughts that we were under surveillance, and we lived with the fear that perhaps Miss Beezel had alerted other store owners, although we didn't know of any others who wrapped gumballs in secret foil.

Jamie, on the other hand, continued to go to her store as if to let her know she had nothing on him. "She's got no proof of anything," he assured us. "So what if our fingerprints are all over the store. We go in there all the time anyway. The cops got nothin'."

This statement was unusual since Jamie was paranoid about leaving fingerprints during capers. Still, the rest of us stayed away until June rolled around. Once summer vacation started, we reentered our comfort zone and it was time for the four of us to introduce Jamie to the grandeur of summer life and all it had to offer. He had always been popular in his own neighborhood but spending all his time with us had caused him to lose touch with his former friends. Once he had been kicked out of St. Basil's, his prior connections eroded and when he entered our world he was exposed to new activities. As a group of seasoned veterans of summer life, we wanted the two months following grade four to be good ones. Over the years, we had developed an endless array of activities in which to partake—activities that involved traipsing through the woods, target shooting, damming up creeks, and chopping down trees to use as material for forts.

We were at that golden age—old enough to leave the house giving only a vague description of our destination, yet young enough to be invisible to most adults. The singular responsibility we had for the entire summer was to be home in time for supper.

During the summer, the only barometer we lived by was the sound of the heat bug. When it buzzed early in the morning and signaled a really hot day, our inclinations turned to swimming rather than fort building. For swimming, we only had two options. Option number one was the reservoir—the rez as we called it—which was usually occupied by high school guys who drove cars and had girlfriends. On days we could get a swim in before the older guys arrived, we always took time for a special ritual. Just before leaving, we'd circle up and tread water while we took a communal leak. This gave us great satisfaction knowing that *our* drinking water came from a different source and the water from the rez was pumped to the homes of the more affluent residents of the neighboring city. The rez was technically off limits because every year some kid would drown and then the local cops started daily patrols to prevent anyone else from enjoying themselves for the remainder of the summer.

"If the cops know someone is going to drown every year and then they're going to have to patrol, why don't they patrol before someone drowns?" Al asked.

"If a high school kid doesn't drown every year, they won't have anybody to dedicate the yearbook to," Jules explained. Unfortunately, his response was said in complete seriousness and acted as a truthful reminder to all of us. The yearbook was, in fact, usually dedicated to a student whose cause of death alternated between drowning in the rez or a car accident. One year the school board had the wreckage of Anthony Thomasini's car towed to the high school parking lot where it remained for several weeks under protests from both parents and students. The idea was to remind everyone to drive safely. Thomasini had swerved off the road on Windbender's Hill and was killed instantly. Since he was so well liked, no one needed to have his totaled Chevy sitting in the middle of the parking lot as a friendly reminder that speed can kill you. The thought confirmed Jules's earlier statement regarding the dedication to students whose death occurred by either drowning or driving too fast and led to a full page in the yearbook. No one had drowned this year but with the possibility of being interrupted at the rez by high school kids, we had little choice for swimming other than option number two.

Option two, the Waterton City Pool, posed several problems. It was noisy, packed with little kids, had too many rules, bathing suits were required, and it was located in the uptown end of the city. The distance was inconvenient enough to force us to take the city bus. This required a wait of an undeterminable length of time, as the buses never ran on schedule. We stood at the bus stop wearing our bathing suits under our shorts and carried our underpants rolled up in our towel. It was important to tuck your underpants well inside so they wouldn't hang out and be seen by strangers. Some of us—Al in particular—had learned this the hard way.

It's a story for another time and one that would most likely begin with the phrase "I'll never forget the day that Al's underpants were hanging out of his towel and got caught on a rose bush...."

Once off the bus, the summer air was permeated with diesel fumes until a few steps took us close enough to the pool to allow for the transition to the smell of chlorine. The same air also carried the familiar sounds of hundreds of voices and shouts, along with an occasional whistle, all melting into a cacophony of indistinguishable conversations of summer fun that we would soon be a part of. After paying the five cents admission fee, we headed for the locker room. The main building also housed the bathrooms and had that unmistakable aroma of chlorine, hairspray, and Juicy Fruit gum mixed with just a touch of urine.

Little kids who had not yet learned to disobey their mothers' demands to not pee in the pool ran inside to use the bathroom. Their bare feet left wet footprints on the hot pavement until once inside they made slapping sounds on the watery cement floor.

The basket girl gave us a numbered wire basket that included a short elastic band with a metal tag displaying the corresponding number. The elastic band we later slipped around our ankle while swimming so we could reclaim our basket. Some of the tougher guys from uptown, wore it around their bicep but, except for Jules, our arms were so skinny the band slid down to our wrists and fell off so we were resigned to wearing them as ankle attire.

Wearing our suits under our shorts made for a quick change and saved us from Al's complaints regarding the embarrassment of having to undress in front of people. The biggest challenge in the locker room was to not let your shorts touch the floor when you got undressed as it was covered with pool water.

No one else seemed to care about the wet floor, so it was just the four of us who were stared at as we stood together on top of one of the benches and stepped out of our shorts. Jules usually tried to ignore us.

The transfer of our underpants from the towel to the basket was, once again, done with masterful precision so basket girl wouldn't see them. It was always the same girl and, because she was cute, we certainly didn't want her to see our underpants. Once again we carefully tucked them inside our shorts—safe from the thorns of rose bushes.

Between her gum smacking and bubble blowing, basket girl always asked people if they had taken their valuables. She did so while pointing to the big sign that was supposed to read:

DO NOT LEAVE VALUABLES
WE ARE NOT RESPONSIBLE FOR ITEMS
LOST OR STOLEN

But somebody had crossed off 'FOR ITEMS LOST OR STOLEN' with a black marker and then added the word PEOPLE! so the sign read:

DO NOT LEAVE VALUABLES
WE ARE NOT RESPONSIBLE F~~OR ITEMS~~
~~LOST OR STOLEN~~PEOPLE!

It seemed the initial message wasn't found to be important enough to be reinstated because once the rewriting had been done the sign remained like that for most of the summer. This led to someone else adding the words:

IF ANY OF US WERE RESPONSABLE, WE WOULDN'T BE WORKING HERE IN THE FIRST PLACE!

In this last addition, the word responsible was spelled wrong and the words **HERE IN THE FIRST PLACE** ran over onto the cinderblock wall as there was no longer any room left on the cardboard.

Basket girl always pointed to the sign because it was impossible to hear anything she said over the volume of her radio. Today she was competing with the Crew Cuts singing "Earth Angel." Fortunately, as pool regulars, we knew enough about basket thieves to only carry a small amount of change with us, usually fifteen cents or a bus token for the ride home, and enough for a frozen milkshake on a stick after swimming. The concession stand near the exit had a good variety of candy bars and they were all kept in a freezer. The first few bites of whatever you bought were always difficult until it warmed up a bit and you could actually get your teeth into it. Sometimes we'd carry a little extra change to get a bag of potato sticks while we were there or, on one special day, when Jules needed extra money for a couple of Baby Ruths. Most kids concealed their change in the button-down pocket of their bathing suit, but these often ripped and their change found its way to the pool drains, which we checked with regularity. We always combined our money and put it in one of Dusty's socks, which was then stuffed into his sneaker and kept under guard. We had discovered his to be the cleanest, with Al's socks definitely off limits if we ever wanted to touch our money again.

The only other things we took from the locker room were our towels and these we spread out where we could find a spot on the perimeter of the chain link fence. The area around the edge of the pool started out as concrete followed by a substance that was once grass but now resembled the dry, cracked earth of a desert. Beyond that area, the lush green of the intended lawn became an unrecognizable mass of yellow straw.

Blankets and towels were spread out and occupied by high school girls covered in baby oil to get the perfect tan. Seventh and eighth graders sat in clumps playing card games and high school kids who were going steady occupied the areas farthest from the water. They spread out big blankets and made out between the lifeguards' rounds when they checked for the prohibited public displays of affection. The entire area was flooded with basket girl's music from WTRY. It was always too loud because basket girl was in charge and had no idea what the speakers sounded like outside the confines of her cage.

Unlike the peacefulness of the rez, our afternoons at the city pool were filled with rock and roll music blaring from loud speakers mixed with kids screaming, lifeguards yelling, and the fragrance of chlorine, Coppertone, and bubblegum.

Once we staked our claim to one of the sparsely covered dirt areas, we'd take a quick dip. As bad as the chlorine was, it was necessary to counteract the abundance of urine from little kids who stood innocently and smiled while they made warm spots in the water. A quick survey of the day's clientele allowed us to plan strategies for our favorite game... bombardment. This, we knew, held a benching penalty from the lifeguards.

Benching was a lifeguard-imposed retaliation, which meant you had to sit on the bench closest to the guard's chair for a designated time—usually five or ten minutes but most of them told us to watch the big clock over the entrance to the locker room and, by the use of the honor system, keep track of our own time. In those instances we implemented self-imposed amnesty and rarely served our complete sentence. Al, who was the quickest and fastest of our group, was extremely adept at escaping unnoticed and rarely spent more than two or three minutes on any bench.

Anything worth doing resulted in a benching penalty and bombardments were certainly worth doing. This was when three or four of us cannon-balled into the water on both sides of two or three attractive girls enjoying a nice swim. A really good bombardment involved that rare mother who had dared to bring young children to the pool. If she sat on the edge watching her kid, and especially if she was the type who didn't want to get her hair wet—that was a perfect opportunity for a bombardment.

Most of the time the benches were full of little kids who had been put there for running or pushing their friends off the side of the pool. Being benched for those types of offenses was a waste of time. If we had to sit on a bench for any part of our pool visit, our offenses had to be worthy of the penalty. Bombardments certainly fit the criteria. By rule, any third offense was cause for a guard to send the offender home. The trick was to not get caught by the same guard more than twice, which left a lot of holes in their system.

All the lifeguards were high school kids except Big Tony. Big Tony had spent a good five years or more earning his high school diploma and had now secured his minimum wage job as head lifeguard. The pool opened at one o'clock, but it was rumored that Big Tony was always there early in the day lifting weights. When the other guards arrived for duty, he was well oiled with glistening sweat that he must've thought appealed to the high school girls.

It was important to keep track of Big Tony's location; he was usually standing around talking to an off-duty female guard. From their appearance, it looked like Tony did the hiring and he liked to keep them happy. For that reason, he never bothered to bench anyone. Any type of infraction that interfered with his socializing was cause to send you home. If we gave any of the female guards real trouble and they called Big Tony, our day of swimming was over. This made our self-imposed rule to stay in areas where we could avoid Big Tony an easy rule to follow.

The benching penalty by most of the guards was usually five minutes, except for Candace Melonovski who started right off with a ten-minute bench and sent you home for a second offense.

Candace thought she was something special but the only two things that made her special in our eyes were her huge tits, and because of those assets, we had changed her name from Candace Melonovski to Candy Melons and enjoyed referring to her in that way. None of us ever referred to her as just 'Candy' or 'Melons.' We always used the two-part name 'Candy Melons,' and it was her we watched hoping for the occasional drop of her whistle that allowed us an enhanced glimpse of her cleavage when she bent down to retrieve it.

We were certainly not the only ones to notice her. Whenever she ascended the steps to take her seat in the elevated guard chair, all eyes quickly turned. She was so aware of the fact she seemed to make a special effort in providing a touch of dramatic flair as she turned and wiggled her ass into the seat. She even looked good wearing the pith helmet, which shaded her eyes from the sun to allow for a better view of kids to bench. Her application of the white gunk all the lifeguards put on their noses had obviously been applied with the care and caution of prom make-up. All this was accentuated by the tiniest of waists and the shapeliest of legs. Combined with her blonde hair and blue eyes, she was irresistible to the high school boys and we figured more than one of 'em had given her melons a squeeze. There was even talk that she dated older guys from the local college.

On one occasion, Candy Melons and her boyfriend, along with another couple, had interrupted a swim at the rez. As the two guys were telling us to get lost and find some other place to swim, the girls were getting out of the car and Candy Melons was wearing a two piece bathing suit. Unlike her lifeguard attire, this gave further evidence that no parts of her, other than her personality, were pretentious. It seemed her only voiced concern on that day was her distress that the one-piece lifeguard suit was causing havoc with her tan lines. As if her guard suit didn't provide for the adequate amount of sun to which the rest of her body was entitled.

Knowing that she was the meanest of the female lifeguards, we usually kept our distance from her area until we were ready to go home. At that point, we always did a five-man bombardment in front of her chair with the hopes that some of the splash actually went high enough to interrupt her leg tanning. Then she blew her whistle and yelled at us, saying we were through for the day and to get dressed and go home. If she decided to bench us, we walked into the locker room in a sign of unified rebellion. At that point, Jamie checked to make sure Big Tony wasn't in the area before he flipped her the finger.

The best day at the pool, however, was the day we now referred to as the Fizzies & Floater Caper. We all brought as many packages of Fizzies as we could get our hands on. Fizzies were flavored disks that were put in a glass of water. They fizzed up like Alka-Seltzer and magically turned your drink into carbonated soda.

Jules positioned himself at the shallow end of the pool and knowing the grape flavored fizzies would do the most damage, the rest of us loaded up with handfuls of purple Fizzies and jumped into the deep end for a synchronized release. Once we were on the bottom, we turned them loose and swam underwater to the shallow end and climbed out. The water beneath the diving boards immediately started to turn purple. People seeing the disturbance screamed, perhaps thinking it was blood or something, and the lifeguards went crazy trying to figure out what was going on. This diversion allowed Jules time to unwrap two Baby Ruth candy bars and toss them into the shallow end of the pool. The fact that they were fresh out of the freezer kept the chocolate from melting off right away and in no time, an unsuspecting mother, standing waist deep, felt one of them bumping into her back. She stood there yelling and screaming as she made her way to a ladder while she pointed to the floater and drew more attention to it. In the midst of all the screaming, the second floater was discovered by another swimmer.

With a purple volcano erupting at one end of the pool and what looked like two floaters in the shallow end, the entire pool saw a mass exodus of frantic people. Lifeguards ran everywhere and people left their towels and encircled the pool to see what was happening.

Soon the entire pool congregation had surrounded the shallow end with all fingers pointing to the Baby Ruths as they bobbed in the vacated water. This was then a job for Big Tony. As head guard, he rescued the day as he took the long rod used for getting debris out of the pool and jabbed at the bar, trying to snag it. People watching continued to scream each time the tip touched the Baby Ruth but failed to move it. Tony became frustrated. "Get the other pole," he yelled to another guard, as the second Baby Ruth bobbed around in the choppy water. "The one with the net on it."

Jules then nonchalantly walked to where Big Tony was poking the Baby Ruth and stood next to him.

"What's going on?" he asked with as much innocence as he could muster.

"Whaddaya think's goin' on? Some asshole took a shit in the pool!" Big Tony yelled. Older women, appalled by his choice of words, gasped at his outburst. At that point, one of the administrators arrived from the office while the second guard continued searching for the net to assist Big Tony in fishing out the floaters. The pool bosses discussed whether or not everyone would have to be sent home while they drained all the water. This was an interesting thought to us as draining the pool would give credence to the rumor that when they did so at the end of the summer, it left an oversized bathtub ring.

"If the health department gets wind of this, we'll be in hot water and could be closed down for the rest of the summer," the administrator yelled at Big Tony. Of course anyone saying anything was yelling because basket girl knew nothing about the outside events and everyone competed with Bill Haley and the Comets as they belted out "Rock Around The Clock." At that point, the second guard had finally netted one of the Baby Ruths and discovered the hoax.

"Hey, this isn't shit," he yelled for all spectators to hear. "It's a candy bar or somethin'." Then he took it in his hand and held it up to Big Tony. "Wanna bite?" he asked jokingly.

Neither Big Tony nor the administrators seemed to see any humor in the question and the few remaining women standing around with children shuddered and left the area. The guards then huddled up with the administrator and with the discovery that the floaters were just candy bars, the decision was made to keep the pool open.

"It's all just a big joke," Big Tony announced. "Just a false alarm."

Despite this reassurance, mothers dragged their kids to the locker room in lieu of taking any unnecessary risks with contamination.

At the deep end of the pool, the water seemed to be returning to its natural composition of chlorine and urine, and the diving boards were reopened.

We laughed our asses off all the way to the bus stop that day. It was a glorious caper that turned out to be another one of those "I'll never forget the day..." stories.

Chapter Seven

Raising havoc at the pool, combined with the building of numerous forts took us through the summer and the bonds of friendship continued to grow. About a week prior to the beginning of fifth grade, Jules brought additional unity to the five of us. Coming from Jules, it was unexpected and out of character. It was late afternoon and we were about to make plans for the following day when he told us he wanted all of us to meet in front of his house the next morning—said he had a surprise. Jamie showed up first and the two of us talked about improvements to the fort we were currently building and he filled me in on his newest idea for getting supplies.

This topic held little interest to me knowing we had the ease of obtaining scrap lumber from behind the Towpath Inn. It always had piles of junk behind it and gave us more than enough lumber. If we needed nails, we made after dark visits to construction sites and filled paper bags. Jamie's idea was an elaboration of the same plan with the addition of commandeering a wagon, which would allow us to take entire boxes of nails from some sites and lumber from others.

"We could establish an inventory of goods," he told me. "We'd have lumber and stuff on hand for anything else we want to build."

I nodded in polite agreement knowing that once such a plan was underway, he would have very little interest in building anything. It was the planning and its execution of stealing stuff that interested him. Before I could actually provide a comment on the idea, Al and Jules came out their front door.

"I want all of us to head over to the railroad yard." Jules announced. "I called Dusty and told him we'd pick him up on the way."

I was a bit reluctant about the idea as I felt Jules was infringing on my rightful territory.

"Why are we going to the railroad yard?" I wanted to know.

"Well, we're not actually going in the yard, just near it. C'mon."

With that, we slid off the porch steps and headed for the train yard. Once we arrived at the tracks, Jules held up a hand to bring our march to a halt. He then withdrew a handful of change from his front pocket and sorted through it.

"Take this one," he said, handing a shiny penny to his brother. "Here, you guys take these," he continued, as he passed out pennies to all of us. "I went through the change from my paper route money," he told us. "These were the shiniest ones I had. I picked them out especially for today."

"What are we supposed to do with 'em?" Al asked.

"Just hold your ass a minute," Jules told him. He finished giving us our pennies and started a second round. "You should each have two. Now pick out a couple of spots on the tracks and put your pennies on them. When the train comes by it'll run over 'em and flatten 'em like pancakes."

This, of course, brought a question from Al. "What if they make the train go off the tracks and crash?"

"They won't." I told him before Jules could respond. "It doesn't work that way."

Dusty gave me a look but then must've figured I was the train guy so I knew about such things. Actually, I had discussed this very topic one day with Mr. Faulk. Flattening pennies on the rails was not really a new idea; kids had been doing it for years. He told me it would take a lot more than a few pennies to derail any train he was engineering.

"So we have copper pancakes. Then what?" Jamie wanted to know.

"I just thought it would be neat if we all did this together and had one." Jules told him. "Kinda like a club or somethin'. Some guys in my class were talkin' about doin' it. They're supposed to look really cool when they're all flattened out."

Al then wanted to know why we each had two of 'em.

"'Cause the guy told me when the train goes over 'em they fly all over the place and sometimes they're hard to find."

"If we're gonna do this now, we're gonna have a long wait. There's no train goin' by here for at least an hour." I knew a freight train went through the yard at 10:10 every morning and it was barely 9:00.

Jules reluctantly saw my point and to kill some time, we walked down the road to the main office of the steel mill. The office had a water cooler with the coldest water on the planet and whoever was on duty would always let us get a drink. As per Jules's instructions, we each carried a canteen on our belt and we'd already drunk most of the water.

"We can fill our canteens at the cooler too," he pointed out. "After the train goes by we can hike somewhere, maybe up the canyon or something."

They were military surplus canteens we bought at the Army/Navy store. Al had some initial concerns on the day we all bought them.

"Do you think real army guys used these or do you think maybe they took them off of dead guys on the battlefield?"

"Yes," Jamie told him. "They took them off dead guys just so they could sell them to us to go hiking in the canyon. I think the one you've got is from a guy who got his head blown off by a grenade!" This comment seemed to end the discussion, although Al was not sure if he wanted to drink from the canteen of a guy who got his head blown off.

Sometimes we took day trips to the canyon behind the steel mill and more planning was required. We had taken Jamie to the Army/Navy store in Troy to purchase canned day-rations and whatever else he needed. His former life as a Catholic had never included anything like hiking up the canyon. On the day we took Jamie, the clerk got all upset because Al was walking around the store wearing a gas mask.

"You can buy it or you can take it off," the clerk told him. "Either way, you can't walk around the store with it on."

Jules told him he looked like a stupid alien and pointed out it cost too much anyway. He then grabbed Al's arm and instructed him on proper soldier behavior. Without enough cash to buy the gas mask, Al settled for a container of camouflage face paint. He took it out on the bus ride home and, after he put some on his face, Jamie grabbed it and passed it around. When we got off the bus, we looked like true soldiers ready for battle. This behavior and new look seemed normal to us, but the other passengers on the bus displayed questioning looks.

Once we arrived at the steel mill and got our drinks, Jules became antsy about getting back to the train tracks. He had planned this event on his own and the timing would be critical. As it turned out, we got back to the crossing and placed our pennies in plenty of time for the 10:10.

We sat a short distance from the tracks in an area of high grass but close enough that we could each see our pennies. Reflections of the morning sun were caught by their sheen and the coins appeared as copper raindrops perched on the contrasting heaviness of the tracks.

That was Jules's plan. It was simple and should've remained simple. Flattening pennies on railroad tracks had been done for years. Put one on, the train goes by, you find it. We were all in agreement with its simplicity. Jamie, on the other hand, saw an opportunity for a dare.

"We should go down there and hold them," he said.

The sheer lunacy of his comment interrupted our thoughts and before any objections could be raised he continued. "You know, hold on to them when the train comes, so they don't fall off from the vibrations. It would be cool. When the train comes, the last one to let go is the winner," he continued.

"Winner of what?" Al yelled. "A coffin?"

"If you don't want to do it, then don't," Jamie told him. "Maybe you're just too chicken to do it."

It was Jules who then took up the fight. "Why do you have to make a challenge out of everything we do?" He sounded angry as he posed the question. "This was just a simple thing all of us could do together. We don't have to make a suicide mission out of it."

"Yeah, well, I think I'm gonna go down and hold mine 'til the train comes. You guys don't have to, unless someone wants to put up a challenge."

Jules stood and stared again. His cheekbones tightened as he followed Jamie toward the tracks. "Okay, smart-ass, you want a challenge, I'll give you a challenge," he responded. "The rest of you guys leave your pennies where they are," he ordered. "Jamie and I will duel it out right here."

As he made the statement, he pointed to the area directly in front of us. Despite Jules's order to remain where we were, we left our protective nest and followed the two of them to the tracks. Jules crossed over and knelt down on one knee while he moved his penny to the rail directly across from Jamie's.

"No, I want the challenge," Al yelled to his brother. "He challenged me first."

"I'm doin' it," Jules responded. "Just leave your penny where it is."

"Just because you're bigger, doesn't mean you make my decisions. I'm doin' it and, if you say no then I'm doin' it up there before the train gets to this spot."

Al was adamant and Jules, realizing there was an underlying compulsion for Al to take the challenge, relented. None of us knew where it was going, but it was no secret that Al and Jamie had been spoiling for some kind of a fight. Al continually questioned Jamie's plans and charts for our capers. He may have been smarter than Jamie, but knew he was no match in any kind of a fistfight. Beating Jamie at a dare would go a long way in future disputes.

"Okay, you do it then," Jules said as he stood. "Get down here where I am so you're both at the same place when the train comes. As soon as either of you takes his finger off the penny, yell 'OFF' as loud as you can, and don't cheat on it. I'll stay on this side of the track with Al. You and Dusty stay over there with Jamie." He then looked directly at Jamie. "Make sure you yell it good and loud. We all wanna be able to hear it."

Dusty and I stood staring at each other not believing what was about to take place. Several silent minutes passed before we heard the distant sound of the 10:10. The low rumble grew as it approached. Al had one knee on the ground with the other leg positioned to sprint from the track at the last possible second. His penny was firmly held under his finger. Jamie sat with his arms locked around both knees, eyeballing his penny and biding his time with an air of nonchalance.

It wasn't until the train made the curve out of the yard and became visible to all of us that he got to his knees and put his finger down. The scheduled blast for the highway crossing sounded and mingled with the bells that coincided with the lowering of the gates. It became clear to all of us that with the roar of the approaching diesel, no one would be able to hear either Jamie or Al yelling the word off.

I looked across the tracks. Jules was crouched behind Al with both hands on his knees like a home plate umpire getting ready to make a call. Dusty and I followed suit and assumed the same position behind Jamie.

The train roared closer and it must've been the engineer's sighting of the five of us on the tracks that made him pull the horn again. This time, it was much louder and sustained for several ear-shattering seconds. Jamie and Al pressed their pennies to the rails and stared at each other. I stole glances back and forth between my two friends and the oncoming train. It was a freighter that had no prior reason to slow as it traveled through the yard. She was coming full bore.

The sound became so deafening; it was impossible for either Jamie or Al to hear me. "Let 'em go!" I yelled. "This is bullshit! Let 'em go!"

Both my friends remained in their positions, staring at the finger that pressed down on their penny. I looked at Al and, unlike other situations of this magnitude, his face showed no fear. With his glare aimed at Jamie, he seemed to have little regard for the oncoming train or his finger for that matter. Jules had shifted his hands to a position over Al's shoulders as if his plan was to pull him off at the last minute despite any stubbornness.

Everything then happened at the speed of the train. I caught a quick glimpse of the engineer's face and saw his look of horror. The horn wailed again, this time with no end to the blast and in the split second before it roared by us, Jamie's hand jerked from the track. Whether or not he yelled "off" was indiscernible and didn't really matter. What we did hear, just after Jamie's release of his penny was the bone-chilling scream from the other side of the train. I placed my hands over my ears trying to drown out everything. Trying to pretend nothing had happened. I didn't know if I was covering the sound of the train or the sound of Al's screaming. I just wanted to get away from there.

The train seemed to go on forever as car after car clicked over the joints of the tracks. Dusty and I fell to our knees as we joined Jamie in an effort to see Al and Jules to try and decipher what had happened. During the hollow intervals beneath the train I spotted their four legs and then, two of the legs crumpled and it looked like Al. He fell and rolled around the ground. The entire scene between the wheels was like watching an old-time movie as the actions flickered by.

When the train finally passed, our vision of Al was one of horror. He was standing again, but doubled over, holding one hand within the other as he continued screaming. He then stomped in circles, remaining doubled over until he stopped to face us. With a pained expression, he raised his right hand in the air and revealed a missing index finger. All of us turned white with fear. I felt sick and knew the thought of my friend losing a finger was about to make me throw up.

"I won," he announced in a choked voice. "Admit it you asshole, I won!" He pulled the deformed hand back into his stomach, continuing to glare at Jamie.

Jamie gave a nod conceding the victory. "Yeah man, you won," he said slowly and then added, "I'm really sorry, man."

"Sorry about what?" This time Al spoke with the calmness of a guy eating ice cream. "Sorry you lost?" As he asked the question, his missing index finger popped up from behind his palm and he started laughing hysterically. "You not only lost, you admitted it in front of all of us!"

Jules was so pissed at the joke he punched Al in the shoulder with a force that sent him to the ground. Rather than get up immediately, he rolled around continuing to laugh.

"I knew you were faking," Jamie yelled back. "There wasn't even any blood."

For the second time that morning, Jules intervened on behalf of his brother. "Bullshit," he said to Jamie. "You're whiter than he is," he said pointing to Al who was still laughing. The discussion that ensued left no doubt in the minds of the rest of us that Al was the victor.

Once the adrenalin settled, we found our pennies and discovered Jules had been right. When the train rolled over them, they took on a life of their own. Finding them proved to be a task, which made Al yell at Jules for only giving two to each of us. We also lost the advantage of finding them from their glint from the sun, which had been lost by the flattening process.

After we each located one, we continued to look for others but only Dusty found a second. We all exchanged comments about the different shapes we had recovered. Al's was more oval than round and he could see a small part of a number.

"Probably part of the date," Jules discerned.

"I'm keepin' this one," Dusty told us, holding up one of the two he'd found. "I think it's better than this other one." Al wanted to know if he could have the other one, just as an extra and Dusty obliged.

We continued to examine our coins and noted the differences of each. Dusty pointed to a mark on his and told us he thought it was Lincoln's nose. It didn't take long to discover that with their individuality, we could each identify our own. To prove the point, we threw them into Dusty's baseball cap and had no difficulty reclaiming each one. Dusty then suggested we go to his house and drill holes in them so we could put them on a string or something and wear them. This detour from the hike to the canyon was unanimously agreed to and in ten minutes we were in his father's garage. Dusty clamped his penny in a bench vice and prepared to drill it. Just prior to the first hole, he thought it might be a good idea to experiment with the extra one he'd given to Al. Reluctantly, Al handed the penny over and it took the place of the one in the vice. When Dusty touched the drill to the penny, the bit skidded across the smooth surface and made numerous scratches.

"Maybe we should make a dent in the coin where we were going to drill the hole," I told him. With a quick search we found a good-sized nail and after making a dent, the second drilling was successful but the bit was too large and the hole went through to the edge. We tried a smaller bit, which worked, but it left Al's extra penny with multiple holes and scratches, and he no longer wanted it.

With the proper bit, we each had a neat hole drilled in our penny and with some string we found in the garage, they were looped around our necks. This done, we decided to head to Beck's Foundry to continue examination of our new jewelry.

Beck's manufactured tank turrets. Not the entire tank, just the turret section that sat on the top. Once these were cast, a big crane set them out in the yard and lined them up in a uniformed grid pattern. At times, there would be as many as fifty or sixty turrets sitting on the ground and it was a great place to play army games. One turret would easily accommodate the five of us and we would climb in and take a gunner's position. We peered out one of the empty spaces where another company, at some point, would insert a cannon barrel or machine gun. We believed the guns for the tanks were probably made in the Waterton arsenal. Daylight streamed in through the hole left for the top hatch.

We often used the turrets as a meeting place and identified the rendezvous turret with letter and number coordinates. Even using the word 'coordinates' established the secrecy of our meetings. In that fashion, we could go across the front row by letter and then count back to the designated number and easily locate turret C-7 or E-12. Occasionally we would pull a trick on Al and give him different coordinates. He'd wind up sitting alone until he searched the yard and heard us talking in one of the other turrets. On this day, however, we all arrived together and selected A-4, a turret on the fringe of the grid. If the foundry workers were in the yard and wanted to chase us out, the fringe area gave us an easy escape route.

It was Dusty who looked at his penny and started the conversation. "If we all have these we should have a name or something to go with them, like Jules said this morning."

"Yeah," Al agreed. "How about we could be the ah...five pennies!" As he said it, his eyes lit up as if revealing the winning answer on a game show.

Jamie showed immediate disgust. "The Five Pennies! Are you shittin' me? Sounds like one of those Pat Boone songs! I'm out on that idea!"

Al was determined to come up with the winning name. "How 'bout the nickel group then? You know, it takes all five of us to make the nickel so we'd have to stick together."

"No! Also a dumb idea!" Jamie responded. And then from one of the few shadowed areas of the turret came the quiet voice of Jules. He seldom spoke in situations like this, but the entire idea with the pennies had been his from the start and he may have figured it shouldn't end in a drawn out disagreement.

"How about The Five-Cent Gang?" he said very quietly. "We could call ourselves The Five-Cent Gang." The solemnness of his comment seemed to permeate the tank turret as we all sat and pondered. I'm not sure if it was the word 'gang' that was in the title that made the name acceptable or if it was the tone of Jules's suggestion that settled the issue.

"Yeah, The Five-Cent Gang, I kinda like that." Dusty agreed.

"I like it too." I chimed in.

"Yeah, The Five-Cent Gang's okay," Al added, although he seemed to have a tone of disappointment at not having the winning entry.

Jamie's final comment sealed the deal. "The Five-Cent Gang, yeah, I can live with that."

So on that particular summer day, in turret A-4 of Beck's Foundry, The Five-Cent Gang was born and a pledge was taken to proudly wear our flattened copper dog tags around our necks. The highly valued treasures secured by kite string were touched periodically throughout the days that followed to ensure their presence. It wasn't something any of us ever wanted to lose. It was Jules, the gentle giant, who had come up with the plan. He had brought the shiny pennies, and most importantly, he had given us a new identity. It was also a day that, although Jamie was still our leader, Al had beaten him on a dare and gained a new respect from all of us. Because of all that, the coins seemed to unite us. We weren't just five kids hanging around together anymore. We were The Five-Cent Gang.

Chapter Eight

It was the end of summer. I sat on my porch the morning following Labor Day and waited for Dusty to turn the corner. I had forgotten Priscilla might be with him and she appeared first. Priscilla was Dusty's kid sister and she had obviously exerted a good deal of energy pedaling her bike up the back hill. She exhaled breaths of white clouds in synchronization with her pedaling. Seeing your breath—another sign that summer was over.

The nickname of Cilla, given to her by her mother, had been immediately replaced by Dusty and me to 'Silly.' Although she posed no threat to our friendship when he and I met in kindergarten, we were entering grade five now, and found that her yearning to tag along on our daily adventures was an annoying imposition. It had started over the summer when we were short a player and put her in right field. Her temporary adoption by our team led her to believe she could follow us everywhere, as if she were one of us. At times, even when issued a loud and threatening warning, she appeared to leave, but then in her stealth-like manner became invisible and covertly trailed us to our destination. In one instance, she overheard us using questionable language.

"I heard you guys. You were saying swears!" She yelled at us. "I'm tellin' Mom."

Throughout that entire day she followed us with a continued warning saying she was obligated to tell her mother and used the incident to blackmail Dusty. She told him she would keep quiet in exchange for being allowed to go with us. At first, his threats of retaliation secured her silence but after a week or so she became more brazen and we found ourselves in the problem-solving process of finding a way to eliminate her demands.

Before any information leaked from her lips, however, our timely redemption came when we happened upon a confrontation between Silly and two of her male classmates. They were refusing to let her pass on her way home from the baseball field. One was holding the handlebars of her bike as he straddled the fenderless front tire and the other was pawing through her basket seeing if she had anything worth eating. It was common knowledge that everyone brought a snack of some kind to the ball field. Our intervention saved the day and, unbeknownst to me, I became her personal hero. I believe it was that incident of heroism that curtailed any tattling regarding our cursing and it was never leaked to her mother.

Today as she neared my front porch, she rode full bore until she neared the curb and then slammed on the brake. Her back tire locked and the bike swung itself to a perfect skid as the tire threw gravel onto the sidewalk. It was the type of sliding skid I couldn't have done better myself. I was well aware that her dress, no doubt selected by her mother for her first day of school, disguised her bike-riding skills and betrayed her true athletic abilities. Dusty and I thought she handled a bike better than any of the guys her age and even some of the older guys but we would never admit that to her.

"Hi Auggie," she called out in her squeaky voice. The greeting was administered with a sing-song cadence and provided truth to the fact that Silly had a crush on me. It wasn't an emotion easily hidden by an eight-year-old.

"My mother's letting me ride my bike to school this year."

"I can see that," I responded. Until now she had been driven to school every day and was only an occasional inconvenience on days her mother couldn't drive her. On those days, Dusty and I had to make sure she got to school and back safely.

"I have to stay with you and Dusty 'til we cross the main road, then I can ride alone the rest of the way."

"Won't we slow you down? You're already ahead of Dusty." As I said that, he emerged from around the corner and, like Silly, was exhaling similar white clouds of fall.

It was clear summer was over and you could always smell that first day of school in the air. It was a scent that designated the return to Public School Number One and included the icy feeling in your lungs as you made the walk and sucked in the cold air. We always walked to school as riding our bikes didn't allow for any meaningful conversations.

The first day of school seemed to be the only school day that was a bit special to Dusty and me and this year Silly was about to ruin it. It wasn't that I didn't like Silly. She was actually pretty funny sometimes. Her awkward grin revealed front teeth that were slightly uneven and a slight spray of freckles covered her nose. She always had a wisp of hair that refused to stay in place and drooped down onto her forehead. She had a habit of skewing her mouth at just the right angle to blow it off so it didn't dangle in front of her eye.

Silly told us she wanted to be a boy and do boy stuff. She actually proved her worth by outrunning, outclimbing, and outplaying most of the guys her age. She was the type who grew on people and she was always cheerful and full of energy.

"No, you won't hold me up," she said interrupting my thoughts. "I'll just ride in circles around you guys so we can all stay together. Whaddaya think of this dress? My mother got it for me for the first day of school. She's *makin'* me wear it. Do you think it's awful?" She pretended she hated it but I could tell she was fishing for a compliment.

"Very pretty," I told her. I didn't mention I was also wearing new clothes, but since it was the first day of school, everyone was caught up in the ritual of the new wardrobe. I saw Silly had a book bag on the carrier behind her seat and I pictured the inside of it. If it was anything like the one I used to have when I was her age it had new tablets and one of those pencil boxes with a slide-off ruler on top and a sharpener on the end as well as some show and tell stuff from the summer. All the little kids had that crap on the first day.

Al and Jules joined us as we left my house and Dusty kept his part of the arrangement and made sure Silly got across Route 32. Once we crossed the highway, however, she ignored her allowance of freedom to ride ahead and pedaled near us as we walked. We slowed our pace, figuring she'd have a hard time staying with us. We knew there wasn't enough room on the sidewalk for her to circle us as she had planned. In a few blocks Jamie joined us and when she realized she was being completely ignored she rode on ahead, pedaling with an angry fervor, leaving The Five-Cent Gang preparing for another year at PS Number One. When we arrived at the schoolyard it was good to see friends we hadn't seen all summer and we talked about stuff we'd all done since school got out as we waited for the morning bell.

Inside, the building held that welcome-back newness of highly polished floors and the lingering scent of cleaning products that made all the areas look as refurbished as the janitor could make them. The blackboards were clean and their trays free of chalk dust. At the end of the first day they would be marred with new spelling and vocabulary words or facts of multiplication and division. Books were distributed with instructions that our homework that first night was to make covers from paper bags to protect them over the coming months of grade five. Some of the kids got real book covers from the store. That first day of the school year was always something special.

On day two it was over because once day one ended, it was just another year of school and a long wait until another summer. The polished floors were gone and, as expected, the blackboards were covered with words and numbers. Select students were honored by being asked to clean the erasers, which meant going outside at the end of the day and clapping them together to rid them of the day's accumulation of chalk dust. Following an incident in grade four, Miss Hannigan put Al on the shit list. He had slapped them against the red brick building and made a crude stick figure which he told everyone was Mr. Murdur. Some of us were waiting to see if word had gotten out to Mrs. Morrisey, our fifth-grade teacher.

She seemed to have the same problem as Miss Hannigan regarding our seating arrangements. Thinking ahead to our more-than-likely separation, we had spent turret time over the summer devising multiple hand signals, which made us fluent in distant communication. We discovered immediately that we should have devoted a bit more time to perfecting our system. On the first day, Al signaled Dusty that he needed to talk to him at recess. Dusty thought he was signaling that he needed a pencil and threw one to him. The pencil hit Sarah Maloney in the back of the head. This was witnessed by Mrs. Morrissey and brought about a punishment of staying in for recess to contemplate throwing pencils, and Al's message went for naught.

We had also decided to keep the identity of The Five-Cent Gang to ourselves for a while but wore our pennies around our necks tucked into our undershirts. We now used them for voting whenever an important decision had to be made. Anytime a question for debate was to be decided, those in agreement tossed his penny into the middle of the group. If your penny wasn't tossed into the pile it was counted as a vote of dissention. The use of the pennies for voting was Jamie's idea and I believe, looking back, it was the pressure of not throwing your penny into the circle being a sign of turning on your friends. To date, all of our votes had been unanimous.

Al's concern was what might happen if some of the older guys in school found out we were a gang and decided to beat us up. "They could beat the crap out of us," he commented worriedly. "Especially if Jules isn't around to protect us." Jules, of course, was isolated from us in Miss Buchanan's grade-six classroom and we only saw him at recess.

"Maybe you should remember that we don't really have any kind of a gang problem here." Jules reminded him. "Besides, I'm the biggest sixth grader in the school."

"Yeah, and besides that," Jamie added, "we're a gang that pulls off secret capers like the guys on TV, you know, the guys who started organized crime. We're not like the enforcers in the movies who're supposed to be tough guys. We fight with our brains."

For those reasons, our gang identity remained undisclosed to the general public. This was definitely a good thing for if we ever did have a physical encounter with other gang affiliates, especially without Jules, we would've surely been badly bruised and beaten.

Chapter Nine

It was a few months into the school year when our first fifth-grade caper evolved. It was the day after Thanksgiving. Jamie and I were sitting in B-14, the designated meeting turret, waiting for the others to arrive. The two of us were engrossed in our respective comic books and there seemed to be a strange quietness in the turret that day. After many months of maintaining my silence regarding Jamie's expulsion from St. Basil's, I felt this might be the perfect chance to satisfy my curiosity. I believed that he was tougher than I was and could probably take me in a fight, so I had waited until just the right time to ask the question. I took a deep breath and lowered my comic book. "Hey Jamie," I began, "Ya know when you were kicked outta school? I don't wanna be nosey or anything, but I was just wondering...why'd you get kicked out anyway?" I figured the nosey part would give him a way out if he didn't want to talk about it and he wouldn't get mad. To my surprise, he never batted an eye— never hesitated with his answer—never even looked away from his comic book.

"Uncontrollable sexual desires," he said with an air of coolness.

His answer caught me totally off guard. "What? Sexual desires! What does that mean?"

"Well, that's what they wrote down. It was just a bunch of bullshit that Father O'Brien wrote on my permanent record."

"Why, what did you do?"

His nonchalance continued. "I squeezed Anne Marie Demsey's boobs." With this comment he put his comic book down and looked right at me. "Well, actually, it was only one of 'em."

"You squeezed a girl's tit!?" With that, I guess Jamie could see he had captured my attention—so he continued.

"Yeah, she was one of the eighth graders who came to our room once a week to help us learn our spelling words. I didn't really need any help, but Demsey was probably the best lookin' eighth grader in the school. When she was assigned to our room, I started to get Fs on the spelling tests on purpose."

Excitement had now replaced my curiosity and I pushed for more details. "Yeah, so what happened?"

"Well, she sits down across from me bein' real nice. Smilin' and everything ya know? Anyway, I notice that one of the buttons on her blouse is undone and I can see part of her bra. For an eighth grader she was kinda built if you know what I mean and I could just imagine what that bra was holdin'. Anyway I kept starin' at 'em. I'll bet by the time she gets to high school she'll be bigger than Candy Melons. Anyway, I kept goin' back and forth lookin' at her bra and her smile, then her bra and then back to her smile. I couldn't even concentrate on the spellin' words she was askin' me. Finally, I couldn't help it anymore and I just reached my hand into her open blouse where the button was undone and copped a feel."

"Oh man! So then what?"

"Ahhh, she jumped up screamin' to Sister Patrice and yellin' that I squeezed her breast. Next thing I know, I'm bein' hit with a yardstick and dragged down the hall to Father O'Brien's office. Then he starts yellin' and tellin' me of my sinning ways and then he called my parents to come and get me."

"This is your last day in this school!" He was yellin'. When he took me back to the room to get my jacket, Anne Marie was talkin' to Sister Patrice in the hall, asking her if she would have to confess to Father O'Brien about me grabbin' her breast. I figured I didn't have to confess anything because Father O'Brien already knew I did it and punished me by kicking me out of school. I wasn't gonna add any Hail Marys to that deal. A few days later, he sent home a formal report. My father left the letter on the kitchen table and I saw it. Father O'Brien wrote that the reason I was kicked out, or 'dismissed from academic standing' as the letter said, was that I had exhibited 'uncontrollable and unwarranted sexual desires.' So now I'm doomed in any school 'cause that's on my permanent record. Probably won't even be able to get a job when I get older."

"Ah, I don't know. They'll probably forget about it by then." My statement was an attempt to make him feel better but we both knew our permanent record was a permanent record. Jamie and I were rarely alone so I seized the opportunity to continue questioning.

"Any regrets?" I asked him. "You know, about grabbing her tits."

He paused, and a smile began to show on his face.

"So c'mon," I pushed. "Was it worth it or not?"

His smile continued, spreading wider across his face and he stared off in the distance as if he was reliving the incident and then, before he answered me, we were interrupted by the voices of Al and Jules and Dusty as they neared the turret. Actually I figured I knew the answer; but I wanted to hear him say it.

As the voices neared the top of the turret, I could hear Al and Dusty arguing about whether or not the knife thrower on the Ed Sullivan Show was better at throwing knives than Tonto. Al had a passion for The Lone Ranger and was not convinced by Dusty's claim that a professional knife thrower could beat an Indian. He countered Dusty's argument by pointing out that Tonto was a professional, too. He was a professional Indian because Jay Silverheels, who played the part on TV, was a real Indian. The argument continued inside the turret with Al adding that because Tonto was brought up by Indians he would've been taught knife throwing when he was just a kid.

"A brave you mean," Dusty interjected. "Indians are braves, not kids."

Jules finally ended the argument with a threat of knocking both their blocks off if they didn't shut up about it. The conversation then turned to the wait we had until the new comics arrived at Miss Beezel's store.

"Yeah, she should put them out on the rack as soon as she gets them." Jules commented.

"Whaddaya mean, as soon as she gets 'em?" Dusty wanted to know.

"They'll be delivered tomorrow. They're always delivered on the last Saturday of the month. They're always sittin' there when I go by at the end of my paper route. I think the guy drops them off like the papers, around three o'clock in the morning or something. Ya know he probably delivers to all the stores the same night."

"And then you're sayin' that she doesn't put them out that day?" Dusty pursued.

"No, none of the stores do. They all wait until the first Monday of the month. At least that's what Miss Beezel does. Eddie does the same thing at The Pit. I never bought any from any other stores."

"I like to get 'em at The Pit," Al interrupted. "I mean where else can you buy a comic book and then sit and read it while basking in free air conditioning in the summer or sipping a good cup of hot chocolate in the winter?"

The Pit was Eddie Pittenger's drugstore, which was located halfway between home and school. Most people referred to it as Pittenger's or the drugstore, but the name eventually got shortened to Pit's place and our final abbreviation, which we thought sounded the coolest, was The Pit.

Al was right. During the school year we got our comics at Miss Beezel's but in the summer, it was a better deal to sit in The Pit. It was much nicer to sit at the soda fountain on a hot summer day and read comics. Once the winter cold set in, we often stopped for a hot chocolate on the way home. Miss Beezel only had a soda machine outside her store and in the winter she emptied it so the soda didn't freeze.

"The turret's plenty cool enough in the summer. Maybe we should spend some time tryin' to get some cold beer and have a turret party." Jamie threw in.

"I'd rather have the new comic," Al told him. "The day it comes out," he added.

Jamie looked him square in the eyes. "Then let's get you one." His face held a big smile. He then turned his gaze toward Jules. "You sure they're goin' to be there tomorrow morning?"

"Yeah, probably. It's the last Saturday of the month. I know 'cause I have to pay for my papers tomorrow night."

Al's face brightened as he was catching Jamie's idea and he turned to Jules. "Yeah, you could take one of the new comics from the bundle and ..."

He was cut short by Jamie. "No, forget that man, we'll take the whole bundle!" He returned his look toward Jules. "What time do you go by The Pit?"

"About six-thirty."

"How much room is in your bag then?"

"It's empty. The house at the end of the alley is my last customer."

"Anybody around?" As Jamie fired the questions, Jules seemed to become more interested in the idea.

"No, not really. Sometimes a car might be goin' by on the highway but no big deal."

"What about the weight. How heavy is the bundle?"

"Not any heavier than a full bundle of papers. I could carry it easy."

"Why do you want the whole bundle?" Al wanted to know. Dusty, already having figured out Jamie's scheme, answered the question for him.

"We could sell 'em in school. We'll keep one of each for us and sell the rest of 'em for half price or somethin'." This revelation was met with remarks of approval from all of us. The Pit was only a few blocks from Jules's house so once he got the bundle home we could sort them out there.

"It would be a good business if we could find regular customers," Jamie continued as he elaborated on the idea. "We could steal a bundle every month but from different stores. Miss Beezel's would be off limits as she might still have the cops casing her place after the Candy Bar Caper but there are plenty of other stores in the city. Stores we rarely go to."

Jamie was right about the money. Usually in the winter we could make a few dollars shoveling sidewalks and driveways. In the summer we mowed the lawns of those same people but customers for kids our age were hard to come by. The older guys took most of the business. Money meant independence from adults. It meant not asking for stuff. It meant taking care of ourselves and buying things other kids couldn't buy. Taking comics from a store didn't really seem like stealing. Once again Jamie reminded us that it was a big company and storeowners had insurance and stuff. It seemed like it would be a harmless caper and in addition to getting the latest issue of our favorite comics, we'd all make a few bucks.

"I say we vote on it." As Jamie said this, he removed the penny from around his neck. "We don't need any further discussion do we?" This time, he threw his penny into the middle of our seating arrangement. Jules tossed his in with no hesitation. I saw Dusty reaching for his and, not wanting to be the last to agree, I grabbed mine and added it to Jamie and Jules's. Al's toss, which always imitated Jules's action, made it unanimous.

Once the idea had been agreed to, it would've been easy for Jules to simply put the bundle of comics in his bag and take them home but, as usual, Jamie had to make a big production out of it.

He took us all outside and cleared a spot in the dirt. After finding a stick, he drew up another one of his aerial view maps depicting the city streets and the route Jules should take from The Pit to his house.

Once the plan was set, we went back to the neighborhood for lunch. When Jamie was about fifty feet into the shortcut to his house, he stopped and turned around to face us.

"Hey Aug," he yelled, "Yeah, it was definitely worth it!" and then he turned and cut through a yard.

Al and Jules looked at me. "What was that all about?" Al asked me. "Was what worth it?"

"Ah, nothin'," I said smiling.

* * * * *

WHETHER JULES ACTUALLY TOOK Jamie's route or not we never knew. At six-thirty in the morning of the Comic Book Caper the rest of us were in bed. The plan was to meet at Jules's house after breakfast. Jamie had set a time of eight-thirty but it was closer to nine when Dusty and I arrived to find Al and Jules and Jamie already in the cellar. The bundle of comics, still tightly bound with wire, sat on an old trunk. It was the same type of wire used to bundle the newspapers and Jules's wire cutters were sitting on the table. A protective wrapper was hiding the top comic adding to Al's eagerness to see the covers of the latest issues, but Jules was making him wait until everyone arrived. It seemed he wanted the event to be ceremonious. Dusty and I entered through the bulkhead door under the porch.

"Good timing," Jules said. "My mother just left for the Laundromat. We've got the whole house to ourselves."

Al was much more irritated. "Why are you guys so late? We were supposed to meet here at eight-thirty!"

Jules raised his hand to silence his sibling and then reached for the wire cutters. With two careful and exacting snips, the wires that crossed each other burst apart and the bundle seemed to exhale a sigh of relief as the comics expanded around their edges. Al wanted to be the first kid in the neighborhood to see the latest Superman episode. He reached in and tore off the protective wrapper.

We were standing in a small circle around the trunk and as the paper was removed, we all stood and gazed in amazement. We shared stares with each other as our eyes looked at the top cover and then back to our friends. Our jaws dropped and remained hung open as we stared in an awkward silence anticipating

Superman's next adventure. Jules had obviously grabbed the wrong bundle. The cover we were staring at displayed a large red Christmas wreath being used as a picture frame around the face of a smiling blonde woman. The expectation of the Superman comic to be revealed turned out to be the third anniversary issue of Playboy magazine.

Within seconds, our wide opened jaws turned to smiles, which escalated to laughs and then whoops and cheers. Our excitement was extended when Jamie took the top copy and let it fall open. He held it up as if he was one of our teachers reading us a story.

"Gentlemen," he said, as he allowed the centerfold to fall open and reveal all the details of the woman on the cover, "Meet Miss December, centerfold of the month!" A round of applause along with congratulations were given to Jules, the hero of the day for making the great mistake.

"There were three bundles sitting outside the store," he told us. "I thought they were all comic books. I just grabbed the closest one."

For the next hour or more, we pawed through the stack and found there were multiple copies of other men's magazines. In addition to Playboy, the cellar floor was soon covered with issues of *Gent, Lipstick, Midnight Lace,* and *Esquire.* Our gawking and dreaming were finally interrupted by the return of Al and Jules's mother. Jules went outside to assist with the laundry baskets and the rest of us put the magazines in an empty carton. It was decided that we would take them to one of the turrets until we figured out what we should do with the extras.

Chapter Ten

Once the magazines were moved to the turret, we all spent a lot more time there. We knew keeping them there for long could be risky. There was never any guarantee the turrets remained at the foundry. We couldn't decipher any set schedule, but periodically, they were loaded onto huge trucks that disappeared down the highway. Anything we put inside them for safekeeping was definitely on a temporary basis. The cranes usually loaded the trucks from the row closest to the foundry so we took the magazines to D-15, which was in the middle of the yard. We had considered the far end until Al spoke up.

"What happens if they decide to start loading from the other end?" For once, one of his questions made sense so we all agreed on D-15.

Dusty was the business manager of the gang and pointed out that, although the price on the cover was fifty cents, we could probably get double the price at school. "A dollar each keeps it simple," he explained. It also worked out nicely with our inventory as we had six copies of six different magazines.

"We can charge guys five dollars for six if they want to buy one of each and save a dollar," he pointed out. With six copies of each we could get at least thirty dollars. Jules reminded us that we said we were going to keep one of each for us to read. The mention of the word 'read' brought laughs in unison along with Jamie's comment of "Where ya gonna read them, man, in the bathroom?" and we all laughed again.

With all the work we'd done and the predicted yield of only five dollars each, Jamie threw out the question of whether this was worth doing again. "Maybe we should move on to something with more profit," he suggested.

Dusty and I agreed, mentioning that selling comics in school was okay but selling dirty magazines would mean nothing but trouble if we got caught. It was a bit beyond our level of risk taking. Al and Jules didn't seem to have any thoughts along those lines.

Before any sales came to fruition, Jamie reported the next day that he had mentioned having access to some men's magazines to one of the eighth graders in his neighborhood who attended St. Basil's. Later in the day, the kid came to his house and offered him twenty-five bucks for the whole stack.

"Twenty-five bucks," Al yelled.

"Yeah, I told him I had thirty magazines. I thought that was the deal. You know, keep one of each for us and anyone else could get a copy of all six for five bucks. Anyway, we could get rid of them all at once, take five dollars each and be done with 'em." Once again we turned to Dusty and, due to his prior concern regarding the selling of dirty magazines, he advised we take the twenty-five dollars and then find another idea for future revenue.

Before Jamie could accept the deal offered by his friend, word leaked out that the eighth grader had Playboys for sale and other offers started to pour in. In the next few days we learned that some of the high school guys at Catholic Central would pay five to ten dollars or more per copy. There seemed to be an actual bidding war underway. Jamie was quick to seize the opportunity and entered into negotiations. The twenty-five dollars offer for the entire bundle exploded into five bucks per magazine.

"Five bucks for each magazine? We'll be rollin' in the dough!" was Al's response when Jamie reported the windfall.

"Well, that was the original deal we made. There could be a minor problem," Jamie told us.

"Whaddaya mean, minor problem?"

"It's Tully, he's my contact guy. He can't give us any money to start. He told me he couldn't pay me until he sold 'em. He's got the customers all right, though. His older brother is in on it with him and he goes to Catholic Central. Tully said he's got guys lined up already."

"Why don't we just sell them ourselves to those guys? We'd probably wind up with a lot more if some of 'em are willing to pay as much as ten dollars!"

"Because for one thing, we don't know who they are. They could even take the magazines and then not pay up at all. Whaddaya gonna do then? Besides, you didn't let me finish. I told him I'd go along with getting paid later but he'd have to give us six dollars a piece. Anyway, if he goes for the deal, we're gonna get a hundred and eighty bucks!"

We all looked at each other. It was clear we had dollar signs in our eyes. We were mentally spending the money as he spoke.

"It's a good plan." Jules said, breaking the silence. "I say we give 'em the magazines and get the money later." Then he turned his gaze to Jamie. "Tell him we'll give him half the magazines. When he pays for those, we'll give him the rest. If he doesn't pay, I'll be comin' around to take care of business."

Again, we looked at each other. For a guy who couldn't get out of third grade, Jules seemed to be the smartest one in the turret. It appeared we had our own personal enforcer for The Five-Cent Gang but I did have doubts as to whether Jules would actually hurt anyone.

The plan worked. Before Christmas vacation, we not only had the money from the first fifteen magazines, but Tully had taken the other fifteen and he and his brother sold those as well. Combined with the money we made shoveling sidewalks over the holidays, we all had fat wallets.

The Comic Book Caper had paid off and our deal was done. At least it was done until the day after Christmas when Jamie lowered the boom on us. We were sitting in J-6 with all but one hole stuffed with newspapers to keep out the cold. The top hole was covered with an old piece of plywood. Inside, we kept warm with the use of clay flowerpots. We turned them upside down and put candles under them. The small drain hole in the pot's bottom let the smoke escape and the heated clay made for miniature stoves. It was a great trick that Jules learned in Miss Buchanan's science class. It turned the iron turret into a toasty igloo. We had also found that sitting on a couple of newspapers kept our asses from freezing. All in all, we were pretty comfortable in our winter fort.

"Whaddaya mean another bundle?" Dusty was furious as he hollered at Jamie.

"It was part of the deal. Tully said he'd buy the magazines but I'd have to guarantee another bundle in January."

"Wow. Why'd you make that deal?" Al's question was so sincere it was almost comical.

"What if the cops are watchin' The Pit?" I wanted to know. "Jules could get caught this time. He's the one takin' all the risks."

"Yeah, what if Jules gets caught?" Al echoed. "He's the one taking all the risks."

"Okay then. I'll go with him," Jamie countered. "And we'll hit a different store this time."

"What store? We don't know any stores! Miss Beezel doesn't sell Playboy!" Dusty was still upset.

"Bell's Grocery carries them." Jules said quietly. "If I start my route a little earlier, I can get over there by six. It's still dark then. I can get 'em."

"If there're two of us, we could grab two bundles," Jamie added. "We can double our money!"

Once Jules was on board, there was no stopping it. On the last Saturday of the month, Jamie explained to his parents that he was going to help a friend with his morning papers and the two met near Bell's Grocery at six o'clock. To Jules's surprise, Jamie had a sled to which he had secured two cardboard boxes. "Great huh?" he told Jules.

Jules eyed the sled, taking particular note of the design. It was much smaller than his own and halfway back it had sides and a back to hold a small child. The entire sled was pink and depicted a woman enveloped in a white fur coat. The coat was adorned with pink fur trim on the collar and sleeves. She held some kind of wand in her hand. Jules continued staring at it with a skewed eye.

Jamie noticed Jules's look. "It's the Snow Queen Fairy," Jamie said, anticipating Jules's question. "It belongs to the girl that lives next door to me. I'll get it back before she even knows it's missing. It'll make haulin' the magazines really easy."

"Why didn't you bring your own sled?"

"Hey, I'm not gonna risk my sled. What if somebody sees us and we have to ditch the magazines?"

Once the sled issue was resolved they loaded two bundles of men's magazines onto it. They had learned from prior experience and made sure they had the correct product. Jules tore off a piece of the protective wrappers before they were loaded and then grabbed a third bundle that contained the latest comics. "For Al," he told Jamie as he loaded them. Jamie, the master planner, had also brought along an old blanket to use as a cover. It also eased the possible embarrassment if they were seen hauling a sled depicting the Snow Queen Fairy, clad in her fur coat. The two figures walked without words. The morning held a wonderful quietness, which was broken only by the sound of the snow as it squeaked beneath their feet.

Later in the day we all met in J-6. Jamie had wasted no time in getting the magazines to Tully on this second go around and had collected half the money in advance. The count was seventy-four magazines and Jamie sat fondling a roll of rumpled bills. With our split today we would each get thirty-seven dollars with another thirty-seven to follow. We were waiting for Dusty's arrival so we could split the money but when he arrived, he brought bad news.

"I think we're gonna have to lay low for a while on this magazine deal. You better hold off on giving them to that Tully guy."

"Too late. Jules and I gave 'em to him this morning. He already gave me half the money. Why, what's goin' on?"

"The guy who owns Bell's Grocery called my father last night. Told him about his magazines bein' robbed and stuff. Then my father called the station and found out this is the second time in two months that this happened. I heard him tellin' my mother about the ones bein' taken from The Pit. Anyway, when The Pit was robbed, they thought it was just some fluke thing.

They even thought it might be the driver or somethin'. Now they think there's more to it. They even said it might be some high school kids 'cause this time they took all the bundles including the comic books. Did you guys take the freakin' comic books?"

"Why did they call your father?" Jamie asked, ignoring any possible risk involved in the phone call. "Do they think you might be in on it?"

"No. Remember his father's the Chief of Police." I said, answering for Dusty.

"Jeeeezus! I forgot all about that."

"The guy called him at home because they're also old friends and thought he might be able to help. Anyway, this could be trouble so you should call your friend Tully and tell him to hold off on selling the magazines."

Dusty's advice had come too late. The Tully boys had wasted no time in distribution of the magazines and when that information got to us we all remained in fear of discovery. Our fear, however, failed to deter our interest in the contents of the first haul we had made. In the weeks that followed, each of our respective bedrooms secretly held an issue of one of the first six magazines we'd stolen. As they were rotated from house to house, the noticeable dog-eared corners of specific pages left evidence of our favorites. In my case, Lisa Winters of Playboy was always number one.

It was the lateness of Dusty's unfortunate warning that prohibited us from rectifying our greed and although the month of December 1956 brought familiarity with the women pictured in the pages of our sacred library, the month of January 1957 proved to unravel pages from a different book.

Al probably summed it up best the day we got the news that a police car was sitting in front of Tully's house. After Dusty gave us the bad news, we sat in silence until Al asked one of his most unforgettable questions: "Do you think it will be a happy new year?"

Chapter Eleven

Within days of the phone call from the owner of Bell's Grocery to Dusty's father, the Waterton police car had relocated itself from the Tully house to the house of Jamie McGuire. It hadn't been much of a challenge for the local police. With only one high school in Waterton, it was the logical place to begin their investigation. This led to rumors that some students at Catholic Central were selling men's magazines. Since Catholic Central was located in the neighboring city of Troy, the investigation was tossed out of Waterton. It didn't take long for the police in Troy to discover the name of the boy selling magazines and, as he lived in our city, jurisdiction was returned to Waterton. The accused student then quickly implicated his eighth-grade sibling. Once the eighth grader was found to be complicit in the crime, he was so scared he would be sent to reform school, he immediately gave them Jamie's name. He also told the officers there were some other guys working with Jamie but he didn't know who they were. This was true. Jamie's philosophy was that The Five-Cent Gang didn't give information to anyone. As he told us, "nobody not in the gang doesn't need to know any of our shit."

Two police officers sat in the living room of the McGuire house and revealed the chain of events that lead to their visit. The living room was an area Jamie referred to as The Forbidden Zone. His mother, wanting to protect the couch fabric, had put a heavy clear plastic cover on it along with her instructions that anytime he wanted to sit in the living room he should sit on that couch. When Jamie told us about the plastic cover, Dusty mentioned his aunt did that too but he thought it was because she was from Germany. This led to a discussion as to whether plastic covers originated with Germans or Catholics. Dusty said his aunt might have been Catholic once, before she married his uncle but he wasn't sure, so we decided the plastic covers were a Catholic idea. Even with the plastic, none of Jamie's friends were to sit in the living room and there was certainly no food allowed in that area. During rare times when Jamie did have a friend over, he always shared his views on the subject and let them take a peek into the room. The one time I was there, it felt like I was looking into one of those rooms in a museum except it didn't have the big rope across the doorway to keep out curious spectators.

Although Jamie hated the room and had initially decided to rebel by not using it, he did find use for the couch whenever his father sat in one of the two unprotected chairs. One of his evening rituals was getting his daily dose of John Cameron Swayze as he read the evening news.

During that half hour Jamie found great amusement once he discovered that sitting on the plastic, he could squirm in certain patterns and make strange sounds that would interrupt his father's TV viewing. Some of the noises were unidentifiable squawks but his favorites were those that emitted an auditory tone as if he was farting. This was also the sound most interruptive to his father and would eventually lead to him being given the alternative of either sitting still or leaving the room.

On this day, when the two cops arrived, they had been escorted into the living room and had been seated on the plastic couch. Jamie's parents had quickly taken the unprotected chairs. After all, who knew where the policemen's asses had been that day. Jamie was directed to sit on the small hassock his father usually used as a footstool.

Once seating had been arranged, the first police officer informed Jamie's parents that the two other boys involved were the Tully brothers. He then leaned forward on the couch and whispered. "I'm not really supposed to reveal their names," and then added as an aside that, "If your son is a friend of the Tully boys, it might be a good idea if he looked around for some new friends. We've had dealings with that family several times prior to this incident."

He then turned and focused his attention toward Jamie. Jamie muffled a laugh as the officer's movements on the plastic evoked farting sounds and the cop's expression was trying to tell everyone in the room that the noise was coming from the cushion, not him.

He started to question Jamie, but then seemed to have an afterthought and he turned back to Jamie's parents. The couch continued making noises and an apparent redness rose from the officer's neck as he spoke. "It was the younger brother who received the stolen property from your son," he informed them. "This, of course, makes Jamie here our lead suspect."

"I don't think you need to refer to our son as a suspect." Jamie's father corrected. Hearing his father jump to his defense surprised Jamie.

"Well, you should be aware that he is in quite a bit of trouble," the other cop interjected, then turned to face Jamie, causing himself the same auditory embarrassment as his partner. "You could help yourself, Jamie, if you would give us the names of the other boys you're involved with and who helped you steal the magazines."

Jamie, who had been instructed by his parents to answer any questions the officers might ask him, was quick to respond.

"No one helped me," he told the cop. "I went out one morning and got them by myself. I used a sled to haul them back here."

His parents' faces showed little patience. After his expulsion from St. Basil's they were having none of it and as far as they were concerned, this latest episode was enough to ground him for the remainder of his life.

"Who would you say is his best friend?" the first cop asked looking at Jamie's mother.

"I really couldn't say," Mrs. McGuire told him.

This response by his mother was a revelation of sorts to Jamie. His parents didn't have a clue who any of his friends were. Never once had they shown any interest in who he was with or what they were doing. When he did invite friends to his house, they drew very little attention as long as they remained a safe distance from the forbidden zone.

The only other information they could possibly provide the cops would come from parent gatherings at school events and Jamie knew this never happened. After he had been expelled from St. Basil's, his mother was appalled at the thought of him having to attend a public school.

"He is a good Catholic boy," she kept saying. "Misunderstood perhaps, but a good Catholic boy. He certainly did not deserve to be forced into a public school," she explained with embarrassment to relatives.

For that reason, Mrs. McGuire never made cookies for the school bake sales and she always ignored invitations to classroom activities. She told

Jamie she would never attend any of *that school's* ridiculous PTA meetings. We, being Protestants, and the McGuires being Catholics also meant separate circles of friends for our parents. Jamie knew they had never met. This made it easy for us to remain friends with Jamie, even after the visit from the police, and continue our anonymity.

"Who was that boy you had over here last week, Jamie? What was his name?" his mother questioned as she interrupted his thoughts.

"Billie," Jamie responded without a moment of hesitation.

"What's Billie's last name?" the second cop wanted to know.

Jamie looked at the floor and shrugged his shoulders. "I don't know," he mumbled. "Just a kid I met in the neighborhood."

This response brought on a sigh of resignation from the cop while the vein in the neck of Jamie's father enlarged itself and began to turn a deep purple. The cop shot his partner a look indicating his thought that further questioning would be futile.

"Look," he said staring down Jamie's father, "if there's anything else you can help us with or any information about this, please give the station a call. If nothing else develops, I'm afraid Jamie here is going to get all the blame and whatever punishment goes with it."

❋ ❋ ❋ ❋ ❋

JAMIE CALLED ME AFTER the discussion between his parents and the cops.

"They got nothin'," he told me. "As far as they know I did it all. Tully would've squealed on you guys but he didn't have any names...besides, he's scared shitless. Thinks he's gonna go to prison."

The way things stood, we all agreed to separate and lay low until school resumed. With that resolve, the telephone became our only source of communication. Mr. Barnes, being an old friend of the store owner, felt obliged to give the matter his special attention and called him with continuous updates on what they'd found out—which was nothing. Silly had given Dusty a lesson on the correct way to pick up the extension in the upstairs hallway without being detected and he listened in on his father's phone conversations. Silly's knowledge of this was surprising. We never suspected she would have such a skill, as honest as she was. Additionally, sharing this bit of covert activity with Dusty meant she understood he might be in some sort of trouble and thus he might be a target for blackmail by her at a later date.

It wasn't until the passing of several days that Dusty and I discerned her telephone skills had more than likely been acquired while listening in on our phone calls, and now we would need to establish a secret verbal code. Between hand signals at school to avoid police surveillance and coded voice messages to confuse Silly, we were becoming fluent in many languages.

As Dusty listened in on bits and pieces of information, he kept me informed of new developments. We didn't know if Jamie would eventually crack and tell on us or, as Edward G. Robinson would say, rat us out. Dusty got pressure from his father who discussed the incident with him and pushed to see if he had heard anything from kids at school.

"If any other kids get caught, will they have to go to jail?" Dusty asked his father.

"No, that's not going to happen," his father told him. "But anyone involved would certainly be going to court along with their parents."

Dusty worried his father would find out he was involved and I knew if his father did find out, the trail would continue to my doorstep. Our parents were certainly aware that he and I were inseparable. If he was caught, I was caught. Whenever I got updates, I relayed the information to Al and Jules. Al, as always, was more paranoid than the rest of us.

"I unscrewed the mouthpiece on our phone to see if it was tapped," he told me. "I saw a guy do that once in the movies. We should all be careful and check our phones. If the cops wanted to, they could tap the phone of every kid in our class—or in the whole school if they wanted to."

I told him that was just movie stuff and he was worrying too much but after I hung up, I unscrewed the mouthpiece to make sure. I didn't think there was any tap in there. I wasn't sure because I didn't know what a tap looked like. Jules, on the other hand, didn't seem to have any worries at all regarding the incident.

When vacation ended and school resumed, the three of us passed Jamie notes and communicated with our hand signals. We figured the cops may have placed hidden cameras in our classroom trying to establish who Jamie's friends were. The best time to actually talk to him was during our bathroom breaks. We stood side by side at the urinals and had short conversations while we were pissing. Dusty told us even the cops wouldn't put cameras in the bathrooms. I thanked Jamie for not squealin' on the rest of us—told him he was still in good standing with The Five-Cent Gang. When things cooled off, we could all get together again.

"The judge put me on probation," he told me. "My parents said if I don't reveal the names of the other kids soon, they're gonna send me to a military school but I ain't tellin' 'em nothin'," he told me. Knowing Jamie, I knew he was true to his word.

Chapter Twelve

With The Five-Cent Gang living separate lives once again, I figured it might be a good time to visit Mr. Faulk. Despite the cold weather, it was still fun to spend the first half hour of a four-to-twelve shift riding the yard goat. I sat in the engineer's seat while he moved a few cars around before we went to his small office to share a snack of peanut butter crackers. Crackers were always kept in good supply in his locker, along with miniature boxes of raisins. On one occasion he gave me the combination to his lock. "In case you ever need an emergency dose of peanut butter," he told me with a smile.

After our snack, I transferred my attention to my grandfather. As the yardmaster, he was well respected by the men—a respect he had earned over his many years with the D&H. There was a good balance of new workers and old timers under his supervision, but since he was nearing retirement, no one had been there longer.

The men knew his role of supervisor never took priority over getting scheduled work done in the yard. Mr. Faulk told me once that many a night when a crew was shorthanded, my grandfather worked alongside the yardmen to keep the trains on schedule and he had the calluses to prove it.

As I sat in the office, I looked out the huge window and imagined it was my train yard—a set of giant toy trains that I could move around the loops and spurs that comprised the twisted mass of rails. Looking at the hundreds of cars in their distinctive shapes and colors always reminded me of a group of trains having some sort of meeting, a train convention or something. The sound of the engines snorting and the uneven rise and fall of their revving diesels were like the sounds I heard from the summer carnival—compressors that ran the rides on the midway producing a growling-like noise each time they needed additional power, and then returning to their natural purring.

I could see most of the yard from the office. On the far end was an area known as the graveyard, which stored cars that were in need of repair or waiting to be scrapped. Other spurs held long chains of cars waiting like hitchhikers for other trains to take them to their intended destinations. Some contained Pennsylvania coal or "Black Diamonds" as the men called it. For me, the entire view was a panoramic paradise.

In the springtime, I could easily view the intricacies of all the tracks in the yard that eventually merged into a straight run that continued as far as the eye could see. Now, the dead of winter brought an early darkness and gave me a different painting. Lights flickered throughout the yard as men carried lanterns and flashlights. Mr. Faulk had returned to the yard goat and the cab was illuminated. I could see his profile silhouetted within the dim light as he maneuvered the small loco around the tracks. Inside the office, the warmth from the potbellied stove served as a reminder that winter had arrived and the crew would soon be given the task of removing snow from the tracks.

I was rarely around past five o'clock. My instructions to be home for supper trumped any thoughts of staying to help in the yard. Occasionally, a phone call from Gramps would allow me to stay and eat supper with him later in the evening. It was then that everyone in the yard who had worked to get the outgoing train in order would take to their lunch pails or "go to beans," as they called it. By eight-thirty, Mr. Faulk would have the eastbound loco onto the main line and begin coaxing the big diesel out of the yard. Thirty-two minutes later we all knew he would have her sitting in the Albany depot, right on schedule.

By the time the men finished supper, a westbound train would be in the yard and the men would grab new clipboards and repeat the car shuffling once again. Just before the shift ended at midnight, Mr. Faulk would bring a second train in on a return run from Albany, shed his D&H coveralls, and punch out at twelve o'clock.

❋ ❋ ❋ ❋ ❋

ONE DAY IN MID-FEBRUARY, I hurried home from school and got to the yard to witness the entire crew of workers standing outside the beehive. When Harold saw me approaching he put his forefinger to his lips motioning me to be silent. When I joined the group, I realized they were all listening to an argument that was taking place in the office. The volume of the two voices carried the entire dispute out to the yard and some of the men were having a chuckle over it. I immediately recognized both voices.

The first I heard was that of Mr. Faulk. "The new loco is having her number changed?" he asked. Mr. Faulk had been with the D&H almost as long as my grandfather and their close friendship could be calculated in decades. It was that relationship which allowed the tone he took, as he demanded an explanation.

"That's bad luck ya know," he yelled. "My God, John, it's almost as bad as havin' a woman on board a ship. They were known to sink ya know!"

"It's not my doin', Ben. Orders for the change came right from the top. Here, I'll get you the work order if you don't believe me." My grandfather's voice was certainly loud enough to hold his ground, but his tone was lacking the irritation of Mr. Faulk's.

"Believe me, I'm on your side on this but I've no choice in the matter," he continued.

The two men had now shifted their positions in the office and we continued to watch them through the glass. The position held by Mr. Faulk placed his head behind the D&H lettering on the window. The late afternoon shadow gave him the appearance of having the D&H logo tattooed on his face. I watched my grandfather open his desk drawer and after he rummaged through a few papers he withdrew a letter and handed it to his friend. Even from my distance, I could see the familiar spacing of the words 'Delaware and Hudson' in bold letters across the top. Like all the company stationery, it displayed the yellow shield of the D&H alongside the letterhead.

My grandfather stood in silence, giving Mr. Faulk time to read the memo. It was a work order from the main office directing the painting of the new diesel along with the number change. He gave him time to read it before he spoke.

"Just like it says there, Ben. It clearly states that the recently purchased diesel is to be painted with the blue and gold of the D&H along with having her number changed from 1508 to 4075. It's a B&M engine. We can't keep their colors on her."

"It's not the color change I'm against, it's just bad luck to be changin' numbers."

Mr. Faulk shoulders slumped as he dropped the arm holding the letter to his side. On one hand he was thrilled about the purchase. The new diesel was an RS-3 made by the American Locomotive Company in Schenectady, which was only a fifteen-minute drive from the yard. The company wasn't the biggest manufacturer of locomotives, but Mr. Faulk believed it to be the best. He also enjoyed being in close proximity to the manufacturer in case he wanted to suggest improvements or discuss any concerns. Recently acquired, the 1508 was only two years old and, according to Mr. Faulk, the best diesel the company ever put on the rails.

He raised the letter and lingered over it as if reading it again might change the wording.

"Like I said, Ben, I'm with you on this one," my grandfather told him, "but it's from the top. You and I have no say in the matter."

"We may not have a say in it, but I'm the one who drives her and I'm the one who could be gettin' the bad luck. There's just no call for it. You do what you want John, but I'm callin' her the '08!"

"It's a registered number with the B&M, Ben. You know that. It's cheaper to re-register than transfer the number."

With that declaration, Mr. Faulk tossed the letter on the desk and left the office. It was only when he appeared on the platform that he realized the crew had played witness to the entire incident. He addressed the crowd as he stepped off the platform. "You idiots got no reason to be standin' around eavesdroppin' on me and John when we're discussin' company business. I'd think ya all might be able to find some actual work to do."

The men separated themselves as if they were the two halves of a giant zipper as Mr. Faulk walked through them. Once he passed, I heard a comment that disturbed me immensely. I couldn't decipher who made it, but someone mumbled, "He's just an old alcoholic who ain't never gonna change his ways."

Before I could look to see who said it, Mr. Faulk stopped and turned his gaze back toward the crowd. Evidently he had heard the remark also. It was then he spotted me standing with the men and his look of anger transformed itself into a warm smile.

"C'mon Auggie, let's you and me go for a ride. I've got to move the '08 down the line aways. You better come along and supervise," he told me. As we walked, he continued with his displeasure of the memo.

"Imagine, the railroad says we've got to change her number. Well, I'll tell ya Auggie, the company can do what it wants, but she'll always be the 1508 to me— just as she was christened. It ain't right changin' numbers like that. It's bad luck."

I had to walk quickly to keep up with his long strides and after boarding the big diesel we moved her down the track and he patted the throttle as he spoke to her.

From that day on he always referred to her as the '08 and no one ever argued with him about it. When he told the men he was taking out the '08 they all knew they could find him on the 4075. I believed my relationship with Mr. Faulk obligated me to honor his continuance of ignoring any change in her number. I do recall one instance when I mentioned it in the presence of my grandfather, which triggered a raised eyebrow in harmony with a forgiving smile.

We drove the engine to a vacant spur, and Mr. Faulk must've felt there had been enough talk and dispute over the number change because the subject was dropped.

"I've got to move her down near the graveyard for a couple of days so they can slap a new coat of paint on 'er. Make her one of the fleet." His continuation of our conversation then turned to the issue of colors.

"What do you think of the colors the D&H uses? You like the blue and gold?" he asked me.

"Yeah," I told him. "I do."

"Yeah, me too. Not as good as black, mind ya, but it's acceptable. I think colors are important for companies. I mean, ya take John Deere now...there's a company that makes a great tractor. A great tractor! But they got the color all wrong. Tractors oughtta be red. I mean, who ever heard of a green tractor? Now, on the other hand, Massey Ferguson hit the nail on the head. Their tractors are all bright red, as they should be."

Before I could respond, he continued with the lesson in color. "Now, you take the Gulf Mobile and Ohio locos. Why they came out with a diesel locomotive that was bright red. Then—on the top part where the engineer sits and down around the wheels— they painted the darn thing purple! It's the most God-awful thing I've ever seen. I mean, would you want to ride around the yard with me if the '08 was painted red and purple?"

"Yeah, I guess that would be kinda weird," I agreed.

After leaving the '08 near the graveyard, the two of us walked back to the yard goat. As we walked, he continued with my education regarding the railroad and I listened and learned everything I could. He had already given me the responsibility to visually inspect any switches we passed during our walks to and from different areas of the yard. He had taught me how the switches worked and how to use the throw bars to move them to change the path of a train. In that lesson, he emphasized the importance of timing.

I was allowed to stay and have supper with my grandfather that evening and after the meal we climbed into his Packard and he drove me home. I could've taken short cuts and walked the distance in less time than the drive, but he never allowed me to walk on a dark winter night. During the drive, I reluctantly confessed that I had heard the comment that Mr. Faulk was an alcoholic. My grandfather evidently picked up on my concern and disappointment. I continued by defending Mr. Faulk and stated that I had never once seen him take a drink and he never smelled like he'd been drinking. I was surprised when my obvious disillusion over Mr. Faulk being an alcoholic brought forth a hearty laugh from my grandfather and, when we reached the house, he switched off the ignition and opened the glove compartment.

"Let me show you something," he said. "I'm an alcoholic too, ya know. As a matter of fact, I think you are too, or at least you might be some day." As he spoke he removed a small pad from the glove box and in the dim light from the compartment he wrote the letters A-L-C-O. He then wrote the word ALCOholic beneath it, capitalizing the first four letters to emphasize the ALCO. I stared at the soiled pad and said nothing.

"You see these letters?" he asked me as he circled the first four. "They stand for American Locomotive Company—the company most of us believe to be the best manufacturer of diesel engines. Men in our business—men who really love trains—like you, and me, and Mr. Faulk, well, we're known as alcoholics."

I sat and stared at the note pad.

"Feel better now?" he asked me.

"Yeah, much better. Thanks, Gramps." With that he returned the pad to the glove compartment and flipped it shut. His huge hand patted my knee and he scooted me out of the car with a reminder to make sure my homework got done or he'd be in hot water with my mother.

When I climbed into bed that night, more than an hour of tossing and turning took place as I relived the events of the past two weeks. The money we'd made, then Jamie being arrested and all of us worrying about getting caught. Today had been a good day with Mr. Faulk. With all he taught me, I always thought he would've made a real good schoolteacher. I mentioned that to him once but he just laughed.

"All I need is a good loco and a lot of track in front of me," he told me. "It's one of the reasons I like engineering the night train to Albany. Night trains just rumble through the blackness," he said, "and on summer nights as I move through that darkness under a starlit sky, I try to imagine the families with kids behind the pulled window shades that are all lit up inside."

As he spoke, his eyes danced and his fingers pointed toward the houses and he twisted them as if he was casting a magic spell over the people living inside.

"I wonder if they wait and listen every night when I sound the horn at a nearby crossing?" His eyes drifted down the tracks that left the yard and disappeared into the distance. It was as if I wasn't there...as if I wasn't any part of what he was thinking and I thought about what Gramps said about being an alcoholic. I understood what Mr. Faulk meant about people in their houses. I was often on the other side of the window. In my own room at night, I always listened for the night trains. The haunting sound that was a strange mix of a horn and a whistle but singularly could be defined as neither. It was a sound that had become a memorable part of my childhood.

Even that night, I knew the silence would, at some point, be overpowered by the low rumble of the night train, and I waited to hear it. The rumble became louder and I pictured it streaking through the rail yard I knew so well: the Delaware and Hudson streaming through the pitch of night; the gate bells sounding to warn approaching cars and the engineer dispensing a piercing blast of the diesel's horn; the same piercing sound that after traveling the mile from its origin to my window was transformed into its lonely wail. It was the 11:32 returning from Albany. I pictured Mr. Faulk in the engine compartment and followed along with him as the train reached the highway crossing. The slight dip between the pavement and the railroad yard caused a thumping sound as each car snaked its way onto the long straight run from Albany.

The thumping of the wheels was like a heartbeat and with each beat I counted the cars as they passed over the indent: thump thump, thump thump, thump thump. It was that mesmerizing sound that finally put me to sleep and just before dozing off, I understood what Mr. Faulk meant that day. I wasn't sure whether he was talking to me or just thinking out loud as if he was reciting a poem. He said, "I have always felt poorly for anyone who has never heard the lonely wail of a distant train as it rumbles through the black of night."

Chapter Thirteen

The police involvement in the Comic Book Caper during our fifth-grade lives had scared all of us, but we eventually put it in our rear view mirror and watched it fade into the distance. Jamie never ratted us out, his parents never sent him to military school, and the Tully boys never went to prison. The events of the crime eventually disappeared into the bleak days of winter and, although spring brought on new energy, it was an unanimous decision during a meeting in C-7 that we had had enough capers for a while. This feeling lasted until the end of the school year at which time Jamie seemed to be getting restless. He was looking for any kind of an opportunity and, surprisingly, it was presented to us by the United States Army.

In most cities across America, Memorial Day weekend designates a renaissance of summer and a rebirth of activities after a long winter's hibernation. It's the celebrated three-day weekend involving picnic baskets, the opening of camps, and getting boats waxed and prepared for the season's first launch. To kids living in Waterton, however, it was overshadowed by Armed Forces Day, which arrived two weeks earlier. In our city, Armed Forces Day was the one day of the year kids got the opportunity to peek inside the Waterton Arsenal.

This massive weapons installation, which divided the city into two unequal parts, encompassed forty-two acres of land and housed facilities in which the military manufactured a variety of weapons. These included ICBM missiles, high-powered machine guns and, most notably, the world's largest rocket. This fact was the reason students attending the Waterton Junior-Senior High School carried garnet-colored gym bags depicting a rocket being launched into space. The missile was our mascot and we were known as the Garnet and Gray "Rockets."

Because of its importance in military standing, the arsenal was completely protected by a four-foot high stone wall that provided the anchorage for a wrought iron fence, that added an additional six feet of height. The iron rails were spaced a few inches apart with the tip of each fashioned into a sharp point.

Anytime necessity required us to walk the entire length of the fence to go from Port Schuyler to the uptown area, it was customary to find a stick and run it along the iron fencing like a piano keyboard. Missing any of the rails during the walk was construed as a prerequisite to bad luck, which meant the acceptance of the task of hitting hundreds of rails was an endeavor of real commitment. It became more complicated if several of us accepted the challenge as we usually got in each other's way. This led to a lot of pushing and shoving until one of us broke from the pack and ran the remainder of the length to become the winner. Even then, the integrity of the champion was questioned as to whether or not every spike had been touched. The fence eliminated the boredom of walking the quarter-mile stretch. It was that same length of the protective barrier that caused us to take the city bus to the pool.

We sometimes joked that the high-walled barrier was there to protect Candy Melons from her large array of suitors. Her father was the base commander and she lived inside the impenetrable walls. She was one of several kids who lived in the arsenal and they were all driven to school in an army-green van. Although none of the arsenal kids went to Public School Number One, we had heard about them indirectly through comments made by Dusty's father. He often got calls at home when some of the older kids from the arsenal got into trouble in the city. The calls were usually from a member of the town council with assurance that the base personnel would appropriately handle any disciplinary measures needed. The councilman always added the importance of maintaining good relations between the military and the city.

Only two access roads allowed entrance into the arsenal and guard houses manned by armed military personnel protected both. With the exception of a few lay people hired for clerical duties, all employees were members of the United States Army and they lived and worked within the compound.

The Saturday designated for the celebration of Armed Forces Day was that one day of the year when the arsenal gates would open, the armed guards would step aside, and all the secrets of military weaponry were revealed to the waiting public. This was a day, which Al, being our weapons expert, cherished above all others. To him, it was better than his birthday. Large cannons were fired throughout the day. Ballistic missiles stood erect on temporary launch pads. Helicopters were placed at various points where we stood in long lines for an opportunity to sit in the pilot's seat and gaze in awe at the multitude of dials and switches.

The greatest magnet for us was the demonstration of the firing of the machine gun, which occurred every hour on the hour. We rendezvoused at the arms building and witnessed the first demonstration of the day, which was focused on the Browning Automatic Rifle. When playing soldiers, it was the Browning we carried onto the battle fields, imitating John Wayne, and shot down the enemy of the day. It was one of many machine guns manufactured in the arsenal and, as explained by the demonstrating sergeant, was about to be phased out in a few years and replaced by a more advanced weapon.

An army sergeant was in charge of demonstrating the weapon and when he spoke, each word in his sentence carried the same monotonous tone. "The Browning Automatic has the capability of firing 500-650 rounds per minute," he announced to the crowd.

This statement, of course, immediately triggered questions from Al who was never reluctant to holler out anything on his mind.

"Have you been in any wars?" and "have you ever killed anyone with it?"

The sergeant then explained that, thankfully, he had never had to kill anyone. This was a bit disappointing. In the several years we'd attended the open house, we had never been introduced to the Browning by anyone who'd killed someone with it. As was the case in the classroom, Al's questions seemed to stir an enjoyable interest within the observing public.

Spectators were then warned that the firing of the weapon was quite loud and everyone was advised to cover their ears. At that point, the sergeant ceremoniously donned his own ear protection, inserted a full clip of ammunition, and fired the machine gun at the area behind him. He first released three or four short bursts and then concluded with the grand finale of a lengthy ten-second discharge, which spewed empty cartridges on the ground as they made their exit from the chamber. When the firing ended, the sergeant turned to face an audience with all but five people standing with a uniformly placed forefinger stuck in each ear. The five of us stood grinning, cherishing the ringing sound in our ears and watched the smoke curling skyward from the hot barrel. Never would we allow such an opportunity to hear a real machine gun be muffled by sticking fingers in our ears. The sergeant made another announcement, which was only known to us by the moving of his lips. Our temporary loss of hearing made it difficult to decipher exactly what he was saying.

We later discovered he told the spectators there was another demonstration scheduled for thirteen-hundred hours. We, of course already had the armory's schedule for the whole day and knew what guns were to be fired and the time of each demonstration. If we had been able to hear his announcement of thirteen-hundred hours we would've known he meant one o'clock. If anyone was confused about the military time reference, Al certainly would have been happy to circulate and translate for any civilians.

Jamie had never been to an open house. This year, as we concluded grade five, he was available to go with us and, for him, it was his first look inside the arsenal walls. While Jules and Dusty and I took in the sites and opportunities that availed themselves to us, Al remained at the armory most of the day and Jamie disappeared. Unknown to us, he was studying the layout of the entire forty-two acres. After disappearing from our group, he sat contentedly in the shade of a large maple tree and studied the guide map that each attendee had been offered at the main gate.

❋ ❋ ❋ ❋ ❋

ON THE WALK HOME, Al stared off into space grinning ear to ear. Prior to our departure, he had witnessed the ceremonial firing of the arsenal's largest cannon and, of course, declined the obligatory suggestion to cover his ears. For the remainder of the day he was a very happy deaf kid.

A week later we sat in F-7 and Jamie's thoughts of the open house surfaced. In his usual exaggerated manner, he withdrew a folded paper from his back pocket and spread it out on the cold floor of the turret. Much like the blueprint of Miss Beezel's store and the drawing of the alley for the Comic Book Caper, the sheet was covered with boxes and Xs. None of us had any idea what we were staring at until Jamie informed us it was an enlarged map of the arsenal grounds.

"It took me a couple of hours to make the big copy," he told us.

We all looked it over, but Al was the first to respond.

"Whaddaya gonna do, break into the arsenal?" his question carried an obvious tone of sarcasm but Jamie seemed to ignore it.

"No, we're all gonna break into the arsenal," he responded. His eyes held the look we had all seen many times. We knew he was dead serious.

"Look," he began. "I've been studyin' the layout of the wall and the fence they've got all the way around the place so people can't get inside but look at this." As he talked he pointed to a square on the map that depicted a swimming pool. It was part of a recreation complex for the families that lived on the base.

"The pool is totally enclosed by another fence, probably to keep little kids and stuff out. If we drop over the outside wall into the pool area, no one will spot us getting in because the pool wall'll protect us. Once we're in, we can pull a commando raid."

At the word commando, Al's ears perked up and his attention became much more focused. "Whaddaya mean a commando raid. What are we gonna do once we get inside?"

"Look, see these Xs I've got marked on the map? This one here is the old civil war cannon that's out there on display and this one is the Honest John Missile they've got sittin' there."

He pointed to the Xs and explained what each one represented. As he continued, he seemed to gain more confidence until he felt we were satisfied that he knew what he was talking about. The fact that he had made a careful study of the interior layout certainly was evidence he had done his homework on the subject. His presentation was so well executed he captured the interest of all of us.

"Okay, so you've got these things marked on here," Dusty responded. "What do we do with them? You plannin' on stealin' 'em?"

"No, that's the beauty of this caper. Look here." He pointed to the top of the blueprint where he had written, 'The Cherry Bomb Caper.'

"I've got ten Xs on here. When we get inside, we each take two of them and plant a cherry bomb with a time fuse. Remember that guy in the movies who stuck the fuse of the dynamite into the end of his cigar so he could get away? We can do the same thing with the cherry bombs, but we can use cigarettes."

"Okay, then what?" I asked.

"Then we get back to the pool, over the wall, and circle around to the used car lot across the highway to watch the fun. Don't you get it? This is an arsenal full of weapons. They'll think somebody's shootin' or something. Those army guys'll be runnin' all over the place tryin' to figure out what's going on...like they're under attack or somethin'."

"I like it," Jules chimed in from his gunner's position in the turret. "But don't you think it's gonna be a bit hard for a bunch of kids to hide cherry bombs with military guys walkin' all over the place?"

"Yeah, normally it would be, but the beauty of this is, we'll do it when it's dark out. Ya know, like one or two o'clock in the morning when nobody's around." He paused and looked at the rest of us.

"Anybody here who can't sneak out of the house?"

We all knew that Al and Jules could get out okay. Their mother was a nurse at the hospital and worked the night shift. It seemed Jamie made the inquiry for the reassurance of Dusty and me. With Dusty's father being the Chief of Police, he may have seen the possibility of some friction. Surprisingly, there was little hesitation with Dusty's response.

"Yeah, I can get out."

Jules followed up with the expected answer. "Yeah, me and Al can get out no problem." "How 'bout you, man, can you get out?"

"Yeah, I can do it," I told him without actually thinking about any specific strategy for doing so.

Dusty pointed out that the blueprint was a good start but we would have to do a lot more planning before pulling any commando raid on the arsenal. He suggested some surveillance and that word alone triggered a positive response. We all agreed and Jamie quickly stated some additional information he'd been thinking about.

"I'll keep working on the plan," he told us. "Each of you will have to take care of some of the details. I'll give you all assignments as soon as I work things out.

We'll go over everything once we get all the timetables."

Once again, the word 'timetables' gave credence to our new caper.

A few days later Dusty helped me rig the screen on my bedroom window. It was one of the long ones that covered both the top and bottom window so we tied strings on the top of the frame so when I pushed it out on the bottom it would hang loose. The strings acted like hinges and allowed me to slip out without having to go through the house. He didn't need anything rigged at his house as his bedroom was fairly isolated from his parents and he could get out easily. His only possible obstacle was Silly but since it would be two or three o'clock in the morning, he knew she'd be asleep by the time he left.

With only a few weeks before summer vacation, we agreed that the Cherry Bomb Caper would be a go the first weekend after school got out. Although Jamie masterminded the details, we all had our own thoughts of how it would work and contributed ideas. A commando raid...on the arsenal...a highly secured federal installation...in the early hours of the morning...our pockets loaded with cherry bombs and time fuses. What could possibly go wrong?

Chapter Fourteen

During the first week of vacation, Dusty and I sat on the curb in front of my house waiting for Al and Jules to wake up and come over. The day was going to be hot. The heat bug was already humming and we discussed possible scenarios for the day ahead. If our daily schedule held to form, Al and Jules would be out of the house and over to my side of the street any minute and Jamie wouldn't be far behind.

I was picking up small pebbles from the uniform piles the street cleaner had deposited along the edge of the curb. Holding them in my left hand, I selected the good throwing ones and tossed them into the center of the road. It was always a good time killer. I waited for Dusty to say something. For several days he hadn't been himself and I wasn't exactly sure what was going on in his head.

As twelve-year-olds, none of us had an inkling of what depression was, so Dusty being depressed about anything never occurred to me. Our emotions, when we bothered to ask one another, were pretty much limited to either being okay or not okay. If a particular idea was being discussed, we were either cool with it or not cool with it.

The two of us had been best friends for so long that we could tell if the other was okay or not okay. It was this alliance that led me to believe that, for some reason, Dusty was not okay and hadn't been for a few days. It was usually this same alliance that kept either of us from probing the reasons for the other's feelings. After three days, however, I was tired of having a best friend whose mind was somewhere else and decided to seek out some answers.

"So, how you doin'?" I asked throwing a good-sized pebble to an oil spot on the road.

"Okay," he lied.

"I don't think you are." I told him.

"Whaddaya mean, you don't think I am?"

"I mean you been mopin' around for three days now like your best friend died and seein' as how I'm supposed to be your best friend, and I'm noticeably still alive, somethin' else must've happened."

There was a long pause before he responded. "I think my father got demoted," he finally confessed.

Dusty's father had been the Chief of Police in Waterton since I was born so this news wasn't good. Normally we didn't like cops but Dusty's father was different. Whenever any of us were at his house hangin' around, he was always pretty friendly and would have a good joke to tell us—usually some cop joke. I sat and recalled one occasion, when we were all at his house and Al asked him if he could see his gun. This followed Al's usual question as to whether or not he had ever shot anybody. Mr. Barnes's response was pretty much the same as the one given by the sergeant who demonstrated the Browning.

After a bit of coaxing from the rest of us, Dusty's father, who was always very safety conscious with his service weapon, removed it from its holster. We all watched with anticipation as he pushed the lever allowing the cylinder to fall open. He tilted the gun and the bullets dropped into his hand. Seating himself at the kitchen table he took the five bullets and lined them up like they were miniature missiles being prepared for a launch.

"This particular gun actually holds six rounds," he told us. "But I always leave the hammer resting on an empty chamber. It's a safety suggestion I learned a long time ago in my training. And if you boys are ever handling a gun, remember that safety always comes first," he added.

He then showed us the empty chambers to prove the gun wasn't loaded and, with a snap of his wrist, threw the cylinder back into place. The sharp sound and movement of this action brought an ear-to-ear grin to Al's face. The Chief then put the revolver on the table and looked Al straight in the eye, probably because he had shown the most interest in the unloading demonstration. "The question now is, is this gun on the table loaded or unloaded?" And then he quickly turned to Dusty and put his forefinger in the air as a signal to remain quiet and not give away the answer.

"It's empty," Al told him, a bit of annoyance in his voice for being asked such an obvious question.

"And that Alfred is how accidents happen." Dusty's father told him. "The golden rule to remember about guns, is no matter where a gun is or where it's been or who's holding it, you always assume it's loaded. There's no such thing as an empty gun."

Al seemed a little embarrassed but I wasn't sure if it was because he'd given the wrong answer or because Dusty's father had mistakenly called him Alfred. Of course, anyone of us would've responded with the same answer as Al that the gun was empty except Dusty who'd heard the lesson before.

The Chief didn't stop there. To our surprise, he continued to tell us all about his gun and its working parts, pointing out that police used single-action revolvers rather than double-action.

"What's the difference?" Al asked him.

"A double-action requires the shooter to cock the hammer back before pulling the trigger," he informed us. "A single-action revolver requires only one action. When you pull the trigger, the hammer cocks back and the gun fires simultaneously. If I used a double-action gun, which would require me to cock the hammer each time before I pulled the trigger, I wouldn't fare too well in an emergency."

"What if you weren't sure what kind it was? Like if you were in a fight and picked up the bad guy's gun and didn't have time to find out?" Al asked him.

"I guess if it was an emergency and you needed to make sure the gun was going to fire when you pulled the trigger, you'd just cock the hammer. Any revolver can be cocked manually."

This seemed to satisfy Al in the event he was ever in a fight with a bad guy and happened to get his gun mixed up with someone else's. The rest of us stood absorbing the information. Al's request to have him load it and go outside to shoot it off, as he put it, was dismissed by Mr. Barnes but he did allow Al to put the bullets back into the chambers before once again snapping it shut. He probably felt this might compensate for Al's disappointment regarding the Chief's earlier response that he had never shot anyone.

Knowing all this about Dusty's father and how we had never had any serious murders or holdups in Waterton, I couldn't understand why he would ever get demoted, as Dusty had said.

"How do you know he got demoted?"

"I heard him talking to my mother the other morning. He told her they were going to put this other guy in as Chief and he was going to be on some kind of trash force."

"Trash force? What's a trash force?"

"I'm not sure," Dusty confessed. "I mean I know it doesn't mean that he's at the station taking out the trash. I think maybe he just has to go after the real stupid criminals who do little crimes and stuff."

I wasn't sure what to say but realized I had to give some reassurance to my best friend. Knowing that his father had been a good Chief of Police, I had to figure there was some other reason for a demotion. "It's probably just something political," I told him.

"What do you mean political?"

"Well, it's what my father always tells my mother whenever he's unhappy with stuff goin' on in Waterton. It's political, he yells. Yells it all the time."

"Yeah, but what exactly does political mean for being demoted?"

"Well, in this case, as my father would say...the mayor's involved in it right up to his ass!"

It was another two days of misery for Dusty before he finally got up the courage to approach his mother regarding the demotion. It was too embarrassing a topic to discuss with the man who was actually demoted and he figured his father probably felt bad and wouldn't want to talk about it. To his relief, his mother gave him a light laugh and sat him down to explain that his father had been put on a *Task Force*, not a *Trash Force*. It was actually an honor to get the position and he would now be heading up a special team of men and would, at times, even be working with some agents from the FBI.

Later that evening, when Dusty's father heard of the confusion he explained a few more details including the need for some amount of secrecy in the matter. The FBI currently had an investigation going on in

Waterton and the fewer people who knew about the
task force the better. That was also the reason there
had been no notice in the paper regarding a new Chief
of Police and, as far as the general public knew, Mr.
Barnes was still the Chief, although from now on he
would be focusing on major crimes and one of the
police lieutenants would assume many of his prior
duties.

Against his father's wishes, Dusty told me about
the task force and the FBI after swearing me to an oath
of secrecy. It had been a strange coincidence that the
two of us had been involved in similar issues of
misunderstanding and I relayed my story of Mr. Faulk
being an ALCOholic and the two of us laughed,
realizing we would probably never understand the
confusing language of adults.

I gave my word along with my sworn oath of
secrecy and, other than telling Al and Jules, who I made
swear to the same oath, I kept my promise. Al,
however, mentioned it a few days later when all of us
were sitting in one of the turrets. He had forgotten that
Jamie was sitting there who, for obvious reasons,
hadn't received the information.

When Al mentioned the task force, Dusty's eyes
glared in my direction. "What did you do? Did you tell
everybody about the task force? You were sworn to
secrecy."

"I made them swear the same oath," I told him
trying to quell his anger.

At that point he turned his gaze toward Al. "And
you shouldn't even be talkin' about it," he told him.

Jamie, now privy to the information refused to let
it go and pressed Dusty for all the details. Dusty gave
him a brief explanation and then made all of us raise
our right hands and take a second vow of secrecy
which would override any previous vows and no word

of the task force was ever to be mentioned outside of The Five-Cent Gang. Besides, we had our own work cut out for us. The Cherry Bomb Caper was to take place in a few days and it was a caper that required precise calculations and split second timing...not to mention camouflage face paint.

Chapter Fifteen

The fact that my presence in the train yard raised no suspicions was one of the reasons Jamie assigned me the task of finding our best entrance into the arsenal. The two areas shared a common border. It had been my responsibility to see what part of the train yard was opposite the pool area inside the arsenal wall. The time for the raid drew near and the afternoon meeting brought all the pieces together.

"The pool is on the opposite side of the wall from the graveyard. It'll be real easy," I told Jamie. As I did so, I pointed to a drawing I'd made. I had come to learn that sometimes Jamie's diagrams and pictures were a good idea and allowed for everyone to see the plan in its proper perspective.

"Graveyard? Whaddaya mean graveyard?"

"It's where they put old trains or cars and stuff they're not going to use for a while." The response came from Dusty. He was the only friend I had taken to the train yard on multiple occasions and was familiar with the general layout. Jamie looked at me for reassurance on Dusty's response and I nodded confirmation.

"It gets better," I added. "There're two freight cars sitting on the track right next to the wall." I pointed to the rectangular representations on my drawing. "We can climb on the top of them and practically jump to the wall. If it's too far, I hid a plank under one of the freight cars that we can use to go from the car to the wall but I don't think we'll need it."

"Any problem with workers bein' around that area?"

"Not at night. The night shift guys never go over there." I told him.

Jamie smiled and nodded. "Nice work." He then focused his attention to Jules. "You get the cherry bombs okay?"

"Yeah, no problem. The guy that gets 'em for the Fourth of July just got his whole supply in. I got more than enough. Even got a break on the price."

"Dusty...how we doin' on the timers?"

"I did some experimenting. I put marks on some cigarettes and let them burn without puffin' on them. I kept track of how much time it takes for them to burn different lengths. I can cut them so we can set them for whatever minutes we want. I figure fifteen minutes at the most if we use Luckies."

"What if they don't go off at the same time?"

"It won't matter," Jamie responded to Al. "They'll be close enough so it'll seem like all hell's breakin' loose. Things look good here. I say as long as we're all sneakin' out anyway, we should pull this caper off around three o'clock in the morning. Any problems with that?" The turret remained silent as we all nodded in agreement.

"If we're gonna enter from the rail yard, I'll meet you guys at the rail crossing at quarter to three."

I looked at Dusty. "Al and Jules and I can meet you at the foot of the back hill around ten of," I told him. Al and Jules nodded.

"So, we'll meet at the crossing right before going into the yard," Jamie repeated. "Anybody here who doesn't have a watch or can't get one? We're gonna need them to light the fuses at the same time once we're in there." Again the head nodding demonstrated a consensus. It was agreed we would meet after supper for a final briefing and then return home and wait for the departure time for the rendezvous.

Before leaving, Jamie took on his leadership role once again and addressed all of us as if we were a platoon going into battle.

"You guys all did a great job on your assignments. This caper is gonna be the best one so far." With that he extended his open hand faced down into the center of the group. "The Five-Cent Gang," he said. Dusty put his hand on top of Jamie's and we all followed suit. "The Five-Cent Gang," we all echoed.

"Yeah, and the Cherry Bomb Caper," Al added.

❋ ❋ ❋ ❋ ❋

WHEN WE MET AT the railroad crossing, Al and Jules had already applied their camouflage face paint. Al would've worn it in school every day if it had been allowed. In all our planning, no one had thought to consider the night sky and, to our horror, we found we would be operating under what appeared to be a moon that had only a night or two remaining before rounding itself to its full face. Our raid would be executed in what seemed like daylight. Jamie had instructed all of us to wear dark clothes for the mission but the only black shirt I owned was my Hopalong Cassidy T-shirt. It depicted a large smiling face of the cowboy and Hoppy's grin was glowing in the moonlight. Jamie gave me a disappointed look when he saw it.

"What?" I yelled. "It's the only black shirt I own. What else was I supposed to wear?" The response was an immediate consensus that, for security reasons, I should wear it inside out.

Our walk from the crossing to the graveyard involved each of us reviewing our assigned targets. Jamie, Dusty and I applied Al's camouflage paint to protect our identity. Once we were in the pool area, we would separate to our targets and then return and rendezvous at zero, three, thirty-two. From there we would make our getaway up and over the wall back into the graveyard. Jamie had set the original rendezvous time for three-thirty but Al felt it would be more precise and military like if it wasn't such an even number. At the pool we were to synchronize our watches, although there had been some dispute how that was done. Again, the key to much of our anticipated success was in the vocabulary of what we were doing and the word synchronized fit the criteria.

Getting over the wall was easy. We didn't need the plank. With a short leap we went from the top of the freight car to the wall. There were no pointed spikes in this area and hanging from the top of the wall left only a short drop to the ground. I then heard Dusty's voice as he spoke to Jamie in a loud whisper. "How are we supposed to get back over when we come back?"

"We can do it like that training thing in the movie *To Hell and Back*," Al told him. "Remember when they had to get over that wall?" Al was referring, of course, to the part in the movie where two soldiers held a rifle between them so the others guys could use it as a step. That was followed by Hollywood stuntmen who climbed over each other's backs and then the soldiers at the top pulled the last man up and over. Although we didn't have any rifles and I knew this method would never work for us, Dusty seemed to be content that there was any sort of a solution to the problem.

The five of us stood with faces that displayed random designs of greens and black paints as if we were Indian braves preparing for battle...the whites of ten eyes peered into our surroundings as we stood staring at each other. This was the real thing. We were commandos about to make a raid on an unknowing enemy. The pool area was filled with shadows of closed umbrellas as they stood in the middle of vacant tables like sentries in the moonlight. Lawn chairs were stacked in uniformed piles at one end of the pool. Initially, the only sound we heard was a chorus of crickets singing in the warm summer air but as we paused to get our bearings, more sounds became apparent and the crickets were accompanied by trickling water along with a gurgling from a floating skimmer. All the sounds seemed to be in harmony with the steady hum coming from the motor in the filtration system. Looking around, I noticed this pool was small and had no lifeguard chair. In the light of day, it was probably occupied by army wives tanning themselves in lounge chairs as they read magazines and little kids splashing each other as they floated around in plastic inner tubes. There was certainly no comparison with this pool to the Waterton pool. This was not a pool where bombardments would be tolerated or floaters welcomed.

We soon discovered the gurgling sound we heard was coming from a trickle of water from a hose dangling over one of the pool ladders. We never would've known that if Al hadn't tripped over it. The fact that he was able to catch himself on the ladder was the only thing that prevented him from falling in. Fortunately, only his left foot went into the water, but the splashing caused some alarm within the group.

"You okay?" Jules asked him.

"Yeah, but I got a wet foot!" Al complained. "And the cuff of my pants is all wet."

We all knew what that felt like from treks in the woods. Any slip of the foot during a stream crossing

would cause a foot soaking and there weren't too many
things worse than a wet foot. This also meant that for
the remainder of the mission, Al had a squishing sound
every time his left foot took a step.

"Don't make so much noise when you walk,"
Dusty told him.

"What do ya expect me to do, fly around the
place? I can't help it."

While we sympathized with him, Jamie
complained about the lack of protocol. "You guys have
to stop talkin' about everything," he whispered. "First it
was getting back over the wall and now it's the stupid
wet foot. We're supposed to be using our hand signals
in here. You want the guards to hear us?"

Without waiting for a response, he opened the
pool gate leading to the main grounds just enough to
see into the outer complex. He gave the thumbs-up
signal indicating the coast was clear and then pointed
his index finger at each of us and then to the outside.
This was presumably the signal that we were supposed
to go out there. Although we had agreed to use hand
signals once inside the wall, we had never actually
discussed what the signals would be. One by one, we
slipped through the gate and took cover behind a bush
or a tree or one of the available outbuildings, trying to
remain in the shadows. Most of our travel at this point
was done on our bellies as we wiggled on the wet grass
and imitated soldiers we had seen in the movies. We
eventually discovered this tactic was not actually
necessary as the entire area at this hour of the morning
was completely void of people. Both entrances
containing the guards were on the far side of the
complex and the remainder of the place seemed to be
in sleep mode.

The only movements now were the five of us
running parallel with our shadows from one area to

another in a hunched-over position. For some reason, we felt displaying our full height would cause some alarm if anyone spotted us. I stopped that tactic after we went our separate ways and I saw Jules and Dusty running hunched over beneath the moonlight. As they loped along they appeared to take on the shape of two demented werewolves.

I then saw Al trying to catch the eye of Jamie. As per the earlier reprimand, he was using hand signals to get him a message. He kept pointing to his face and shrugging his shoulders. He was signaling that some of his camouflage paint had smeared into one of his eyes and he was having trouble seeing but the back of Jamie's head never got the message. It wasn't until the raid ended that I discovered what a face point followed by a shoulder shrug designated. I was also too far away to make any contact, so Al was forced into combat with only one good eye and a squish-emitting left foot.

With each of us armed with cherry bombs and cigarette fuses, we attended to our assigned targets. In the fifteen minutes that followed, we set the bombs. The striking of each match sent out a flicker of light and unintentionally informed each of us of another's location. It was during the setting of my first fuse that I realized we had forgotten to synchronize our watches. I checked mine and noted that it read three-twenty. We were supposed to begin lighting fuses at three-fifteen so I figured I was close enough to being on schedule. Like Jamie had said, they would all go off close to the same time and that would be good enough.

With all bombs ready to explode, we reconvened in the pool area. Everyone but Al. Dusty was first to show concern. "Where's Al?" he asked no one in particular. We all looked around as if waiting for him to magically appear.

"I'm gonna go look for him," Jules whispered. "He had that old cannon display that was right out in the open. There're a lot of lights in that area. Maybe he had trouble getting to it or got caught or something."

Al had been given the old cannon specifically because it was in the open and he was the fastest runner in the gang. His plan, which he had told us prior to the mission was to run at full speed to the target and then, as he put it, become one with the cannon. Jamie grabbed Jules's arm. "Wait a couple a minutes. He'll probably show up. Don't forget, it was Al who wanted our rendezvous time to be zero, three, thirty-two, rather than on the half hour. What time is it now?"

We looked at the watches we'd forgotten to synchronize and we each called out a conflicting time, making us realize another miscalculation in our caper.

Jules swiped Jamie's hand from his arm. "If you guys wanna climb over the wall and head out that's cool with me. I'm not leavin' here until I know Al's okay and not in any trouble."

True to his word, Al had made it to the civil war cannon beside which was a pyramid of antique cannon balls. Beneath the streetlight, he had, indeed, become one with the cannon. Even his blurred eye that watered and sent tears down the right side of his face had not been a deterrent. Stopping frequently to wipe his eye with the bottom portion of his T-shirt had caused several delays in getting to his targets but the old cannon was a prize for the taking and Al had no intention of omitting it from his mission. In addition to his sight problem, he took time to roll his wet pant leg up to his knee and then smeared camouflage paint on it from the knee down. Now being one with the cannon, he set his cigarette timer and dropped the cherry bomb down the huge barrel.

Jules left the pool area to begin the search for his brother but before he got fifty feet from the pool gate, the cherry bomb Dusty had set under the base of an ICBM missile exploded into the night air. It only took that one explosion to elicit a flurry of activity. Brightness rained down from spotlights that we had never noticed during the daylight hours. Yelling could be heard in the distance and was then interrupted by a second explosion and then a third and a fourth.

Dusty and Jamie and I remained in the pool area trying to make sense out of what was actually happening. The wall we had climbed over earlier, which had provided protection and a blanket of darkness, was now lit up like a summer afternoon at the beach. Another cherry bomb exploded from somewhere and the detonation coincided with a siren that started as a low moan and slowly worked its way to a feverish and scary howling.

"We've got to take a chance on the wall," Jamie yelled over the siren. "We can't go out that way," he was pointing to the arsenal grounds as he yelled. "We're still protected by the pool fence if we can get over the wall."

"What about Al and Jules?" I hollered back.

"No time now," he shouted. "We've got to get out...lights or no lights!"

"I agree," Dusty yelled. "We can't do anything here for either of them. We need to get to the rendezvous point as planned and hope they can get out somewhere else and meet up with us."

More cherry bombs exploded in the midst of the bright lights and sirens and Al searched frantically for any dark place in which to hide himself. He knew the final cherry bomb in the barrel of the cannon would be going off soon and its eventual explosion would surely bring attention to that area. His one-eyed visual search of the surroundings gave him a glimmer of hope when he spotted a car parked under a large tree in a small cul-de-sac. It seemed to be part of an unused area of the grounds and secluded enough to offer protection. In his best werewolf running position he squished his way to the car and crawled under it. As he lay there he studied the undercarriage through his remaining good eye. He was breathing heavily and his left foot still felt much heavier than his right, reminding him of why he couldn't run as fast as he usually did.

Although he felt safe for the moment, he needed to contemplate his next move. Then, as if by magic, everything stopped and reverted back to normalcy. The spotlights were turned off and their giant bulbs transformed themselves from a sunshine hue to dimming pieces of filament until they faded out and rested in their off positions. It was as if this absence of light was a signal for the siren to end its screaming and the arsenal grounds returned to the light of the moon. The brightness that had brought on an earlier discussion and cause for alarm now seemed dull in comparison to the absence of the security lights.

It was then Al heard a nearby voice and by cranking his head a bit he could see past the right rear tire and he spotted a guard in military attire. He was standing next to the civil war cannon and talking into a hand held walkie-talkie. The voice was just audible enough to allow Al to overhear most of the one-sided conversation.

"Yes sir, no sir, that's affirmative sir. Yes...just some kids, we think not much more to it than that. Yes sir, Private Kirchenbaum thought he heard them over in the pool area. Yes sir, he checked it out but no one was in there. He climbed up on the wall and said he saw some kids running through the train yard but didn't really get a look at any of them."

Al closed his right eye which was now burning from the paint and continued to listen, feeling both relief for his friends' safety along with a bit of despair for his own predicament, knowing they would surely not return to save him.

"No sir, I don't know who tripped the siren. I apologize, sir. Yes sir, I realize it's the middle of the night and families are trying to sleep. No sir, they won't be coming. We contacted them when the siren sounded and told them it was a base issue. Yes sir, Kirchenbaum and I have closed down both gates and locked down the security bars. No vehicles will be getting in or out until we get back. Yes sir, total lockdown."

As Al continued to ponder his fate, he heard a second voice. This time it was much closer than the guard at the cannon. It was the voice of a woman and it seemed as if it was coming from inside the vehicle. This seemed impossible, as he surely would've known if someone had gotten into the car. Before the mystery could be solved, he became gripped with fear when he noticed the car was beginning to move. It wasn't until the woman spoke again that he realized the car's movement was not actually forward. It seemed to have more of an up and down bouncing motion. The woman's voice became louder and she was yelling "Just like that, yes...just like that." And then she got louder and louder and the car seemed to bounce with a greater amount of energy. "Don't stop," she yelled, and then continued her chanting of "Just like that, just like that!"

By now, Al realized that the voice was coming from inside the car and whatever the woman was doing was obviously being done right. He eventually considered the possibility that someone (or two someones) were doing sex things in the car and they were doing it right above him. He didn't have any sexual experiences himself, but he had heard stories of

what happened in the back seats of cars at drive-in
movies or lovers' lanes and began conjuring up a
variety of images of the event above him. He closed his
good eye and became comfortable as a shower of "just
like thats" continued to rain down from above. His
thoughts were then interrupted by what sounded like
the crushing of gravel. He opened his eye and found
that this time, the car *was* moving forward and was
indeed, crushing gravel as it inched away from him.
Evidently the frantic activity inside the vehicle had
either dislodged the parking brake or moved the gear
shift into neutral.

As he and his friends had done so many times in
the past, he imagined a movie scene that related to his
predicament and saw himself as the hero who had to
choose between remaining perfectly still on the railroad
tracks or be crushed to death by the oncoming train. Al
closed his good eye again, stiffened his body, and kept
his arms close to his sides in hopes he would survive
that oncoming train. The car continued to inch its way
down the slightest of slopes until it traveled
approximately the same distance as the length of his
body. As it moved away, the woman's voice continued
with loud yelps and accolades confirming his lovers'
lane theory and when the crushing of gravel stopped,
he opened his good eye and found himself staring up at
the huge maple tree under which the car had been
parked.

The moonlight was shining down through the
branches and they swayed gently in the warm summer
breeze giving the entire area a strobe light effect, which
compounded the surrealness of the moment.

Finding himself with no vehicular protection, he
stood and looked around to get his bearings. As he did
so, he glanced at the car, which now displayed a woman
in the back seat. She was facing out the rear window

and arching her back; the window now a cinemascope of bouncing breasts. Unlike her darkened neck and shoulders, her breasts, which had obviously never seen any sunlight, reflected the brightness of the moon as they bounced up and down to her continuous chant of "just like that, just like that."

It then appeared that the woman realized the car had moved from its protected location beneath the tree and, for the first time, she leaned her body forward to peer out the window and Al saw her face. Even with her tussled hair in total disarray, her beauty was unmistakable. It was the face of Candy Melons. Al continued to stare at the two giant mounds of vanilla that having been denied the sun by her lifeguard attire were now jiggling amidst an ocean of well-tanned skin. All he could imagine was two huge bowls of vanilla pudding, jiggling with every movement.

As he gazed in awe, the final cherry bomb exploded from within the cannon and echoed throughout the complex. Candy Melons looked frantically out the rear window of the car searching for the source and now seemed bewildered as to why the car was no longer parked beneath the tree. The explosion caused the floodlights to return and painted the car with a hue that both enhanced and complemented her two assets.

Al stood with his mouth hanging open and gawked at the window. With no one around to ask a question, he asked himself if this reciprocal arrangement would've been better between the two of them if he had two eyes from which to view her two melons.

Candy, on the other hand was looking straight into the painted face of, what she felt, was a would-be attacker. Her vision of Al was one of horror. He stood in the strobe light with one eye skewed and a face

smeared with black and green paint. The dewy grass
and perspiration had smeared the paint in all directions
which caused the colors to run down onto his neck. He
was obviously a murderer made scarier by the
appearance of one black leg that for some reason had
the pant leg rolled up.

In one hand he held a tree limb that he had
grabbed when he stood up. In the dark it gave the
appearance of a weapon...perhaps a machete.
Appropriately, Candy Melons let out a horrifying
scream. In the melee that ensued, the guard returned to
investigate the latest explosion from the cannon and
arrived as the back door of the car opened and Candy's
male companion rolled out of the car with his pants
around his ankles. In Candy's panic to leave the scene
and avoid the attacker, she had pushed the guy out of
the car.

The guard, avoiding further reprimands regarding
the siren, was instead blowing a substitute whistle in
hopes of gaining assistance from the other guard. It
was then that Candy attempted to climb out of the
back seat and fell on top of her companion, a position
previously very familiar to her since the return of the
blackout. When she fell from the car her flowing skirt
covered her companion's head and his arms flailed
beneath it as he tried to free himself.

Candy Melons then stood and continued
screaming as she used one arm to unsuccessfully cover
herself and yanked on the handle of the front door of
the car. It was then that Al recognized the figure on the
ground who was trying to get his pants on. It was the
one and only Big Tony.

Candy continued to point at Al and, in the chaos,
screamed for Big Tony to rescue her. "Murderer," she
yelled. "There's a murderer with a knife under the
tree!"

Al turned and ran behind the tree and then continued on and took refuge behind a small building. The guard arrived and between huffs and puffs, he babbled into the walkie-talkie. "Turn off the goddamn lights," he yelled into the box.

The floodlights faded once again and Candy was no longer in the spotlight of fame. The guard then discovered her in all her glory as she yanked on the door handle. Big Tony was now upright and, although shirtless, had at least recaptured his pants and a slight amount of dignity.

Knowing Candy was the daughter of the base commander, who had already been awakened by the siren, the guard realized he was in a delicate situation. His attention to detail was the distraction Al needed and while the guard interviewed the screaming daughter of the colonel, he made for the gate.

Jamie and Dusty and I sat in the used car lot across the highway. We had witnessed the second coming of the lights followed by the constant blowing of the whistle. After many anxious minutes we saw Al's familiar silhouette running toward the exit. We couldn't hear the wet foot and could only imagine the sound of the step...squish, step...squish as he made his escape. From nowhere, a second figure appeared from the darkness and we were certain it was the guard who had seen Al running for the exit. We figured even with a wet foot, the guard would be no match for Al's speed. We were still unaware that he only had one eye and the blurriness was continuing to give him vision problems. A Ford station wagon provided protection for us as the triangular flags of color surrounding the car lot flapped in the breeze.

Dusty quietly urged him on. "Come on, come on," he kept saying. "You can beat that guy. Run your ass off, man."

As both figures neared the guard house, it was me who noticed it first. "It's not the guard chasing him, it's Jules!"

As I said the words, Jules appeared in the light and fell in behind him. In his search for Al, he had remained in the shadows waiting for the right moment to move and look around. When Al made his run for the exit, he had spotted his brother and followed the same path. The guard was somewhere on the grounds trying to remain calm on the walkie-talkie and explain to the commanding officer that the final explosion was just a leftover firecracker. His second responsibility was to comply with Candy's wishes to not involve her.

"If my father finds out I was out this late after curfew, I'll be grounded for a month," she told the guard. "We were just sitting here talking and then I saw a colored man lurking around under that tree. He had a huge knife or a sword or something. I think he was getting ready to attack us," she continued.

It was probably the story of the colored man that saved her reputation, as well as from being grounded. When the guard explained to the colonel what had transpired, he omitted any reference to his daughter being in the area. Other than the initial call to the second guard to be on the lookout for a colored man wielding a machete, the story of the stalker remained within the confines of the base. That call, however, did reach the Waterton Police Department's scanner and news and a description of the attacker eventually got back to Dusty as he overheard his father relaying the story. It came with a warning to Dusty's mother to make sure that in the future all the doors and windows were locked before going to bed.

It had been an exhausting raid. The morning sun was just beginning to shed the early light of dawn when we split up to go our separate ways. During the walk home, Al relived and relayed his experience with Candy Melons. This time, we had the questions and Al was required to supply the answers. After telling us the story, he filled in any voids in our conversation by yelling "just like that" and then we'd all give an envy-filled laugh as we thought about his adventure. Although Al was the only one present at the car fiasco, Candy Melons became something special to all of us that night. She wasn't just Candy Melons anymore, she was the "just like that" girl and the phrase "just like that" became our new battle cry.

During the weeks that followed the raid, we spent many days at the pool making our usual bombardments on unsuspecting females. Through it all, we gawked at Candy Melons with a greater appreciation. We watched for a change in expression as we bellowed "just like that" with each cannonball we landed in front of her guard chair. Throughout it all, she remained expressionless, indicating to us that she was either dumber than we thought or just plain clueless.

As the summer drew to a close, I thought about my conversation with Jamie grabbing the tits of an eighth grader and about Al, who had witnessed the bouncing breasts of Candy Melons and I couldn't help but feel that life was passing me by.

Chapter Sixteen

Sixth grade proved to be the best year ever as The Five-Cent Gang honed our skills under Jamie's tutelage. Jules was the most popular kid in school, even among the eighth graders who had left him behind in grade three and as his entourage, all five of us spent time wheeling and dealing throughout the school year.

We learned that mischief led to after-school detentions and since discovering the advantages of The Pit, detentions took time away from our entrepreneurial enterprises.

It was the one store that stood among the houses that lined US Route 32 and like the houses on either side, it was a long skinny building with the highway running past the storefront and a dirt alleyway behind it. The dirt road in the back was primarily used for access to the yards of the houses or, in the case of the store, it was used for deliveries. It was The Pit that had provided the Playboys we had stolen and it was The Pit where we usually stole our comics.

The owner and sole employee was Eddie. He was an old guy, probably in his late forties, who usually had a Pall Mall hanging from his lips. Eddie had the unique ability of being able to dangle a cigarette in his mouth without ever taking a puff or removing it to talk until the complete length was one long ash. If it happened to be dangling from his lips while he was scooping ice cream into a cone, kids often became worried that it might drop off and find a resting place on their scoop of pistachio or butter pecan. If so, Eddie passed the ashes off as free sprinkles.

During the school year, The Pit often became a quick stop either coming or going between home and school. In the cold months we stopped to get warm and grab a cup of hot chocolate. During the hot days of July and August, our visits were lengthier. Those were days we could sit at the counter and take advantage of the air conditioning.

With our sixth-grade school year drawing to a close we occasionally stopped for a soda before going to the field to shag some fly balls. If the new comics were in, two of us would keep Eddie busy at the counter while the other three stuffed the latest issue of Green Hornet and other superheroes into our jackets. If he was on the phone in the back room, we would steal items from his wide variety of display cards. Eddie was real big on display cards and they held stuff we could use or sell to our friends at school.

Since this was the new routine we had adopted throughout our entire sixth-grade school year, it added to the money we already made from snow shoveling and lawn mowing. We always had enough for cigarettes, baseball cards, and other things we wanted that Eddie kept out of reach or inside glass display cases.

We made some good money that year and just before school ended for the summer, the four of us were promoted to grade seven and Jules had been elected as president of the eighth-grade class. Our beliefs had already been confirmed that each year offered more seniority and moving up the ladder allowed for freedoms and privileges in the school halls and outside during recess. We knew the next couple of years would be even better as the seventh and eighth graders pretty much ran the school. During our rehearsal for the promotion ceremony, however, Mr. Murder lowered the boom on all of us when he made the unexpected announcement that the next two years of Public School Number One were being extracted from our lives.

"The good news," he began, "is starting next year, the seventh and eighth grades from all the city schools are being combined with grades nine through twelve and you'll all be attending Waterton High School, which will now be known as the Waterton Junior/Senior High School."

While this may have been good news to Mr. Murdur, who would be rid of us, it was a disaster in our minds. After spending our entire lives in PS Number One, waiting for the day we would be the eighth-grade rulers of the kingdom, we were going to be demoted to the bottom of the pile again. It was like kindergarten all over.

Jules, being able to take care of himself, was not as alarmed as we were. For Jamie, Al, Dusty, and me, this new development most likely meant an end to our financial enterprises and the possibility of losing Jules's protection. Following Mr. Murdur's news, we waited for that last day of school to arrive which would open the doors on our final summer together.

With only a few days of school remaining, Al and Jules were helping their mother move boxes and Jamie was serving a week of after-school confinement by his parents. With three of the five missing, there wasn't much sense for Dusty and me to go to the ball field. Having limited alternatives, and since it was a hotter than normal day, we decided to make a Pit stop. It was certainly hot enough to justify stopping for a 'beer' while we looked over issues of comics we hadn't read yet. A beer was Eddie's concoction of a root beer soda with a shot of pure vanilla.

Our entrance that day was pretty much the norm. The door triggered a bell to let Eddie know he had a customer. The place was deserted and, not seeing Eddie behind the soda fountain, we figured he was in the back room on the phone. He spent a lot of time in the back room, yapping with people. When the bell sounded, he usually emerged from the back. Some days he met us with a cheerful greeting and we would hang out and order a beer. On days he was grumpy we would keep our visit short and make a quick exit.

The long narrow structure of the building dictated a compression of the store's items and made for a claustrophobic interior. It was narrow to begin with and the arrangement of merchandise inside left room for only one long aisle that ran from the front door to the back. The only interruption to the structure was the single wall that ran the entire width of the store and partitioned off a small area that Eddie used for his office. It also had a door leading out to the back alley for deliveries. We'd never been back there, but the curtain was usually open and it was furnished with a desk and a few filing cabinets. He usually pulled the curtain closed if he needed privacy but we could still hear his end of any phone conversations—his end being a bunch of grunts and an occasional number. We figured he was just ordering more supplies or display cards. Jamie insisted he was taking down numbers because he was a bookie and he was taking bets for people. He always closed the curtain if he was finishing a phone conversation and there were regular customers around but he never seemed to bother if we were the only ones in there.

Other than newspapers and cigarettes, it didn't seem like he sold much merchandise. The left side of the store held display racks for magazines and greeting cards.

Opposite the magazine rack, Eddie had configured a small area with an always-vacant table for two. It sat next to the rack holding local newspapers. He had separated that area from the soda fountain with a homemade wooden bookshelf and added height to the shelf with more display cards. These held items that customers pulled from their elastic restraints and brought to the cash register. He had added a new card recently as the old one that once held twelve folding fishing knives had only two left. The other ten we had stolen over the past several weeks. Each of us kept one and the other three we sold to classmates.

His new display card held cigarette lighters. These were advertised as 'Vu-lites' as the bottom half was clear plastic and you could see the lighter fluid inside. They had tiny colorful figurines in them that bobbed around as they floated in the fluid. One had a baseball player in a crouched position prepared to field a ground ball. Dusty joked that the guy would drown in the lighter fluid before the ball ever got there. A quarterback with a cocked arm along with other sports figures added to the collection. The first day the card was displayed, Al laid claim to the one with a hunter aiming his rifle. A dog stood at the hunter's feet with a paw raised and his nose pointed to the target. Once Al made a claim, I called dibs on the one with a pair of miniature dice inside.

Like the fishing knives, the lighters would be easy to steal. We had honed our skills greatly since the days of the Candy Bar Caper and no longer worried about cops. Besides, with Jamie's insistence that The Pit was a front for gambling, we figured Eddie didn't much care about losing knives and lighters. If he was a bookmaker, it explained why he was always on the phone and never took precautions to guard the display cards or put them out of reach. He must've known that ten knives were gone from the knife card and he hadn't sold any.

Despite the dust and clutter, The Pit was a good place to hang out. We were accustomed to the familiar scent of old wood that emanated from the magazine rack and provided a smell of stains and varnishes that had been applied decades ago. These were kindled by the summer heat and, with no circulation, hung in the air and mixed with the aroma of newsprint and musty greeting cards that had been there since their initial arrangement. The huge overhead fans sat idle giving no movement to the strips of year-old fly paper. They had once hung like elongated springs but had lost most of their natural curl long ago. Their lack of stickiness posed no threat to the flies that used them as if they were deserted air strips; landing, getting a brief rest, and then taking off again—layovers en route to Big Lizzie's litter box in the back room. Big Lizzie was a twenty-two pound stray that Eddie had named after Elizabeth Taylor.

The entire floor was hardwood. The cut nails used in the original construction had loosened over the years and the floor creaked and moaned as it fought the weight of the customers. Like the rest of the store, the hardwood had seen little upkeep over the years. Other than a few spots along the way, it was badly scuffed and had turned a barren gray and lacked any finish. If the bell over the door went unheard, the creaking of the floor acted as a secondary warning system of entering customers. Knowing where the creakiest spots on the floor were, we sometimes stood in front of the magazine rack and rocked back and forth on our heels until Eddie got pissed off.

"Stop rocking or stand somewhere else," he yelled.

Normally, The Five-Cent Gang occupied five of the six stools at the counter and on the day Dusty and I stopped to kill the afternoon, we sat on the two padded stools we always used. Once seated, the smell of the old wood and varnish was replaced with a fragrance reminiscent of my house on Christmas morning. Not so much the scent of the tree but more the mixture of the afterglow of opened gifts. Perfumes and sachets mingling with bath powders and scented soaps—gifts my father gave to my mother. The unleashed fragrances escaped as they sat in their glass containers no longer adorned with ribbons and colored papers; Christmas smells that lingered and filled my nostrils as I walked past the tree.

Eddie had lined the shelf behind the soda counter with bottles of perfumes and gift boxes of little soaps, giving The Pit that same familiar smell. The bottles and boxes were doubled in number, as they stood back to back with their reflections in the big mirror. The scented perfumes overshadowed but failed to completely erase the aroma from the adjacent tins of pipe tobacco and cartons of cigarettes. To fill up additional space, another display card sat next to the perfume bottles. This one held pipes and, as we didn't choose to smoke out of a pipe, we didn't care that they were not within our reach. If we smoked at all, we would opt for a pack of Luckies and always use an out-of-the-way vending machine to avoid adults.

The appearance of items behind the soda fountain never changed. Eddie held the belief that things on the shelves only showed the dust of time if they were touched by his huge hands. Touching left marks of fingers and thumbs but without any touching, the uniform layer of dust went unnoticed. Other than the perfume bottles, Eddie adhered to his philosophy of convenient display cards and in addition to the pipes, his wide variety included Gillette razors, matching sets of hair combs with brushes, and a card full of dust-covered nail clippers.

If we spun around on our stools, the comic book rack was in easy reach. Eddie's rack didn't spin like the one in Miss Beezel's store. It couldn't spin because the store was so crammed. Eddie had wedged it against a glass case full of every kind of candy bar imaginable. They were all five cents except the Powerhouse bar that cost ten cents and was so big you had to either split it with a friend or save half to eat later. Another inconvenience in The Pit was that Eddie didn't stock any penny candy or have a gumball machine. Miss Beezel had both along with a better variety of comics, but hers were harder to steal.

Eddie was sitting behind the counter reading a magazine when we got there. The full-length ash of his Pall Mall was about to fall into the centerfold. He must've read our minds as he gave us the usual greeting when we sat down.

"So, is it hot enough today for a couple of beers?"

"Yeah, two beers," Dusty echoed back. When Eddie referred to the doctored drink as beer it was more or less Eddie's way of making us feel older, or maybe like the tough guys that we weren't. When he first stumbled onto the concoction he had hit on a goldmine. We were all immediately addicted to the vanilla's irresistible sweetness and the unique taste it added to the root beer. A straight root beer soda was fifteen cents but if you ordered a beer, Eddie added a nickel more for the shot of vanilla. It didn't matter. Once the drink was invented, we always had him add the shot.

We still had a bit of cash left from winter snow shoveling and most of our regular customers would stay on and have us mow lawns all summer. We also got a few bucks from stuff stolen from The Pit and, in a few days, we'd be adding Eddie's new Vu-lite cigarette lighters to our inventory.

Eddie began the ceremony of fixing our drinks. "So, you guys must be happy about bein' away from the books for the summer eh? How long before your parole kicks in?"

"Three more days," Dusty responded. "School's just a bunch of crap anyway."

"I read in the paper they're movin' grades seven and eight up to the high school next year. That's you guys, isn't it? That'll be a big change."

He must've sensed our rejection of the idea. "Hey, just think of all those extra women you'll have up there. You guys'll be makin' out like bandits."

We both ignored the comment and watched as Eddie pulled out the paraphernalia for the ceremonial beer making. First came the hour-glass silver bases, which he placed on the counter in front of each of us. These were followed by the insertion of the white cone-shaped paper cups. He took them one at a time and shoveled in a scoop of crushed ice, then grabbed the root beer hose and pulled the trigger to fill it.

"You said you wanted shots too, right?"

"Yeah, we both want shots." Dusty confirmed. "Make 'em good ones, will ya Eddie?"

Eddie slid the first soda under the pump and oozed out a long shot of vanilla syrup into the drink and set it in front of Dusty. He was about to grab mine to repeat the process when the phone rang. He eyeballed the back room and then stared back at my soda as if trying to determine which took priority. He then addressed Dusty who was sitting nearer to the spigot of vanilla. "Can you shoot a shot of vanilla in Auggie's drink for me? I gotta get the phone."

"Yeah, sure," Dusty told him and he took the soda. He leaned his lanky frame over the counter and pushed down on the vanilla spout. Then he looked at me. "One more for good measure," he laughed and added a second shot. He then reached over with his own cup and added a second shot to his drink. It wasn't the first time he'd done it. Whenever Eddie was on the phone, anything in the store seemed to be fair game. If he wasn't within earshot of the counter, he had no line of vision to see anything going on out front. At least that's what we always thought. We never knew about the mirror that allowed him to see the entire store. Fortunately for us, it was there for a different reason than to catch us stealing shots of vanilla.

* * * * *

BEFORE EDDIE WAS OFF the phone, there was a knock at the back door and without any invitation, the door opened. The sunlight spilled into the back room and silhouetted a man who completely filled the doorway. It was only as he turned to close the door behind him, that the sun was allowed to peek through and make him visible. The man was a big fat guy and he breathed heavily as he withdrew a handkerchief from a pocket and wiped his forehead. Eddie was a big man too, but this newcomer dwarfed him. He shifted his weight and wheezed more long breaths of air between his movements. As he stood catching his breath, he noticed Dusty and me at the counter and pulled the curtain that separated the store from the back room. Their voices became low and muffled but we could still hear bits and pieces of their conversation.

"...early," Eddie said, sounding surprised, letting us know he hadn't expected him.

"envelope...on time...Thursdays from now on," came from the fat man. His voice continued, "Hotter 'n hell," he said and then added something about a "drink of cold water?"

"Help yourself." Were the last words we heard from Eddie before the fat man pushed the curtain aside and stepped into the store.

He eyeballed the soda fountain and then squeezed and wheezed his way between the wall and the end of the counter to get behind it. In the florescent light of the store, we could now see he was even fatter than we first thought and Dusty was kicking my foot in a coded silence of ridicule. I inhaled deep breaths through my nose to keep from laughing. Any thoughts I did have about laughing were quickly dismissed when the fat guy looked directly at me. For the first time I noticed one half of his face was covered with a purple blotch that encompassed a good part of his forehead and continued down over one eye and most of his left cheek. It was ugly and scary at the same time.

Until that moment I thought fat people were jolly and good-natured but this fat man didn't seem in any way to be jolly, or happy, or full of fun of any kind. His stare held a streak of anger or meanness. He said nothing to either of us as he began flipping up the lids of the compartments that held different flavors of ice cream. Following a short look at each flavor, he slammed the lid down. Eventually he found the one containing the crushed ice he'd been looking for. That one he left open as he searched for a glass. Dusty and I watched with a mixture of fear and curiosity. Since his emergence from the back room he had said nothing. He simply exhaled snorts of heavy breathing from a mouth that dispensed small sprays of saliva. His short-

sleeved shirt was soaked with perspiration, which
included big rings of sweat under his armpits. The skin
on his arms reflected a wetness that matted the dark
hairs. His arms were stubby, and looked almost
deformed. He grabbed one of the silver hourglass bases
but, unlike Eddie who always inserted a paper cup
before scooping some ice into it, he dipped the entire
base into the ice compartment and brought it up half
full. He then began a search for the hose to fill it.

"Water's the hose on the end." Dusty told him.

"How'd you know I wanted water?" His question
was strategic and anything but friendly.

"I heard you tell Eddie." As the words left Dusty's
mouth, I knew he had made a big mistake. For some
reason, I knew we weren't supposed to hear anything
that had been said in the back room. My suspicion was
immediately confirmed.

"What else did you hear, kid?" His voice was
abrupt but held no tone of anger. He seemed to be
fishing with a pretense of friendliness.

I returned the earlier kick on the foot I'd received
from Dusty to try to warn him to be cool about what
he was about to say.

"Nothin'," he told him. "I just heard you say
something about getting a drink of water."

I knew Dusty well enough to know that he had
gotten the message my kick had sent him. His voice
sounded nervous. The fat man used the hose and then
lifted the drink to his mouth and drank the water
straight down. He reached for the hose and filled it
again. This time he looked at me as he did so. "And
what about you? What did you hear? "

"I didn't hear anything," I confessed. Like Dusty,
my voice was tight. Even I didn't recognize the speech
sounds I was making. "You really can't hear anything

out here when Eddie's back there. We were talkin' out here anyway."

He took a step sideways and stood squarely in front of me. "What's your name, kid?"

"Auggie."

"And what about you, what's your name?"

"Dusty."

"Well, you two look like good kids so I guess you know when grown-ups are talkin' it ain't polite to be listenin' in on their conversations, right?" As he spoke, his eyes were focused on me and his hand fell on top of mine. His fingers were fat and puffy and he squeezed my hand with a continued pressure as he spoke. The grip became so painful I thought he was going to break the bones in my fingers. "Am I right there, Auggie? Do you not listen to grown-ups' conversations?"

"Yes sir," I told him. "I mean no sir. I don't listen to other people's conversations."

"Good boy," he responded, releasing his grip and then he patted my hand as if being friendly. He gulped down the second cup of water and tossed the container into the sink. The cup clanged as it hit the stainless steel and the remaining ice hit the basin like tiny pebbles. The sounds brought Eddie from the back room.

"Everything all right out here?"

The fat man gave a quick look at Dusty and me before answering. "Yeah, everything's fine and dandy," and then he wheezed again.

He looked at Eddie and nodded toward the back room. Eddie went back and the fat man squeezed his way past the end of the counter and followed behind him. His sweat-soaked shirt had caused it to stick to his back and pull it up over his waist. As he waddled through the doorway, the raised shirt revealed a holster attached to his belt. It was holding a small gun, which appeared even smaller due to his immense size. It looked like Dusty's father's gun—his .38 service revolver. I felt my face get cold and then hot. It was like the blood drained out of me and then fled back in again.

If Al had been there he could've told us exactly what kind of gun it was. Whenever we took time to read our comics, Al often had his face buried in the latest gun magazine.

The fat man talked to Eddie again and, like before, the voices were muffled. Three words that did drift out and come through very clearly were, "two kids" and "counter."

This time the curtain was left open and I saw Eddie hand him an envelope. I remembered Jamie's comment about The Pit being a front for bookmaking and wondered if the envelope was full of money. The fat man then wasted no time in leaving and his departure had no good-bye or other words that friends might say to one another. When he opened the door, the sun had moved just enough so that I could see his yellow car parked in the alley. When he started it up, we could hear the throatiness of the muffler.

"Glass packs," Dusty said. "He's got glass pack mufflers. I bet he's got that car all souped up. Prob'bly goes like a bat outta hell. I bet he even had it painted yellow just so people see him comin' and get out of his way."

As events unfolded in the weeks that followed, I realized it was one of those times that maybe we had been in the wrong place at the wrong time. Maybe what happened that day was our punishment for stealing or other things we'd done over the past two years. We had no business seeing what we saw or hearing what we heard. Actually, we didn't really know what we saw or heard. Most importantly, we never should've told

Jamie, the catalyst of chaos, about it. He was the one who pointed out that big businesses like Miss Beezel's store and The Pit could afford to have stuff stolen.

"It's practically expected and besides, the insurance company will give 'em their money back," he told us.

Once he heard about the fat man, he wouldn't let it go. Thanks to Jamie, the incident at The Pit would not be the last time we would see the yellow car or hear the wheezing or see the stained face of the man who packed a revolver.

PART II

INNOCENCE LOST

Chapter One

It didn't take long for Jamie to catch wind of our encounter with the fat man. A few days after the incident at The Pit, we met at B-17 for a regularly scheduled meeting. Dusty and Jamie arrived before I did and once Dusty mentioned the incident to Jamie, he was furious that he hadn't been there to witness the event. Questions abounded as he pumped Dusty for information. In Dusty's compliance, the details became more intricate which prompted even more invasive questions.

"Whaddaya mean he was carrying a gun? What kind was it? Could you tell what caliber it was? Was it loaded?" The questions came fast and furious as Jamie visually pieced together the chronology of events he had missed. Of particular interest was the passing of the envelope, which, he assumed, was full of money. "How much do you figure was in it?" he wanted to know and "Where do you think he was taking it?"

Soon the questions turned to statements like "I told you that place was a bookie joint! I'll bet that fat guy was collecting money from the bets Eddie makes. That's why he's always on the phone."

By the time I arrived at the turret, I could see that my warning to Dusty not to say too much about the fat man had gone unheeded and Jamie's thoughts were already in high gear. I sensed another of his capers coming into play. Obviously, we had to mention something to the others, but I told Dusty not to get too detailed. I knew Jamie would see some kind of angle in the moment. The two were still discussing the incident when Al and Jules showed up and this led to a rekindling of what had happened for their benefit.

When Dusty repeated the story for the two of them, other events unfolded that he had omitted during the first version along with the addition of a few hyperboles. This led to more questions from all three of them. Al, of course, was more upset about missing an event involving a revolver and pressed Dusty for all the details about the gun.

"The one time we can't make it to The Pit and all kinds of shit happens!" He directed his barking toward Jules as if it was his fault they had to help his mother that afternoon. Jamie, on the other hand, was equally upset but seemed to be more curious than angry about not having been there to actually witness the obese stranger first-hand.

When the discussion died down, other topics emerged ranging from plans for the summer to what school would be like next fall. We were still depressed and angry at the move to the junior/senior high school or The Big House, as Al called it. We were missing our rite of passage to complete our elementary school to its end and none of it seemed fair.

Jules had already started to hang out with some of the high school kids and was feeding us information about what was in store for us in September.

"The seventh and eighth graders are stuck in the basement rooms all day with crabby teachers and no windows," he told us. "Other than that, it's no big deal. I mean you have to change rooms for different subjects and ya don't get to go home for lunch, but other than that, it's pretty much the same." He neglected to mention there was more homework because he never did any homework anyway, making it a topic that didn't really matter.

"They're gonna split us up too, ya know," Dusty mentioned. "We're gonna get stuck with kids from all the other schools from uptown. I don't wanna be with those guys."

"Some of us may still get to be in the same classes." Al was optimistic as he spoke. "We could ask the principal or the teacher or somebody to see if we could stay in the same room, or maybe we could swap schedules with some kids from uptown."

"It doesn't quite work like that," Jules told him. "You get a homeroom and then the homeroom teacher hands you a schedule and that's it. You don't have anything to say about it. They don't even ask what extra subjects you want to take. All the guys have to take shop class and make birdhouses and shit. The girls go up to the third floor and learn how to cook and work on the sewing machines. I heard a guy last year cut off two of his fingers on one of the big power saws and they had to get an ambulance. They even gave the ambulance guys the two fingers that were on the floor to take with 'em. Blood everywhere, man."

This story brought renewed interest in attendance at The Big House until Jamie interrupted. He was in one of his customarily thoughtful dream states.

"Well, you know what I'm thinkin'?" his question was casual and somewhat distant, "If this is our last year of school together in old PS Number One, this summer's caper might also be our last. So I'm thinkin' it should be extra special. You know, somethin' we can all remember for a long time."

"Like what?" Dusty's voice held an air of caution. We had all been through enough of Jamie's capers to know that if he wanted to do something special, it would be something the rest of us should be leery of.

"Well, I was thinkin' about that fat guy that took the envelope full of money from Eddie. Maybe we could come up with a plan to steal the envelope. He probably picks one up every week."

"Are you crazy?" Dusty's voice now held a tone of anger. "First of all, we don't even know if the envelope had any money in it and second of all, you didn't see this guy. And why do you think he carries a gun?"

"I think the 'why do you think he carries a gun' question would technically be classified as a third of all," Al added.

"Yeah, well, whatever the case, this is not a guy you want to mess around with!"

"Dusty's right," I chimed in. "This guy isn't somebody you want coming after you. I mean, what's your big plan? You gonna wait out in the alley behind The Pit and tackle him?"

"Maybe we could all jump on him," Al said, maintaining his usual optimism. "Two or three of us could knock him down and somebody could grab his gun so he couldn't shoot us." And then Al looked at Jules. "You could take him couldn't you? I mean if we got him on the ground."

Jules pretended not to take the plan seriously and laughed as he answered Al's question. "I don't know, from what these guys are sayin' he might roll over and sit on me."

Jamie, however, persisted and seemed to be ignoring any obstacles to his initial idea regarding stealing the envelope.

"Look," he said, dismissing our reluctance. "Let's just see if he shows up again next week and picks up another envelope from Eddie. At least that'll tell us if it was just a one-time thing. If he shows up again, it'll tell us something."

"Yeah...it'll tell us he showed up again." I yelled. "So what? We still won't know if there's any money in the envelope."

Dusty chimed in with more reasons, hoping the others would be in agreement with me. "What difference does it make? Who cares if there's money in the envelope or not? I'm sure not going after some big mean fat guy who's carrying a gun. I'm not interested." Dusty was adamant with his statement and I nodded again.

Jamie seemed resigned to defeat in the category of a big hold-up and the conversation drifted back to plans for the summer and Candy Melons and what new things we could do at the city pool. Most of the people had caught on to our floating Baby Ruth routine.

Less than twenty-four hours later the conversation regarding the fat man was revisited. With only two days left before summer vacation, recess time was fast and loose and Jamie used the chaos to call us together. Teachers were as eager as we were to see the end of the year and structured activities in the schoolyard disappeared.

Jamie motioned for us to convene in one of the exterior alcoves that were normally off limits. I guess the teachers thought if there was an earthquake or something the alcove would collapse and we'd be crushed to death but it was a good meeting place if we needed privacy. Once Jamie got us in the area, he wasted no time in bringing up the permanently tabled subject of robbing the fat man.

"Okay, how about we just use the fat guy as part of a detective game?"

"What do you mean a detective game?" Al wanted to know.

Dusty immediately interrupted the conversation. "Wait a minute. Who said anything about the fat man in the first place? I thought we settled that."

Jamie kept talking as if he had never even heard Dusty's objection to the continuation of any plan involving the fat man.

"Well, we won't rob him or anything, we'll just follow him and see where he goes and what he's up to. You know, maybe he makes other stops."

Al, who had yet to venture any serious objections, seemed to take an interest in this new approach. "How you gonna follow him when he's in a car?"

"We can use our bikes, especially if he stays in the city. He can't get around that fast."

"What if he spots us?" I asked.

"That's just it. That's part of the game. If he spots us we lose."

"We could lose a lot more than the game!" Dusty protested. "The rest of you didn't see this guy," he reminded those who hadn't been at The Pit.

Once again Jamie continued as if immune to any negativity regarding his ideas. "First of all, what's he gonna do if he does spot us? He can't leave his car in the middle of a city street to chase us and, even if he could, you said he's too fat to ever catch anybody. You don't think he's actually gonna pull out his gun and start shooting at some kid because he might be following him on a bicycle!"

Jamie's arguments were all valid but, because Dusty and I continued to voice objections, the idea was put on hold until we could meet in the turret for a final vote. Al did add the suggestion that if we could get enough evidence, we could turn him in to the police and probably get a big reward, but no one seemed to be in favor of that idea.

It was another two days before all five of us were together again but whenever Jamie wasn't around Dusty and I lobbied with Al that this was one caper or game as Jamie put it, where we had to draw the line...a plan we agreed none of us would get sucked into.

❋ ❋ ❋ ❋ ❋

A FEW DAYS LATER Jamie's new caper began. The discussions behind his back had obviously not been persuasive enough to overpower his own lobbying efforts, particularly since it was only a game and there wouldn't be any direct contact with the fat man. We all knew from Dusty's initial telling of the story, the fat man had told Eddie that pick-ups would be "Thursdays from now on." With school out for the summer, Jamie insisted on starting right away so the following Thursday, we were all assembled at The Pit to begin phase one of our new caper.

During the days leading up to the meet, as Jamie referred to it, he had once again convinced the rest of us that the detective game would also be a great activity to break up the monotony of summer. It never occurred to us that summer *had* ever been a monotonous time of year. We had always found that fort building, along with swimming at the rez, gazing at Candy Melons or throwing floaters into the pool was entertainment enough. We never thought to question why chasing a yellow car around the city on our bikes would improve our summer fun.

So when Thursday rolled around, Jamie was in his designated place inside The Pit. As he hadn't been with Dusty and me the week before, he felt he should be one of the inside guys and get to see the fat man for himself. As always, he had drawn an elaborate chart on a large piece of paper. It depicted the layout—one of Jamie's favorite words—along with a drawing of the alley that ran behind the store and the houses on the opposite side.

Al pretended he needed clarification as to what the house renderings were as they had been done in haste. He was tired of Jamie's diagrams and used any opportunity to get under his skin. "Why did you put this garden full of tomato plants across the alley? I don't remember them being there." As he asked the question, his finger ran over the row of scribblings.

"They're not tomato plants, asshole, they're houses. I had to draw up the whole layout in a hurry." Jamie's voice held an impatient tone, as he hated to be questioned about anything.

The plan was for me to sit on my bike between two of what looked like tomato plants and wait for the yellow car to leave The Pit. I would then pedal off in an inconspicuous manner and find out exactly where the fat man went after he left. Being given the task of following the car was honor enough to cause me to lower my resistance to the plan and succumb to vanity.

It was no surprise, being the fastest on a bike, to have been relegated to tailing the yellow car once it left The Pit. The surprise was Jamie admitting that I was the fastest by assigning me the task. He may have been the owner of a fancy Schwinn Racer that could go Mach speed, but in a head-on race, he could never beat me to the finish line. The only time he had won was when my chain broke mid-race and I claimed he won by default. Everyone else agreed. So on day one of the game, Dusty, who was there for moral support, sat with me while we waited for the yellow car to arrive. Al and Jules sat inside at the counter drinking beers and looking innocent, and Jamie stood at the display rack containing greeting cards. He pulled cards at random and pretended to read verses touting accolades for kids' graduations or well wishes for June weddings. In the midst of them all were a few leftover Halloween cards that Eddie hadn't bothered to remove.

The position Jamie had selected allowed for a perfect view of the back door and anyone entering. The privacy curtain was wide open and he awaited his first glimpse of this bigger-than-life adversary who would supposedly scare the shit out of him—much scarier than the witch he was looking at on the card directly in front of him. The fact that he had placed Jules at the counter as a possible buffer zone was an indication that he believed most of what he had heard.

I was perched on my bike seat and was losing some of the circulation in my hands as I unconsciously tightened my fingers on the handlebars. The bike was leaning against one of the houses allowing me to rest both feet on the pedals. My eyes switched their focus from the back door of The Pit to the dirt roadway.

Dusty sat on the ground with his knees pulled up, encircled by his arms. He rocked back and forth as he stared at the lower portion of my bike. I could tell he was either in deep thought or had noticed something from his eye-level vantage point. I knew he wanted to say something.

"What?" I asked him.

"I was just checking our repair job on your chain. I thought you were going to replace that with a piece of wire." He was referring to the piece of string that we had used to reattach the broken links some time ago. The string had been there for over a week and was now covered in residual grease and hardly noticeable. When we first made the repair, the string was white which served as a nice reminder for me to replace it with wire.

"Yeah, I keep forgetting. Remind me tomorrow."

"Actually you should get one of those replacement links that just snaps in and makes a new connection. Hate to see you lose another race."

"I didn't lose the race. It was claimed a default," I reminded him. "Besides, Mr. Faulk said he might have a rivet or something he could put in the chain for me next time I'm at the train yard."

"Yeah, well this string isn't going to hold much longer."

"Maybe you should talk to Al if you want to discuss real chain problems. He's the one who has to tuck his pant leg into his sock 'cause he doesn't have a chain guard. Yesterday he said he was gonna make a new guard out of cardboard."

If Dusty had a response, it was cut short by the dust at the entrance to the alleyway. It was our signal that a vehicle was turning in off the highway. For a brief instant, it seemed like the world was rotating in slow motion. First the cloud of dust moved as if a mysterious force was carrying it along the ground and then, ever so slowly, the chrome grille and hood of the yellow sedan emerged as if the dust cloud was giving birth. The entire car became visible and, even from our distance, the mellow hum of the pipes could be heard as it emerged from within the cloud. The scene made the moment much eerier than it needed to be. I raised my hand to give Dusty an unneeded signal. He too had seen the cloud and witnessed the same eeriness.

"You sure you want to do this?" It seemed my best friend was offering an honorable way out. "This whole idea was pretty rushed. We could wait 'til next Thursday to give us time to get a better plan," he continued.

"No, I'll do it today," I told him, realizing for the first time as I said the words that it was, in fact me doing the doing. Everyone else would be at a safe distance waiting for my report regarding the fat man's itinerary.

We sat in silence and watched as the car rolled to a stop and, leaving the engine running, the fat man began the chore of getting out of the car. Despite the wide door of the sedan, he had difficulty climbing from behind the wheel and had to assist himself by grabbing onto the door handle. Even from our distant view, he emanated powers of scariness and cruelty and I questioned myself again as to whether or not it was a good idea to go chasing after this man and his yellow car.

"Besides, it'll break the monotony of summer," I told Dusty and then realized my bleak attempt at humor went unnoticed.

Once fully emerged, the fat man withdrew a handkerchief from his back pocket and dabbed it across his forehead. We couldn't see the sweat from where we were, but we both knew it had to be there and he was patting it with his fat stubby arm. From his forehead, the wiping continued downward to include the purple swatch on the left side of his face. We continued staring as he waddled his way through the back door of The Pit and, after several minutes, reappeared. He opened the trunk of the car and tossed in what looked to be a white envelope; similar to the first one we'd seen Eddie give him. He slammed the trunk shut and then squeezed his way back into the driver's seat.

As he drove away, his tires threw off a mixture of dust and gravel. The cloud that had brought him emerged again and escorted him out of the alley as if he was hidden in a cocoon. This was my cue to start pedaling and as I left to follow, Dusty put his hand square on the middle of my back and gave me a strong push to send me on my way.

Chapter Two

Mr. Faulk rummaged through a tray that contained a mixture of screws, nails, and springs along with an assortment of other miscellaneous items. They were all items he kept in an otherwise empty Hellmann's jar. He had dumped the contents onto the workbench in the D&H break room and was searching for anything that would hold my bicycle chain together. Dusty's assessment that the string would have a limited life span had been correct and had brought about an abrupt end to tailing the fat man. Before the chain broke, I realized keeping up with him on the long stretch of the arsenal wouldn't have been possible anyway, even with a good chain.

I opened one of the packets of peanut butter crackers he had tossed me as he apologized for being out of raisins. I broke off one of the crackers and offered it but he waved it off as he picked up various pieces of hardware and scrutinized each one as a possible repair part.

My bike was sitting behind us supported in its inverted position by the handlebars and the seat. The broken chain sat in a heap on the workbench and Mr. Faulk had taken a few minutes from his schedule to act as a bicycle repair man. Knowing his eye for detail and the meticulous nature at which he tackled any task, I was confident that my ride home would entail a completely fixed chain and my bike would be better than new. This was further evidenced by the fact that he had removed his glasses from his coveralls and was wearing them to search for what he now jokingly referred to as the missing link. Everyone in the yard knew when he put his glasses on he meant business. He didn't like wearing them in public, confessing to me he felt they represented the onset of old age.

"We'll find somethin' that'll work," he said more to himself than to me as he continued sifting through the mess of hardware. I watched his long fingers as they worked the pile, fingers I knew were strong and had a grip of steel when needed. Between the sounds of his humming and the scraping of nuts and bolts around the tabletop, we talked and laughed. He always had good stories to tell about the railroad or some worker who'd done something stupid or how some of the crew would pull a joke on one of the guys. Most of the stories involved workers I had come to know and were now funnier because I could put faces and personalities with the vivid descriptions of his accounts.

Today, while perched on my stool, he detoured from his story telling and took a different tact.

"Where'd this happen?" he asked me. "This chain thing I mean. How far did you have to push it to get here?"

"I was on this side of the arsenal," I told him.

"Kinda out of bounds for you on the bike isn't it? Not that it's any of my business," he continued. "The fact that your granddaddy is my boss as well as my best friend doesn't mean I go runnin' to him regardin' any little thing his grandson is up to." He stopped his search for the needed hardware and tilted his head to peer at me over the top of his bifocals. "That's the thing about friendship ya know. Ya can't cross one friend if it means you have to betray the confidence of another. Life's a bit confusing about things like that. I just mention it because I think you told me once that the arsenal and uptown are off limits for you on the bike."

"Well I wasn't actually past the arsenal. I was almost there and getting ready to turn around and head back home when the chain broke," I lied.

It was the first time I ever lied to Mr. Faulk, a man who had been my friend for as long as I could remember. I felt ashamed for not telling him the truth and, at that moment, a feeling of anger toward Jamie crept up inside me. For some reason I believed it was his fault I had lied. It was his fault that I was doing a lot of things I never would've done before.

Mr. Faulk resumed his search through the hardware until his next comment broke the silence a second time. "Between you, me, and the fencepost, I don't know why the government had to come in here to our fair city and build that arsenal square in the middle of town anyway. All those guys do in there all day is shoot off machine guns and design rockets that'll blow people up. We got too much of that in the world today." And then he paused as if waiting for my agreement or dissention on his motion. Before I could put together what I felt would be an acceptable comment, he continued.

"It's a lucky thing you didn't go all the way to the other end of the arsenal on your ride. That fence they got keepin' people out must be a half a mile long on the front side. Goes the same distance here in back along the train yard. Why, we coulda used a lot of that land for some extra spurs of tracks. Lord knows we need 'em. The funny part of the whole thing is, that fence they got for security doesn't do anything on this side. All ya gotta do is stand up on one of the freight cars in the graveyard and ya can see right into the place.

Prob'bly could jump right in there if you wanted to. Some security," he added, as he picked up a small rivet out of the menagerie of items spread out on the workbench.

It was almost as if he had knowledge of the entire raid we pulled on the arsenal—how we stood on the freight cars and hopped the wall. I feared he had perhaps seen our footprints or maybe had been questioned the next day. I felt uneasy knowing he might suspect that I was involved in something like that.

"I'll put this rivet in the chain for now. It's not the best solution but it's certainly better than that piece of string you had on there. Tomorrow, on my way into work, I'll stop at the hardware store and pick up a proper link you need to fix this chain once and for all. I can't have you breakin' down at some inopportune moment." He looked at the rivet more closely. "This should hold 'til then. Suppose you were a secret agent trailin' a pack of bank robbers or something today?"

Again, I thought about the accuracy of his guess and how I followed the fat man and how close to the truth Mr. Faulk was with his comment.

"I can pay for the link myself," I told him. "I mean if you don't mind picking it up."

"Tell you what partner," he said with a smile. "I'll put the fifteen cents on your tab." With that comment, he rustled my hair with a gentle hand. For such a slender man, he was one of the strongest in the train yard. Yet with all his strength and responsibilities, I had never once seen him angry or lose his temper with the men. And being a religious man, I had never heard him swear or use abusive language like most of the other workers. I had no idea a day was about to come when I would witness his temper getting the better of him. It proved to be a day that changed the life of each member of The Five-Cent Gang.

❊ ❊ ❊ ❊ ❊

WHILE MR. FAULK MADE final adjustments to my bike chain, a solitary figure, some six blocks away, entered the yard of Jamie McGuire. It was the only time Jules went there alone and the only time he climbed the steps of the back porch and knocked on the door. When Jamie came downstairs, he was so surprised to see Jules on the porch he stood speechless. His friend was noticeably alone and Jamie's first thought was Jules was there because he wasn't happy with something that involved the gang—perhaps the comic book caper or the raid on the arsenal.

"We need to talk," he told Jamie. "Outside."

"Yeah, sure, what's going on? Where is everybody?"

"I needed to talk to you alone. I'm not sure where Al is. I told him I'd catch up to him at the turret. You hear anything from Auggie yet?"

"No. I mean I guess everything went as planned. He's supposed to fill us in at the turret."

"Yeah, well, I figured I'd come over here and if you were ready to go, we could walk over together and talk on the way. You got everything you need?" Jules was always serious about things, but today he seemed tense and anxious. There was no evidence of his usual smile that displayed his white even teeth; no nonchalance in his attitude.

It was rare that the two of them ever stood this close together and Jamie now noticed a distinct difference in their sizes. Over the past year, Jules had filled out some and it fit well with his natural physique. He had not only added two inches to his height, but the contours of his upper body stretched his year-old T-shirt taut across his chest and there was no floppiness or space between his sleeves and his biceps. His visible strength continued as veins bulged from his forearms. In some ways, with Jamie's dark hair and rugged appearance, observers seeing the two of them walking together would guess them to be brothers. Jamie was a contoured smaller version and blessed with the same even white teeth and deceptive smile. After a few steps, Jules began the conversation, the topic of which surprised Jamie.

"This thing you mentioned, you know, about following the fat man for a game."

"Yeah?"

"Well, I been thinkin' about that other thing you said. You know, about maybe trying to come up with a plan to get the envelope. I'm thinkin' that you're right about him picking up money from different places and maybe we should try and get it. I was also thinkin' that depending on what Auggie found out today, that if the guy's picking up other envelopes from different places, we should maybe wait until he gets all of them."

"I'm not so sure the rest of the guys will go along with that idea."

"Well, I'm thinkin' we bring it to a vote. I'll take care of Al. I mean he'll vote whatever way I tell him to. With you, that makes the majority. Dusty and Auggie'll have to go for it."

"They may have to go for it, but I'm not so sure they'll have to go through with it. Why are you changing your mind, anyway?"

"I've got my reasons and they're my own. The main thing is, I'll back you on the plan but it's gonna have to be your idea. Bring it up today if you want to, depending on what Auggie found out or wait a couple of days, but not too long."

The two walked another block in silence before Jules spoke again. "How much do you think might be in the envelopes? I mean, I'm guessing if you're right about Eddie being a bookie or something there might be a couple a hundred or so."

"Yeah, and if that fat guy is picking up envelopes from other places we could get ourselves a good take. We might even get a couple hundred bucks each." Jamie's voice now held an air of excitement as the thought of planning a real crime with split-second timing was a possibility. It would be the master plan he'd always talked about when they could actually rob someone.

"He couldn't even go to the cops if we robbed him," he said aloud as he pondered the possibilities.

❋ ❋ ❋ ❋ ❋

AL AND DUSTY SAT in the turret awaiting the arrival of the others. The conversation focused on their choice of which super power they would choose if they were limited to just one. Dusty had opted for flying while Al had chosen x-ray vision, explaining it would allow him to see through girls' clothes. As exciting as the thoughts were, Al became impatient.

"Where the hell are they? Do you think the fat man spotted Auggie and kidnapped him? I mean, why is he so late getting here? He shoulda been here by now."

"Relax man. Auggie knows what he's doin'. Even if the guy did spot him, he'd never catch him. Like Jamie said, what's he gonna do? Get out of his car in the middle of traffic and run his fat ass after him? Even if something happened, Auggie's on his bike. I mean, he can fit through places a car can never get through and he knows every yard and alley in all of Port Schuyler all the way to the arsenal. He even knows his way around uptown." As Dusty spoke, he remembered the piece of string holding Auggie's chain together but thought better of mentioning it.

* * * * *

THE DEBRIEFING TOOK PLACE as scheduled and after I explained the broken chain was my reason for being late, talk returned to the next phase of the game. It was agreed that further surveillance was needed during the days ahead. We made small talk but Jamie made no mention in the turret regarding the possibility of robbing the fat man. Jules guessed it was a suggestion he would save for a more opportune time, but gave him a knowing glance when we split up. This delay by Jamie allowed for the opportunity for Jules to discuss his own motives for a robbery with his brother. Later that evening, as the two sat in Al's bedroom, Jules made his pitch.

"I talked to Jamie today about a plan to rob the fat guy."

"What do you mean rob the fat guy? I thought that was all settled? We weren't going to have anything to do with that. It was just a crazy idea."

"I need the money," Jules continued. "Actually, we need the money."

"Why do we need the money? I thought we were doin' okay."

"I've been puttin' some money away and I talked to Mr. Billings down at the appliance store yesterday about getting Mom a washer and dryer for the house. You know, so she doesn't have to spend all day every Saturday down at the Laundromat washing our clothes and stuff. Anyway, he's got a used washer and dryer I can buy right now, but I'm a little short and I figure if we could rob that fat guy I'd have enough. Even if I didn't, you could chip in from your share."

"How much are you short now?"

"A hundred and forty-two dollars."

"A hundred and forty-two dollars!" Al echoed. "What if we rob the fat guy and he doesn't have that much on him?"

"Well then, I guess you start saving your money too until we get enough. I mean, the hook up for the washer and dryer are already in the basement and Mr. Billings said he'd deliver the stuff and connect it himself."

Al sat in quiet contemplation. Being the older of the two it had been Jules who had taken over the man-of-the-house responsibilities when their father died. All Al knew about his father's death was that he'd been hit by another car and died in the accident. Jules knew differently. His father, in a drunken stupor, had been the one who had caused the accident. His father was known for spending most of his time in bars and had certainly fallen short in the roles of father and husband. This was information that Jules would never reveal to his younger brother, but the fact remained that he was in charge and was the self-appointed protector of the family. With no response from Al, Jules continued.

"Do you think it's easy for Mom to spend all her time taking care of us? This is something we can give her together. Even if both of us keep saving, she'll be old and gray by the time we could afford it. Besides, Mr. Billings could sell the used machines to someone else. We could never afford new ones."

"What about the other guys?"

"It's like I told Jamie, with you and me voting with him, it's three against two. We're either The Five-Cent Gang or we're not. This will tell...and as far as the money goes, why we need it is none of anybody's business so just keep your mouth shut about Mom and stuff."

Chapter Three

Several days passed before Jamie broached the subject of changing the game. In that first round of surveillance we discovered the fat man was covering too much distance for me to stay with him, especially on the long stretch of the arsenal. It was a section of the city where all drivers, knowing there were no stoplights, took full advantage of the half-mile distance. Other than the used car lot opposite the arsenal's entrance gate, there were no side streets.

The surveillance problem was solved when Jamie posted Al at the opposite end of the arsenal to continue my tail. Without the possibility of turning on to a side street, spotting the fat man when he reached Al's end was easy. The one time I followed him from The Pit he made one other stop before reaching the arsenal stretch. It was a small grocery store and when he came out he, once again, opened the trunk of his car and threw an envelope into a satchel.

With our new plan, I followed him to the arsenal and then called Al. We used pay phones and two rings meant the fat man was on the way. It was a system that worked to perfection and on the second run, Al picked up the tail and followed him as he made three more stops before disappearing onto the major highway.

We continued to meet at the turrets to discuss our findings and the game dominated our days. Surprisingly it did turn out to be fun and it remained that way until Jamie pushed it to the next level.

"We need to know where the fat man ends up if we're gonna steal the money." After making the slip, he gave an awkward glance toward Jules.

"Steal what money?" I demanded.

"Yeah, what money, who said anything about stealing money?" Dusty chimed in.

With the information accidentally dispensed to the rest of us, Jules took the lead before Jamie could answer my question.

"Jamie and I have sorta been talkin'," he said. "We think we can maybe get a plan together to get the envelopes the fat guy collects every week. We haven't really done any kind of a caper since the cherry bomb raid. We should end on something better than that if we're gonna have a final caper like Jamie said. The arsenal thing didn't really go as planned."

"Yeah, well that's exactly my point," I argued. "It didn't exactly go as planned. Suppose stealing from the fat man doesn't go as planned either. We're not talkin' about some guard catching us blowing off cherry bombs. You weren't sitting at the counter when that fat guy came in The Pit and almost broke my hand off...and that was for doing nothing!" I added.

Dusty then spoke with all the logic of a police chief's son.

"We talked about this over a week ago...we decided no way on trying to steal the envelopes. We said we'd just follow the fat man for a game."

"Actually, we didn't decide," Jamie corrected. "I mean, we never brought it to a vote. We just kinda said we wouldn't try to rob him."

"Jamie's right," Jules chimed in. "If we're gonna make a final decision on this, we need to vote on it and make it official."

"No way, man, I vote no," Dusty said without hesitation. Although he had already cast his vote verbally, he pulled his penny from around his neck and held it in his hand, letting us know he wasn't going to throw it into the center. Jules retrieved his penny and tossed it in. "I say we take the fat guy for every cent he's got."

"I gotta go with Dusty on this one," I said. "Sorry, Jules. Too much weird shit could happen with that guy—and don't forget, man, he carries a gun."

Jules looked at his brother. "Al, what do you say?"

"I say we do it," talking more to his brother than to us as he tossed his penny into the center. Jules then looked at Jamie. "Up to you, man," he told him. "What's it gonna be?"

Jamie used his usual dramatic flair to make a big deal out of his decision, as if we didn't know what he was going to do. The idea for robbing the fat man had been his from the beginning. Now, he was going to make the final decision as to what the vote would be, as if it was Jules's idea, not his.

"I gotta go with Jules and Al on this one," he said, throwing his penny in with the other two.

It was the first time a decision made by The Five-Cent Gang hadn't been unanimous and we sat in silence in our obvious division. As our code of honor dictated, Dusty and I both knew decisions by votes had to be carried out and we were now bound to rob the fat man whether we liked it or not.

"I guess that settles it then," Jamie said. "We keep going with our surveillance and then I'll come up with a plan to rob the fat man."

"What if he catches us?" Al asked.

"Maybe you should've thought of that before you voted, smart ass," Dusty yelled back.

"Nobody's gonna get caught," Jules assured us. "And we're all gonna make some good money out of this deal."

"We'll need to talk about more surveillance," Jamie decided. "I'll set up a plan tonight and we'll go over details tomorrow."

With the discussion concluded, the three yes voters retrieved their pennies from the middle of the circle and replaced them around their necks, but the discord revealed in the vote carried through when we left. Dusty and I took one path from the turret and the affirmative voters left in a different direction. The two of us discussed the risks we would be taking and the lack of wisdom in stealing from the fat man. The plan Jamie put forth the next day would have to be fool-proof.

He must've spent a good portion of the evening planning the robbery. His presentation was one of the best he ever put forward and even Dusty and I were convinced that we at least had a chance of pulling it off. If any miscarriages did occur, the plan was structured so none of us would be identified. Additionally, accounting for the physical attributes of the fat man, he wouldn't be able to catch us on foot and chasing us in his car wouldn't be an option.

For the next two weeks, we worked on little else. We each carried a small notebook that contained the locations and phone numbers of every phone booth along the fat man's route. We also discovered he started his collections from an office in an old bell factory. He left the building with the satchel and threw it into his trunk. From there, he started his weekly pickups and each stop yielded an envelope that he tossed into the satchel. Once he finished and returned, the bag was taken inside. Al had the factory outlook and kept track of his comings and goings. We all wrote down notes and shared information during meetings in the turrets. Al made extra notes about things he thought comical and added how funny the fat man looked going in and out with his satchel.

"Like he's a big fat doctor or something," he told us.

The plan was to take the satchel while he was inside his second to last stop on his return trip to the factory. The last stop was at the city drug store and he parked on the main street. The stop we had selected was a barber shop. For that collection he parked in the back alley and there was never anyone around when he went inside. It was agreed that it would be better to forfeit the money in the final envelope if we could grab the bag in the seclusion of an alley.

We had timed him on his stops and the shortest time we ever clocked was two minutes and twelve seconds. The barber shop was closer to three minutes. Jules had assured us that with a crowbar he could get the trunk open and he and Al could grab the satchel and get away in under a minute. They would then take it to a second alley where we would be waiting and each of us would take a few envelopes. We outlined different routes we would take on our bikes and rendezvous at turret H-4 where we could safely count the money and then split it up. It all sounded so simple even Dusty and I became believers, and the talk and thoughts of what to do with the money added to that belief.

Anyway, that was the plan. It was simple and probably would've worked, but we never found out.

Chapter Four

It was a lazy Sunday evening. With only four days to go before the robbery, we were hangin' out at Dusty's house. Jamie said we should just get together to relax. "It's what they did in the Ma Barker movie when she and James Cagney had the gang holed up in a cabin before pulling a job," he told us.

When we arrived that evening, Dusty's mother was preparing trays of cookies and mini sandwiches and we assumed they were for us. There was nothing promising on the Ed Sullivan Show so the five of us went upstairs to Dusty's bedroom to play a relaxing game of Monopoly. During an argument over how many houses equaled a hotel, several cars pulled into the driveway and we soon discovered Dusty's father was holding a meeting with the members of his task force. The hors d'oeuvres and other goodies were for the men who convened in the study located directly beneath Dusty's bedroom. There was a heating vent in the floor and the voices below us were audible enough to hear the conversations. When they first arrived, everyone was engaged in small talk until Dusty's father called the meeting to order. He sounded very official as he got the men's attention.

"I appreciate you taking the time to come here on a Sunday," he began. "This meeting is more or less meant to be off the record, but due to some recent information from our inside man, our hand is being forced. It appears Wenzel is making a move this Thursday, so the operation we discussed last week regarding our plan for the end of the month is out of the picture."

Phrases like 'off the record' and 'recent information' and 'inside man' were so similar to the police jargon in the movies, we had no recourse but to continue listening as the conversation drifted up through the heating grate. No doubt Dusty would've put a stop to it if some advance notice had been given, but seeing as how we were sort of innocent bystanders, it was more embarrassing to announce ourselves than to listen in.

"Shhh," Jamie said as he put a finger to his lips and signaled the rest of us to be quiet. He then motioned for us to get closer and the five us crept on all fours to the heating vent. We got down on our bellies and surrounded it with our heads touching. We looked down on the tops of the men who comprised the task force.

"They're G-men," Al whispered.

Jules then poked him in the ribs and in a low whisper told him to keep his mouth shut. At that moment, the huge doors to the study rumbled open and Mrs. Barnes entered with the tray of food she had prepared. The men made space by moving their briefcases and manila folders as she maneuvered herself through the room and set the tray on a small table in the corner. When she left the room, Mr. Barnes continued and as he talked, he removed a large cloth that covered an easel.

The five of us fought for space on the small vent and we bumped heads as we maneuvered ourselves for the best vantage point.

The board was covered with photographs and from our aerial perspective they were arranged in a fashion much like the family tree my mother had once shown me. Dusty's father pointed to the pictures and continued addressing the task force.

"Move over man," Jules whispered to Dusty. "I can't see any of the pictures."

"If I move over, I won't be able to see them either. It's my house, remember?"

Dusty's father continued with the information on the easel. "As you can see, I put Provinzini on the top of the chart because he's running the local syndicate action. We still believe they set up shop here in Waterton because we're a small town that doesn't draw much attention. Everything going on upstate is funneled to Provinzini and four times each year the money is transferred down to the city. For those of you who haven't been working with us on this, the guy pictured directly below him is Harold Wenzel. He's our main focus. Provinzini's running the show, but Wenzel is the weak link."

At that comment, Al bent his arm to show us his muscle and pointed to his miniature bicep as he made a face to agree with the weak link comment. It was that action that forced out some muffled laughs and triggered continued miming of comments throughout the meeting. As a natural comedian, he turned our covert spying operation into opportunities of comic relief.

"He's the one person who can turn evidence on every one of these other clowns," Mr. Barnes continued. As he spoke he made a sweeping gesture over the pictures of the other men on the easel. "Wenzel keeps the books, organizes the files, and oversees the money laundering. According to our guy on the inside, he's going to make the quarterly run to

New York City on Thursday. We need to nail him when he's in possession of the books and he always takes them with him on the New York runs. According to information we've received, he'll leave the old bell factory here in Waterton around three o'clock and head over to Troy. We know he's going to Troy first because Provinzini has to okay the final figures on the books before he leaves. There's no way Wenzel can go to the city without them. He'll also be carrying a large amount of cash, but that's secondary on this. We're after the books. Anything else we might grab will be gravy."

Mr. Barnes then instructed the men to open their folders and look at the first map before he continued.

Al then pantomimed the opening of a folder and then added a look of shocked surprise as he looked inside.

"He'll most likely take the Green Island Bridge to Troy. Prior surveillance has told us he always uses that route when he meets with Provinzini. It's convenient, quick, and easy for him to get to. That said, the fact of the matter is we don't care what route he takes. We're not picking up any surveillance until he comes back into Waterton."

The bridge comment once again set Al into action as he mimed the driving of a car and then feigned an accident as he went off the road. Our tenuous position, which didn't allow for any noise from above, made his actions funnier than they actually were and all of us fought to muffle our laughs.

"I know where that bridge is, my father uses it for a shortcut to Troy too," Jamie informed us.

"If you guys don't shut up, we're all gonna get caught." The warning from Jules temporarily ended further talking.

At this point of the meeting, Mr. Barnes pinned a second sheet of paper on the easel while he continued.

It looked like a diagram that Jamie might draw and contained a map of streets in Waterton along with highways that wound their way out of the city.

"Jamie, did you give Dusty's father caper lessons? That looks like one of your drawings." Al's comment received an elbow to the rib cage and a dirty look from Jules.

"After Provinzini okays the books, we know Wenzel will return to Waterton, head east somewhere along here, and head up Nineteenth Street. From there he can shoot straight up to Interstate 87." Dusty's father indicated the route with the end of a ruler as the men looked on.

We all saw the similarities of the chart and the plan and how they mirrored illustrations Jamie always made.

"This is like an adult caper," Al whispered to Jamie.

This time Jules put a hand over his brother's mouth and gave him a dirty look, but none of the heads in the study looked up and we remained silent as Mr. Barnes continued.

"Once on 87, he's got a clear shot to the Thruway which he'll obviously stay on all the way to the city."

A question then came from one of the task members. As we could only see the tops of heads, he was identified to us by the raising of his arm as he leaned forward to ask the question.

"Shouldn't we tail him all the way from the factory to the city?"

"No need to," Dusty's father replied. "We'll be called from a car stationed at Provinzini's house to let us know he's on the way. He'll take the same bridge back and we'll pick him up once he's out of Troy and back into Waterton.

There's only one other place locally he can pick up the interstate and we'll have them both covered. As a precaution, we're even putting a team on a third route but he'd have to drive through a lot of city traffic to Albany which is at least an hour out of his way. If you check the second page of your packet, it designates each of your locations and the location of the other agents involved. Some of them are on duty tonight and couldn't be here so look the information over carefully. We'll have men stationed in several strategic places and you need to know where your team members are."

"How reliable is this information you're getting?" another agent asked.

Adhering to Jules's earlier reprimand, no words were spoken but more squirming ensued as we jockeyed for position to get a look at the agent who asked the question. In the process, Al's head bumped into Dusty's and he winced in pain. Jamie rolled over holding his stomach and then put a hand over his mouth to keep from laughing. Mr. Barnes continued with the meeting.

"It's first rate," Dusty's father told the agent, which coincided with a thumbs-up from Al. "We've had one of our own on the inside for over six months now. If he says Wenzel is leaving the factory at three and heading out, you can take it to the bank. When this guy picks up 87, we'll be all over him. Bob's car will pursue from a reasonable distance and radio Ted at the toll booth to give them a heads-up." As Mr. Barnes said this he used his ruler to point to the agents who would be involved. He then continued pointing to other men as he explained the plan in detail.

"Taking him once he's through the toll booth will be handled by Ted and Frank who'll be in the car stationed here." Once again he used the ruler to tap the diagram. "They'll fall in behind Wenzel as soon as he gets on the Thruway. From what we've been told he'll be alone. He's one of the few involved in the money laundering who's not recognizable. He's primarily a pencil pusher, strictly a behind-the-scenes type of guy."

"Is one team there enough?" The question had come from a bald-headed agent who wiped cigarette ashes off his lap as he spoke.

As he continued with his comment, Al whispered, "Yeah, one team will be enough but we're gonna need five or six guys to clean the ashes off your pants," causing Jamie to take another roll on the floor and cover his mouth a second time.

The agent continued with a comment regarding the amount of time the force had invested in breaking these guys. When I heard the word breaking, I couldn't resist getting in on the fun of acting things out the way Al was and I took the pencil I had in my pocket and broke it in two. This sent Al into a laughing fit to the point that he had to crawl backward on all fours to get away from the heating vent.

The meeting droned on as Dusty's father continued and Dusty gave all of us dirty looks and started pulling us away from the grate.

"If you read farther down in your notes, we're not using just one team," his father told the men. "We'll actually have three teams with Bob and Roger coming through the toll booths behind them, and we've got the State Police sitting at mile marker 110. Ted and Frank will have plenty of time to pull him over before he reaches the state boys. We don't expect to get any resistance from this guy. Like I said, he's a pencil pusher, plain and simple. He'll most likely be calm when he's pulled over, thinking it's some kind of routine stop. He's not the type to panic. Keep in mind the info we've got on this guy along with the wiretaps means he's either gonna turn state's for us or take a long vacation on the feds. We figure with an additional offer of witness relocation, he'll give us the entire operation. He's not the kind of guy who would have much success in a federal penitentiary."

Mr. Barnes called for a brief break before he fielded any more questions and encouraged the agents to take advantage of the food Mrs. Barnes had provided.

"Coffee's on the way too," he announced.

Everyone began discussing the plan and the conversations gave us the diversion needed to return to the Monopoly board and talk quietly.

"You guys are real assholes. I could get in big trouble if we get caught listening in on his meeting."

The apologies that were returned were not the most serious as they were provided through a variety of snorts and laughs.

"Wow, your father really is the head of a task force," Al whispered, trying to sooth the moment. "Did you hear how they're gonna get that Wenzel guy?"

"Of course. We all heard it. We were layin' right there with you." Dusty told him.

"Who do you think that Wenzel guy is?" I asked Dusty.

"I don't know. Probably one of the guys my father's been after. He's workin' on something big, I know that. He's been pretty secretive around the house. I got a quick look under the cloth once and saw the pictures. It's full of guys he's after."

Jamie was quick to seize the moment. "Who else's picture is on there?"

"I don't know. I didn't get a good enough look. I just know it's a bunch of pictures of guys he's after. I'm not supposed to be messin' around with stuff in his study."

Just as things were calming down, Al kicked over his glass of orange soda that had been sitting on the floor next to the game board. Everyone watched in horror as the pool of orange left ice cubes behind and headed directly for the heating grate. It moved slowly and everyone seemed to be horrified at what was about to happen.

Just prior to reaching the vent and spilling down onto the lap of one of the men, Jules ripped off his T-shirt and threw it onto the pool of soda bringing it to a stop. We all looked at one another and exhaled a synchronized sigh of relief.

"That's it," Dusty yelled. "Time for everybody to go home!"

"What about the game?" Al asked. "I've got all these houses and stuff on my property."

"We can finish it tomorrow," Jules told him. "We gotta get goin' too."

"Can we do that?"

"Yeah," Dusty told him, still irritated. "Just leave the board where it is and come over in the morning."

As we left Dusty's room that night, I may have been the only one who noticed the glint in Jamie's eye. It was a look I'd seen before. A look that appeared when his wheels were turning. It wasn't a look I liked seeing.

Chapter Five

Monday - Changing The Plan

Monday morning we reconvened to finish our game of Monopoly, although the encouragement from Jamie to do so held an ulterior motive. After eavesdropping on the task force, he had time to think things through and before we continued our game he was coaxing Dusty to let him see the board in the study. It didn't take much to get the rest of us in the spirit of detective work and all of us joined in on the urging. We wanted to see the pictures of the men we had heard about when their descriptions drifted up through the heating vent. Reluctantly, Dusty led us downstairs and into his father's study.

He pulled the heavy doors apart. The chairs that had been arranged for the meeting we'd witnessed were still in place and were facing the big easel that sat in the front of the room. It held the board that was covered by a piece of cloth and Dusty carefully removed it and revealed photos of the arch enemies of the Waterton Task Force. The guy in the top picture fulfilled our expectations of a criminal. A snarled lip added a look of evil and meanness and the label beneath the picture read, 'Carlos Provinzini—Crime Boss'. As Dusty's father had said at the meeting, the guy named Wenzel was directly below him but his picture was a disappointment. He looked more like a science professor than the henchman for the mob I'd been expecting. My thoughts were interrupted by Jamie who was scanning other photos further down the board.

"Holy shit! Look at this," he yelled. "It's a picture of the fat man!"

We all focused our attention on Jamie's discovery and stared at the face. Although the man depicted seemed a bit thinner and displayed more hair than the man that collected the envelope in The Pit, it was unmistakably the fat man.

"Look at this!" he said pointing beneath the picture. The name printed under the photo read, 'Vincent Malducci—Enforcer'.

"Do you guys see the connection here?" Al held one index finger on Vincent Malducci and pointed his other to Harold Wenzel. "This guy Wenzel works for the fat man. I'll bet that money he's takin' to New York on Thursday is probably the money from all the envelopes."

"I think it's the other way around." Jamie pointed out. "I think the fat man probably works for the Wenzel guy. That's why he's the one on the top of the chart."

"Yeah, well either way, if he's takin' all the money to New York like Dusty's father said, maybe we should try and steal it from him instead of messin' with the fat man. I mean, look at the guy, he probably doesn't even carry a gun."

Dusty's fidgeting and glances toward the window indicated to me he was getting uneasy with the length of time we were spending in the study. His mother was outside in the garden but could return at any moment.

"We better get out of here," he told us and he grabbed the piece of cloth and replaced it over the easel.

Jules wasn't so quick to dismiss the idea of robbing Wenzel. "We need to discuss this new possibility," Jules said. "But Dusty's right; we need to get out of here. We can talk outside."

As we walked toward the turrets, the conversation immediately turned to changing our plan and Dusty expressed his concern about using information from his father's task force to set up a caper.

"We should stick to the original plan," he argued. "It may not get us as much money as robbing that Wenzel guy but the plan we've already got is pretty good and we don't have any kind of a plan for stealing that other guy's money."

"I agree with Dusty," I chimed in. "To try and add anything new now isn't a good idea, besides, we already voted."

Jules, on the other hand, wasn't so easily convinced. "Listen, Dusty's father said the guy is going to New York on Thursday. That gives us three days to come up with a new plan and we can always take another vote."

Arguing with Jules was not as easy as arguing with Jamie. Since he was older, when he contributed his infrequent comments, they were not to be taken lightly.

Jamie focused his stare on Dusty but his comments seemed to be aimed more toward Jules. "Your father said that guy was going to take the Green Island Bridge to Troy. That's the old D&H Bridge. Nobody even uses it anymore. It would be the perfect place to pull somethin' on him."

"I say we get our bikes and check out the bridge," Jules added. "Any objections on doing that? I mean we'd just be takin' a look, that's all." No one voiced any objections and the late morning sun found us pedaling our bikes past the forbidden area of the arsenal into uptown Waterton.

Our bikes reflected our personalities. Jamie, of course, had the newest Schwinn on the market, which sported a chrome light mounted on the handlebars accompanied by a matching chrome horn. Being fully equipped for night riding, he also had side reflectors within the spokes of the front and rear tires. Jules, on the other hand, had streamlined his by removing both fenders. Al's bike was lacking the chain guard, not because he had adopted his brother's streamlined look, but because he procrastinated in its reattachment. For that reason, he rode with his right pants leg rolled up to reveal a grease-covered sock. He also rode with two playing cards clothes-pinned to the front fender frame so they flapped in the spokes and made it sound like a motorcycle. This feature was never discussed in the presence of his mother once she made mention that she'd played three games of solitaire one afternoon without winning a game and then discovered she was missing the three of clubs and the nine of hearts.

Dusty's bike always brought him to the ball field well prepared. He had such a love for the game of baseball that he made a quiver for his Louisville Slugger, which had become an integral part of his bike. He went nowhere without it, along with his glove that was looped on his handlebars and a baseball that he wedged under his seat. My bike was adorned with stickers for the Brooklyn Dodgers. Not because I liked the Dodgers, but because my father bought it second hand and it was the favorite team of the kid he bought it from. I was discouraged in attempting their removal after I took one off and some of the paint came with it. Al solved the problem when one of his frequent questions was actually a solution.

"Why don't you just become a Dodger's fan?" he asked me.

The five bikes moved in single file past the arsenal as we rode uptown.

The D&H Bridge had finished serving its purpose years earlier with the completion of the Congress Street Bridge, the new, state-of-the-art four-laner a mile down the highway. The entire time we were there that morning, not one car crossed over. Once the Congress Street Bridge was built, the D&H was only used by a few of the locals as a back road into Troy. When initially built, it opened up a line for the railroad and a set of tracks paralleled the two lanes provided for vehicles. The massive iron girders coupled with huge wooden beams combined to form an architectural masterpiece of its time and it had been the premiere crossing over the Hudson River.

Although it was still safe, the imbedded wooden road trusses were now worn from many years of use and when cars crossed over, their tires hummed from the echo of the girders. Even the D&H railroad, which contributed most of the initial cost and continued maintenance, had ceased running trains on the line that connected the two cities. Jamie was quick to point out how the isolation provided a perfect place to separate Wenzel from his money.

The five of us stood in the middle of the bridge and looked down as the Hudson flowed beneath us. It was a narrow passage at this point, one reason the bridge had been built in this location. The embankments on either side were an easy climb and paths that led to the water provided evidence of guys who took their .22s to the riverbank and shot at carp and the occasional white eel. Areas of bare turf near the water were littered with empty cartridge shells and indicated the ideal vantage points for shooting. The same areas held an assortment of candy bar wrappers, cigarette butts, and beer cans. Posted signs leading to the bridge were riddled with bullet holes, which provided further evidence of the bridge's lack of traffic.

A path leading from the lower embankment to Waterton wound itself into a small patch of trees and then continued out onto the city streets of uptown. We all stared at the water rushing below us until Jules broke the silence.

"Whaddaya think?" The question was thrown out as if he wanted our input, but I knew he was asking Jamie. What did Jamie think was what he wanted to know.

"Dusty's father said that Wenzel guy will leave the factory at three o'clock, It's probably a ten-minute drive to right where we're standin'," Jules continued. "Any ideas?"

Al, who had no idea that the question was being addressed to Jamie, volunteered the answer. "We could shoot one of his tires out and when he gets out to fix it, one of us could sneak up and steal the money," he responded.

As crazy as the idea sounded, it wasn't totally dismissed by Jamie who was deep in thought. He continued to stare at the water below.

"I don't think we need to shoot out any tires, but this bridge wouldn't be a bad place if we could stop his car some other way. I think we need to make a new plan."

With that statement, Jules called for an immediate meeting right there on the bridge and a vote was taken to forget about stealing the envelopes from the fat man's car and rob Wenzel on Thursday. The decision was again decided by a vote of three to two. Immediately, Jamie began giving us a few details of the new plan. This confirmed my notion that the decision had been made the night before, and Dusty and I remained skeptical.

We stood on the bridge as Jamie talked but, for once, his ideas seemed to be less than adequate. Unlike his prior efforts in our other capers, it lacked efficiency. Since this was the biggest one yet I was concerned about flaws that left possibilities for errors. Additionally, Dusty was afraid his father's position on the task force would be compromised. As the word compromise wasn't one we actually used with any amount of frequency, his exact phrasing was "I don't want to screw up my father's job."

Jamie's idea was to stop the car and somehow get Wenzel out of it.

"Maybe I could run out in front of his car and fake an accident," he said, "pretend he hurt me. When he gets out to see if I'm okay, one of you guys can grab the money."

The omission of details in the idea apparently caught Jules by surprise also. In the silence that followed, we stood with our own thoughts until Jules addressed him.

"Don't fuck it up," he said. "You know what I'm talkin' about, right?"

The fact that he had used the 'F' word had caught the attention of all of us. Not that we hadn't heard it before, but it was seldom used within our group. We were pretty much limited to calling someone an asshole, or using the word bullshit, or the phrase pissed off. Not being Catholics like Jamie, the rest of us might also throw in an occasional jeezus if there was something a particular situation warranted. But the 'F' word was pretty much out of bounds and something we figured Jules used now that he was hanging out with guys in high school. We'd certainly heard guys toss it around whenever they kicked us out of the rez. It was never 'get outta here,' it was always 'get the fuck outta here' or 'you fuckin' guys can leave now—maybe go to the kiddie pool.'

Jules telling Jamie to not fuck it up meant that Jamie better make every detail of the new plan totally foolproof and leave no room for error.

"This isn't like one of our baby capers we pulled. If you're gonna plan this thing you make sure our asses are covered, and that means all our asses!"

"Yeah, and you have to have the plan ready by tomorrow," I added. I caught Dusty's eye in an attempt to signal that my comment might dissuade the others and encourage a return to Plan A. Stealing the envelopes out of the fat man's car might mean a bit less money but the plan was simple and didn't leave much room for error.

"I'm not done yet," Jamie responded. "I'll get it all worked out. I say we all go home and get some lunch and then meet back at the turrets."

"If we want to draw charts and stuff, we should have more room than the turret. We can meet in our basement." Jules responded. "There's plenty of room there and a big table we can use. Everybody plan to be there at one o'clock."

With the rendezvous set, we biked back past the arsenal wall. The sidewalk was narrow and, for most of the ride we rode in single file. That, combined with all the huffing and puffing, didn't allow for much conversation. I guessed most of us were thinking about the new direction we were about to take.

The fact that the vote called for a new caper may or may not have changed our lives. None of us will ever know if the original plan we aborted would've been successful. Although I was initially against it, it held no complexities for its execution; there was no dependence on split-second timing. Dusty and I agreed that the new plan was dangerous and held catastrophic possibilities.

We didn't know what Thursday would hold. We didn't realize we were going to be real criminals. As Jules pointed out, this was no baby caper. It wouldn't be a day of switching gumballs on Miss Beezel or tossing Baby Ruth candy bars into the city pool or setting off cherry bombs in the middle of the night. On Thursday we were going to steal money. We were somehow going to stop a car and rob a guy.

In the days of planning that followed, the idea that we were taking money from an organized crime syndicate was something that never really registered. In our minds, we were simply outlaws like Jesse James or Billy the Kid—and we were about to rob the stagecoach.

❋ ❋ ❋ ❋ ❋

JULES'S SUGGESTION TO MEET in his basement was another of his good ideas. Jamie brought a big roll of paper, which we spread out on the large wooden table and all of us worked to create a diagram of the bridge, the paths, and anything else we felt pertinent. The plan took shape with input from all of us and Jamie evolved into a bona fide team leader. When Al asked, "What if the guy sees us and later picks us out of a police lineup?" The question was immediately met with laughs until Jamie pointed out it wasn't so dumb.

"Well, maybe the lineup part was dumb," he said. "But we may want to think about wearing disguises or something."

Following that response, Al's questions were no longer seen as frivolous. Any time one of us asked something, the concern was given consideration and we agreed questions from anyone had to have a reasonable answer or solution.

The idea of disguises seemed like a good idea for those of us who would be out in the open. As Al had been The Lone Ranger for Halloween, his was a logical choice.

"The Lone Ranger mask will be perfect and anybody seein' me will just think I'm with some kids playin' cowboys and Indians," he reasoned.

That gave Jules the idea to dress as Tonto and was finalized when Dusty said he could get a wig with braids that Silly had worn in a school play.

After more than two hours of drawing and talking, we were convinced we had a plan that fit the criteria Jules had set forth. "Maximum reward, minimum risk," he had told Jamie. It was statements like that which made us wonder why Jules had been held back in third grade.

As the caper took shape, our excitement seemed to overpower any previous concerns and by the time Dusty and I left the meeting, we were discussing how each of us would spend our share of the money.

"Before I buy anything for myself, I'm getting Silly something," Dusty told me.

"Whaddaya mean?"

"She's always moonin' over that green bicycle in Farnsworth's hardware store. I don't know why she likes green so much, but if that's what she wants, I'm gonna buy it for her and park it in her bedroom so it'll be there when she wakes up. Maybe for her birthday. Then I'll buy myself something cool. What about you? What are you gonna get?"

"I don't know. We probably shouldn't buy too much right off or spend money on anything real big. You better think about the bike for Silly. It might look suspicious. Besides, we don't even know how much we're gonna get."

"Jules said we should get a lot. Maybe four or five hundred dollars each."

"Yeah, we'll be like rich land barons or somethin'."

Tuesday - A Rope And A Hatchet

We continued to use Al and Jules's basement as our meeting place. Al felt we needed a special name for the cellar.

"Ya know," he said. "Like we have coordinates for the turrets, we should have a code name for the cellar."

I made mention that the office in the train yard was called the beehive as it was where all the action took place. This was immediately accepted as the name for our meeting place if for no other reason than to appease Al so we could get back to the plan.

When we arrived Tuesday morning, we each had the items we'd been assigned to bring and put them on the table. Al contributed his Lone Ranger mask and cowboy hat and what was left of his always-present container of camouflage paint. Dusty kicked in a blond wig with fashionable braids along with a large S-hook that his father used to hang paint cans from the ladder. I brought a length of rope that was criticized by Jamie for being too short. Jules said he had a piece of rope that we could tie to mine to give us enough length. My piece would obviously never reach from the bridge to the ground. Jules placed a triangular-shaped rock on the table along with some twine and his hunting knife.

"Where's the nail?" Jamie asked looking directly at Al. "And the ten cents for the phone call?"

"I've got the money," he responded. "It's upstairs in my room. I'll make sure I've got it Thursday. And a nail's easy to get. We've got plenty of 'em around here." "No!" Jamie yelled. "That's not what we agreed on yesterday. We all had assignments and we would bring all the stuff we needed. Suppose you're at the phone booth and all of a sudden you realize you don't have any money to call Auggie. How're we supposed to know Wenzel left the factory? Or you're supposed to be letting the air out of the tire and you don't have the nail or something to do it with?" As he finished speaking, he took a deep breath and exhaled slowly before looking at Jules and throwing his arms in the air. "You said don't fuck it up, remember? Well, he's your brother, tell *him* not to fuck it up!"

Jules raised an eyebrow and gave Al a frustrated look. "There're some roofing nails in the coffee can over there. Go get one and put it on the table and when we run through this tomorrow, I better see a dime or two nickels comin' outta your pocket."

Jules disturbed tone continued as he turned his attention to the table and picked up the blond wig. It was as if he wanted to shift the focus from his brother to someone else and he targeted Dusty. He stood with a force that caused his chair to fall backward and held the wig high in the air. "What's this supposed to be? You said your sister had a wig with braids. You didn't say anything about it being blond? Did you ever see a blond Indian?"

Dusty had failed to mention that the school play in which Silly achieved stardom was for her leading role as Heidi. Before he could respond, Jules leaned forward and pushed the wig closer to Dusty's face. "Does this look like hair an Indian would have?"

"Well, I figured maybe we could dye it black or somethin'," Dusty stammered out.

"Yeah, we could get some black stuff at the store and dye it black." This echo came from Al who was tactfully intervening in the dilemma. "It'll be pie easy," he continued.

"You mean easy as pie," Jamie corrected.

"No, I mean pie easy. I like to say pie easy."

"Say what you want, but it's supposed to be easy as pie and everybody knows it."

"Hey, you say tomato, I say tomahto, you say easy as pie and I say you're an asshole." This response from Al was so ridiculous it brought a round of laugher from all of us and the disagreement in semantics was the tension breaker we needed. At that point Jules put the wig on and, having a head much larger than Silly's, his appearance added to a second round of laughter. When it settled, Jamie looked squarely at Jules. "We'll make it black for the caper," he assured him.

He then asked Jules what the rock was for as it hadn't been on his list.

"I'm gonna get a piece of wood and make a genuine Indian tomahawk. I'm gonna use the twine to attach it to the wood. Might come in handy if we need a weapon."

"If you want it to be genuine, I don't think real Indians used twine." Dusty countered.

"And the knife?" Jamie continued, ignoring Dusty's comment.

"More of a real weapon...ya never know. That might come in handy too." It was the type of comment that was followed by a moment of silence and, in some small way, brought forth the reality of what we were about to do.

With the initial inventory completed, we continued reviewing our assignments. Dusty's job was to block the road to the bridge after Wenzel split from the main thoroughfare. We figured there wouldn't be any other cars to worry about, but Jules said we shouldn't take any chances.

It was Al who solved the problem. "The city guys are patchin' Sixth Street. They've got a whole bunch of those Road Closed signs in the back of the truck and nobody's ever around the stuff when they're workin'. I can steal one."

When he told us his intent, none of us considered that a year ago, the stealing of the sign would've been a caper in itself and would've been preceded by hours of planning. Now we thought nothing of stealing a sign in broad daylight from the back of a city truck.

"You sure you can get it?" Jamie questioned.

"Yeah," Al assured him and after looking around at the group tacked on "It'll be pie easy."

This time no one made any semantic corrections.

"I'll go with him," Jules said. "I can keep a lookout or something and make sure we get it."

"Okay, once you get the sign set, you'll move up to here," he told Dusty as he pointed to an area of high grass just before the entrance to the bridge. "If everything goes well, you just stay there. Even if the guy gets out of the car to chase Al, he's not gonna know you're there so just sit tight. You can leave later."

"I still think I should have a disguise." Dusty told him.

"You and Auggie don't need disguises. Nobody has any chance of seeing either one of you. You're layin' in the grass and Auggie's down on the ground under the bridge. We already discussed this."

Jules interrupted the debate as he addressed Jamie. "What are you wearin'? You said you were gonna look around the house for somethin'."

"I'm still lookin', but I'll get somethin' by tomorrow, no sweat."

I shared Dusty's concern that we were the only two without disguises and we had discussed the application of camouflage paint. It was my job to wait under the bridge and get the satchel when Jules lowered it down with the rope. If Wenzel happened to look down, I'd be staring him right in the face. I mentioned my concern again, arguing that Dusty and I should at least wear camouflage paint. Jules nodded, agreeing it would be better for all of us to not be recognized.

Wednesday - The Rehearsal

When Dusty and I entered the beehive, Jamie had already arrived and was spreading black paint on a bike we'd never seen before. Jules had used the paint the night before to cover the Heidi wig, which hung from a makeshift clothesline. When Jamie saw the can he decided to use the leftover paint to disguise the bike. Al was sitting at the table wearing his Lone Ranger mask and hat. He toyed with several nickels and dimes that sat in front of him as if trying to decide which ones would work best in the pay phone. Dusty and I focused our attention on Jamie.

"Where'd you get the bike?"

Jamie was nonchalant with his answer. "Grocery store," he told us. "I just waited outside for some kid to go in and get somethin' and I hopped on it and took off."

This was another type of caper that, a year ago, would've taken days of planning and diagrams. He then looked toward the table where Al was sitting with his collection of nickels and dimes.

"Hey Al," he yelled. "Stealin' this bike was easy as pie!" The words 'easy as pie' were intentionally drawn out and when he got to the last word he moved his paint brush in the air to draw an exaggerated sized P, I, and E in the air. He then pantomimed an exclamation point accompanied by a cork popping sound made with his mouth as he placed the dot at its bottom.

Al pretended he didn't hear him and said nothing as he continued to paw through his pile of coins.

Jules also remained quiet and focused his attention on the wig he had transformed from Heidi to Tonto. Before painting it, he used electrical tape to add a piece of rope on each braid and made them longer. The effect left him with a hairpiece that no self-respecting Indian would endorse. His last-minute painting had also failed to cover all of the blond hair on the top. The two-toned effect gave it the appearance of the hair of the girl who worked at the local deli counter.

Satisfied he would look more like an Indian, Jules placed the wig on his head and sat at the table. He had clothes-pinned one of the elongated braids onto the makeshift clothes line and, as it had dried in that position, the right braid stuck straight up in the air. Al looked up to see the one braid aimed at the ceiling and let out a howl.

"You look like one of those cartoon characters who just saw a ghost." Jules pushed the braid down to find it was only a temporary solution. As he stood, it returned to the scary ghost position as if in slow motion.

Jamie was focused on the stolen bike and felt it was sufficiently disguised and called us together. We sat at the table and stared at the diagram of the bridge and its surrounding areas.

It was Jamie's idea to have a dress rehearsal and for the first time, he noticed Dusty was wearing his army helmet.

"Why are you wearing that?" He seemed perturbed as he asked the question.

"Insurance," Dusty told him. "I'm gonna wear camouflage paint too. If I have to get in the action, I'm not stickin' my real face out there. You guys all got disguises."

"But your helmet's always fallin' off when you wear it. What about that?"

"I'll wear the chin strap tomorrow. It'll be good 'n' tight."

"Then I'm gonna need something else to. The camouflage paint may not be enough," I told the group. "I'm not gonna be the only one to get caught."

"Then just get an old hat or something if it'll make you feel better," Jules said.

"You could wear a Yankee cap. Then nobody would ever suspect it's you," Al added.

Jules then focused his attention on Jamie. "What about you?"

Jamie produced a brown paper bag from his pocket. He opened it, placed it over his left fist, and held it up to display the holes he'd cut for his nose and two eyes. The two ovals he'd cut for the eyes and the triangular nose opening resembled those of a carved Halloween pumpkin.

"I'm gonna wear this. Nobody's gonna see me anyway so it doesn't matter if it's not some store-bought costume. As long as Wenzel can't see my face it'll be okay."

Jules exhaled a breath of frustration. "Okay, now that everybody has a disguise, let's get on with the plan." As he made the statement, he again pushed his pointy braid down to his cheek. This time he held it there.

"This is no different than doing a school play," Jamie started. "We need to have a rehearsal today so we'll know if anybody's missing anything." He then looked at Al. "Did you get the road sign?"

Al pointed to a corner of the cellar where the sign leaned against the wall. We sat in momentary silence and looked at each other around the table. Al in his Lone Ranger attire, Dusty wearing his army helmet, Jules holding down one of his Indian braids to prevent it from pointing to the ceiling, and now Jamie had put the paper bag over his head. No one said what he was thinking, but I'm pretty sure we all wanted to make some kind of a remark, particularly about Jules's upright braid, but making fun of Jules was never a good idea. Additionally, he had finished tying the stone to the tree limb and the homemade tomahawk sat on the table with a menacing appearance. If the robbery didn't work, we would at least give the Wenzel guy a good laugh.

"I think we've made the plan for the caper as simple as we can," Jamie began. "I just want to review it one more time before our rehearsal so listen up." As he went over each of our roles, he pointed to the designated places on the huge drawings that matched our locations.

"Al will wait here and call Auggie as soon as Wenzel leaves the factory. Make sure as soon as you hang up you haul ass and get to the bridge," he added. "Take the same route we timed yesterday. With the shortcuts you took on the bike, you'll be there in plenty of time." He then looked at me. "Aug, as soon as you get the call you ride to the woods, here," he told me, pointing to the rendering of the trees on the chart. "Leave your bike there and get to the bridge. Don't forget to signal me that everything's okay and then hide down here." Again, he pointed to the chart where I would take my place. He then glanced back at Al. "When you get to the bridge, you lay low here in the high grass with Jules, on the left side of the bridge entrance. I'll be here on the right. The two of you wait there in the high grass until the car bumps me off the bike."

Jamie's voice was calm and his hand steady as it moved over the diagram and pointed out each tactical maneuver we would take. It was then Dusty's turn for instruction.

"Dusty, as soon as Wenzel turns off the main road onto the bridge road, you put up the Road Closed sign and wait there until the caper ends and you see Auggie heading back to the woods. Once he's got the money and is headed for his bike, you take down the sign and get outta there." Jamie then scanned the rest of us. "Don't forget, Dusty's the extra man if anybody needs help. Just yell "Geronimo" and that's his signal that something's gone wrong and you need him. Otherwise he stays put and just handles the road closing."

"I'll be here," he continued, "on the entrance to the bridge, opposite Al and Jules. I'll pretend to be fixing my bike. It'll be impossible for Wenzel to make the right turn onto the bridge unless he slows to almost a complete stop. When he does, he'll be going slow enough so I can pull out and force him to hit my front tire. As soon as he hits me, I'll fall over and pretend I'm hurt. He'll have to get out of the car to see if I'm okay and, when he does, that's when Al sneaks up and lets the air out of the rear tire."

Al had been given that job because he was the fastest runner and would easily outrun Wenzel if he saw him and chased him on foot. With no air in one of the tires he couldn't use the car to go after anyone.

Jamie then continued with the briefing. "While Wenzel is checking on me, Jules will run to the car, get the satchel, hook it onto the rope with the S-hook, and lower it down to you, Aug." He then returned his focus to Jules. "Don't forget to tie the rope and the hook and everything as soon as you get to the bridge so it's ready to go...and make sure it's out of sight. Once the moneybag is lowered down, Auggie grabs it, heads to his bike and heads up Nineteenth Street and takes the back route back here to the beehive. We'll wait here and count the money and split it up when he gets here."

We all felt the plan was pure genius and during his review we paid close attention. He covered every detail as he outlined where we were supposed to be and what we were supposed to do. When he finished we set up the beehive to act it out. Jules, who agreed it was a good idea, overruled Al's protest against the rehearsal. Within minutes the beehive was transformed to represent the bridge and the surrounding area. We used a chair for the car, empty boxes for high grass, and an old sheet served as the bridge.

After acting out the robbing of Wenzel several times we needed a break. This time even Jules agreed. The tension brought on by our anxiety was running high. Everyone felt they knew their assignments and we were all tired of the repetition. This was confirmed with Jamie asking Jules if he thought we were ready to go and got an affirmative nod. Jamie suggested a few more run-throughs after lunch but groans and complaints signaled the contrary.

"We'll take the afternoon off," Jules informed us. "Everybody meet here after lunch tomorrow. We'll do one more quick run-through and then go to the bridge together. Make sure you bring everything you're supposed to." As he made the statement he looked directly at Al and that ended the discussion.

❀ ❀ ❀ ❀ ❀

DURING THE WALK HOME from the beehive, I told Dusty I had to meet my grandfather at the railroad yard to do some chores. It was one of the few times I remember lying to him, but I needed some time away from The Five-Cent Gang and could think of no better place to spend it. I knew Mr. Faulk wouldn't be there until the afternoon shift arrived, but I could hang out among the workers and lose myself in the daily routines. To my surprise, when I entered the office, I found Mr. Faulk talking with my grandfather. Their tones were whispered as if they were sharing some secret information.

Mr. Faulk's back was to me and my grandfather gave me a greeting, which seemed a signal for their conversation to end.

"Look who's here," my grandfather said, and Mr. Faulk turned to greet me as well.

"Hey, you're just the guy I need to see today," he said. "You gonna be here for a while?"

"Yeah. How come you're here? Aren't you working the late shift today?"

"Well, I've got some special business in the yard today—thanks to your grandpa here. But first, I think we might need some nourishment."

He motioned for me to join him on the outer platform in front of the office and we sat together on a bench in an area shaded by the building. As if by magic he pulled out a package of peanut butter crackers and a can of orange soda. He sent me back inside to retrieve paper cups and we ate and drank our fill. It was just what I needed to keep my mind off the D&H Bridge Caper.

When we finished, he tapped my chest with the back of his hand. "C'mon. There's somethin' I want to show you."

I followed him to the graveyard and he suddenly got very quiet and looked around as if to see if anyone was watching us.

"Wait'll you see what's over here in the graveyard," he whispered. "Do you think you can keep a secret?"

"Yeah, I can keep a secret." I told him.

"I came in early today after your granddad called me with a special surprise. That's what we were discussin' when you got here. Come on!" He then grabbed hold of the sleeve of my T-shirt and pulled me along. Once we got to the coal cars, he continued further to an area that was hidden from view by freight cars that were well beyond repair. He pointed down the tracks, but I was still baffled as to what I was supposed to be looking at. I was also hard pressed to know why he was still whispering. Not only were we in a totally secluded area of the yard, but surrounding noises made it difficult for me to hear him. As he whispered, he continued to point beyond the boxcar nearest us and it was then I saw the old steam engine.

"I pushed her into this area just before you got here," he told me. "A real beauty, isn't she?"

I stood and stared at the vintage locomotive that had now become the obvious target of his pointing finger. A small section on the front part of the engine looked like it had recently been cleaned a bit in comparison to the rest of it. Mr. Faulk continued to whisper with excitement. "It's an old Baldwin," he said. "Came into the yard last night, hitched on the back of the renegade. Other than your grandfather, it seems like no one even knows she's here. I took a few minutes this morning and put a rag to 'er to see how she'd take to bein' cleaned up a bit."

"What're they gonna do with it. Is she gonna be used on the line?"

He continued with his secretive tone. "That's just the thing ya see, no one seems to know what we're supposed to do with her. Your granddad's tryin' to figure out why the railroad hauled her here in the first place. Nobody seems to know nothin' about it. From all that I can tell from lookin' her over looks like she's in good runnin' shape. I mean, they won't be usin' her for regular runs or such but I'm thinkin' maybe sometime you and I can sneak over here and get her stoked up and cookin'. Take her for a spin around the yard. Whaddaya say to that? I'd like to get her all cleaned up though first," he added. "I got this little area of the brass piston housing done so far," he said pointing to a small area that, contrary to the remainder of the engine, gleamed in the sunlight. He continued in his excited tone and with his hand wrapped around my arm he walked me from front to back and told me all about the Baldwin. As we walked, he pointed out her graceful lines and told me her history.

"This particular engine was built in 1919," he told me. "Only two of 'em made that year. Here, step up here and get in." As he said that, he boosted me into the engineer's compartment. Once in the cab, he flipped down the hinged coalman's seat. "Stand up on this," he told me. "Now, move that lever over your head and slide that panel back."

At first glance, I couldn't find any lever. "It's there," he said pointing. "It's hard to see because it's been modified. In the old days they made the sliding panel into a secret compartment." I then saw the small lever and followed his instructions. The panel over my head slid back.

"See what I mean?" he continued in a whisper. "It's actually an access hatch in case someone needs to get up there and work on the steam pipes," he explained. "But during prohibition, men hid liquor up there on return runs from Canada. They nicknamed it the bootlegger's hole and the engineers could fit as many as twenty or thirty bottles of liquor up there.

Then they divvied up the orders throughout the rail yard once the train got in. Oh, I'd venture to say more than one train rolled into a yard with a drunken engineer if ya get my meanin'."

After telling me of the bootlegger's hole, he pointed out the window of the cab and started yelling. "Look! I think there's some G-men out there tryin' to get our liquor!" he shouted. This was followed by machine gun noises from his invisible machine gun as he mowed down the G-men. "Check the other side," he yelled and for several minutes the two of us fired our imaginary machine guns as we shot at G-men and protected our contraband.

Before closing up the bootlegger's hole, Mr. Faulk boosted me up to look inside. With the help of his flashlight, I described the pipes that carried the steam to propel the old engine. Once he was satisfied with the information, I closed up the hatch and he explained the various instruments and how the old engine differed from the new diesels.

We used the cleaning supplies he had brought down earlier and set to work restoring the controls in the engine compartment. It was exactly what I needed—an afternoon of playing engineer and listening to stories of bootleggers and bandits and prohibition. The departure for home to eat supper came much too quickly.

* * * * *

LYING IN BED ON summer nights was a time when sleep usually came easily. The head of my bed was positioned at the window and allowed me to smell the fragrance of the night air. Even rainy nights were special. Whenever a gentle rain fell on the outer sill the screen severed the drops as they came through and sprinkled lightly onto my face.

On the night prior to the bridge caper, however, even the familiar feel of the warm air washing over me accompanied by the steady rhythm of crickets failed to bring sleep. I could find no comfortable position or conjure any pleasant thoughts that night. My head filled itself with thoughts of the D&H Bridge and my mind raced as I mentally rehearsed my role. I visualized the satchel of money being lowered to me in the same way we had practiced with Jules's gym bag. It had been easy in our rehearsals to slip the handles from the big S-hook and pretend to carry it to my bike.

Jamie would stop the car. I knew that. He would drive the bicycle in front of the vehicle and be broadsided. His was without a doubt the riskiest job in the caper, but I believed I had the most important role. It would be me that would carry the money from the bridge to the beehive. As I tossed from side to side, the white-laced curtains moved gently away from the windowsill and their hems washed over my face before they returned and pressed themselves against the screen. They seemed to inhale and exhale as dictated by the breeze.

It had been over a month since the spring curtains had been replaced by the summer ones. The changing of the guard my mother called it. "Time for the summer sheers," she always said. And each year they were carefully removed from the shelf in the linen closet and, even though they had been hand-washed before storage, they would be hand-washed again. They were much too delicate for machine washings. While they soaked, I was called upon to set up the drying racks. It was a ritual that required much attention to detail as the assembled racks held hundreds of sharp pointed nails that would be used to hold the curtains in place as they dried. Taking up as much space as they did, the racks were set up in both the living room and dining room. They had pencil marks from previous years to ensure they were always set to the exact dimensions. Once washed, the curtains were stretched to their full length, to 'size them' as she called it, and then she poked their edges over the tiny nails to hold them in place. She always whistled whenever she did things she enjoyed around the house and sizing her curtains was a whistling chore. Now as the breeze moved them and they washed over my face I could feel the slight stiffness from the starch. I thought once again of what I would do the next day and how disappointed my mother would be if she knew of our capers.

As difficult as it was to empty my mind to allow for sleep, I thought it ironic that the last thing I remember feeling were the summer sheers and the last thing I remember hearing was the sound of the night train.

"It's three different notes," Mr. Faulk had told me once. "They just seem to go together the right way if you know what I mean," he continued. "And all the manufacturers use those same three notes." Lying in bed that night, it was that haunting sound that brought me sleep or, as Mr. Faulk described it—harmonious dissonance.

Thursday - The Bridge

Al played his part as instructed. Dressed in his Lone Ranger hat and mask, he took the additional liberties of adding his canteen to his belt and peered incessantly through his army-green binoculars. His focus was aimed at the parked car outside the old bell factory. The car hadn't moved since his two o'clock arrival, nor had the magnified lenses revealed any other movement in the area. With his patience approaching the breaking point, the door of the factory opened and the man whose picture he had seen on the task force bulletin board emerged from the building. He carried the same large leather bag as the fat man and, after opening the door of the car, slid it onto the front seat before climbing in behind the wheel.

As instructed, Al pedaled to the phone booth and called me to set the plan in motion. Today's signal was not two rings followed by a hang-up. Today he was told to sacrifice his dime and wait for me to answer. Everything had to go right.

"He just left," he panted into the phone. "He's in a big black car and he's got the leather bag with him. It's the fat man's doctor's bag. I saw him put it on the front seat. Make sure Jules knows it's on the front seat, not in the trunk. This'll be easier than we thought."

The call ended abruptly and I knew Al was on his way to the bridge. I, in turn, rode the one block to the wooded area, left my bike among the trees, and ran to take my position under the bridge. As I ran, my arms gave an exaggerated wave to Jamie who resembled someone doing jumping jacks as he returned an acknowledgement. Once I was under the bridge and Al arrived, all the players were in their assigned positions. Our planning was about to pay off.

Had Al waited and witnessed what happened prior to Wenzel actually leaving the factory, the plan may have been aborted. In his haste to call me, what he didn't see was soon to throw our plan into a tailspin.

Unknown to us was the knowledge that this particular run was not the usual operation that occurred on Wenzel's quarterly trip to New York. It was the one time of year that money was funneled to the East Coast from St. Louis, Cleveland, Chicago, and Detroit—all cities included in the money-laundering process. It was a run that, because of the amount of money involved, required an armed guard.

After Al's hasty departure from the factory to make the phone call, a second man emerged from the building. It was the man who assumed his customary role of bodyguard and protector of Provinzini's money whenever trips of this nature took place. The man was fat and wheezing and normally drove a yellow sedan but today his assignment was to protect the contents of the bag.

Before getting into the car, he opened the door and placed a double-barreled sawed-off shotgun in the front seat where it was cradled by the satchel and rested between him and the driver. He then stood and looked around as he withdrew a handkerchief from his back pocket and wiped the perspiration from his head. First from the back of his neck and then from his forehead. After climbing into the passenger seat he felt the uncomfortable bulge of his pistol against his back and, before Wenzel drove off, he removed it from its holster and placed it inside the satchel.

* * * * *

WHEN I REACHED THE bridge I hollered up to Jamie and relayed the information of the leather satchel being in the front seat, which he passed along to Jules.

Looking up, I could see the coiled rope holding the S-hook as it sat on the outer side of the railing. I was glad it was Jules who would be taking the bag from the car and lowering it to me. We had discussed an alternate plan of Jules grabbing the key out of the ignition if Wenzel put the money in the trunk but having it on the front seat would now be easier. As gentle as Jules was in our daily routines, he could also be tough when a situation presented itself. Despite Wenzel appearing to pose no physical threat, we all knew why Jules was the guy picked to grab the money.

Although my position beneath the bridge allowed for a good deal of safety, it denied me any view of what actually took place that day. When I heard the car approach, my heart raced as it did the night before during my mental rehearsal. When it slowed to make the turn onto the bridge, my chest tightened and my mouth and lips went dry. Not until I looked at my hands did I notice my clenched fists. I heard the thump of the car hitting the bike followed by a cry from Jamie as I envisioned him falling to the ground. I didn't know if the cry was part of the act or if he was actually hurt. That was something we never discussed during our rehearsals.

Once Jamie was down, the next minute of my life was encapsulated in a blurred flurry of auditory discrepancies. Jamie's cry was accompanied by the slight squeal of tires as they skidded on the mix of gravel and blacktop. I then heard a car door open followed by yelling. The river below me made just enough noise to prevent hearing the entire wording of what was being said, but my ears picked out key words. Words like 'dumb kid' and 'hospital' and 'give me a hand.'

Hearing a second car door open alerted me that something was wrong. The first door had never been

closed and I wondered why a second door had opened?
Who would be giving a hand? Was someone else in the
car? My questions were answered when I heard a
second voice.

I continued to listen and my mind's eye tried to
put a scene to the sounds. More yelling was followed
by footsteps running on the bridge. First toward the
Troy end with exclamations of "You little shit," and
"you fucking little bastard, you're dead, do you hear
me? Dead!" All this followed by more voices and the
shouting from the two strangers became mingled with
yelling from the familiar voices of Jules and Jamie.
Jules's voice came from one end of the bridge, Jamie's
from the other. More footsteps followed. This time
slower, accompanied by a wheezing sound. It was the
same wheezing I heard when Dusty and I sat at the
soda fountain in The Pit. The thought of the fat man
and the possibility of his presence on the bridge
brought on an icy fear and I wasn't sure if my legs
would now be able to move. I heard more
yelling...grunts...a   scuffle...until   the   slower,   more
labored footsteps moved back toward the car. I wanted
to return to the woods or, at the very least, step out to
see what was taking place but my legs were
immobilized.

More shouts from one of the stranger's voices
yelling "Get him. Get that fucking asshole! You see
what he's doing? Get that bastard!"

My blood ran cold when I heard the first of two
explosions. I knew enough about guns to recognize the
blast of a shotgun. A second shot rang out and I heard
Al's voice scream in a high feverish pitch. "I've been
shot! I've been shot!"

* * * * *

WHEN WENZEL MADE THE turn onto the back

road leading to the bridge, Dusty was so low in the grass to avoid detection, even he didn't see the fat man in the front seat. This meant the option of yelling Geronimo never came into play. Our first knowledge of the fat man's presence wasn't until Jamie poked his stolen bike in the path of the front bumper. There are no appropriately descriptive words for the look on Jamie's face because the brown paper bag draped over his head hid any look of fear or shock. There was most likely reciprocity in the shocked faces of Wenzel and the fat man as they gazed upon a cyclist riding around wearing a paper bag over his head. To compound the value of their surprise, following our final meeting in the beehive, Jamie had taken it upon himself to add adornments to the bag. None of us knew if this was in response to the exasperation exhibited by Jules when he first saw the plain brown disguise. Jamie took the remainder of the roll of twine home with him and glued strips of it onto the bag, transforming it into something that resembled a brownish wolf man. He had also cut shorter strips and added twine eyebrows and an uneven mustache below the triangular nose hole. Needless to say, it was a sight the two occupants of the car had never seen before.

When Jamie went down, the front tire of the car rested squarely on the rim of the bicycle tire and pinned him to the pavement. The shock of seeing the fat man in the passenger seat combined with an impact greater than expected had been cause for the shout en route to the ground. If that hadn't been enough to instill panic, the bag shifted during the fall and only one of Jamie's eyes was privy to an eyehole. The second hole was positioned somewhere around his right ear. Both Wenzel and the fat man were perplexed as to how a kid had come to be on the bridge—not to mention a kid riding a bike with a paper bag over his head that resembled some type of beast.

Whatever the reasoning, the fat man viewed the accident as a severe inconvenience. With money, books, and weapons in the vehicle, it was no time for him and Wenzel to be in an accident that might lead to police involvement. He also realized it wasn't a good time to have to produce any kind of identification to the authorities.

"You stay in the car," he barked at Wenzel. "I'll see if the kid's okay. If he is, I'll give him money for a new bike and we can get the hell outta here. We don't have time for this shit."

"What if he's hurt? It doesn't look like he's moving."

"If he's hurt, we'll throw him in the back seat and run him up to the hospital."

"What about the doctors and other personnel?"

"Hey, we ain't gonna stick around. We'll dump him in front of the emergency room and get the hell outta there." Malducci got out of the car and before checking on Jamie he leaned in through the open window. "Whatever happens here, you say nothin' of it to Provinzini. It'll be both our asses if he hears of this. You understand what I'm sayin'?"

Without waiting for an answer, he approached Jamie and leaned over him. Jamie was still struggling to get out from his pinned position. In addition to the immovable weight of the bike, the cuff of his pants was caught on the pedal. With the twisted mask allowing only limited vision, he continued struggling and cursing as the fat man looked on.

"That was pretty dumb kid, you okay or do you think you might need to go to the hospital?"

As Malducci pulled on the bike to free him, the Lone Ranger left his position with the roofing nail in hand to let the air out of the back tire. Jules reached for his shoulder to stop him. "Forget the tire," he told him. "We didn't figure on the fat guy bein' in the car. Christ, didn't you see him get in at the factory? Why didn't you tell us?"

Al shrugged. "There wasn't any other guy when I called. He musta got in later."

"No way you can do it now, if he turns around we're all dead."

"I can do it," he told Jules as he jerked the hand off his shoulder. "He's busy checkin' on Jamie. Besides, this is my part of the caper."

Once Al left, Tonto was about ready to leave his hiding place and get the money when something favorable occurred. He first thought he would have to wrestle the driver for the satchel and felt for the security of the tomahawk but before he left the tall grass the fat man called to Wenzel. "Come out here and give me a hand with this kid."

It was the opportunity Jules needed. Wenzel got out of the car and walked to the front. Before he reached the fallen bike, the fat man had yanked Jamie to his feet. Jamie adjusted his bag mask and, once again, seeing the fat man and realizing he was in his grasp, he yelled and yanked himself free. He then turned and ran to the Troy end of the bridge.

"Christ, I'd better talk to him," Malducci grumbled as he walked in the path Jamie had taken. "He might go to the cops or some shit. Looks like he's okay. I'll give him a few bucks for the bike and give 'im a hint that he should forget about it. You stay with the money."

Jules had taken advantage of the distraction Jamie offered and was at the car. Wenzel had left the door open and reaching in to grab the satchel was easy. As he pulled it from the seat, Wenzel turned and spotted him. As startled as he was to see a bag-headed bike rider, he was in no way prepared to see the sight of an

Indian in full war paint. Tonto stood erect. He wore no
shirt and his painted chest was impressive as the
rippled muscles gleamed with sweat. Like the war paint
on his face, the bone-like chest designs had been
applied with a combination of camouflage paint and his
mother's lipstick. The Indian braid had been somewhat
tamed but still stuck out parallel with the ground.

Wenzel saw Jules holding the bag and leaped
toward him. Jules put the bottom of the bag on
Wenzel's chest and pushed him back with a force that
sent him to the ground. Wenzel then grabbed Jules's
ankle to prevent his escape and, having no other
weapon, Jules pulled his homemade tomahawk from
his waistband and brought it down on Wenzel's temple.
The release of his ankle was immediate as Wenzel
rolled over and groaned from the blow. Once freed,
Jules ducked behind the car and crossed to the waiting
rope, put the S-hook through both handles and
lowered the satchel.

The fat man was halfway down the bridge and
gasping for air when he heard the moaning from
Wenzel. When he turned he saw Tonto lowering the
money bag and then spied the Lone Ranger letting air
out of one of the tires.

"Hey, you little shits," he yelled. "You fucking
little bastards! You're dead do you hear me? Dead!"

He instinctively reached for his gun forgetting he
had tossed it into the satchel. Now realizing what was
happening, he ignored Jamie and started back to the
car. Jules turned and grabbed Al. "Forget the tire, that's
enough!" he yelled. "Get outta here. Go down the road
and get Dusty outta here too. We need to split up. I'll
go this way through the grass."

The fat man continued screaming curses while he
yelled to Wenzel who was still on the ground. "Get
him. Get that fucking asshole! You see what he's

doing? Get away from there, you little bastard!"

When he reached the car, he leaned into the open door and grabbed the shotgun. Raising it to his shoulder, he fired a shot at Al.

"I can't believe this. We're being robbed by a bunch of kids," he said to no one in particular. He fired the second barrel and I heard Al scream "I'm hit, I'm hit!" It was the same cry I had heard him yell hundreds of times on our battlefield of play when he feigned taking a bullet from a German soldier. But being hit this time had been followed by a shotgun blast. A blast that possibly resulted in the tearing of his flesh or ending his life. His scream was followed by Jamie's voice hollering "Run, Al, run!"

It was then I noticed the dangling leather satchel, now in plain view. My mind was racing so fast; I hadn't seen it at first as it sat there, twisting on the S-hook just a few feet away. Jules had done his job. It was now my turn to execute the final step of the plan. Getting the bag off the hook and getting it back to the beehive was my responsibility. Without it, anything that happened on the bridge was senseless.

For some reason, hearing Al yell and knowing he'd been hurt in some way or maybe even shot turned my fear to anger. The strength returned to my legs and I stood to get the satchel. In my panicked haste, I slipped on the loose dirt and slid a few feet down the embankment. When I looked up, I was staring at the bottom of the swinging moneybag as the rope securing it to the bridge acted like a pendulum. It hung there–moving in slow motion. Above it, I saw the loose ends of the knot connecting our two ropes together as they twirled in synchronization with the satchel. I stood to remove it from the S-hook but found the slip I'd taken had moved me down the bank just enough to put the bag out of reach. In one desperate leap, I jumped up and found myself clinging to the satchel. My cheek pressed against its side and, as the rope stretched a bit my feet struggled to gain traction on the dirt. With my toes just scraping the ground, I tried to use the weight of my body to gain more traction. But that same weight made it impossible to remove the bag from the hook and to let go didn't seem like a viable option. It was then I looked up and saw the horrible face of the fat man as he leaned over the railing. He had thrown the shotgun into the car after spotting me hanging from the satchel. The rope slowly rotated from its natural twist making his appearance circular and dizzying as I tried to focus. He was soaked with perspiration and from the end of the dangling rope I heard his labored breathing. Fat stubby arms emerged from his sweat-soaked shirt and his obesity continued all the way to his hands, with fingers that were short and puffy like miniature connected marshmallows. He panted and grunted as he cursed and pulled me upward with a fat-hand over fat-hand motion drawing me nearer to him. "You're dead kid. When I get you up here you're dead. You hear me?"

It was then I had to decide if I should release my grip from the satchel and fall to the underbrush. In doing so, the money would be gone. The fat man would win. I considered my options as the exertion of each pull on the rope caused huge drops of his August sweat to drip down and fall on my hands and the top of my head and the back of my neck. Crazy thoughts raced through my mind. Mr. Faulk, my mother and her summer sheers, and Al lying dead in the grass, killed by a blast from a shotgun.

The knot in the middle of the rope neared the fat man's grip and the purple birthmark on his cheek was now more visible. In that instant, the decision whether or not to release my grip was overridden by my fall to the ground. I hadn't consciously let go of the bag and it wasn't until I hit the ground that I realized I was still holding it. I fell hard with the bag on my chest and I looked up at the bridge. I stared directly into the sun trying to discern the unrecognizable figure who stood at the railing. When the figure moved he blocked the sun and I saw it was Tonto, his entire wig now askew but the unmistakable braid pointing its silhouette toward the sky. The blade of his hunting knife glistened as he held it in his hand. The knife he had just used to cut the rope and send me spiraling downward.

He had returned to the bridge following the gunshots. He had heard the cursing and seen my predicament. He once again used his tomahawk to land a blow on the head of the fat man. Whether it was the force of the blow or the weakness of the twine holding the rock to the stick, we'll never know. It was the last blow the tomahawk ever made as the rock flew out of its nesting place and into the Hudson. The fat man fell to his knees and clutched the rail for support. Wenzel was still dazed but had pulled himself to a standing position and steadied himself against the car. He scanned the pavement in search of his glasses that had been dislodged by the tomahawk. The last thing he saw before passing out was the sight of an armed soldier running toward the bridge screaming Geronimo because Dusty had also come running at the sound of Al's yelling. Somewhere he had picked up a stick, which gave the appearance of a rifle to a dazed Wenzel. Jules gave a wave to Dusty to get back.

"Everything's under control here," he yelled. "Get outta here." He then leaned over the railing and hollered down to me. "You okay?" I could see his war paint was smeared from its mix with perspiration.

"Yeah, I think so," I told him.

"Everybody up here's okay too. So get going!"

He then disappeared from sight and I lugged the satchel to the woods. I turned once and looked back to see Wenzel helping the fat man to his feet. He was pointing in my direction. The fear of being followed crept into my thoughts and my only hope was that Al had time to let plenty of air out of the tire.

Chapter Six

The weight of the satchel was something we had never thought to discuss and it turned out to be much heavier than expected. I used both hands and carried it in front of me but it banged against my knees and made the short run to the woods more difficult than anticipated. Once I reached the fringe, I glanced back a second time and saw the fat man had regained a standing position and was clutching the railing for support. Wenzel was nowhere in sight. I picked up my bike and slipped the handles of the satchel over the right side of my handlebars and started down the dirt path toward Congress Street.

Before leaving the protected area, I stopped and used my T-shirt and erased what I thought were any remaining signs of camouflage paint. I pedaled out onto Congress and for the first time realized just how populated the area was. It made the first leg of the ride look more suspicious than I'd anticipated. A kid on a bike wasn't an unusual sight to onlookers, but the satchel on the handlebars was not the kind of bag any self-respecting sixth grader would lug around. I pedaled the several blocks needed to get me to the side streets and quiet neighborhoods. The bag continued to hinder my progress as it hit my right knee with each upward pedal stroke. All eyes were on me as I rode. People wondered what was in the bag. I knew when they walked past me their thoughts told them I was carrying stuff I'd stolen. They no doubt wondered where I was taking it. I knew people would call the police as soon as I rode by. Every black car I spotted seemed to be driven by Wenzel and the fat man sat next to him, pointing a gun out the window.

The ride up Congress was a bit of an uphill run and with the combination of afternoon heat and the weight of the bag, I was exhausted. Any initial surge of adrenalin had dissipated after the first few blocks. When I made the turn onto Sixteenth Street I rode my bike into a small park, leaned it against a shade tree, and dismounted. I sat on a bench and tried to catch my breath. A summer breeze came from somewhere and I welcomed the change from the heavy heat of the ride. The sweat rolled off my forehead and my chest pounded. I put my hand on my heart with the hope of slowing it down. It was then that I looked at the bag and thought to open it. The contents needed to be examined. Suppose it wasn't money? Suppose I was sweating my ass off for a satchel full of reports or newspapers or magazines?

I removed the bag from the handlebars and set it on the ground next to the bench. The brass clasp had a small keyhole but when I pushed the button, it snapped open. At least Wenzel had seen no need to lock it. I pulled the two sides apart like jaws of a giant shark and peered inside. It was dark in the bag and the shade from the tree made it even darker. Looking in, I didn't see any money, only two black books...most likely the ledgers Dusty's father had discussed at the big meeting. My heart sank. It looked like all we had stolen were a couple of books. An emptiness crept inside me as I realized our folly. My eyes then shifted their focus to something shiny that was wedged into the side of the bag—a gun. I pushed the ledgers aside and reached my hand in to touch it. It was then that I noticed the familiar green of dollar bills under the two books— bundles and bundles of money. It was more money than any of us had hoped for. The entire bag was filled with stacks of five and ten dollar bills, each stack secured by a rubber band. My earlier paranoia became greater as I realized the renewed urgency of getting to the beehive. I started out again but the bag magnified the difficulty of pedaling on the lumpy grass and when I stood to force my bike over the knoll, my pedal went down with a familiar crack. It was a sound I knew well. I had broken the chain again. The words of Mr. Faulk echoed in my mind. "I can fix 'er now or she'll go on ya when ya need 'er most," he had said, handing me the new link.

"No, that's okay," I told him. "I have to get home. I'll put it on myself this afternoon." But I hadn't, and the link I needed was sitting on my bedroom dresser.

❋ ❋ ❋ ❋ ❋

THE FAT MAN STEADIED himself on the railing as he looked down at Wenzel. The driver had regained his feet but fallen a second time as he tried to assist Malducci. The fat man's weight made it an impossible task. Wenzel was a frail man, and still dazed from the tomahawk blow Jules had delivered to his temple. Malducci, having experienced the same fate, was also still reeling a bit as he struggled to stand and steadied himself. In Wenzel's case, the blow had done more damage than intended and he was having difficulty with his balance. After walking from the vehicle to the railing, he became woozy while trying to help Malducci and he fell at the feet of the fat man.

Both men remained somewhat in shock from the recent events. Provinzini's ledger books along with the annual flow of cash from the four largest East Coast

Syndicate operations were gone. Malducci's head throbbed as he analyzed his predicament brought on by the recent occurrences. Were they kids or not? Had there been a mix of kids and adults? Whoever hit him on the head was certainly no kid. Was it a random robbery that had coincidentally gone in their favor?

The fat man could see Wenzel was in no shape to drive and, not being the sympathetic type, picked him up like a rag doll and threw him into the back seat. He then examined the rear tire. He had interrupted Al before any great amount of air had been released and felt confident he could get to a gas station to inflate it. Before getting into the driver's seat, he yanked the stolen bike from beneath the front tire and with an effortless toss it sailed over the railing and into the Hudson River. He turned the car around and as he headed off the bridge toward Congress Street, he rubbed away the dried blood brought on by the tomahawk. He spotted an ESSO station and pulled in.

"Help you sir?" The question came from a skinny kid wearing a green uniform shirt that sported an ESSO emblem on one side and the name 'Howard' embroidered over the opposite pocket.

"Put some air in that back tire there for me, will ya?" Malducci's voice told the attendant. It was more of an order than a question. "I gotta make a phone call. You got a pay phone inside?"

The attendant pointed to the outside corner of the station where a phone was visible. "Right there, sir. I can get you change inside if you need it."

Malducci ignored the offer and was half way to the phone booth when the attendant spoke again. "Sir? You'll have to move the car over to the air pump for me."

"Keys are in it," he hollered over his shoulder. "Just take care of it and don't worry about the guy in the back seat. He's just takin' a nap."

The phone call to Provinzini was not pleasant from either end. Malducci's head was still throbbing as he assured his boss that whoever the bastards were who hit them on the bridge, he would find them. Neither man displayed any concerns for Wenzel who was still moaning in the back seat. Only the attendant seemed to show any sympathy when Malducci returned from the pay phone and he mentioned the man seemed to be sick and perhaps needed a doctor. Malducci dismissed any thoughts along that line as he removed a wad of bills from his pocket, peeled off a five, and handed it to the kid. The attendant was still staring at the bill in his hand when the fat man pulled out of the station and headed up Congress.

❋ ❋ ❋ ❋ ❋

THE BUSTED CHAIN LEFT me no choice but to ditch the bike. I pushed it to an area of the park that contained several bushes and small trees. I removed the satchel and pushed the bike in, hoping it would fall once it got into the growth. The bushes, however, were thick enough to support it, which forced me to climb my way in and push the bike to the ground. In the process, my arms were raked by thorns and started bleeding. With satchel in hand, I calculated the distance to the beehive to be a bit over two miles. It was a distance that would be difficult with the burden of the heat. I was desperate enough to contemplate Jamie's tactic of looking for a bike to steal, rationalizing the theft by telling myself I'd return it when I came back to get my own.

Before any decision was made, I spotted another black car as it passed my side street and continued up

Congress. This time, it was not the paranoia that made me see the fat man—it *was* the fat man. He was behind the wheel and looked from side to side as he loafed the car along, a big whale, trolling for fish I thought. His window was rolled down and exposed a fat elbow. I froze as I tried to blend in with the shade tree that gave me little protection. If he began weaving in and out of side streets, I knew my trek to the beehive would be difficult. For a brief moment, I considered hiding the satchel and going it alone. Without the added weight I could climb fences and take other shortcuts I was familiar with. The thought was erased when I considered the consequences of arriving at the rendezvous without the money.

Just prior to his car moving out of his line of vision to my area he spotted me. I heard the throaty muffler as he accelerated and pulled into an empty driveway. Tires squealed and knowing he was turning around to make a return run, I sprinted across the street and dove into an area of high grass between two houses. I dropped to my stomach with the satchel at my side. I didn't see how he could possibly know where I was. The car lumbered by, still trolling. I listened to the lone exhaust as he went the distance to the end of the street and then turned around. I watched as he drove by again back toward Congress. This time he turned and went a block north to Seventeenth Street. I still heard the car but when he passed I had no line of sight unless I turned my body around. I waited. Seeing nothing on Seventeenth, he drove a street past me in the other direction to Fifteenth. If I had any chance of taking a favorable direction to the north, this would probably be the only opportunity. My eyes searched the area for more protected places that allowed for a way out. I needed a miracle of sorts, and the miracle I needed fell upon my ears. It wasn't a miracle I saw or felt, it was a miracle I heard. It was the sound of harmonious dissonance.

The 4:37 was coming in to the Nineteenth Street Station. I knew once it arrived it would come to a stop and sit for three minutes while the station clerk threw the mail sacks on board. I pictured Mr. Rosemont sitting in the engineer's compartment ready to take her in and end his shift. If I could make the three blocks to the tracks, it would be a four-minute ride to the safety of the yard.

The run to the train would've been difficult without the satchel or a black car circling the area. My arm strength had been pushed to the limit, and my shoulders ached but I was determined to get the bag three more blocks. The 4:37 was at a standstill when I maneuvered myself around the back of the station platform. I had watched it slow and come to a halt as I moved at a frantic pace. I needed to get to one of the empty freight cars at the back of the train. I knew it was the only place that allowed me any hope of getting on board and once it started down the track, I would have little or no chance of climbing on.

The warnings of Mr. Faulk rang in my ears as I ran in a crouch toward the waiting boxcar.

"I know you see guys in the yard hop on moving trains all the time, but don't you ever go tryin' it," he warned. "Those guys do it every day and know what they're doin'. It's no game and it's dangerous."

Rosey gave a blast on the horn and the pistons forced a slight movement of the train. First a foot backward, then it lurched forward and sat motionless once again. I moved toward the boxcar without the precaution of checking for onlookers. Hopping the train was my only hope of getting away from the black car and I had abandoned any pretense of avoiding being seen.

I was within steps of the freight car when the train made another jerk forward. Rosey gave what I knew was the final blast of the horn and then began to ease the train out of the station. I ran alongside in the unsure footing of sloped gravel and, realizing there was no possibility of climbing onto a moving train while I struggled with the weight of the satchel, I pushed the bag into the open boxcar. I took hold of the grab bar as the train began to pick up speed and before I could get into the car, my feet were taking steps on the ground that were separated with high leaps. When a foot left the ground, I seemed to float in the air before the next would hit. It was just a matter of time before my legs would concede to the momentum of the train and I would be forced to release my grip or be dragged along. Even the release at this speed would be dangerous. Warnings about train hopping were always accompanied by stories of those who'd been dragged under to their death.

Once again I was hanging from the end of a decisive rope and once again, the decision whether I should let go or not was made for me. From the inside darkness of the boxcar a hand emerged, reached over my back, and grabbed my belt. The hand pulled me into the car with a force that landed me on my stomach. A smell of hay filled me as I was face down in the remnants of feed in a car that recently transported cattle. The force of the throw had knocked the wind out of me and I rolled over slowly to look at the man who'd saved my life. He stood over me. His legs straddled mine and I pushed myself to a seated position. He was a man well over six feet tall and, from my vantage point, he had the appearance of a giant.

I knew immediately he was a hobo. Mr. Faulk had taught me all about hoboes. His clothes were rumpled and covered with stains of grease and past meals. As he peered down, he removed a piece of straw from his mouth with one hand and lifted a worn fedora with his other as if he was greeting an old friend.

"You best stay seated as you are, sonny. Ridin' the rails in a standin' position isn't always the best way to travel."

"Hoboes ain't to be trusted," Mr. Faulk always said. "They ride for free and they steal for food. You'll be wise to remember to never trust a hobo."

In my seated position, I scooted myself backward. He, in turn, took a step back and I felt better with some distance between us. The satchel pressed against my back and I reached around and pulled it forward into my lap.

"Big bag for such a little boy," he pointed out. "Runnin' away from home are ya? Goin' off to see the big wide world?" The train was now out of the city limits and the sun streamed through the trees giving the hobo's face continuous flashes of shade and sun. During the sun flashes, his artificial smile revealed teeth that were uneven and colored with a slight tint of green.

"Yeah, I'm runnin' away," I told him.

"So what's in the bag there? Seems like it's bigger than you are."

"Just clothes and stuff."

"Stuff? What kinda stuff? Maybe we should have a look see. Why I can even help you sort out stuff you prob'ly don't need."

I was afraid of him. That hobo. Several thoughts raced through my mind. The ride from Nineteenth Street to the safety of the train yard was just minutes away and I knew to avoid being seen, hoboes always jumped off as the train slowed going into the yard. Once in the yard, I knew places to hide where I could rest undetected and then take a safe route to the beehive. I only had to stand my ground for a matter of minutes. The hobo stepped forward and I, in turn pushed myself back. This time, I pushed open the latch on the satchel and slid my hand inside. I'm not sure why. I had no memory of the gun being in the bag until I felt the metal. I dug my heels into the floor to push myself away a second time but my back had reached the end of the boxcar. The hobo grinned and, without saying a word, took another menacing step toward me. I withdrew the gun with little idea of what I was about to do.

This time his smile disappeared and he stepped back. "Whoa, whoa, there fella. I ain't meanin' to do ya no harm now. Is that thing real?"

"Yeah, it's real," I told him. "And I know how to use it." The gun shook in my hand and I cocked the hammer as I answered him.

"Easy now, sonny. You don't need to go shootin' anybody now. I was just fixin' to help ya that's all. I mean I pulled you onto the train didn't I? That should count for somethin'."

The words were barely out of his mouth when my nervous grip caused the gun to go off. The sound of the shot rang in my ears and the gun fell from my hand. The bullet sailed passed the hobo's ear and, as he backed up with a yell, he failed to notice I now sat empty handed. Seeing his reaction of fear gave me the confidence to continue and I regained control of the gun. The train was beginning to slow as we neared the last crossing before the yard.

"Jump off!" I told him. "Get off right now."

"But she's goin' too fast yet. Let me at least wait until we slow down a bit more."

"Do it," I said and cocked the hammer once again. Without hesitating, he grabbed his own small bag from the shadows and jumped. I scrambled to my feet and when I got to the door and glanced back, I spotted him limping away from the area toward a small meadow. I tucked the gun into my belt and pulled my shirt over it as I breathed a sigh of relief knowing in another minute or two I would be safe in the yard. I would get the bag to the beehive. I had gotten away. I had eluded the fat man and hopped the train undetected. There would be no reports to the railroad. I fought off a hobo with my pistol and, in my telling of the story, I would be the hero of the day.

What I didn't know was just before being pulled onto the train I *had* been seen. Seen by a man in a black sedan who frantically chased the train all the way to the yard.

Chapter Seven

When the train came to a stop, I climbed out of the boxcar and pulled the satchel out behind me. I had regained the strength in my arms and was now close enough to the road that ran to the neighborhood that the trek would be fairly easy. I waited while Mr. Rosemont climbed out of the engineer's compartment and started toward the office and then I crossed a set of empty tracks to the graveyard. Once there, I knew I could use the deserted cars for cover and rest before I took the back road leading to the neighborhood.

I was about to leave the protection of the cars when my blood turned to ice. A black sedan drove over the crossing and I didn't feel there was any possibility of a coincidence. The driver pulled off the road and parked. The car door opened but the driver remained seated. It was then we looked directly at each other, he from the seat of his car, me amidst the graveyard. The fat man climbed out and headed in my direction. The cars in the graveyard were never connected which allowed me to go between them and I began to put as much distance between us as possible. Although hampered by the weight of the bag, I knew he could never move as fast as I could.

When I reached what I thought was a safe distance, I got on my knees to see if I could spot his feet. He was closer than I anticipated so I slid the bag under the car and crawled in after it. I pushed the satchel into one of the large cavities in the underbelly of the car and then crawled forward to fit myself into another. I watched as his feet moved toward me and he came close enough that I heard him wheezing.

He then stood directly alongside the car I was hiding under and his heavy breathing became more distinct. The platform I'd wedged myself into was not entirely big enough to hold me and I grabbed anything I could to keep from falling to the ground. I watched as his feet turned from side to side, as he scanned the yard. My heart pounded more than in the park or during my confrontation with the hobo. My arms began to ache again, this time from the strain of holding my weight to keep me from falling on the ground.

It was then a second pair of feet became visible and before I recognized the voice, I was relieved to see the cuffs of the familiar pinstriped coveralls of Mr. Faulk.

"Can I help you stranger? People aren't supposed to be in the yard here. Railroad property you know."

Although I welcomed an ally, I feared for my friend. I knew when he encountered strangers in the yard he protected it as if it was his own house and it was my doing that brought the man here. I was sure Mr. Faulk could tell he was no hobo and I was also sure that neither of these men would back down from the other. As I waited, my arms started to tremble from the stress of holding my body weight.

"I lost my dog," the fat man told Mr. Faulk. "Jumped out of my car there," he continued as he pointed to his car. The black sedan sat with the motor idling and the driver's door still wide open. "Thought I saw him run over this way."

"Be that as it may, you can't be walkin' around this area. I'd certainly be willing to take your phone number and if you tell me what your dog looks like, I'll be glad to give you a call if we spot him." It wasn't a friendly offer. It was more of a request to leave the area, and I knew Mr. Faulk wasn't buying the lost dog story.

"I really don't think I can leave here without him." The fat man returned. Like Mr. Faulk's tone, the voice of the fat man had no friendliness to it and I felt fear again for my friend.

"Everything okay here?" It was the voice of Harold. His feet, along with the feet of three other men became visible as they all stood at Mr. Faulk's side.

It was Mr. Faulk who then spoke again. "I think we're okay. This fella here says he lost his dog and I told him we'd keep an eye out. Call him if he wants." This time Mr. Faulk exhibited a tone of finality. His comment was followed by a lengthy silence.

"I'll check out on the highway," the fat man responded. "Maybe he ran over in the other direction." His feet then turned and he headed toward the car.

"What the hell was that all about?" The question came from Harold.

"Not sure. But I'll bet you dollars to donuts it wasn't about any lost dog. Check back on this area every once in a while. I wanna make sure that guy, whoever he is, doesn't come back." As the men left, I heard a comment from Harold trail off in the distance..."Good thing we came along, Ben. That guy might've sat on ya and crushed ya to death."

When the men left, I fell to the ground. My arms still ached from the strain and, before moving again, I rubbed them to get some of the feeling back. The boxcar that gave me needed protection was one of many in the graveyard and I remained beneath it as I watched the fat man walk to his car.

When he climbed in, Wenzel was sitting up in the back seat. As Malducci eased the car down the highway he stared into the rear view mirror and addressed him. "I'm gonna tell Provinzini I need twenty-four hours to get the money back."

Wenzel remained upright but said nothing. He couldn't say anything. Jules's blow with the tomahawk had done more damage than the fat man realized.

"Until I figure this thing out, you keep your fuckin' mouth shut about it being a bunch of kids, you hear me?" Malducci warned. "I don't intend to be a laughing stock, getting taken by a bunch of little assholes. I think I know who one of 'em was. Think I saw him once at Eddie's place and when I get my hands on him I'm gonna get the money back and then rip his fuckin' heart out!"

❋ ❋ ❋ ❋ ❋

BEFORE I RETRIEVED THE bag, I dragged myself from beneath the car to catch my breath and survey the area. Without knowing the intentions of the fat man, the thought of leaving the satchel where it was crept into my mind. I knew, temporarily, it would be safe to leave it wedged under the car. That thought became permanent when Mr. Faulk's voice came from behind me.

"Auggie?"

I turned to face him and he eyed me up and down. "What are you doin' over here?"

Before I could answer he hit me with another question. "You all right?"

"Yeah, I'm okay." I felt him scanning me up and down and I knew his keen eyes weren't missing an inch. He studied the smeared camouflage paint I'd missed, the bloody scratches on my arms, a T-shirt and pants badly soiled and hair that was wet with sweat and pasted to my forehead. His gaze shifted from me to the highway and to the area the black sedan had been parked and then back to me. Any one of these signals would've required an explanation to any other adult but my friend asked nothing. He simply wanted to know if I was all right.

"C'mon, we'll go over to the locker room and get you cleaned up," he told me. "You look like you were in a fight with an alley cat."

"N-no, that's okay," I told him. "I gotta go, I've got stuff to do for my mother. I promised her I'd do it this afternoon." It was the second lie that week I bestowed on my teacher.

"Okay, you're the boss." But as he said that, he stole a second glance toward the area in which the black sedan had been parked. He then stood and waited for me to leave. I didn't turn around as I headed toward home but I could feel his eyes watching. Not watching with any doubts, but watching in his protective manner until I was out of sight. I knew the satchel would be safe until my return, but it gave me little comfort at the thought of entering the beehive empty-handed.

Chapter Eight

When Jules entered the beehive, Al was seated on the edge of the table. Dusty was examining his right arm in a desperate attempt to find a mark of some kind.

"What's going on with him? You all right?" the question came from Jules as he inquired about his brother.

"I got shot," Al told him.

"Whaddaya mean, you got shot?"

"When the fat guy used the shot gun, he shot me. That's what I mean!"

Jamie's voice came out of the corner of the room. "He didn't get shot anymore than I did."

"I did so. Tell 'em Dusty."

Dusty was still examining the arm in search of a gunshot wound. "Actually Al, I'm having a hard time finding anything."

"It's right there. Look," he said pointing. "Right there!"

Jules was now at the table and joined the examination process. "You mean that little red mark right there?"

"It may look like nothin' to you but it was where one of the bullets grazed me. I'm the one who took the bullet."

Jamie had taken an earlier look at the wound and continued to defend his prior statement. "If anything, it might've been one of the bb's from the shotgun. Looks more like you scraped it on a tree limb or something. The skin's not even broken."

"Well, I still say I was shot in the act of a robbery."

Jules, now convinced of Al's overreaction, changed his focus. "No sign of Auggie?"

"No, but it's gonna take him a while to get here. He's gotta go all the way up Congress and then cut through a bunch of side streets with that stupid bag on his handlebars."

"Maybe we should walk down the street and keep an eye out," Dusty suggested.

"We'll wait here, according to the plan," Jules said and there were no further comments or counter suggestion from Jamie or anyone else.

❋ ❋ ❋ ❋ ❋

WITHOUT THE BAG, I was able to cut through Beck's and use the turrets for cover and I saw no further sign of the fat man. When I entered the cellar, Jamie was the first to question the absence of the bag.

"Where's the money?"

"Yeah, where's the bag?" Al echoed.

Dusty was the first to notice the scratches of dried blood along with other telltale signs. "Are you okay, man? You look like shit. What happened to your arms?"

"Yeah, but before I say anything, I need a drink of water."

Jules motioned to Al to go upstairs.

"The money's safe," I told them. "I had to leave it in the train yard but I hid it under one of the cars in the graveyard. I ran into some problems." I then realized I still had the revolver stuck inside my belt and, seeing an opportunity to allay their disappointment of not having the money, I withdrew it and slapped it down on the table. All eyes fell to the gun and I was immediately besieged by a barrage of questions.

When Al returned with the water, he turned his attention to the gun, for him, a bigger trophy than the cash. Jules, realizing it was loaded, quickly took it from him and removed the cartridges. It was then passed around for all to inspect while I told my story.

In my retelling of the incidents from the bridge to the beehive, I held the attention of everyone. Having a captive audience, I felt I had the right to add embellishments and the expressions on their faces begged me to continue during my pauses for gulps of water. My soliloquy left out none of the details. I described my flight from death from the fat man, the breakdown of the bike, the run to the train, and the hopping onto the moving freight car.

I had their full attention and continued with the telling of the menacing hobo who I drew and fired on before I forced him to jump from the moving train. I included every detail that preceded the culmination of the chase through the train yard. It was all there for the taking.

Each of us, in turn, relived our own part in the caper inventing and exaggerating as we did so. The details we included could not be disproved with any credibility, but served to enhance the day's events. Al's claim of getting shot during the robbery, as unlikely as it was, was not disprovable and we were forced to live with it.

For me, the laughter was a mix of amusement and fear as questions remained in my mind regarding the fat man, what he saw of me, and what was to follow. When the tales of our adventure came to an end, our thoughts turned to the money and what our next move would be.

Jules tried to ascertain how much money was in the bag until Dusty explained that from what I told him he could figure out a reasonable guess when he got home and did some calculations. Jamie wanted to know more about the rantings of the fat man and Al wanted to know who was going to get to keep the gun. Our leader sat and considered our next moves.

"We need to focus on getting the money and getting it to a safe place. If this fat guy is still around he could be watching. Did he see any of you guys on the bridge?"

"He didn't see me real good on the bridge, but he may have seen my face in the train yard," I confessed. "I didn't have any camouflage on or anything then."

"If he saw you and he's going to continue to hunt us, we may have only one option."

"What are you thinking?" The question came from Jules.

Jamie's face took on the familiar look I'd seen too many times as he took the gun down from the shelf and held it high in the air. "We've got his gun here," he said. And then changing his voice to his best Edward G. Robinson impression added, "Yeah, we'll have to rub him out, see?"

Al and Jules laughed but Dusty and I glanced at each other. We knew he was dead serious.

Chapter Nine

The unresolved future with the fat man led to another night of restlessness which was extended when my mother initiated a rude awakening on Friday morning.

"August, I thought you told me you left your bike at Dusty's." She didn't seem to care that I was sleeping when she made the comment.

I rolled over trying to make sense out of what she was saying but before I could respond, she continued. "He must've brought it up here this morning. You better get yourself up and get it. It's going to get hit where he left it. It's half on the sidewalk, half in the street. I don't know why he left it there. He knows better than that."

Still making no sense of what she was saying, I dragged myself from the bed and after dressing, found her proclamation to be true. My bike, upright on its kickstand, was standing in front of the house, half on half off the sidewalk. I pushed through the front door and descended the porch steps. It was unmistakably mine. Parts of bushes were still entwined in the spokes and the broken chain dangled from the sprocket.

In my confusion to reach it, I never noticed the yellow sedan parked a few yards away and as I reached for the handlebars, a vice-like grip ensnared the back of my neck and nearly lifted me off the ground. My knees were forced to the sidewalk and, for the first time, I noticed the car. I was pushed toward it and a fat hand reached around to open the door and threw me into the front seat. It was done with the ease of someone tossing a newspaper.

My entire body was gripped with fear and my chest tightened. A hand on my head pushed me farther down on the floor of the passenger side. He had me. I sat facing the rear of the car, wedged between the dashboard and the seat. I knew my life was over. The car's engine revved up and the throaty mellowness of the glass packs was a sound I now feared. I felt the force of the U-turn before the sedan headed down the hill toward the highway. This was the man who crushed my hand as I sat in The Pit. The man who probably killed people every day, I thought.

The imaginary chest bands tightened and continued to make breathing difficult. I tried not to look at him—I didn't want to see his face or the ugly purplish hue. It wasn't until we were on Route 32 that he spoke. "August," he started. "You seem surprised to see me. Guys like you—you always mess up somewhere along the line."

I sat trembling, feeling ready to throw up, and said nothing.

"I figured you left your bike somewhere between that park and the train you hopped."

I remained silent with my knees dug into the rubber floor mat.

"By the way, I want to thank you for leaving that nice sticker under your bike seat. You know, the one with your name, address, and phone number. Mighty thoughtful of you."

My throat was tight and dry. If he was waiting for me to say something, I couldn't.

"Nothin' to say smart ass?" The back of his right hand came down hard on my shoulder as he asked the question. "Okay then, I'll do the talking and tell ya what's gonna happen this morning. First, we're gonna pull into Baine's field down here and have a quiet talk, only this time you're gonna do the talkin'. We're gonna discuss just where you put my leather bag and then, if I need your help to get it, you're gonna help me."

As he talked, I stole a glance at the door lock. It was pushed all the way down which eliminated the possibility of opening the door and jumping out. He noticed my glance and pulled out a large hunting knife, seemingly from nowhere. It was shaped like Jules's knife but much larger.

"Go ahead," he told me. "Reach for the door. I'll cut your fingers off if that's what you want. Is that what you want, kid?"

I spoke for the first time since I'd been thrown into the car. "No sir."

"Good. Now I want you to understand that this doesn't have to get ugly between you and me. You get me my bag and we both go on our merry way. It's that simple." With that, he pulled the car to a stop and switched off the ignition. Baine's field was only a short distance from my house, but it was isolated from the highway. It was a deserted field we used for pick-up games on summer afternoons. No one else ever used it with the exception of two weeks in July when the carnival came to the city and it came alive with the giant midway.

After Malducci climbed out, he leaned in, grabbed my arm, and yanked me out the driver's side door. My hip dragged across the gear shift and one foot got caught in the steering wheel. To free my ankle, he used his vice grip on the back of my neck once again and yanked me the remainder of the way.

He dragged me from the car and his grip held me off the ground until we reached the riverbank. The pain was sharp and unending. Unlike the gradual slope below the D&H Bridge, the bank that bordered the field was steep with a straight drop of thirty feet or more. At the base was a narrow ledge of shale and small boulders before a second drop of a few feet to the water.

He continued to hold me by the back of my neck and pushed my head down to see the rocks below us. "I thought this might be a nice private place to have our talk." Again, I remained too scared to speak. "So all you gotta do now is tell me where you put the fuckin' bag. I don't figure you left it on the train so it must either be in that train yard somewhere or you lugged it all the way home and stuck it under your bed or maybe in your closet. You want to give me an answer?" As he asked the question he tightened his grip on my neck and pushed my head down farther. The pain caused a new aching. I struggled to find an answer as I stared at his shoes.

"It's in the train yard," I told him with a voice I didn't recognize.

"Good. That's good. Now where in the train yard?" This time, he relaxed his grip a bit but not to the point that allowed for an escape. When I didn't answer immediately, he threw me to the ground and I rolled to my back as I fell. He straddled me, in much the same fashion as the hobo had. His huge frame intercepted the sun and as he rocked back and forth, its brightness took turns blinding me and showing me his size. During the intervals I saw him—saw his sagging chins that revealed rolls of sweat and wet circles that ringed his armpits. Once again, the knife appeared from nowhere. He reached down and grabbed a handful of my T-shirt and lifted my torso off the ground. He was about to speak again when I caught a flash of movement behind him. With the movement, the knife fell from his hand and he released his grip. The scream he emitted was not one of anger as he fell to one knee, but a shriek of pain.

I realized something had hit him in the back of his head that caused his reaction. Someone was standing behind him and the figure was holding what looked like a baseball bat. The blow that had caused the fat man to drop me had come from a well-placed hit. The bat landed a second blow with full force on the side of his knee. I shielded my eyes, then in direct line to the sun, and witnessed a third blow that caught his left side. He clutched his ribs and buckled over.

I then saw the attacker. It was Dusty, his lips clutched tight as he swung again and again with the fury of a crazy man. The fat man raised his arms in defense and turned and faced him from his kneeled position. He knocked the bat from Dusty's hand and grabbed him by his belt buckle. It was my turn to help Dusty. The only grip I could get on the Louisville Slugger was the fat end but, once I had it, I swung it valiantly with little or no aim and landed minor blows to his blubbery arm and shoulder. The fat man's focus remained on Dusty, which allowed me to get to my feet. With the bat reversed, I took another swing and caught a hip. Malducci turned on me and the three of us formed a triangle with Malducci still on his knees and his back to the cliff. This time when he spoke, saliva spewed from his mouth and the purplish hue of his face was a deeper red.

"I've had all I'm gonna take from you little shits," he yelled. "You wanna play fuckin' games? You're playin' with the wrong guy."

I took another hard swing with the bat. He leaned back to avoid the slugger but it was just enough to spin him off balance. With his arms flailing, he began a slide down the embankment and clawed at the grass. There he held himself with the slightest of footholds leaving only his arms and head visible to us. His puffy hands continued clutching the grass and I relaxed the bat in my hand and turned to face Dusty. Malducci reached out in a desperate attempt at survival and grabbed the cuff of my pants. He pulled me down and my legs slid toward him. Dusty grabbed one arm as I became the rope in a tug of war.

"C'mon, kid. Help me up here. I wasn't really gonna hurt ya." His voice now held a tone of desperation.

Dusty and I were too busy struggling to say anything but I figured any guy who was gonna cut my fingers off for looking at his door lock was not to be trusted.

"Listen," he continued. "You guys help me up here and I'll tell you what. You can keep the money in the bag. Yeah, keep all of it. I won't take any." As he spoke, the clump of sod he was using as a foothold began to crumble beneath his weight. He sunk farther down the embankment and pulled me closer to the edge with him. His face tightened and his grip moved from the cuff of my pants to my sneaker. Dusty had moved behind me and now struggled with both hands under my armpits as he strained to keep me from going over. I knew from Malducci's look, he was about to take the thirty foot drop.

"He's going over," I yelled. "Pull me back!"

"I can't hold you."

"He's got my sneaker!"

"Take it off, kick it off or somethin'!"

I dug the heel of my sneaker into the ground and frantically worked my foot out. The action coincided with the final crumbling of the fat man's footing and he disappeared. I recalled the caption under the fat man's picture on the easel that contained the word enforcer as I listened to the sound of a scream as he fell to the rocks. Somehow it seemed the scream, along with his last desperate attempt to save himself, was out of character for such a tough guy.

Dusty and I were both exhausted and I collapsed backward into his arms. We sat like tandem bobsled riders and stared up into the morning sky. It was blue and cloudless and, from somewhere, the heat bug buzzed. It was going to be a very hot August day.

"We better look," Dusty said after a brief respite. Still exhausted, we moved to the edge on all fours not knowing what to expect. The fat man lay motionless at the edge of the river and for the first time he looked very small to me. His body appeared bent from the fall to the ledge. He looked all twisted and, even from our distance, we could see a dark pool of blood that oozed from his head onto the rock.

"It's blood," Dusty announced. "That stuff coming out of his head. That's blood, man," he repeated. "Probably came out when he hit his head on those rocks. He's definitely dead."

We remained on all fours and backed away before standing.

"Thanks, man," I told him. "How did you know where I was?"

"I was rounding the corner to your house when I saw him grab you and throw you into the car. Lucky he only came to the field or I wouldn't have been able to keep up." We stood staring at each other until he broke the silence once again. "Well, at least now it's over, right? I mean we should get outta here." His voice held an unfamiliar tremor.

"It's not quite over."

He looked at me confused. "What? Oh, you mean that other guy? The guy who was driving the car?" And he then remembered the reason he was going to my house in the first place. "That's right. You don't know yet. The guy driving the car? He's dead, man!"

"Dead?"

"Yeah, I listened in on the..."

"No, that's not what I was talkin' about." I interrupted. "I mean, that's good that he's dead...I guess...but..." I stepped to the edge of the riverbank and pointed to the corpse below. Dusty looked down but still didn't comprehend our problem until I pointed it out.

"He's still holding my sneaker."

❋ ❋ ❋ ❋ ❋

WE BOTH KNEW GETTING the sneaker was necessary and it turned out to be an ordeal. To get to the fat man, we had to hike to an area that allowed for easier access to the lower bank of the river. At the body, we found Dusty's earlier thought had been accurate. We stared at the pool of blood that had oozed from the fat man's head and now blackened the rocks. He laid across the small boulders in a position that didn't seem to look normal. One of his legs was bent beneath him, twisted and misshaped from a bone that poked through his pant leg. I tried to avoid his eyes but they stared at me as I yanked the sneaker from his grasp. Dusty, not so squeamish at the sight, poked at him with a stick and made the suggestion that we take his ring as a souvenir but then, figuring it might be evidence that could trap us later, dismissed the idea.

A full hour passed before we retrieved the sneaker and began the walk home with Dusty's bike between us. We rehashed the morning's events and the importance of getting the sneaker. Jamie, of course, would've been worried about fingerprints. Our comments were spoken intermittently in sentences sprinkled with nervous laughter as each of us tried to disguise our fear. To lighten our mood, we played a game and made up headlines of what the newspaper would say if we had left the sneaker there. Headlines like: 'Police Search For Cinderella Boy In Local Murder' and 'Police Seek Killer—If The Shoe Fits, Arrest Him!' The humor blanketed our fear and our shame.

Dusty filled me in on the eavesdropped conversation his father had had with the agent who had been working undercover as one of Provinzini's men.

It was Silly who picked up the phone and put a finger to her lips to silence Dusty when he emerged from his bedroom that morning. When she mentioned some guy got shot, Dusty forced the phone from her hand and picked up on the tail end of the conversation. From what he heard, Wenzel never did get his head right after being tomahawked by Jules. Provinzini, not realizing the extent of the damage, had questioned Wenzel to the point of frustration. Finally, suspecting that Wenzel and Malducci had been in on the heist together, he decided to put him out of his misery. According to the agent, a single nod from Provinzini and Wenzel was given two shots to the back of his head before anyone could spit.

"It all happened so fast, Dave, I couldn't have stopped it if I wanted to," the agent told Dusty's father. "If you ask me, the guy was acting like he'd had a stroke or something. He seemed disoriented and he was slurring his words," he continued. "Now Provinzini's got the word out and is hunting for Malducci."

Dusty's telling of the phone call was followed by more silence until he evidently felt the need to continue.

"Anyway, the fat man and the other guy are both dead so what are we supposed to do now?" His question was one I had no answer for. I wanted to suggest that we should burn all the money and forget we ever did anything on the bridge or anywhere else. Nothing, in our minds, was resolved. Sooner or later someone was going to find the body and that would involve the police and an investigation. Had we left any clues? What was going to happen then? After seeing Dusty's reaction to the dead body, I believed I was more scared than he was until midway back to our neighborhood, he stopped and let his bike fall over. He took a few steps, fell to his knees, and puked his guts out.

❋ ❋ ❋ ❋ ❋

WE REACHED THE NEIGHBORHOOD and agreed we should talk to Jules and Al. The four of us went immediately to the beehive. Dusty and I told our story and what had occurred during the morning. Al, of course, was full of questions as we told of the fat man and our exaggerated heroics. The telling of the tale seemed to diminish our fears somewhat and the lumps in our throats and tightness in our chests dissipated. Jules listened intently and remained silent until we finished. When Al began to fire questions, he raised a hand to silence him.

"Sounds like nobody knows anything about us."

"Whaddaya mean?" I asked him.

"If the driver guy is dead, like Dusty says, and you two killed that fat guy, there's nobody left that knows anything except us. I mean, it sounds like they didn't tell anyone else what happened. I'm not sure why, but it doesn't matter as long as nobody knows about us."

"What about the gun?" Al asked his brother.

"Stop worryin' about the freakin' gun. I'll take care of the gun. We need to decide what we're gonna do with the money."

"It should be safe where it is," I told him. "Nobody ever goes near the graveyard."

"When we talked yesterday, Jamie didn't like the idea of the graveyard," Al reminded us. "He said we shouldn't leave it there too long."

"I say it's safe where it is. Nobody goes near that area. That's why they call it the graveyard," I argued. "Besides, Jamie's not here now. We're here and we need to decide what to do."

"I don't doubt that the money is safe for now," Jules confirmed. "I just think we should move it where we have more control. You said yourself that you don't usually hang around that area so it might look suspicious if you're always over there. You know, you'll need to keep checking on it. The rest of us can't be wandering around the train yard like you do."

"Jules is right," Dusty added. "We need to get the bag where we have more control over it. What about one of the turrets?"

"Too risky." As Jules spoke, he rose from the crate he'd been using as a seat and paced the floor. "They move the turrets around too much. We didn't do all this work to lose the money now."

"There is one other place in the yard we could put it." As the words left my mouth, I regretted what I'd said. The use of the train yard could easily involve Mr. Faulk, the person I most feared disappointing.

"Where?" Jules wanted to know.

"There's a special train car," I said with reluctance, upset because I had committed myself to the divulgence of a confidence. "It's near the graveyard. It has a secret compartment that no one knows about. Well, no one except me and Mr. Faulk. They used to hide liquor in the compartment during prohibition. Mr. Faulk told me about it."

"Does he ever go in it?"

"No, it's not something you can go into." With that comment I realized a possible way out of my dilemma and continued. "I don't think the leather bag would fit into it." My negative tone continued. "It's too big. We'd have to transfer the money to other bags and stuff. We should probably find another place."

But Jules liked the idea and pressed me for more details. It was a good move, even if temporary, to secure a safer place for the money. "We should probably get rid of that bag anyway. I say we vote," Jules said.

Having been the one that suggested the idea, I felt committed and four pennies were thrown onto the table where the entire robbery had been planned. It was the first time any vote was taken that didn't include all five of the flattened pennies.

In the course of the morning, we had covertly obtained police information regarding Wenzel, done away with the fat man, and voted to move the money. All of it done without any advice from our leader.

Following the discussion with Jules and Al, Dusty and I went home. He promised to keep an ear to the extension and listen in for any new information. I spent the afternoon doing anything that took my mind off the disfigured body we'd left lying on the rocks. Any callers, which included my mother's friends who needed answers to questions regarding their astrological charts, became my enemies. With each ring of the phone my heart raced and my chest tightened knowing it might be the police calling to make an arrest, or at the very least, wanting to question me for some reason.

The sound of the everyday act of the mailman placing letters in the box on the front porch forced me to the living room window in anticipation of possible trouble. On numerous times I felt sick and realized I should've joined Dusty on all fours when he lost his breakfast.

It was late afternoon when my mother picked up the ringing phone and spoke the words I dreaded hearing. "Yes, he's here, just a minute," and then pointed the receiver at me with a motion to take it from her. It would certainly be the police. My heart came to a complete stop and my body flashed cold, then hot, then cold again until she relieved the tension. She covered the mouthpiece and whispered, "I think it's that Jamie character."

The conversation was short. I said nothing about the incident with the fat man, knowing our phone was probably tapped by now. I told him we voted to move the bag and, figuring he knew what I was talking about, remained as vague as possible. He threw questions at me until I interrupted and told him I couldn't talk on the phone. He switched gears and started yelling, telling me we shouldn't have had any meeting or any kind of a vote without him and he wanted everyone to meet at the turrets that afternoon. I thought for a guy who was always worried about any of us leaving fingerprints and stuff, he was giving away a lot of information if the cops were listening in.

"That's not possible for me," I told him. "I can't get away this afternoon. I've got stuff here I've gotta do." It was my first outward act of defiance to our appointed leader but surprisingly he backed off from his demand.

"Tomorrow morning then," he compromised. "I'll call Jules and Al and come to your house around eight. The four of us can walk over together and meet Dusty there. Tell him we'll meet at D-7."

Chapter Ten

I had expected the Saturday morning walk to the turret to be filled with more questions about the money and the bootlegger's hole. Possibly, we'd make the plan to move it. But when Jamie arrived, and joined Al and Jules and me who were waiting outside in the street, our discussion regarding the money was tabled. He was all excited and immediately spilled out information about the cops finding the body of the fat man on the riverbank.

"A couple of guys were fishing in their boat and saw the body," he told us. "It was all over the news this morning. They even put a photo of him on TV. It was him all right. We should go to the river and watch 'em move the body and stuff."

"We can't go over there, man," Jules told him.

I realized then that Jamie was the only member of The Five-Cent Gang who hadn't been told about the prior day's activities.

"Why not?"

"'Cause he's the one who did it," Al told him as he pointed to me.

"Whaddaya mean, did it? Did what?"

"Him and Dusty, man. They're the ones who pushed the fat man off the cliff. They killed him, man!"

Although I had misgivings regarding the death of the fat man, I remained silent realizing for the moment

Jamie was eyeballing me with a new kind of appreciation.

"Whaddaya mean he did it? Are you shittin' me?"

"No man. Auggie and Dusty killed him. Knocked him off the cliff with Dusty's baseball bat," Al continued. A pantomimed motion of a bat swing accompanied his comment.

We all watched as Jamie's jaw dropped a few inches. It wasn't often we saw him speechless. Before Jamie responded, Jules confirmed Al's statement and reiterated the fact that none of us would be going anywhere except the turret.

"We need to keep our focus. We've got other things to take care of first. We can't be showin' up at the scene of the crime. The less interested we are in Baine's field, the better."

The thought that we wouldn't see any of the local police action was most disturbing to Al, who pointed out there would probably be barricades of yellow tape and a chalk outline on the rocks where they found the body. Jules seemed to ignore the statement and urged us to start the walk to the foundry and, until Dusty joined us a few minutes later, Jamie peppered me with questions about sending the fat man over the cliff. When I was slow to respond, Jules and Al continued to fill Jamie in on all the details—details I was tired of hearing and thinking about.

Once at Beck's foundry we realized that, compared to the beehive, the turret seemed too cramped for our meetings. Everyone but me seemed to think we were home free regarding the fat man and the talk turned to the money. Jamie didn't like the idea of putting it in the bootlegger's hole despite the assurance by Jules that it would only be temporary. Jules then reminded him that we had already taken a vote and the issue had been settled. The one thing we did agree on was that none of the money should be spent for at least a month. Until then, it would be safer in the old steam engine than stuck under the freight car in the graveyard. Al's idea was to split up the money and each of us hide our own share. It was Al's second idea of the day to receive a veto from Jules.

As reluctant as I was to touch the coveted leather satchel again, I knew the burden of moving the money was on my shoulders. I was not only the one person who knew which boxcar it was under, but I had knowledge regarding the workers' schedules around the yard, and when they went to beans. Since the money would have to be moved at night, I was the only one who could point out which areas leading to the box car would be most protected by shadows. Sneaking out after midnight was simply another task that Jamie's leadership had added to our repertoire of skills. If we moved the money after midnight, Mr. Faulk's shift would be over and his keen awareness of anything unusual happening in the yard wouldn't be an issue.

"We'll need some smaller bags," I told Jules. "The satchel's too big to fit inside the compartment."

"No problem. My mother's got a whole bunch of old pocketbooks down here in the cellar. She said she's giving them to the church for a rummage sale or something. We can use some of those."

"We're gonna use pocketbooks?" Al asked. "I don't think that's anything real crooks would do. Why don't we just put the money in some paper bags?"

Jules looked at me for an answer.

"We need something stronger; bags will rip and stuff. The pocketbooks will work. I've got an old gym bag we can use too. We need to have soft bags we can squeeze into places."

"I'll draw up a plan this afternoon," Jamie informed us. "Maybe we can meet at the beehive again."

"No." I told him. "No more plans and charts and stuff. If I have to move the money then I'm in charge of the caper and just two of us will do it; I'm picking Dusty." All this was said without a glance toward my friend but I knew he'd stand with me.

"I've gotta go too," Jamie insisted.

This time it was Dusty who voiced his objection to Jamie's going along. "Yeah, sure, why don't we all go?" His arms flailed as his hands almost hit the top of the turret. "We can run around the yard and make all kinds of noise and stuff! Why don't we just carry big signs that say don't worry, we're only here to move some stolen money?"

For several seconds, the space became more of a tomb than a turret. Other than taking a vote during his absence, no one had questioned Jamie prior to this recent decision.

Jules broke the silence. "Auggie's right. We can't all be going in there, makin' a lot of noise tryin' to sneak around." He then focused his attention on me. "It would be good to have a third guy though. He could keep a lookout while you and Dusty transfer the money." As he spoke, he nodded his head toward Jamie, indicating he would be the one doing the looking. To further solidify the third person to be Jamie he pointed out that if he went instead, Al would want to go along too and, with no disrespect to Al, four would be too many.

To set the plan in motion, I researched the status of the moon with my mother. She was delighted to see we shared a common interest and I learned that the new moon was in Venus rising or something. The main thing was, when I pushed her on it, she meant it would be dark that night and a good time to move the money. Transferring it to the old steam engine seemed to hold some urgency and the darkness made it immediately possible.

The idea of the pocketbooks hit some resistance just before leaving the beehive.

"I still don't think we should be using this thing to hide our money," Al objected holding up a giant red pocketbook covered with matching sequins.

"And look at this thing." This time he grabbed a blue fake leather job accompanied by a matching hat and after putting them on paraded around the room.

"Am I fully coordinated?" he asked in his best imitation of a woman's voice, which made even Jules give a laugh.

Jamie lifted the other two bags from the table and slung the one resembling leopard skin over his right shoulder with a black patent leather number over his left. "I kinda have to agree with Al for once," he said. I'm not so sure we want to be seen carrying these huge things around. Each of the bags suggested that Al and Jules's mother seemed to have an addiction to really big pocketbooks with a lot of zippers and compartments. Jules solved the problem when he rolled them up into long cylinders and stuffed them into the old gym bag identified by the Waterton High School logo. It was an unwanted hand-me-down from my cousin and no sacrifice on my part to donate it to the cause.

Oddly enough, once on the back hill, Jamie and I each took two of the purses out of the bag and put them over our shoulders before we met Dusty at the crossroad. I gave Dusty the red one and in that wee hour of the morning, the three of us sashayed to the train yard under a starlit sky. We were commandos once again...on another dangerous caper...and we were ready...armed with our jackknives and pocketbooks.

Before entering the yard, we crouched in the light of a streetlamp and, using a stick, I drew a sketch in the dirt showing them the layout to include the boxcar with the money, the location of the Baldwin, and where Jamie should stand to keep watch. It was my version of a blueprint, which I hoped set a precedent for any future capers drawn up by Jamie. I think we were all tired of his fancy plans and charts.

We went straight to the boxcar to unload our bags before Jamie went to his lookout post. At the boxcar he insisted on seeing the satchel before leaving and the three of us crawled into the pitch-blackness of the train. I then realized my decision to eliminate flashlights during the caper was an error in judgment. While it prevented any light from flashing out into the yard, it made finding the bag more difficult. Eventually I located it and Dusty and I tugged it out of its hiding place and it fell on the ground between us.

I pushed the mouth of the bag open but the anticipated view of the money was a disappointment to all of us. Our cramped quarters, combined with the darkness, allowed no visible opportunity to see anything inside the bag.

"Drag it outside," Jamie ordered in a loud whisper. "Let's look at the money."

"No way. We can't be messin' around out in the yard. Just fill the bags here." As I gave him my response, I removed the two ledgers that covered the bundles of tens and twenties and set them near the outer edge of the track. There was just enough light to see them and Jamie picked them up and fanned through the pages.

"What are you doing?" I asked him. "It's too dark to see anything in those."

"I'll bet these are lists of all the places the fat man got his money and stuff. We'll have to get rid of these. We can take 'em with us and bury them with the bag."

Dusty responded with an edge to his tone I had never heard before, as if he was now suddenly in charge. "Just put 'em down for now and go keep a lookout."

The two of us then worked methodically. I reached into the bag over and over with both hands and removed stacks of bills. Dusty, in turn, filled the pocketbooks.

"Don't fill 'em too much," I told him. "They won't fit in the compartment if they're too fat. They look big on the outside but these things aren't like our knapsacks."

When all the money had been transferred, we pushed the pocketbooks from under the boxcar along with the empty leather satchel.

"Feel around on the ground," I instructed Dusty. "Make sure we didn't miss any of the bundles in the dark."

Once free from the belly of the boxcar, Dusty signaled to Jamie and the three of us carried the bags to the Baldwin. The steam engine towered above us as it emitted a silhouetted presence of the history it represented. Even under the sparseness of the new moon, the brass adornments glistened with the glow of restoration and provided evidence of Mr. Faulk's love and devotion to his prize.

Jamie returned to his post and Dusty and I tossed the bags into the engineer's compartment. We climbed in and I pulled the coalman's seat down much the same way I had done with Mr. Faulk. I slid open the door to the bootlegger's hole and, one by one, took the bags from Dusty and wedged them into the compartment, relieved to find the space was large enough to hold them all.

Dusty signaled once again to Jamie and we left the yard through a night stillness broken only by an occasional shout from one distant worker to another or the sound of a tool pounding on a switch or the coupling between two cars. I had heard these sounds many times during the daylight hours but they now seemed alien in the black of night. Dusty carried the satchel and, although its only contents now were the two ledgers, he held it tightly to his chest as if the money was still inside.

Our plan was to cut through Beck's foundry and weave between the turrets. It was familiar territory and an easy way back to the neighborhood. We had decided to hide the satchel somewhere in the area of the turrets and return the following day to bury it. As we neared the foundry Jamie spotted an easier method of disposal. "Look!" he shouted. He pointed to an area on the fringe where someone on the night shift was using a fifty-gallon drum as an incinerator.

"It doesn't look like anybody's around. If nobody's watchin' the can, we can drop the bag right into the fire. It'll be nothing but ashes in the morning." It was a spontaneous resolution but we all agreed, knowing it would be easier and safer than burying it.

"Gimme the bag," Jamie told Dusty. "You guys wait here and I'll go over and throw it in."

Dusty loosened his grip somewhat and then, before handing the bag to Jamie, removed the ledgers.

"What are you doing? We gotta burn those too. They're evidence."

"I'm keeping these." As he said the words, he pulled the ledgers to his chest and held them in much the same way as he had been holding the satchel."

"Keeping them?" Jamie shouted. "You can't keep those. If anyone catches us with those books it's big freakin' trouble, man. What are ya gonna do with 'em anyway?"

"They're the evidence my father needed for the task force. Remember? He told the guys he didn't care about the money. They just needed to get the books. I'm giving them to him."

"Giving them to your father!" Jamie's voice was reaching a dangerous pitch and displayed a combined tone of anger and disbelief. "You can't give them to your father. What are you talking about?" He then looked at me for support to dissuade my friend's idea. "Say something to him will ya?"

Before I could answer, Dusty continued. "Hey, it's not like I'm gonna just hand them to him or something. I'll have to figure it out but you're not burnin' them."

"We have to," Jamie continued in anger.

"Then, I say we vote on it," Dusty demanded.

"We can't vote on it, there's only three of us here. I say they have to go into the fire right now. If that's not good enough for you then I say we vote tomorrow, and we all get a say."

Dusty stole a glance in my direction searching for a look of support. He knew a vote tomorrow would be no guarantee of him keeping the books.

"Yeah, well three is a majority of The Five-Cent Gang and majority rules. I say we take a vote here and now and whatever we say tonight stands."

"Yeah, sure, and you two are gonna stick together on this. What kind of a vote is that?"

"The same kind we had when you voted to change the plan of robbing the fat man to the bridge caper," Dusty told him. "You and Jules wanted that and Al does whatever Jules tells him. You think that was fair?

And now me and Auggie are killers! You think that was fair either?"

Jamie's jaw tightened as he clenched his teeth. His cheekbone rose and fell in unison with his breathing. He had been eliminated from a vote the day before and now was being pushed into a vote that he knew he would lose

"I gotta go with Dusty on the vote idea," I told Jamie. I was as tired as Dusty was regarding the trouble Jamie always managed to get us into.

"Well, I vote I take the books," Dusty said, without letting the discussion continue.

"And I say we burn them," Jamie countered, and then both of them turned to me. Dusty continued to clench the books to his chest while Jamie's eyes met mine with a piercing look that burned right through me. His eyes flashed with anger. I deliberately waited a few seconds before answering and, when I did so, my stare never left his. "I vote Dusty takes the books."

"Of course you do!" He hesitated as he surveyed the area as if for an unknown ally to appear and save the day. "Then you burn the fuckin' bag!" he yelled as he threw it to the ground and started through the turrets. After a few yards he stopped, turned, and pointed a finger at Dusty but looked at me as he spoke. "Don't come cryin' to me when he gets caught with those stupid books and we all go to prison!" he yelled. Without waiting for further threats, Dusty and I made our way to the incinerator while Jamie continued out of Beck's toward the neighborhood. Once Dusty tossed the satchel into the fire, we turned just in time to see Jamie's back fade into the darkness.

Chapter Eleven

None of us were the same after the D&H Bridge Caper. The ordeal placed a wedge that divided us into differing factions and for the remainder of the summer we played a waiting game. Dusty and I, being best friends and with the confrontation with the fat man as a common denominator, continued to spend time together. Most days we went to the city pool but there were no longer any bombardments or getting benched or even ogling over Candy Melons. We used much of our time to discuss the money and, despite assurances from Jules, we were worried about Al spending too much too fast and maybe even talking too much.

The newspapers spent days on the murder of the fat man. It started with a front-page story and then continued throughout the week with follow-up articles. The initial story following the headline told of a gangland killing of a notorious gang enforcer. Most people who had seen Vincent Malducci around Waterton were not surprised. Follow-up stories were vague and revealed very little factual information.

Dusty's father appeared on the local television stations and gave only sketchy details, stating it was an ongoing investigation. There was never a mention of an occurrence on the bridge or stolen money or ledger books. Additionally, there was no mention of a man named Wenzel. The death of the fat man was simply a gang-related killing. It was only because of the extension phone that The Five-Cent Gang gained information the general public lacked. But even within our small circle, no one had any idea of the amount of money hidden in the Baldwin and it was usually the only topic of discussion on the increasingly rare occasions when we saw each other.

At one point in the investigation, there was word of some possible money involved. When that leaked out, rumors spread like a virus in barbershops and beauty salons as well as discussions around office water coolers. Residents imagined the fat guy from the riverbank hid some money somewhere before the mob bumped him off. Everybody in town had an opinion regarding the amount and who stole it and where it might be hidden.

Although the robbery changed all of us, Dusty and I were the hardest hit. We were only twelve and still trying to figure out whether or not we had actually committed murder. Neither of us was certain. We didn't want to believe that we did, we wanted to believe that the fat man fell. When I argued the point that we made him fall, Dusty was quick to counter and reminded me that we acted in self-defense. "We couldn't have helped him up if we wanted to," he told me. "Besides, if we did, he would've killed us."

I couldn't argue with his logic and wanted to believe everything he was saying even if it was to ease my own conscience. Jamie's phone calls continued but usually to make sure I was checking on the money. It was also a concern held by both Al and Jules. Al was hot to spend his share and he had a list ready of all the rifles he planned to buy. Those thoughts and conversations were instrumental in Jules's reassuring us that he'd keep him in line.

"When we split up the money, I'll take Al's share," Jules told me. "I'm gonna have to give it to him a little at a time. He's liable to spend it all in one day buying guns and camouflage paint and a bunch of other shit."

Chapter Twelve

A week after the robbery, Jules received a phone call from the football coach who encouraged him to try out for the freshman team. Even though he had been held back in grade three, the coach explained he was age eligible. There was no mention during the conversation regarding the coach's thoughts that Jules's size and strength would be a great asset to his offensive line. With his acceptance of the offer, the traditional August practices left us without a valued companion and Al floundering for the camaraderie of his missing brother. Dusty and I sometimes took Al to the pool, but usually it was just the two of us. We didn't see Jamie often and the fact that he wasn't around much didn't seem to matter to anyone.

During one of the trips to the city pool, Dusty spent the entire bus ride wearing a huge grin. It was the first time since the fat man went over the cliff that he displayed such an obvious sign of joy. When I questioned him on what was so funny, he told me he'd fill me in at the pool. After a quick swim, he told me he had worked out a formula to figure out how much money was in the bag. He was the business guy and mathematician of the group and so I had no reason to doubt his claim. We were sitting on our towels on our usual isolated dirt patch near the Anchor fence that surrounded the pool grounds.

"First, you take the dimensions of the bag," he began. "I had to guess at those but I think I'm pretty close. Then I put stacks of play money together until I got an inch of paper." There're at least two hundred bills in an inch. His logic continued and the more he talked, the more believable his system became.

"So then I figured out how many one inch stacks would fit in the bag and guessed half of them would be stacks of five dollar bills and half would be ten dollar bills. I mean you saw them right? That's what you said you saw."

"Yeah, yeah," I agreed. "So come on, what did you come up with?"

"Well, according to my calculations, a person could fit twelve bills on the bottom of the bag...four rows of three."

As he talked he pointed in the air to show me the twelve piles. "Did you know a bill is two and a half inches wide by five inches long?"

By now I realized he was busting my chops and wanted to make me work for a final dollar amount. "Stop bustin' me," I yelled. "How much was in the bag?"

"Well, according to my calculations, if the bag is fourteen inches high it could hold one hundred sixty-eight stacks of bills. That means eighty-four stacks of tens and eighty-four stacks of fives with two hundred bills in each and that, my friend, gives us a grand total of..." and then he stopped and took a bite of his frozen milkshake.

I yanked on his arm, dislodging the candy bar. "Stop screwin' around," I demanded. He sat there laughing. "Tell me how much is in the bag!"

He picked up a twig and smoothed out an area between our towels and wrote the number in the dirt. He intentionally prolonged the process as he started with a big dollar sign followed by a two, five, two, zero, zero.

"What? Are you tellin' me you think there was twenty-five thousand, two hundred dollars in that bag?" I didn't believe his figures but I was certainly hopeful as well as a little scared.

"Not exactly," he said still smiling and then he laid down on his back and took a bite out of his candy bar. "What I'm sayin' is we each get twenty-five thousand, two hundred dollars."

Before I actually believed him, he repeated the entire process of his calculations and they weren't figures I could argue with. The afternoon was then spent dreaming of what we would be able to buy with the money, once we split it up. We talked about cars, and yachts and maybe even buying a private jet. Our initial dreams of cameras and rifles and such were just buds on a tree. Now we had enough to buy the entire limb or even the whole forest.

It was a figure that required a meeting. Although the papers had said nothing of stolen money, intercepted phone conversations revealed that Provinzini and other bosses were still looking. The thought that we shouldn't spend any of it for at least a month was something we would have to consider.

When Jules and Al and Jamie were given the estimated dollar amount, retrieving the money became an even bigger issue. All we talked about was the stuff we were going to buy and how much of our shares we would put away for sports cars and motorcycles when we got a license. Al wanted to get a car immediately.

"I'll just have it delivered and park it in the driveway so I can sit in it. I can still start it up and listen to the radio and stuff," he argued. "Or, I could probably buy a tank if I wanted to."

When I wasn't with The Five-Cent Gang dreaming about the money, I spent my time with Mr. Faulk. He not only provided a needed break from the pressure of getting the money and splitting it up, but time in the yard provided opportunities to check on the bootlegger's hole. Mr. Faulk's love of the Baldwin made the task easier. On days when yard work was slow, he spent time working on the antique steamer and I was his willing assistant. On more than one occasion I took time to slide open the door of the secret compartment and reach inside to feel the pocketbooks.

As days grew into weeks, questions to my grandfather revealed that the railroad didn't seem to have any immediate plans for the engine and within those weeks, she was shined and polished from top to bottom. While we made restorations, I learned more about the antique locomotive than I ever learned about the diesels. Each lesson coincided with the area we brought back to its original condition. Occasionally my grandfather stopped by to make an inspection. Some comments were not encouraging as he warned Mr. Faulk about the pitfall of getting too attached.

"You're going to get her lookin' like new and then they'll take her away from here," he warned with a laugh.

Mr. Faulk also laughed at that notion, telling me, "I don't think anyone even knows the old gal is here."

I was convinced Mr. Faulk had the upper hand when it came to the Baldwin and the disposition of the antique was the least of my worries. It was the excuse I needed, however, to call a meeting and set a plan to get the bags out of the bootlegger's hole and split up the money. If, for no other reason, we could all go our own ways and Mr. Faulk would be out of any involvement.

Chapter Thirteen

The ledgers that contained incriminating information on Provinzini and other crime bosses remained under Dusty's watchful eye. Once they were hidden in his room, he confessed to me he intended all along to turn them over to his father.

"I didn't like the bridge plan from the beginning," he told me. "We got the information from listening in on my father's meeting. I felt like I was sorta cheating on him. I figured if we got the bag it would be okay to split up the money but if I could get the books for him it might make up for stuff."

Although his rationale made sense to me, I knew the others would be dead against it. That thought came to fruition when he presented his plan to drive by the rear of the police station where his father parked his car and toss the books inside. Jamie immediately rejected the idea.

"If somebody sees you we're all screwed," he told him.

"No way. If I'm seen in the area, I'll have the excuse that I'm there to see my father. I even put a library book in the back seat so I can say I needed to get my book out of the car. It'll be the perfect excuse if anyone sees me," Dusty persisted. "And don't forget, I hang out at the station as much as Auggie hangs out at the railroad yard. Nobody's gonna think anything of me being there."

The others still didn't buy it.

"If something screws up, every one of us will have his ass in a jam," Jamie countered. "All it takes is one little slip."

"Yeah, maybe we should vote on it," Al suggested.

"There's no voting on this." Dusty shouted back with adamancy. "None of us would have any money to spend on anything if it wasn't for listening in on my father's meeting. Now he could lose his job because his whole plan got messed up. If he doesn't get the ledgers then I may have to tell him the whole story."

This threat put an end to the discussion. Everybody sensed the finality of Dusty's tone and his determination to return the ledgers.

Surprisingly, the plan worked easier than either Dusty or I imagined. On the day of the delivery, I went with him in the event he needed a lookout. We circled our bikes behind the police station and saw that his father had left the front window down. We never even parked the bikes. We rode by and Dusty tossed the books inside and they landed on the driver's seat. It couldn't have gone any smoother. The books were tied together and, at Jamie's insistence, had been wiped clean of any fingerprints.

Dusty had been right. The ledgers turned out to be of great value to his father and the Waterton Police Department. During the weeks that followed, arrests were made. Charges were brought against Provinzini and several other crime bosses up and down the east coast. We followed the reports in the local newspapers and evening broadcasts. Some stations tried to link the arrests with the recent murder of the local enforcer, the 'Riverbank Slaying' they called it. Mr. Barnes became somewhat of a local celebrity and Dusty's guilt about eavesdropping seemed to dissipate with his father's redemption.

Only bits and pieces of information remained available to us on the extension line. The task force had been decommissioned and Mr. Barnes no longer had an agent relaying information from the inside. One thing the informant did tell Dusty's father during his last phone call was that there were others out there that the information provided by the ledgers failed to net during the arrests. It was a statement we would not forget.

"These guys know the money is still out there somewhere," the agent told Mr. Barnes. "And they're not going to stop looking for it until they get it—and the guys who took it. From what I understand there was a lot more money with the books than we anticipated. Seems like it came in from all over the East Coast for their annual laundering party. I don't think whoever has it will stay healthy very long."

That conversation necessitated another meeting and because the turrets continued to feel cramped, we agreed to meet in the beehive. The summer was about over and the plan was to get the money during Labor Day weekend. It would be another midnight raid and moving all the bags from the Baldwin required either one trip by all of us or several trips by a few.

"The more trips we make, the more chances of getting caught," Jules pointed out.

Jamie offered to make a plan but with the recent coolness of the group in their feelings toward each other, it was said with more nonchalance than his former attitude of assertiveness.

"I don't think we need to make a big deal out of it," Jules continued. "We don't need any more charts and drawings." He looked at Jamie as he made the comment. "We'll just pick a night and all go over and get the bags. We can bring 'em here. We'll make sure it's a night my mom is working. We can either count it and split it up then or wait and do it the next day. If we get the bags on Friday night, we can do stuff on Saturday morning when she goes to the Laundromat."

"I'll check on the moon," I volunteered, remembering the fiasco at the arsenal. "Hopefully it'll be dark out that weekend."

The talk then turned to the money and Dusty took over the discussion. "If the calculations I did were even near being correct, we're gonna have more money than we know what to do with," Dusty reminded everyone. "Even though we have it, we need to agree on how we're gonna spend it. The agent on the phone wasn't bullshitting when he told my father the guys are still lookin' for it. Bein' kids, they won't suspect us, but we have to be cool about it."

"Dusty's right," Jules confirmed. "We should all pick just one thing we really want that's not too expensive and get that. Stash the rest. Maybe every couple of months we can buy something and just keep sayin' it's from money we made mowin' lawns and stuff."

"I'm gettin' a shotgun then," Al informed the group.

"Yeah, well that's all you're gettin' for now," Jules told him. "I'll hold on to the rest of both our shares."

For the moment, Al seemed content with the knowledge that he would get a shotgun. Dusty had already confided that he was getting Silly the green bike she dreamed of and I had my eye on a new .22 rifle. Jules was noncommittal and said nothing while all the time he thought about the down payment for the washer and dryer. He was smart enough to know if he gave Mr. Billings all the money at once it might look suspicious.

Jamie's idea was to make us all famous. "I'm gonna get a movie camera. We can dress up and make a gangster movie."

We sat and prioritized the things we were going to buy. We were about to get thousands of dollars each and we had a lifetime ahead of us to spend it if we were careful. Until then, the only decision for each of us to make was where we would hide our own share of the money.

Whatever our plans were, they were interrupted by Al's constant concern. "What are we gonna do with the fat man's gun?"

"We're not gonna do anything with it," Jules told his brother. "I'll get rid of it myself."

This decision by Jules without any type of discussion or vote triggered more questions from the rest of us.

"What are you planning to do with it?" Jamie asked him.

"Figure I'll throw it in the Hudson. Maybe take it apart first and throw it in a few different places."

"What about firing it? We've still got the bullets and everything. We should take it to the woods and shoot it off. We've still got the five bullets. We could each shoot it once." Al's suggestion seemed to appeal to Dusty and Jamie. I had had enough of the gun and didn't really care if I got to shoot it again.

"Not a bad idea," Jamie chimed in. "We could go to the woods, shoot it off, and then you could get rid of it. We'll have to wipe it clean, even if it goes in the Hudson. I'm not so sure even the water will wash off the fingerprints if the cops ever find it."

"I didn't figure we'd all be involved in getting rid of it," Jules told us. "It might look bad if someone spots a bunch of kids throwing something into the river."

Surprisingly, Dusty was in agreement with Al and Jamie and without the formality of a vote, Jules put the bullets into his pocket, tucked the revolver into his belt and we were off to fire our prized possession.

Once we were on the path surrounded by a high growth of weeds and trees, Al started bugging Jules to let him carry the gun. We stopped at a decaying cement bridge where we often stood to fire our .22s. The overpass was more of a passageway to allow some of the local farmers to drive their tractors over the creek to tend to their gardens. There were a few logs a short distance away and they were a convenient place to put bottles or cans. While Dusty and I looked around for some targets, Al got the bullets from Jules and loaded the pistol.

"I'm puttin' the empty cartridge in from the bullet Auggie shot," he told Jules. "You know, for safety, just like Dusty's father told us."

The comment was made more for proving Jules had made the best choice of who should load the gun rather than any idea of being safety conscious. As Mr. Barnes had pointed out, it only prevented the gun from going off if it was accidentally dropped on the ground.

Feeling it was safe, Al started waving it around in the air as if he was shooting invisible bad guys until Jules told him to stop messing around with it or he'd wind up shooting somebody. As the warning left Jules's mouth, Al pulled the trigger not realizing the cylinder would rotate and the hammer would fall onto a live cartridge. The revolver discharged with a loud bang and in much the same way it had leaped from my hand when I fired it on the train, it seemed to jump from Al's hand and fell to the ground.

We all turned and everyone's eyes fell on Jules who was standing where the gun had been pointed. His red T-shirt became darker and his face paled as he reached down to feel for the blood that soaked his chest. Al remained frozen with fear and the shock of what he'd done.

Jules, who had felt no pain from the bullet, took a reluctant glance downward to assess his wound. It was then he saw the bullet hole in the canteen at his side and realized the fluid soaking his shirt was from the steady stream of water squirting out of it.

"You asshole!" he yelled as he picked up the gun. "This is exactly why I have to watch over you every freakin' minute. I told you to stop waving it around." We all knew if the shot had been fired by anyone else, Jules would've most likely thrown them into the creek.

Al stood speechless and we all eyeballed the canteen, still oozing water until Jules ripped it off his shoulder and threw it into the woods.

Whether he was the least concerned or wanting to break the tension of the moment, Jamie spoke first. "That was your bullet, man," he yelled at Al. "You fired it and that's it. You don't get another turn. There're only four shots left."

Dusty started to say something to agree that the shot was Al's turn with the gun when the air was shattered with four loud explosions. When we turned, we all witnessed the last of the four bullets hitting the water, sending small droplets high into the air as they pierced the surface.

"That's it," Jules yelled. "The gun's empty. The bullets are all used up and I'll get rid of this thing tomorrow. Is everybody happy now?"

Most of the walk home was done in silence. And, presumably, on the following day, Jules threw the gun in the Hudson. We never saw it again...and we never asked.

Chapter Fourteen

On the Wednesday before Labor Day weekend, I made a visit to the Baldwin. I arrived at the yard early in the afternoon to check on the pocketbooks before Mr. Faulk arrived. My presence around the old steam engine was now so common it brought little attention. To my surprise, Mr. Faulk was in the office with my grandfather and several workers were milling around outside. It was much the same scene as the day the two men argued over the number change which, by my calculations, had never resulted in a curse to anyone or any shower of bad luck.

When I got closer to the office, the similarity to the argument regarding the change of an engine number became more apparent. Mr. Faulk and my grandfather were going at it again only this time, to my surprise, my grandfather was uncharacteristically raising his voice in response to Mr. Faulk's tone.

"No right!" I heard Mr. Faulk yell. "No damn right whatsoever!"

"It wasn't yours and it never was," my grandfather responded.

"You may want to keep out of the way of this one," Harold told me as I approached. "Your granddad and Ben have been goin' at it now for about fifteen minutes. Prob'ly best to steer clear today." As he made the remark, Mr. Faulk emerged from the office pushing so hard against the screen door it swung fully open and slammed against the side of the building. He then stomped down the stairs from the platform.

Unlike the scene I'd witnessed several weeks earlier, this time there appeared to be more involved than a number change on one of the diesels. Mr. Faulk glanced toward me but said nothing. When he passed, he grabbed me by the arm and half dragged me along with him. After taking a few steps, he stopped and turned to face my grandfather, who had followed him out of the office and now stood on the platform.

"Ya know John," he said. "I've only got a couple of months left until retirement and I was feelin' kinda bad about that...about leavin' you and the train yard here." As he made the statement he released me and made a sweep of his arm indicating the entire yard. "After today," he continued, "I don't think I'm gonna care much anymore about leavin'. The fun's kinda gone outta this place, if you know what I mean."

Even at my age, I sensed the tension as he spoke the words and I was saddened to see such a disagreement—a disagreement I felt could possibly destroy the long time friendship of two men I felt so close to.

He then returned his gaze to me. "C'mon Auggie, I've got to move the yard goat. You can give me a hand."

"Okay," I told him. "But I was gonna go over and do some polishing on the Baldwin."

"Can't," he yelled. "It's gone. Gone first thing this morning! The railroad decided to get rid of it. Sold it for junk...junk! Do you believe they could do such a thing to me?"

"You mean they're gonna take it out of the yard?"

"Not gonna take it...they already took the darn thing! That's what I'm tryin' to tell ya boy...it's gone. Took it right out from behind my back."

Before my heart sank, my stomach turned. I wanted to believe what he was saying wasn't possible. I had just been there two days ago and worked on it. It was beginning to look like new. How could it be gone? I yanked free of Mr. Faulk and ran to where the Baldwin had been sitting for the past several weeks. The empty space where she had rested was now a void on the tracks and again I felt nauseous. Visions flashed through my brain. The bridge...gunshots...running to the train...the hobo...the fat man, lying rumpled on the rocks...a pool of blood. All of it...over...gone. None of us had anything now. Realizing the emptiness of it all, no more questions to Mr. Faulk seemed necessary. The why or how didn't matter anymore. The Baldwin had been taken to be melted down. Would it be used for spare parts? Would someone find the money? Would finding it lead to The Five-Cent Gang? I searched for a way out. I thought of the fat man and his confrontation with Mr. Faulk. If the money was found, Mr. Faulk might think he was the one who put the money in the Baldwin. It didn't have to lead to us. And in the midst of it all I thought about a critical question the police would ask. If the fat man hid the money in the bootlegger's hole, where did he get a Waterton High School gym bag?

Chapter Fifteen

I was sick to my stomach all the way to the meeting. It was held in the beehive and I struggled for the right words to dispense the news of the Baldwin's disappearance. None came. To accommodate Jules's football schedule I called everybody and scheduled it for the afternoon.

I wanted the meeting to be brief and when I made the phone calls to everyone, made no mention regarding the events surrounding the sale of the Baldwin. I knew any information in advance would generate immediate questions and addressing the group of four would be easier than separate phone conversations.

Relationships in The Five-Cent Gang were already strained from recent disagreements and my deliverance of the bad news sent it to a feverish pitch. I kept it simple, knowing the hollering to follow would take care of the rest. "The Baldwin's gone," I told them.

"Whaddaya mean gone?" Jamie yelled out.

"I mean gone. As in the D&H sold it and they moved it out of the yard last night. I went over to make a final check on the money before we moved it this weekend and it wasn't there. Mr. Faulk told me they shipped it out for scrap."

At first a silence hung in the air as the news provided each of them with individual thoughts and disappointments. There would be no shotgun for Al, Dusty wouldn't be purchasing the bike for Silly, the washer and dryer for Jules's mother, Jamie's camera, and my .22. Everything was gone. The expected hollering finally broke the silence. Al did most of the yelling but he seemed to be more upset over the loss of his purchasing power for the shotgun. He hadn't quite grasped the entire picture regarding the loss of the money.

Once the initial shock subsided, the questions began to flow. "Where exactly did they move it to?" was the first question from Jules. It was asked in his usual calm tone after a lengthy deliberation of silence, as if he felt the question would provide some form of hope; the money in the Baldwin was still retrievable.

"All I know is Mr. Faulk said it was coupled to a train going to Philadelphia and from there it could go anywhere. He seemed to think that whatever they were going to do with it had already been done. He said they would more than likely take off whatever parts they wanted and then melt down the rest of it."

Jamie paced the floor of the beehive while he looked up and yelled curses at whatever part of the ceiling happened to be above him.

Dusty asked another hopeful question. "Are you sure he's not just tricking you because he knows you like the old steam engine?" His question was sincere enough but I knew that kind of a trick wasn't something Mr. Faulk would pull. It wasn't his style of humor.

"It's gone," I assured him. "It and the money."

The remainder of the day was spent in a wide variety of depressive moods. Our misfortune included brooding over the many hours of planning, the narrow escape from death, and now living with fears and worries about the cops figuring it all out. And even worse, we knew that could lead the men who were looking for us to actually finding us. We had a lot more to worry about than just losing the money.

Chapter Sixteen

Labor day weekend was solemn. We had not only lost all hope of our riches, but we had to face a strange world on Tuesday when we started our new lives at the Waterton Junior/Senior High School. It turned out to be an event that proved to be more of a nightmare than we had imagined. When the four us entered that first day, we were joined by former sixth graders from all five elementary schools in Waterton— a melting pot of kids who would be bound together for the next six years. Hundreds of us were herded into the auditorium and were met by two teachers who barked orders. They directed us to the front rows and told us to sit and be quiet.

Eventually, a woman who failed to introduce herself stood on the big stage, which, except for the lone microphone was completely barren. The auditorium smelled of summer air that was hot and stale. The worn cushioned seats were ripped and small holes were made larger as kids picked at the padding, pulled out wads of the itchy stuffing, and shoved them down the backs of friends who were sitting in front of them. The unidentified woman wasted no time in getting the chaos underway. Between squeaks and squawks from the microphone, she informed us that she would read a list of names. These groupings were what she termed homeroom assignments and at the conclusion of each list, those students called were to meet in the rear of the auditorium. We were then given schedules and as I looked at the kids in my assigned group, I realized I would never see any of The Five-Cent Gang again.

The seated herd dwindled as students were grouped and taken away by teachers wearing questionable smiles. I watched as Al and Dusty and Jamie left one by one with their individual homerooms. Al, in particular, had a look of despair as he joined his group and they paraded out through the huge double doors that led to the hallway. This process, later explained by the teachers, allowed us to meet students from other schools and learn to work as one big team. In that first hour in our new home we were thrown in with a mixed bag of uptown kids. Each time I entered a new class I scanned the room in search of Al or Dusty. Even seeing Jamie would've been a comfort. The few familiar faces from PS Number One were those of kids who weren't actually kids I'd ever spent any time with. I needed to see the faces of The Five-Cent Gang. The information Jules had given us over the summer had seemed superficial compared to the actual rude awakening.

The school was a three-story structure and our seventh-and eighth-grade rooms were housed in the basement. Each room had one small window near the top of the outside wall. Only students seated near the wall would benefit from any daylight that might seep in through the bar-covered concrete enclosure, the top of which was at ground level. Every teacher seated us alphabetically so even that possibility was eliminated for me.

Once the daily routine got underway, I rarely saw any of The Five-Cent Gang. Other than Dusty and I having gym class together twice a week, we only saw each other during lunch. Even then, one of us would be forced to sneak to the other's table. Homeroom groups had assigned areas and were forced to sit together. Cafeteria monitors prowled the lunchroom with clip boards and whistles. I rarely saw Al and never ran into Jamie. When I did see Al, it was the only time during the day when our paths crossed—en route to fourth period. I was on my way to science class while he headed to math. We routinely passed each other notes like spies exchanging covert information that identified our feelings about the school. Things like "this school sucks" and "how long until we graduate?" Sometimes he would cut his own lunch period and eat with Dusty and me and on those days his note would read "see you at the feeding trough." Even those notes failed to reflect his old form of humor like our days together in School One. Nothing about Al seemed the same since the incident on the bridge. Actually, all of us had changed...but Al seemed to take it more to heart and his mind was often somewhere else. Even during the occasions when he ate lunch with us he never said very much and there was an obvious void where his sense of humor had been.

The schoolwork they threw at us was unfamiliar and difficult. Every day we were inundated with questions about things completely foreign to kids from School One. English teachers asked whether verbs were transitive or intransitive and math teachers used letters instead of numbers.

Kids from the uptown schools seemed to know one verb from another and they accepted letters in the arithmetic classes as commonplace. Learning in School One had been limited to reading, writing, and the normal types of arithmetic. We may not have known much about this new stuff, but no one could out spell us nor was anyone faster with long division.

Unfortunately, I never recognized any useful correlation between the amount of time spent on the learning of long division and the actual amount of time spent in its use.

Even the ride to and from school was like a bus ride to hell. Not having school buses like other cities, Waterton made arrangements with the city bus company, and three buses were put on a special route to the junior-senior high school. We had to pay to ride and used our tokens to board buses that were overcrowded. Layers of smoke from the cigarettes of upperclassmen filled the buses as drivers ignored the no-smoking signs, most being too scared to try and stop any breaking of the rules. Kids who smoked were the same ones who laid claim to seats in the rear of the bus and expected to be treated as royalty. From the moment we rolled out of bed until late at night, when the new phenomenon of homework was completed, the entire day was an ordeal of horrific proportions.

When Dusty and I discovered that naming verbs and diagramming sentences wasn't our niche in life, we avoided looking stupid when called on by teachers by giving clever or comical answers. We obtained reputations as class clowns and would-be troublemakers and spent more time than necessary in the office and in the after-school detention room.

None of us ever got to see Jules, who continued to be occupied with after-school football practices and Saturday games, although he didn't seem to mind. His prowess on the field combined with his good looks and congenial personality caused his popularity to soar. When he wasn't playing football, he was surrounded by teammates and cheerleaders.

And so it went. The stage had been set. Our departure from PS Number One, which coincided with the failure of the D&H Bridge Caper, was the beginning of the end of The Five-Cent Gang. With the absence of daily contact, we fell into our own routines. It was only Dusty and me who remained close and it was only during our quiet moments together that we discussed the bridge or the demise of the fat man—the common bond between us.

The days dragged on as each of us struggled with strangers sitting next to us, work we couldn't absorb, and more teachers in a single day than we had had during our entire time in School One.

Jules had managed to scrape together the down payment for the used washer and dryer, but with afternoons devoted to football practice rather than lawn mowings, he slipped behind in his payments. The machines had also seen a constant need for maintenance and spare parts and, Mr. Billings, perhaps feeling somewhat obligated to make amends, offered Jules part-time work in the store.

Jamie, who had always been a good ball player, made the basketball team and coaches for the high school squad drooled as they eyed the future. Even in grade seven, he showed promise to be the best ball handler the school had seen in many years. Dusty and I also made the team, which allowed us to have front row seats on the bench as we cheered for Jamie.

Al, the odd man out, gave the debate team a go only to find his style of questioning and lack of patience was too argumentative. Complaints from teammates and his failure to adopt the advisor's strategies caused him to lose interest and he left the team. Rumor had it that the coach encouraged his leaving. He then began to spend more time alone than was probably healthy.

By the time our second year rolled around, Dusty and I had become friendly with the guidance counselor and managed similar schedules. With the exception of woodworking class that rotated with study hall, Miss Colton had kept us together. She was an older woman with all the motherly attributes of a teacher in PS Number One and when time permitted, we hung out in her office and made small talk.

＊　＊　＊　＊　＊

AFTER OUR SOPHOMORE YEAR, Jamie moved to Boston. There were no parties or parades sponsored by any of the gang, but his departure was a great disappointment to the basketball coach who had already moved him up from junior varsity to varsity. Although our friendship had cooled over the years we said our goodbyes and promised to keep in touch. It was one of those promises that kids make that are sincere at the time but have a weak follow-through— the kind of promise you make after two weeks at summer camp and everyone says they're your best friend and they're going to write every week. After he moved, we exchanged a total of two letters. The one I received from him listed a phone number that I carefully tucked away in the box containing my baseball cards and the other was my response to let him know that school still sucked and he wasn't missing anything.

Dusty and I made occasional visits to The Pit, usually on Saturdays. From what we could tell from our visits, Eddie was still making book and if anyone was searching for the money, it didn't seem we were suspect in any way. As we progressed through school, there were times when older kids bullied the vulnerable and thought they were tough, times when I wanted to step in and say "Yeah? Did you ever kill anybody? 'Cause I did!" But I kept my mouth shut. We all did. We kept our mouths shut and lived with it.

Chapter Seventeen

Before Jamie arrived in Boston, his parents had laid the groundwork regarding his education. His mother, having had enough of public schools, initiated a chain reaction when she instructed his father to encourage his current coach to contact his future coach who contacted the school administrator and the wheels were set spinning. With that done, Jamie's arrival was most welcomed at St. Mary's by Irwin Shoemaker who had been the instigating leg of the phone chain. Irwin held the prestigious title of varsity basketball coach. His follow-up investigation confirmed that Jamie was the player he needed to replace his premier guard whom he had lost to graduation.

Other than confirming Jamie's basketball skills, neither the coach nor the administrator undertook any further vetting process. There was never a mention regarding his disciplinary record prior to his arrival nor would they have shown much concern regarding the third-grade groping of an eighth grader's breast if there had been. Even Jamie had come to realize that an incident that occurred in elementary school lost its punch over the years and the overused and threatening phrase of 'permanent record' wasn't as permanent as everybody thought it was.

His proficiency at the guard position coupled with an already well-established team allowed him to fill the vacancy needed by Coach Shoemaker. Simultaneously, Jamie's desire for a sense of belonging, partially due to the absence of The Five-Cent Gang, was also filled.

The gradual change in his behavior had started in Waterton when, to play ball, he had been forced into an academic standard to remain what the school termed player eligible. During his freshman year his natural ability gave the coach the foresight to have him dress for varsity home games. His playing time mounted and allowed him to gain the experience needed for the next level. In his sophomore year, he was given a permanent position on the varsity and by mid-season, he was a starter. He proved to be a court general who was blessed with both natural ball-handling ability and a deadly outside shot. His move to Boston at the start of his junior year was welcomed by the new school, and at St. Mary's he found a home. The years added some height and he stood just under six feet. His good looks and strong features remained and, like Jules, the combination of charm and athletic ability brought great popularity with his classmates, especially the girls.

With his clean slate, he toed the line at St. Mary's and dismissed the antics of former heroes like James Cagney and Edward G. Robinson. Although the failure of the D&H Bridge Caper, along with the deaths that followed was in the distant past, the incident had left a bad scar regarding any idea of 'capers.' His new set of peers would've no doubt dubbed that kind of behavior as reckless...even juvenile, which left Jamie to become the consummate athlete. In addition to his natural ability with a basketball, he was an elusive running back on the football team and one of the best shortstops the school had seen in many years.

Living his new life, he was surprised when, not too long after his arrival, he was summoned to Father MacNamara's office, which was housed in the parish church. He had never met Father MacNamara and things had been going well but during his walk to the office, the old fear of the permanent record syndrome crept into his thoughts. He had only been to one Sunday service since his arrival and the mass had been given by a priest from another parish as part of a Catholic exercise they referred to as community rotation. Not knowing exactly where the office was located, he went to the door of the church, which he found to be unlocked. When he entered, it seemed to be a much different venue from his one-time Sunday visit. The interior stood in a dim nakedness. It was a much larger church than the one he left in Waterton and, as he stood waiting for his eyes to adjust from the brightness of the sunlight he'd left outside, he breathed in the smell of old wood and studied the interior with more scrutiny than his previous visit had allowed.

The tops of the pew rows rippled on both sides as they cascaded from the rear of the church toward the altar. They seemed to be never ending and the two sides cradled a center aisle, adorned with an intricately designed carpet. The aisle was long, and seemed to narrow as it neared the altar. Jamie studied its appearance. The aisle to the altar resembled a path to the gas chamber or perhaps the path an outlaw of the old West walked to the gallows. The carpet seemed to narrow, and the paralleled benches seemed to draw themselves together as the progression moved forward. For a brief moment, he recalled the view of the railroad tracks as The Five-Cent Gang waited for the train that flattened their pennies. In fact, feeling the coin under his shirt, secured by a silver chain, that had long ago replaced the worn twine, gave him a lift of courage. Like other memories, it came and went with the circumstances.

The light flowed in soft rays from the meticulously placed, five-tiered chandeliers that hung like illuminated grapes over the pews on both sides—chandeliers that had been placed according to the plans of an architect many years ago. They were not as bright as they were during his attendance at mass, not as bright as needed on Sundays to allow the congregation to view the words on the pages of the hymnals—the congregation of older, bi-focaled people.

The area where Jamie stood was the space where binoculars might be necessary to see the priest clearly on a given Sunday. It was the preferred pew for his own seating. As he absorbed the interior and all its beauty, the opening of a distant door broke the silence. Such was the echo that it was difficult to decipher the direction the sound had come from. First the agony of the hinge as the door opened and closed followed by the distinct clicking of the heavy latch. They were sounds that went unheard when parishioners were present and made the slightest stirrings in their seats. The clicking was replaced with the shuffling of feet until Jamie noticed a small figure of a man appearing near the altar.

He genuflected and then turned and walked toward Jamie. His hunched frame, draped in his cassock, was silhouetted against the stained glass above the altar behind him. The priest glued his gaze to Jamie and walked the entire length of the aisle before Jamie realized he could've made the priest's journey a bit shorter if he'd met him half-way. A step before reaching him, the priest extended his hand.

"You must be the Jamie lad," he greeted. His grasp was weak, Jamie thought, but the tone of his voice seemed young and friendly, betraying his age and frail appearance.

"Yes, I am. And you're Father MacNamara?"

"Oh no," the priest responded almost apologetically. "I'll be happy to serve as your guide and take you to him though. Finding your way in this maze is somewhat difficult for people who don't quite know where the good Lord put all the doors and exits and whatnot. Sometimes I wonder if God confuses us in His house so we can't find our way out," and then after hesitating added, "or perhaps he doesn't want some of us to find him when our time comes." He again sounded apologetic as he waved his arm in a small sweep to indicate the vastness of the church.

"I'm surprised you heard me come in," Jamie told him, as if seeing some need to make conversation.

"Oh, I didn't," the priest responded, and then stopped talking with no further explanation as to how or why he happened to enter the church. He led Jamie down the center aisle toward the altar and stopped once again and genuflected. He then rose and walked to the door of his original entry. He seemed to have a rather apathetic attitude regarding Jamie's adherence toward the reverence of ceremony and spent no effort in turning to witness his guest's action at the altar.

Jamie was just Catholic enough to follow suit and genuflected before following the priest to the door. As the priest passed through he made no effort to hold the door and the hinges that had given a forewarning earlier creaked again. Jamie was forced to move quickly and reached for the door to prevent its closing as he followed the priest into a long hallway. It was an interior walkway, the length allowing for a pew on each side that mirrored each other. Compared with those in the church, these were much longer and evidenced the painstaking intricacies of workmanship as they sat with their ornate backs against the wall.

Jamie trailed behind the swishing cassock as he admired the beauty of the hallway and its tunnel-like appearance. The bottom half of the walls behind the benches was fashioned with inlaid panels secured by hand-hewn stiles and topped with intricately cut chair rails. The walls then curved upward and were filled with stain glass murals illuminated by the streaming sunlight that brought their images to life. The vaulted ceiling was accentuated with thick beams—beams that were so enormous and straight, that they underscored the impression that the building of the church could only have been done in another lifetime. Beams like these were certainly unobtainable in modern construction.

The thirty-foot hallway seemed to stop at the far end where a single step led to a much smaller altar than the one in the church. The raised platform held a chair and a small desk, the top of which was covered with a velvet cloth, evenly draped over the ends. A large book, presumably a Bible, rested on the table and was opened to possibly display a passage of great importance. A brass candleholder sat beside the book on its left, within which were the remains of a candle with a blackened wick. On the right side, an inkwell coupled with a quill indicated its use by a priest who might have sat and calligraphied his thoughts, as did priests of earlier centuries.

The altar did not end their walk, however, and the old priest turned at its base and took a few steps to another entryway. This time, he held the door and, with a gesture of his arm, motioned Jamie inside.

It was only when the two of them were in the office, the priest spoke again.

"It seems Father MacNamara isn't back yet," he explained. "He went outside earlier...wanted to plant some bulbs before the fall frost settles in. He'll be wanting his tulips around the parish come springtime, don't ya know." His tone was once again as friendly as his initial greeting and Jamie felt a bit more at ease.

"You should have a seat here," he motioned. "I'm sure Father MacNamara will be back shortly." And after a pause, lifted his index finger in the air and added, "I'll go out and see if I can find him and put a little push to his derriere." As he made the statement, he put his hand on his own behind and demonstrated by pushing himself toward the door that evidently led to the courtyard. As he reached for it he turned to face Jamie once again.

"Did I ever introduce myself?" he asked. And before Jamie could answer, he continued. "Probably not," he said. "It's that old age thing you know? Didn't mean to be rude." He then started to go to the door, still giving no introduction and stopped again leading Jamie to believe his name was finally coming. "And you shouldn't believe any tall tales about me that Father MacNamara may tell you." And then he left.

Once alone, Jamie surveyed the room. Unlike the church and the hallway, this area was more modern. The bookcases that lined the walls supported sets of books that leaned in disarray. Some were near their falling point, as if the last reader had failed to return them properly to their assigned places on the shelves. Others had folded papers stuck within them, which protruded from the tops. A variety of knick-knacks was scattered to seemingly add a touch of home while serving as weighted bookends. The center of the room held an oversized desk, the top of which was smothered by piles of books and papers, mimicking the disorganization of the shelves. Short intervals of wall space held evidence of past years. Artifacts, diplomas, and ornately framed pictures—mostly of priests were askew and arranged in no particular order. Most of the photos had one face in common, a priest who stood smiling for the photographer. He was either shaking hands with another diocesan leader or a layperson, seemingly a public figure. The largest picture in the office hung behind the desk beside a crucifix and depicted the same priest shaking hands with President Kennedy. More impressive to Jamie was the picture that caused him to leave his chair and get a closer look. It was a photograph of the priest shaking hands with Carl Yastrzemski. In the lower right hand-corner of the picture was the inscription:

Father Mac,
Thanks for all your help...
Yaz!

This notation confirmed Jamie's belief that the priest pictured in each of the photos was Father MacNamara.

It was several minutes of staring at the photo of Yaz and the priest standing on home plate at Fenway before the door from the courtyard opened. Jamie turned to receive a cordial greeting. The man entering was dressed in khaki pants and a flannel shirt. He stole a second glance at the photo to confirm the man entering was indeed the priest he had been summoned to meet.

"So you're Jamie McGuire," the man in khakis started out. "And how are you getting along here at St. Mary's?" he wanted to know. As he asked the question he extended his hand. "Father MacNamara," he stated with authority.

Jamie's confused expression caused the priest to look at himself and he motioned to his attire with his hand.

"Oh, my appearance is not what you quite expected," and before Jamie uttered a word, he continued as he took a seat at the big desk. "I was just doing some yard work out back so I'm a bit informal today." His demeanor was warm and emitted an air of trust. Jamie thought if he was anything like the priests he usually encountered, he was doing a good job of hiding it. Father MacNamara had caught Jamie so off guard the question was restated. "So, things are going okay?" he inquired again.

"Yeah, okay," Jamie told him. "Things are okay."

"Coach Shoemaker tells me you arrived just in time to fill in for us at the starting guard position. A position we were a bit worried about I might add. The fact that you're an Irish lad warms me heart," he continued, adding a bit of a brogue. "Between you and me, the coach is much pleased with your relocation to Boston."

"Yeah, well one of the things I knew I'd miss when we moved here was playing basketball so it seems like a good fit for me too. Timing seemed to go right all the way around." As Jamie responded he knew he was talking too much and giving out too much information. He needed to give the priest short answers to specific questions. Find out what he wanted to know and why he'd been called there and then be on his way.

"I'm sorry to bring you out on a Saturday, but actually it's your basketball skills that are the cause for me asking you to stop by." As he spoke, he looked at his watch and followed the action by glancing at the clock mounted between two of the bookcases. It was as if he was checking them for synchronization. "I have a minor problem and thought you might be able to help me out a bit. But before I tell you what's what here, I think the best way to explain is for both of us to sit here for a few minutes. We'll have to be quiet though. Think you can humor me?"

"Just sit here you mean? And not say anything? Yeah, I guess I can do that."

For a little over two minutes the ticking of the wall clock produced the only sound in the study. Jamie grew restless and Father MacNamara intermittently glanced at his watch. Jamie then heard a noise coming from what seemed to be an area below them.

"Ah, like clockwork," Father MacNamara whispered as he lifted his arm and used his index finger to tap the face of his watch. "It's the boys from down the street, Jamie. Give a listen now. See if you can decipher what they're up to."

The two sat in silence once again as the noises continued from beneath the floor. The priest pointed to his watch. He then caught Jamie's eye and pointed to his desk calendar that sat amidst the clutter and continued in his whisper. "Once the weather turns cold, they come every Saturday at this time. There's five or six of 'em. They break in through a loose window down there in the basement." As he made the statement, Jamie heard a louder noise.

"There," the priest announced as if to prove himself right. "That's them opening the window; it's got a broken clasp on the inside and they push it open. Now listen."

He continued to speak in his loud whisper, and rose from the desk to act out each scene that transpired below them.

"Once they get through the window it's a fair drop to the floor but they always seem to make it without killing themselves." He paused and waited for several resounding thuds to hit the floor before continuing. "Then...after about an hour or so they leave through the back door and go around the side of the building and put the window back in place so it doesn't get noticed. I guess they figure if we know it's broken we might fix it you see."

"If they're breakin' in, why don't you just call the cops?"

The priest continued as if Jamie's question had gone unheard. "Listen now," he said as he tilted an ear toward the floor. He acted as if this motion would assist him in hearing more of what was going on. The next few sounds were unmistakable to Jamie. The bouncing of a basketball mixed with the familiar squeaking of sneakers on a hardwood floor.

"The gymnasium's right below us," Father MacNamara whispered with a smile. "They'll play ball for a while and then steal sodas from the machine in the hallway. They're quite ingenious, too. It's one of those machines that has the bottles laying horizontal...you know, the kind you put the money in and pull the bottle straight out. Anyway, what they do is, they go into the kitchen and get some cups and a bottle opener and take the darn tops off the bottles. The soda runs right out into the cups. They get most of the soda out that way too." The priest's words almost seemed to have a ring of admiration for the thieves.

Jamie began to get a bad feeling that he was going to be asked to catch these guys in the act. As if things had come full circle and he would now be the one to interrupt a caper of other kids. His immediate thought was to make the first move and avoid any self-involved policing. "If you know they're coming every week and they're breakin' in and stealing stuff, why don't you seal up the window or just go down there and catch them in the act?"

"Well, ya see Jamie...that's just the thing. You have to understand, that when these kids break in here, I know exactly where they are and what they're doing. Out there on the street, I have no idea what trouble they could be getting themselves into. I'm afraid if I told them they were welcome to come in and use the gym it would spoil their fun. And then there's the red tape of insurance if anything happens to them and, the short of it is, I don't want to end it. I want to organize it—and that's where you come in."

"Whaddaya mean where I come in?"

"These boys are pretty good ball players, but it's all street ball for these kids. They're seventh and eighth graders mostly. Some will try out for the freshman team next year. A couple might even make it, but most won't. But, for those that don't, it won't be because of a lack of skills; it'll be for a lack of coaching and a lack of discipline on the court. They need to be taught how to take what they've got and be part of a team. I've watched them on the playground. I can tell you right now, every player down there is a one-man show. There's no teamwork, just every man for himself. Why I've seen hard fouls delivered on the court in my day but these guys—these guys will use an elbow and knock another's teeth out, not to mention the cursing that goes on. How far do you think they'll get playing like that?"

Jamie sat in silence and, having no response, Father MacNamara continued. "And the guys who don't make the team...what do you think they'll be doin' after school gets out? Why they'll be hanging out on street corners or running drugs or, worse yet, using drugs themselves. Now I realize with your background, you never had to worry about such things and never got into any trouble yourself, but ..." the priest's voice trailed off almost as if he knew things about Jamie's past that no one else would know, things no one else had access to.

"And you want me to teach them teamwork?"

"Teamwork, yes, but also the basic fundamentals and etiquette of the game. They'll listen to you, Jamie. We've got no one here at the church that can come close to your skills; the kids are already talking about this year's high school team. You're a known factor to these guys. There must've been someone who gave you a helping hand once...someone who helped you hone your skills in athletics. Maybe now it's your turn to pass that on," he urged.

Actually, there hadn't been anyone in particular that had ever given Jamie a hand, but he let the comment go. Father MacNamara, or Father Mac as he was later instructed to address him, continued as he explained his plan.

"Look, you show up on the playground some afternoon and play a little ball with these guys...you know...just a quick pickup game. Then you nonchalantly suggest they get a team together; you can mention that you'd be willing to talk to me about letting them use the parish gym for weekend practices. Tell them if they're good enough you could probably get them into the church league and play teams from other parishes."

It was a plan that didn't meet with instant rejection, but not a plan that Jamie was exceptionally eager to accept.

When he left the office that morning, one thing was clear—the hand of Father Mac was nothing like the hand of Father O'Brien who ruled St. Basil's and had condemned him to a lifelong label of a breast-grabbing deviant. Actually, Father Mac was not like any priest Jamie had ever talked to and, realizing his only leadership role with peers had simply involved capers, he promised Father Mac he would give it some serious thought. The priest was more optimistic than Jamie regarding the future decision and after Jamie left the office he picked up the phone and called the aging Father Thomas, the priest who had failed to identify himself. The conversation was short but made the aging Father Thomas, who had absolutely no idea of how the game of basketball was played, breathe a huge sigh of relief.

"He said he'll think about it," Father Mac said into the phone. "I think you're off the hook."

❋ ❋ ❋ ❋ ❋

ANOTHER PHONE CALL, UNKNOWN to Jamie, was made later in the day. The call was to Coach Shoemaker, and Father Mac suggested it would be a good thing for the parish and the sanity of Father Thomas if Jamie accepted the challenge of coaching. The coach, a long-time parishioner, pulled Jamie aside after Monday's practice and mentioned that he'd heard about Father Mac's offer.

"Teaching is one of the best ways to learn," he reminded Jamie. "You'd also be doing Father Mac and the entire Catholic organization a favor of which you're now an integral part. It'll be a great service to the church."

Midway through the week, Jamie reluctantly called Father Mac who was delighted to hear that he would take on the challenge.

The priest had been correct in his assessment of the players. The initial practices revealed much talent but little teamwork. Practices were held three nights a week and Saturday mornings. As they progressed under the watchful eye of Father Thomas, who had gladly accepted the demotion to assistant coach and team manager, the team gradually grew stronger. Jamie mirrored the drills and practice format used by Coach Shoemaker and the team of eight took shape, but not without pitfalls. In the beginning, players took shortcuts, or ignored the plays all together. Cursing was rampant and elbows continued to be thrown. On two occasions, Father Mac approached Jamie with information regarding complaints about team members not doing well with their schoolwork.

"I can't be their tutor as well," Jamie told Father Mac. "I'm having enough trouble getting them to learn the plays!"

During discussions, Father Mac pointed out that patience was required and perhaps the use of different methods. Jamie began to realize that his team was cut out more for capers and often spent time thinking about what he could've accomplished if he had them with him in the old days.

There were only five teams in the church league and after playing each team twice, the record for St. Mary's Parish stood at three wins and five losses. The last game of the season found Jamie coaching only five of his eight players. Two others were serving a Saturday detention and a third was thrown out of the game in the first quarter for giving the ref the finger.

But Coach Shoemaker had been right. Jamie had learned a lot from the coaching experience and much of it was about himself. He learned leading people in ventures other than capers—worthwhile ventures— could be rewarding, even if the road was a bit difficult. When the season ended, the praise from Father Mac was genuine and the proof continued when the following fall rolled around and all three of his eighth-grade players made the freshman team.

"Others will come now," Father Mac told Jamie. "I'll bet you'll have a whole roster. You'll be turning them away."

The thought of a second year of coaching didn't sit well. Jamie had a myriad of things to do as a senior. How could Father Mac even expect such a thing, he wondered? But after receiving a letter of praise at the conclusion of his first coaching season...holding it...reading it...on parish stationery...he learned he had a new friend and confidante in a man he had grown to admire.

Chapter Eighteen

My senior year coincided with two tragedies. Just as celebrations surrounding our upcoming commencement were about to begin, my grandfather suffered a heart attack and died. In mid-June, just two weeks later, Mr. Faulk passed away from the same fate. It was as if the two men were bound together in death, much the same way they had been throughout most of their lives. I was never sure whether it was my closer connection to Mr. Faulk or the combined loss of the two men that caused me to feel a deeper sorrow. The funerals put a heartache on the celebratory times I had planned and, in many cases, I declined invitations to activities associated with graduation.

Dusty and I had been looking forward to our final summer of freedom before going off to college. I would now be leaving with the absence of two people who had played such a huge part in my life and my upbringing. I even considered postponing my departure to sign on as a railroad worker to be close to my grandmother.

But as Dusty's father said on more than one occasion "college may mean more book learnin' but it beats the alternative." His reference was made regarding some of our classmates who had already received draft notices and would soon be off to boot camp—the prerequisite to Viet Nam.

* * * * *

MR. FAULK'S FUNERAL WAS held on a Wednesday. Mourners were plentiful. In addition to his wife with whom he had shared a loving relationship for over fifty years, a large gathering of family and friends shared their grief at the interment. It was certainly no surprise that a good-sized contingent of railroad men stood together at the outer fringe. As I stood with my parents, I returned a grim smile of acknowledgement to Harold and Winks and Binky. Their true identities were somewhat hidden by their formal dress, absence of railroad hats, and manicured appearances. I had a similar experience the night before when I looked at Mr. Faulk in his casket. The lack of his railroad attire combined with his pinkish cheeks and lips made him appear as a stranger. The following afternoon mourners caravanned from the church service and encircled the oak coffin adorned with brass fixtures and numerous bouquets of flowers. The two seemed contradictory. Mr. Faulk would certainly have been more partial to a large brass train whistle. I stared at the tattered D&H railroad cap that had been placed ever so lovingly in the midst of the large spray of flowers that covered the coffin. The spray was comprised of yellow roses and blue forget-me-nots signifying the colors of the Delaware & Hudson.

The absence of my grandfather was a noticeable void to those in attendance. It was at his funeral that I last spoke with Mr. Faulk and we reminisced about the train yard days and the fun we had.

My friend had died in much the same way he had lived. It had been a very quiet and peaceful passing. According to his long-time family physician, his big heart just gave out. I was one person who had grown to know that if anyone had a big heart, it was Benjamin Faulk. A flood of emotion filled me as the minister droned on with phrases and prayers. I felt like my mind was weaving in and out of his verbal fabric. Bits and pieces of what he was saying became intertwined with my own memories that Mr. Faulk and I had shared. Some of the minister's comments evidenced what I already knew about the man while newly shared anecdotes revealed characteristics I had never been privy to. The service concluded with one of the grandchildren providing the soft ringing of a train bell.

Some of his closer friends had been invited to attend a smaller gathering at the Faulk home and since my parents were not going to attend, I caught a ride with Harold. As we left the cemetery, we both heard the low wailing of the 4:37 in the distance and I'm quite sure we both envisioned the afternoon routine we had been part of so many times. I wondered who was driving the yard goat that day. As Harold pulled his car out of the cemetery, we both sat with our silent thoughts.

Once at the Faulk residence, I spent most of the time conversing with old railroad friends. Winks, who had added great width to his waistline over the years, kept a close watch on the buffet table. The homemade dishes prepared by the churchwomen were difficult for him to pass up. None of us from the yard stayed long and after paying my final respects to Mrs. Faulk, Harold drove me home.

* * * * *

IT WAS THE FOLLOWING Saturday that the phone call came. My mother answered and I could tell from listening to her end of the conversation that it was Mrs. Faulk.

"Yes, he's right here, I'll put him on," she said and handed me the phone.

I was both surprised and curious as I greeted her. She was the last person I had expected to hear from.

"Auggie, this is Irene Faulk. I'm sorry I didn't think of this the other day when you were at the house, but Benjamin left a letter here for you. I could've given it to you then but I guess I just had so many things on my mind that..."

"No, that's perfectly okay," I interrupted. "I certainly understand."

"Well, I was just calling to tell you that if you wanted to stop by and pick it up, I'll be home all day today and most of tomorrow. Other than church in the morning, I'll be here. Or, if you're going to church, I could bring it with me."

Not having been to church in several years, I opted for the first suggestion. "No, that's okay. I could come over today and get it if that's all right with you."

"Oh Auggie, that would be fine. Again, I'm sorry I forgot to give it to you when you were here last week."

With the conclusion of the phone call, I dialed Dusty's number. Mr. Faulk's house was out in the countryside and Dusty had a car.

"Hey, I need a lift to Mr. Faulk's house and my dad's got the car today. It's out past Delatour Road. Can you drive me out there?"

"Yeah, sure. Remind me again why we're going?"

"His wife just called. He left me a letter or something and I'd like to pick it up. She said she'd be there all day."

I knew Mrs. Faulk from her occasional visits to the office, but the only time I had been to her home was the recent gathering after the funeral. On that day, I hadn't noticed its exterior. Today, as Dusty pulled his Chevy into the driveway, the well-manicured lawns and shrubbery were visible reminders of the care and patience of my old friend. Mrs. Faulk was peering from the curtained window as Dusty killed the engine.

"I'll wait here. You're just running in to get the letter right? Besides, it's probably a personal thing."

Dusty's assumptions were correct but once inside, I found that Mrs. Faulk had other plans. After greeting me at the door she invited me to sit in the living room.

"Would you like to invite your friend in? He's certainly welcome. He doesn't have to sit outside in the car."

"No, he's fine." I told her. "I told him I was just coming in to grab the letter. I don't want to hold you up from stuff you have to do today." She left for the kitchen and promptly returned with a tray holding two teacups, some cream and sugar, and a small ceramic pot of hot water. While waiting, I looked around the room and my eyes rested on the old photograph that sat on the mantel. It was a black and white picture of Mr. Faulk standing with my grandfather and some of the yard workers. Behind them was a large diesel loco with some of the men leaning on it. The photo was sandwiched between what looked to be their wedding picture and another old photo of people I didn't recognize. It was evident from the wedding picture that Mrs. Faulk had been a beautiful woman in her day. Over the years, she had gained more weight than she probably cared to admit and her graying hair had been left untouched by artificial colorings. Mr. Faulk was as thin in the photo as he was at my grandfather's funeral. With his gawky frame and crooked smile, I knew it had been his warm ways that had caught the eye of such an attractive woman.

When she returned, she noticed my focus on the railroad photo. "One of Benjamin's favorites," she said, setting the tray down on the coffee table between us.

"Your grandfather is in that one too. Probably what made it one of his favorites. Two worse ALCOholics I've never known."

As she spoke, she poured the hot water into our cups setting the teabags to work. On this day, the word 'alcoholic' brought a smile to my face. I recalled my disappointment when I first heard the term and the explanation that was later given by my grandfather. This memory was interrupted as she lifted one of the cups by its saucer and passed it to me. "Help yourself to milk or sugar," she continued.

"An old term I know. Probably before your time but I'd guess you'd be considered an ALCOholic as well," she said laughing.

"Actually, I am familiar with the term and, if I was considered to be one, I believe I'd be in very good company," I assured her.

She then picked up a letter that had been sitting on an end table next to her chair. "You can read this at your leisure," she said. "But I can tell you what it's basically about. Benjamin confided in me that he had an old shed just a few miles up the road. Something he was renting from one of the locals. He said he kept some railroad memorabilia in there and if anything ever happened to him he wanted you to have it. Anyway, he gave me this letter so you would have proof the stuff was to go to you if anyone asked. He told me that he put directions to the place in there too. Never been there myself. Other than that photo he always kept here on the mantel, most of his railroad stuff is packed away down in the basement. Lord knows what else he's got up there in that shed or barn or whatever. I'm not sure what arrangements he had with the fellow who owns the place either so you might want to get anything you want out of there before you up and lose it. If there is anything worthwhile, that is."

I set my teacup down and took the envelope. For a brief moment, I sat and stared at my full name written in his familiar scrawl. It was probably the only time he had ever used my last name. I was either 'Auggie' or 'Kiddo' whenever we had been together.

"Well, I thank you for letting me know about this," I said indicating the envelope. "I think though, if there is anything of value in the shed, you should certainly have it."

"Believe me Auggie, the contents of that place are the least of my worries. I've got enough railroad memorabilia in this house to fill a museum. I may even be calling you to take some of that stuff off my hands. Our attic and cellar are filled with the junk! Take what you want from the shed and leave the rest to the demolition crew which will no doubt follow right behind you."

When I returned to the car, Dusty said nothing about the long wait. I presumed his silence was in respect for my relationship with Mr. Faulk. As he pulled out of the driveway, I opened the envelope.

"He left me some stuff in an old shed," I said tearing it open. "The directions are supposed to be in here. Mrs. Faulk said it was just a few miles away."

"Well then let's check it out. What's it say there?"

"Well, first it explains that anything in the shed is to be mine. Following that, it doesn't say to turn around, but if you want to check it out, you should turn the car around. We're going the wrong way. It's got directions and then it's got the name of some guy here...a Mr. Kittle, followed by a phone number."

After making a two-mile drive in a straight line up the highway, we made the left turn onto the side road indicated on the explicitly drawn map. Another mile on that road brought us to the 'X' that marked the spot where the shed was to be found. In its place, however, was a much larger structure than we had anticipated. So much so that we debated the accuracy of the directions or the location marked on the map. Dusty pulled in and kept the car running while I got out and walked around. When I spotted the padlock on the big door, I smiled. I turned and signaled Dusty to kill the engine and I waved him out of the car.

"For Chrissake! It's got a padlock on it. How're we supposed to get in?"

I looked at the combination lock and smiled again. "Easy," I told him. "We simply dial forty-five right, eleven left, and sixteen right." Dusty gave me a quizzical look wondering how I would know the combination.

"Good old Mr. Faulk," I said. "This is the combination lock from his railroad locker. He told me I was the only one he would ever give the combination to. He said it was for emergencies—you know...in case I ever needed to get a snack. He used to keep those little packs of peanut butter crackers in there and little boxes of raisins. When he gave me the combination it was one of his lessons, a memory thing so I wouldn't forget the numbers."

I spun the dial for the combination as I relayed the story to Dusty.

"First, you have to remember that to shoot this lock off you'd need a Colt .45." I stopped at the forty-five indicated on the dial and started in the other direction as I continued. "Then, he told me to remember that when he gave me the secret to the lock, I was eleven years old." I stopped at the eleven and reversed direction once again. "And sixteen, he told me, was the age I'd be when I started to see girls as something other than yucky, as I always called them."

As I finished the story, I spun the dial to the last number. We both heard the slight clicking and as I yanked on the lock it popped open. We took hold of the massive door and opened it just enough to get inside. What confronted us was a sight we never expected. From what we could see, there was only one item. We stood and stared in awe. Inside the barn—the so-called storage shed—was a set of train rails. There on the tracks...in all its glory...sat the Baldwin.

She looked amazing. Anything that could have been polished had been and anything that could have been restored had been. She looked like a steam engine right off the ALCO assembly line. I stood staring, thinking yes, now I understand what Mrs. Faulk had been referring to and then spoke aloud. "Yes, Mr. Faulk, you truly were an ALCOholic!"

Dusty's mouth continued to hang open until he spoke. "Hooooly shit! Are you kidding me? Memorabilia is one thing...this...this is...hooooly shit!"

"No, this is much better than holy shit," I told him. I realized from his tone that he had no idea what he was looking at. His response was in seeing a perfectly restored steam engine but Dusty had never seen the Baldwin in the light of day. "This is the loco!"

"You mean this is the loco of its day?"

"No, I mean this is the loco! The one we put the money in! The loco that went missing! Don't you remember it? The bootlegger's hole! We've come full circle, man! We're back to the mother lode!"

"You don't think the money's still in there do you?"

"Well, I don't know, but I can't imagine Mr. Faulk squeezing himself up into the hole, so you tell me. I mean this thing's probably been sittin' here since it disappeared."

The two of us wasted no time in getting to the engineer's compartment. I threw down the coalman's seat and stood on it to slide back the door to the bootlegger's hole. The inside was in total darkness and Dusty retrieved a flashlight from the car. Even with the help of the light, I didn't see any of the bags. A gnawing sense of worry grew in my gut. I yelled for him to push me farther into the hole and, once I got my head inside, I detected another cavity. As I aimed the flashlight down the crevice, I could see a soiled section of a bag wedged down between two metal plates. It was out of reach, but satisfied with my find, I hollered to Dusty to pull me out.

"Either the bags are still in there or Mr. Faulk killed a leopard and stuffed it away," I laughed. "I saw some of the red sequins too so there's no reason they all aren't in there. There's a second cavity beyond the hole and somehow they must've fallen down into it. It's behind this plate," I said, pointing to the area behind the engineer's control panel. "There's no way I can reach them the way they're wedged down in there. We're going to need a pole with a hook or something to pull them up, but sure as hell, they're in there!"

"How do you think they got moved? Do you think Mr. Faulk found them and moved them? Do you think the money's still in there?"

"Jeezus...you're starting to sound like Al! How do I know? We'll have to pull 'em outta there." For the first time since entering the engineer's compartment, I noticed an envelope wedged into the throttle assembly. It was similar to the one Mrs. Faulk had given me and once again it had my full name written on it. I opened it to find a lengthier letter than the note he'd left me and I read it aloud. Like my name on the envelope, the letter was in Mr. Faulk's scrawled handwriting.

Dear August,

If you're reading this letter, you are now the proud owner of my cherished Baldwin I say mine because I purchased it from the Delaware and Hudson for one dollar. It was your grandfather, as you can now guess, who oversaw the transaction. Because the deal was what some people might perceive as being a bit shady, very few people knew of it.

I don't know if you remember my brother-in-law (Bull). He was a steel worker who once owned his own company. He moved houses for people I don't mean the contents either. Bull moved entire houses! Anyway, when retirement loomed in my headlights, your granddad sympathized with my affection for the Baldwin and, with Bull's help, we moved her to this barn. He still had much of his moving equipment and he viewed getting the Baldwin out of the yard secretly in the wee hours of the morning as somewhat of a challenge. I have to admit...it was fun! I wish you could've been there.

Your granddad and I even staged that big argument in the yard to throw everybody off the track. It took a lot of convincing to make him do that. It wasn't really in his nature. Many times I wanted to tell you the story but neither of us wanted to put you in a compromised position. A few other men who had worked for Bull lent a hand and then Bull made them take a vow of silence. Which meant a lot more than the lack of silence on the night we moved her. As you can imagine, there was much cursing and swearing. (All from Bull and his crew of course)

Anyway, I've cleaned her all up good and proper like she should be and she's yours now Kiddo to do with as you please. As far as the Delaware and Hudson knows, she was sold for junk and sent to the graveyard years ago. Your granddad took care of the paperwork. I guess they thought we'd put her out of her misery.

I pay the rent on this barn monthly but have always kept it six months in advance so you've got some time to decide her fate. If you wish to continue renting, contact Mr. Kittle (I put his phone number on the letter with the directions). He knows about the Baldwin so don't worry about that. He's a man you can trust. I also told him about you so you shouldn't have any trouble here. You and I sure did have some great train times together didn't we? So have fun Auggie, and take 'er around the tracks once in a while for me!

Fondly,
Mr. Faulk

P.S. If my wife didn't let on about the Baldwin, it's because she's pretty cagey...but she probably knows! That woman has always been the love of my life but I never could hide nothin' from her!

* * * * *

I PUT THE LETTER down and for a brief moment, Dusty and I just stared at each other. We then discussed what things needed to be done and in what order we needed to do them. We agreed that rescuing the pocket books and making sure the money was still intact was our first priority. If the money was secure, we wanted to count it. In the years since the incident, rumors had spread about a robbery connected to The Riverbank Murder and news stories reported amounts ranging from thousands to millions that had disappeared in a mysterious holdup. None of the written accounts ever mentioned any money and during the trials that followed, none of the statements made by the syndicate guys ever mentioned money. It had always been a point of irritation to us, being the ones who actually had the money, that we never knew the answer either. It was time to find out.

After looking around the engine compartment, we found a chain in an equipment box, which had a hook on the end. Dusty pushed me into the hole once again. The chain was too heavy for what we needed to do but by hooking the flashlight over a protruding bolt in the hole, I was finally able to snare the first of the bags. When we pulled it up, I realized it was the Waterton gym bag and the felt missile on the face of the bag was smeared with grease. Dusty's hands shook a bit as he unzipped it. We found the contents just as we left it...stacks of money. Each stack was wrapped with a band, but the numbers stamped on them were contrary to what I had seen the day of the robbery. The stacks of fives and tens were still in there, but they had only been the top layer of what the satchel held. Underneath the initial stacks were bundles of fifties and hundreds.

Dusty made the comment that I should've learned to count zeros more accurately.

"Yeah, well I was kind of in a hurry that day if I remember correctly. Besides, it's our good fortune now." I responded.

Retrieving the remaining bags was a bigger problem. They had fallen so far down in the cavity they had become wedged against the side. I broke a handle on one of them trying to pull it loose and after the handle broke, the flashlight became dislodged and fell into the hole. Having no light to work with, Dusty pulled me out and I climbed down so we could assess the situation.

"The chain is too damn heavy for what we need and now the light's broken. I think we should assume the other bags are okay as far as the money goes. I say we put the gym bag back up there and lock the place. We can come back later with the right tools and a better light to work with."

"What about counting the money? We need to see how much we've got here."

"We're not going to know how much we've got without the other bags anyway. And don't forget, this money doesn't belong to just us. We've got to split it up among The Five-Cent Gang. Maybe we should all be in on the count and then divvy up."

"Whoa there big fella!" Dusty's voice held an air of caution. "I'm with you all the way with The Five-Cent Gang and I agree we need to have a five-way split on whatever's in the bags, but right now you and I are the only two who know the money exists and where it is. Until we decide exactly what we're gonna do, I say we keep a low profile. First off, we don't even know where Jamie is and Al still thinks the fat man and that other asshole are dead because of us. He's gone way off the deep end. He's likely to give the money to the cops or see if the dead guys have kids or something and give it to them!"

Dusty's objections were valid and we agreed to leave the money on the Baldwin until we could figure a safer place to hide it. The train had protected it all these years but with Mr. Faulk dead and gone and two teenagers hanging around the building, things could get a bit hairy. We both agreed we needed to sleep on it. A five-way split would certainly take place but it would happen at our say-so. If only two of The Five-Cent

Gang knew of the find, it was best it was Dusty and me. Our longtime friendship had given us the closest bond of any pair. The money had to be made safe. It wouldn't be buried in the woods or under Dusty's front porch like the old days. We would sleep on it. We would find a safe place to hide the money.

❀ ❀ ❀ ❀ ❀

TWO DAYS PASSED BEFORE Dusty presented me with his idea. Actually, it was his father who brought the suggestion to light. The two of them sat at the kitchen table having a casual breakfast.

"Hey Dad, you're a detective. If you had to hide a bunch of important papers, where would you stash them?" His father took no time with his response.

"Writing your memoirs are you?"

"No, seriously Dad, where would you put them?"

Mr. Barnes closed his newspaper and, setting it on the table, focused his attention on Dusty. "Well, in my experience, I've found that really clever thieves hide things where people can see them. You know, they employ the 'hide in plain sight' theory, someplace the item belongs and looks so natural in the environment it goes unnoticed. For instance, if you wanted to hide a book, the best place might be in a library. The bigger the library the better. Or, if you wanted to hide a key you should put it on a key ring. So with that in mind, you tell me...where would you hide a stack of important papers?"

"I guess in that case, I'd put them in the in-basket on your desk. Stuff seems to sit untouched forever in there."

"Well there ya go!" His father laughed. "Problem solved."

When Dusty relayed the conversation, he added his own solution for our problem. "I figure the best place to hide the money is with a lot of other money. So we put it in a bank!"

I continued staring at him and said nothing.

"We get a safe deposit box," he continued. "My parents have one and they're the only ones who can get into it. The bank's not even allowed to know what's inside it. We can get one in both our names. The money won't be any safer than that!"

It sounded too easy. "Can we do that?"

"I don't see why not. I mean, we have to pay a fee or something but we'll just take it out of the money that's in the bags."

We decided to investigate the possibilities and the following week we drove to Troy to check with one of the bigger banks. Dusty's father was well known and Waterton offered too much exposure. Two kids having to explain safe deposit boxes to their parents was an obstacle we wanted to avoid.

The Troy Savings Bank offered anonymity and on our first visit we opened savings accounts. We took one hundred dollars in small bills from one of the bags, knowing fifty dollars each wouldn't raise any suspicions. As planned, I waited until the woman filling out the forms was engaged in her work before I threw the nonchalant question at her. "What would be the procedure if we wanted to get a safe deposit box?"

The woman eyed me and then returned her glance to the form she was completing. "For you?" Her voice held a note of skepticism.

"Well, we each were thinking of getting one."

"You have a lot of valuables do you?" Her question was unexpected but Dusty came back with the perfect answer.

"It's for baseball cards," he told her. "We have a lot that are pretty rare. Worth a lot of money. They're only worth anything if they're kept in their original condition." This response not only seemed satisfactory but brought us her full attention.

Seeing he had her interest he continued, telling her he possessed one of the 1954 Ted Williams cards that was part of the collection from the Wilson Franks Company.

Her expression told him she had no idea what he was talking about.

"Wilson Franks is a hot dog company that originally distributed the cards and now they're nearly impossible to find," he explained.

"Yes," she acknowledged. "I know about Wilson hot dogs. Didn't realize they'd gone into the baseball card business."

"Well, anyway, I've got one." Dusty lied. "It's probably worth a hundred dollars by now. We've got a lot more too, only they're not worth that much, at least not yet."

Although the woman didn't seem to know anything about baseball, or Ted Williams, or the Red Sox, she seemed to understand the value of their worth. After seeing the size of the box, we were certain we needed two and Dusty made arrangements for his. Not having turned eighteen yet, I needed a parent's signature and left the bank with an application for the second. The signature was easily accomplished when Dusty bribed Silly, who had impeccable handwriting, to sign my mother's name.

Two weeks after our discovery of the Baldwin, the money was secured in two safe deposit boxes. It took three trips as we carried our school gym bags into the vault and made the transfers. Our initial trip involved a bit of paranoia and I insisted we cover the money packets with baseball cards in the event our gym bags were inspected by the guards. As a bit of humor, we named our safe deposit boxes Ray and Ethel in honor of Dusty's uncle and aunt. The names allowed for future discussions of the money without actual references.

The most fun we had was in the counting. Our original discovery that only a few stacks contained tens and twenties proved to be true and almost all the other stacks were fifties and hundreds. Because of the darkness and the urgency of the task, the denominations weren't visible the night we removed them from the stolen satchel and placed them into the pocketbooks. Dusty's original calculation of the number of stacks was surprisingly accurate but it was the amount in each stack that gave us thoughts of expensive things to come.

We agreed the money would go unmentioned to Al and Jules and Jamie until after graduation. After graduation, however, Ray and Ethel remained in hiding. We discussed revealing the money to the others and how it should be dispersed and spent. One of several concerns was Al's discretion once the money was in his pockets. We would have to rely on Jules, who was now the manager of Mr. Billings' appliance store, to keep him in line.

After Jules blew out his knee in a playoff game against Hudson High, his football career ended. Being industrious, and always careful to ensure his mother's welfare, he put in thirty to forty hour workweeks at the appliance store. He had replaced so many parts on the used washer and dryer he had purchased during his freshman year that he became extremely adept at repair work. With Mr. Billings in failing health, he relied heavily on Jules and gave him the promotion, which meant a salary in lieu of his hourly wage. With school completed and his knee excusing him from the draft, his salaried position allowed him to spend extra money without being noticed if he played it right.

On the other hand, Al wasn't the frugal type and the recklessness he displayed during his youth had gotten worse. His whole attitude changed as he searched for an identity. The few times our paths crossed, his conversations involved his eagerness to join the marines and go to Viet Nam and fight the good fight, as he put it.

When the summer ended, I prepared for college. I'd been accepted to Cortland State and planned to establish a career as a physical education teacher. Options were limited and it was more suitable for me than teaching English and telling kids about verb tenses. Dusty enrolled in a six-month training program for police work and assumed a role in the Waterton Police Department. Al, despite arguments from Jules and his mother, remained true to his word and enlisted. None of us had any idea where Jamie was or what capers he had involved himself in. Wherever he was, he was due his equal share and that meant someone would need to find him. Dusty and I remained patient...there seemed to be no hurry. Ray and Ethel could wait.

Chapter Nineteen

My senior year had changed my life considerably. The loss of my grandfather and Mr. Faulk combined with the return of great wealth had all been unexpected.

Jamie, on the other hand, was discovering a different kind of transition and toward the end of his senior year, he sat in his bedroom with several letters scattered around him. Each offered different options regarding scholarships. Small schools that pledged a completely free education in exchange for his ball-handling skills and larger schools that offered partial scholarships. The state school and its offer of the guarantee of on-campus employment to pay for his tuition had been crumpled and thrown to the waste basket in the corner...although missing the basket gave Jamie a momentary thought to perhaps reconsider. The letter getting the most attention was a school in New Hampshire offering a full scholarship. The competition would be good and the distance not so great from Boston.

His first hope was to get the golden letter from a school in the Big East Conference. He hoped for a school where he could compete against some of the best. His first choice, of course, was to stay close to home and attend Boston College. To date, no letter had come forward.

He never knew if it was a coincidence, or fate, or
the combination of the two that caused the phone to
ring that morning. It was a call from Father Mac
summoning him to his office.

Jamie's coaching of the parish team during his
senior year had brought him much closer to the priest.
The two had become such good friends that a phone
call asking him to stop by the office was now
commonplace and left no need for his former state of
paranoia. If anything, he was called to intervene on
behalf of one of his players who was in one type of
scrape or another.

During the season, his Saturday morning arrival to
practice was always earlier than necessary. It allowed
time for Jamie and Father Mac to sit, drink coffee, and
discuss the team and anything else on Jamie's mind.
Occasionally Father Thomas would join them. Even he
had become swept up in the phenomenon of the parish
team and had taken to drawing up plays and offering
them to his young coach—no matter that these plays
were rarely used or tactfully used once the outcome of
the game had been decided.

Father Mac had been correct in his assumption
that more than eight boys would be interested in trying
out the second time around. The fall turnout was so
great in number that Jamie, under the advisement of his
mentor, made rosters for several teams and scheduled
inter-squad scrimmages rather than send would-be
hopefuls back to the streets.

All of this produced a much better second year of
coaching. More discipline, combined with rules that
allowed for a no-nonsense approach to the game, gave
the players structure. When the final selections were
made, Jamie had a squad of ten players that took the
league by storm. The league had grown to eight teams
and when the regular season ended, the players

encouraged a tournament in which St. Mary's walked off with the first-place trophy. The season ended with the presentation of individual trophies at a dinner that included parents and a few church officials.

Jamie continued to gain prowess for his own play at St. Mary's which, when added to his organizational skills involving the parish team and surrounding activities, made Father Mac quite happy with his protégé. His skills led to many of the letters that now surrounded him. Letters that were appreciated, but none were so well received as the thoughtful note from Father Mac who, once again, sent kind words and congratulations when the season had ended. Although college was in his sights, being recognized by a priest he had grown to respect and admire meant much more than any scholarship.

With the successful season under his belt, Jamie's walk to the parish office was enjoyable. Unlike his first visit that had been filled with questions regarding the reason Father Mac had sent for him, today's meeting was most likely to tie up loose ends regarding storing the equipment or maybe even to get his recommendation for a coach for next season.

The door used most to gain entrance to the parish office was the one that led to the courtyard where Jamie had first seen Father Mac enter. Jamie, for reasons of his own, always entered through the front door of the church. Since his initial visit, the entrance into the enormous structure, followed by the small rounded door to the walkway, had become a ritual. He was no longer a stranger to the hallways and passages and he lingered through them, studying their beauty.

As habit dictated, he arrived carrying two cups of coffee from the corner store. Father Mac was sitting behind his cluttered desk and he peered over the top of his glasses and gave a discerning look at the papers in his hand. The usual greeting was omitted as Jamie handed one of the cups to Father Mac. Uncharacteristically, the priest got right to the point.

"How's the search going? Did you pick a school yet?" As he asked the question, he set his cup on the desk and selected a letter from his pile of clutter.

"New Hampshire's still pretty high on the list," Jamie told him. "They're offering a full ride and they play some tough schools."

"I was hoping you might stay closer to home. You do realize I need a coach for next season. I figured if you were in the area I might be able to talk you into it. You've got a great start here with these kids. I'd hate to lose the momentum now."

"Can't stay in the area if I don't have any offers. Some of the smaller colleges have sent letters but they're either offering partial scholarships or are so small, I may as well be playing at St. Mary's."

"What would you think if I told you I was on the phone this morning with Boston College? And what if I told you they were interested. You keep tellin' me you'd give anything for a Big East offer." He shifted his look from over-the-top of his glasses to the paper in his hand and then back to Jamie. "Maybe you should put up or shut up." This time he was smiling.

Jamie sat for several seconds with no words spoken.

"Well?"

"What are you tellin' me? Are you saying they're offering a scholarship? I had pretty much written them off."

"Not a full scholarship, but they've seen enough of your play to offer a partial that will cover most of your costs. The other part, of course, could be paid for if you could find a job..." his voice trailed off.

"So I should start looking for a place to bag groceries? Is that what you're tellin' me?"

"No, that's the good part."

"Good part?"

"After talking to BC, I made a few calls of my own. Realizing we've never paid you for any work you've done here at the parish the last two years, I had a little discussion with Bishop Douglas about giving you work right here."

"What work?"

"Coaching, lad." Father Mac responded somewhat surprised. "And that's not to say you've ever asked for anything either, because we both know you never did. Anyway, long story short, with back pay and future pay from us you could certainly make the two ends meet."

"Future pay. What kind of future pay?"

"Aren't you listening to me, boy? We still need a coach for next year. We can certainly work around your schedule. So you see, this deal is more for me than you, when you think about it. I don't have time to be looking around and interviewing people for a coaching position, and we both know it's out of the realm of possibility for Father Thomas to take over." He then paused, looked around as he cupped a hand to his mouth before continuing, "even with the help of God Almighty. I probably shouldn't tell you this, but he came in here one day and asked if someone should say something to the two fellas on the team who, instead of making a nice soft lay-up, jump way up over the rim and slam the ball down into the hoop?"

The two shared a laugh at the cost of Father Thomas.

"I guess he was afraid they might bend the rim."

They laughed again before Jamie told Father Mac there really wasn't any decision to be made or thought to be given. Not only was Boston College his first choice, he had also admitted to himself that he could do great things with the parish team if he continued. Attending BC meant four more years of developing more than a team, he could put an entire system together. It was an opportunity to give something back to Father Mac.

Part III

ABSOLUTION

Chapter One

I still don't know why Dusty and I let the money sit for as long as we did. Perhaps it was because the separate lives of The Five-Cent Gang showed no need for its immediate use. Perhaps we were just too scared to take the next step.

Dusty was making a living protecting the fair city of Waterton, Jules was managing the store, Al was in the army, Jamie was somewhere in Boston, and I was running up college loans that were going to be taken care of by Uncle Ray and Aunt Ethel.

College proved to be friendlier than high school and by the time my junior year rolled around, I had learned the advantages of setting up my own schedule. Tuesdays were intentionally light and by two o'clock I was usually at Higby's Tap Room having a few beers with classmates. On one particular Tuesday the drinking turned into a minor binge and I didn't get back to my apartment until well after eight. When I arrived, one of my roommates met me at the door.

"You know a guy named Dusty?" he asked me.

"Yeah, he's a friend of mine from back home."

"Well, some guy called. Told me to give you a message, said he didn't know whether you knew or not, but he's dead."

"Dead! Who's dead?"

"That guy—Dusty. The guy who called said he was dead. Said some asshole shot him in Bell's Grocery Store or something like that and said you should give him a call as soon as you get home. He gave me this number." He handed me a torn piece of paper as he relayed the information.

"Who was it who called? What the fuck was his name?"

"He didn't say, man. He just gave me that number and said you should call him as soon as you get home, and then he hung up."

My body went cold...then limp...and a hot nauseous feeling swept over me. Hearing that Dusty was dead just wasn't believable. There had obviously been some confusion in the retelling. I needed more than a phone message. Other thoughts ran through my mind which included the fear that somehow the possibility of being caught with the money had come to fruition. If Dusty had been killed, or at the very least shot, was it linked to the money? Did something happen while I was here at school? Did he get caught in the wrong place by the wrong people? Were the rest of us in danger? I stared at the crumpled piece of paper in my hand and went inside and dialed the number not knowing who would be picking up the phone on the other end. It was a Waterton exchange, but not a number I recognized. After two rings, the voice came across the receiver.

"Billings's Appliance Store."

"Jules?" I questioned, relieved to hear a familiar voice. He wasted no time in relaying the details.

"Yeah. It's Dusty, man, he was shot over at Bell's a couple of hours ago...walked in on a two-bit punk robbery. He was on his way home after work. He was still in uniform, ya know? I guess the guy freaked...just shot him, man...he didn't have a chance in hell. The whole thing's a fucking mess. All over the news. I wasn't sure if you were getting it out there as it's more of a local story. Anyway, it just happened a few hours ago."

"No, if there was anything on the news here, I didn't get it," I told him, realizing that when Dusty was gunned down I was sipping a cold brew and bitching about midterms.

"I'll get some shit together," I told Jules. "I'll drive home first thing tomorrow," I added, realizing I was in no condition to make the two hundred plus mile drive. "No way I can drive tonight. I've been drinking all afternoon." As I said the words, I wondered what Jules would think of me for drinking while Dusty was being shot.

"What about school?"

"School can wait. I'd better get home and see if there's anything I can do."

"You sure you don't want to wait until I get more info? I can call you tomorrow and let you know what's going on here. Why don't you hold off?"

"I'll see you when I get there…tomorrow."

"Okay. Probably best you come to the store."

When I got home on Wednesday, I was nursing a bad hangover and still suffering from the emotional drain of Dusty being dead. I made a quick phone call to Jules and told him my immediate need was an hour or two of sleep and then I'd catch up with him. I was about to call Dusty's father when the phone rang and Mr. Barnes was on the other end.

"How did you know I was home?"

"I'm a cop, remember? I know everything going on in Waterton. So how are you?"

"As okay as can be expected," I told him. "Better than you I'm guessing. How about Mrs. Barnes?"

"Taking it pretty hard as you can imagine. Cilla seems to have been hit the hardest. Anyway, I was calling to let you know you don't have to stand on protocol. The paper states that viewing hours tomorrow night are for family but don't let that keep you away. If anybody is considered to be part of our family, it would be you."

Mr. Barnes' voice was strained as he spoke into the phone. After thanking him for his call, I assured him I'd be there.

● ● ● ● ●

VIEWING MY LIFELONG FRIEND in a casket wasn't a burden I was ready to shoulder and I intentionally arrived late to the funeral home. Mr. Wilson greeted me at the door. He was a stately man whose friendly face was accentuated by an elongated handlebar mustache that, over the years, had stretched itself beyond his cheeks. If anyone had ever been destined to be a funeral director, it was Mr. Wilson. He greeted me by name, having seen me through numerous funerals of my own relatives over the years. It was as if he was that friendly uncle everyone had and it was that kind of calmness and reverence that made him well liked within the community. He was the designated overseer of the Presbyterian deaths while the Nobleman Funeral Home two blocks away attended to any Catholics who died. Other than his soft-spoken voice when he greeted me, the initial quietness was overwhelming.

The fragrance of flowers overpowered the interior and muted conversations were taking place within small clusters of relatives. Considering the evening was for immediate family, there were a lot more people than I anticipated. The occasional sound of a squeal combined with running footsteps from a private area on the lower level provided evidence that a few children were present.

I bypassed the mahogany stand holding the guest book. It stood adjacent to a small chrome tripod holding a card that read 'Services for David F. Barnes.' I read the card and realized I was probably the only member of The Five-Cent Gang who knew Dusty's middle name was Foster—a fact sworn to secrecy on a lazy summer afternoon during our childhood when we each reluctantly revealed our well-kept secret. An old memory flashed into my head and rewound a vision of Al sitting on my chest trying to get Dusty's middle name out of me. He knew it began with an F and, in a playful way, was threatening me with raised fists. He was so pathetic in his attempt to be tough that I couldn't stop laughing.

"Frank?" he questioned. "Is it Frank? I know...it's Ferdinand isn't it? Tell me or die," he threatened. Dusty sat nearby grinning ear-to-ear knowing his secret was safe. Amidst my laughter, I finally yelled that I would tell him if he got off my chest. Al reluctantly complied and when he got off I told him I had to get on my bike first because once I told him, Dusty would want to kill me and I needed a fast getaway. Dusty remained smiling...knowing my sworn oath was my bond. I mounted my bike as Al stood in anticipation and I started toward home. As I pedaled down the path I hollered over my shoulder. "The F stands for Fartface," I yelled and I heard Dusty laughing as I disappeared over the small hill we'd been sitting on.

As an interruption to my reverie, Mr. Wilson's hand touched my shoulder and brought me back to the vestibule.

"You can sign the registry later if you like. I think David's parents are anxious to see you."

I entered the main viewing room wondering if I was still wearing the remains of a grin from my moment of reminiscence.

The scent emitted by the many bouquets and the sprays covering Dusty's casket became more pronounced. The familiar faces of Dusty's parents seemed to loom out from among the clusters of relatives. Each was separately engaged in quiet conversations with people who were not familiar looking, visiting relatives perhaps.

A young woman sat in the first row of chairs with her back to me and I struggled to remember the name of his recent girlfriend. Nina? Myra? A name I should know. Although we'd only met once over pizza, I should remember her name in my offering of condolences. But he was my friend I thought with a slight touch of bitterness. She should be offering me condolences. Dusty and I went as far back as kindergarten and she was just some Johnny-come-lately. I felt a bit of resentment over her top billing.

It was Dusty's mother who first noticed me and she left her husband's side to approach and give me a motherly hug. She stepped back and revealed eyes that were red and puffy. There wasn't really any need for words between us. Our history was deep. It ranged from days she had made Dusty and me fluffer-nutter sandwiches, to giving us rides to basketball practices, to her words of caution when we drove off in his first car. With my hand in hers, she led me to the casket and as we approached, Nina—or Mina, whatever her name was—stood and turned. Like Dusty's mother, her eyes were red with grief and when she faced me, I immediately saw how lovely she was and wondered how the beauty of this woman had escaped me during our one and only meeting. How had my best friend snared such a woman and how during that first meeting over pizza had I not noticed her enchantment?

When she saw me, she threw her arms around my neck and clung to me as if we now had so much in common. We stood in that embrace at length until she released her grip and stepped back. It wasn't until then, when I looked into her eyes that I saw the familiarity of past days. It wasn't Nina or Mina or a person with a name I couldn't remember. I was looking at the grown up face of Silly.

The usual circumstances surrounding adolescence had separated us when she reached the gum-smacking era of seventh grade. I was a freshman then and unlikely to see her in school. Grades seven and eight were still imprisoned in the school's basement. Those kids were looked upon as young inconveniences and were given the same lack of recognition by upper classmen as we received when we were sentenced to serve our two-year term in the dungeon. Even their cafeteria times kept them isolated from the rest of the school. When I made my frequent visits to Dusty's house, she was either behind the closed doors of her bedroom with forty-fives blaring on her record player or monopolizing the telephone. During those rare occasions when she ventured from her room to get a snack from the kitchen, her hand covered the lower half of her face to save her the shame of me seeing her braces.

During the entire time, her pseudo-absence was perfectly acceptable to Dusty and me who had far more important things to deal with. We were getting our driving permits, followed by licenses which led to buying a car, which we felt would certainly lead to getting more dates. We were just too busy in those days to be bothered with the former tagalong.

And so Silly and I had separate social circles. Neither of us knew of the other's existence during a period of six years or more—six years in which the caterpillar had spun a cocoon and metamorphosed into the most beautiful butterfly I'd ever seen. I stood speechless. She not only took me by surprise...her beauty took my breath away. Her auburn hair was no longer restrained by braids. It was full and fell softly on her shoulders. A small ringlet crept out from its assigned place and rested on her forehead. The same uncontrollable wisp of hair that, as a kid, caused her to skew her mouth and blow upward to temporarily get it off her face. It had now become an integral part of her beauty as it rested to one side and no longer induced any incentive to be wisped away.

I continued to stare, and for the first time, noticed the deep blue of her eyes that seemed to sparkle despite her grief. Over the years, the spray of freckles across her nose had diminished and the braces that had made her self-conscious had been successful and provided her with a beautiful smile.

"I'm glad you came tonight," she said. "I was hoping you would. Dad said he called you." Before I could respond, she took my hand and led me to the back of the room. I had no idea where we were going but was more than willing to be taken. When she sat me down in one of the folding chairs in the last row, she spoke as if the void in time away from each other had never occurred...as if her appearance had never changed and as if she was just Silly as she always had been. It seemed there had never been any revelation in her mind nor did she display any attitude of 'Now I'm beautiful so everyone get out of my way.' She was the same wonderful Silly with the same wonderful air about her.

"I know this sounds a bit sacrilegious," she said solemnly, "but I've really got to get out of this place. Did you drive?" Without waiting for an answer, she continued. "Of course you drove. It's too far to walk from your house. You drove didn't you? I mean you have your car here?" Before I could answer a second time, she began again. "I'm sorry, Auggie. Am I rambling? The doctor gave Mom and me something to calm us down but it seems to be having the opposite effect on me? Am I rambling?"

As she sat next to me, she continued to hold my hand and clutched it a bit tighter. I studied her face with what I hoped was an unnoticeable stare and I continued to absorb how breathtakingly beautiful she was. I started to address her as Silly but stopped myself. The old nickname didn't quite seem to fit either the occasion or her appearance. Cilla also seemed a bit awkward being the pet name used by her parents, so I settled for the compromise of a shorter version of both.

"Look, Cil," I said. "Why don't you sit here a minute and collect your thoughts. I should talk to your parents and pay my respects and then I'll take you home. Sound okay to you?" She patted my hand. "Okay, I'll wait right here."

I talked briefly with Mr. Barnes and his calmness led me to suspect that whatever the doctor had prescribed for Dusty's mother and Silly had made its way to his medicine chest also. I then spent another few moments as I stood and looked down at my best friend. There could never be the appropriate amount of time needed for the mental reminiscing I needed, to review all that had occurred in our shared lives. The Five-Cent Gang was now a penny short. I felt grateful that no one was near as the lump in my throat prohibited talking with anyone. I thought of the other members. Al was somewhere in the dense growth of 'Nam, probably asking everyone questions. Jules was a voice on the telephone relaying Dusty's death by proxy through my roommate, and Jamie's whereabouts was unknown. And then there were Ray and Ethel keeping each other company in the bank vault.

I needed to talk to Dusty, to get his advice. Getting himself shot wasn't fair to any of us. I squeezed the mahogany rail of the casket, realizing for the first time that my hand was so close to my best friend. I was angry that he died. Angry he'd been taken away from me—anger that was mixed with melancholy and grief. My thoughts returned to Cil and, for some odd reason, I felt sick knowing Dusty had never been able to get her the green bicycle she wanted. And all because when the money was recovered she had suffered the misfortune of growing up.

After mentally reliving a few other memories with Dusty, I explained to Cil's parents that she was extremely upset and had asked me to take her home. This information seemed to be somewhat of a relief to Mr. Barnes who knew his daughter was worn out. She had gone nonstop since the initial impact of hearing about the incident at Bell's. He had driven to Burlington and picked her up from school as soon as the news had been delivered. The ride back to Waterton had been tear-filled and the emotional stress continued as funeral arrangements took their toll. Dusty's death hit his sister especially hard, perhaps harder than her parents. Mr. Barnes also knew she was safe in the care of their second son...an honorary title I had been given many years before.

Chapter Two

Although I wanted more details regarding the shooting, the conversation during the drive to the Barnes's house was small talk. "So, how's UVM treating you?" I asked her.

"Okay. You know. Burlington's a bit different than Waterton, especially being a college town. There's a lot to get used to. First time away from home...low man on the totem pole, being a freshman and all that kind of stuff, but I'm getting used to it; I've got a good roommate."

"Any plans for your major? You were always pretty good in math if I remember."

"You remember," she said with a surprised tone. "How would you know? You didn't even know I was alive in high school." She then tempered her comment with a slight laugh.

What she said was certainly true and it stung to hear her say it. I guess I hoped she hadn't noticed my ambivalence to our relationship during those years. It was then I realized I had no idea who this woman was or what she thought about anything in life. I was meeting a woman I now called Cil for the first time and the little girl I had known as Silly no longer existed. If I wanted to get reacquainted it would be a new beginning.

"How about you?" she asked, breaking the brief silence. "How's it going at Cortland?"

"Okay. You know, it's far enough to be away from home but close enough to get back here when I need a good meal or to get some laundry done. It's probably a bit easier for me than your situation. Being a junior, I've got the lay of the land...routines down...and I'm living in an apartment with a couple of other guys. It's small, but free from dorm life and dining hall food."

"Could we go somewhere? I don't really feel like going home." Her question indicated either a lack of attention or little interest in my state of affairs and I hoped it was due to the medication she'd taken.

"Yeah sure. Where would you like to go?"

"Somewhere quiet, maybe somewhere we can get a drink...I just need to relax for a while."

The thought of Silly being old enough to drink threw me again. "There's always Sully's," I suggested.

"Sully's might be a little too loud, if I remember correctly."

Remember correctly? Exactly how much growing up did this girl do while I was away, I wondered. "Well, Mike's been bringing in live music on weekends but it's usually pretty quiet on weeknights. Dancing to the jukebox doesn't hold much popularity with the locals."

I took her lack of response regarding Sully's to be a yes and I turned onto Seventh Street.

"It hasn't really hit me yet, ya know?" she said. "Dusty's death I mean," she added.

"Yeah, well, it all happened pretty fast. I'm not sure it's hit any of us yet."

I pulled into Sully's and saw I'd been right with my prediction. Only two other cars sat in the parking lot and I recognized Mike's as one of them. When we entered, he was behind the bar and, other than an old guy nursing a drink, the place was deserted. Mike was a high school friend who had avoided the time-consuming necessity of a higher education by taking over the management of his father's tavern. Sully's was already a lucrative enterprise and some of Mike's improvements were bringing in even bigger crowds on weekends, live music being one of them. I gave him a nod and he set down the beer mug he was drying and threw the bar towel over his shoulder. He gave Silly an appreciative glance and came out from behind the bar to greet us.

I realized he had no idea who she was, so to save him any embarrassment I interrupted his staring as he approached. "You remember Dusty's sister, Priscilla," I said, more as a statement than a question. Whether he did or not didn't matter.

"Yeah, sure, how are you?" he responded, as if she was someone he had talked to just last week. He then snapped back to the moment.

"I'm sure sorry about Dusty," he told her. "I'm planning on getting over to the funeral parlor tomorrow afternoon. Nights here on Fridays get pretty hectic if ya know what I mean. I'll try and get to the funeral Saturday too if I can get away. Dusty was a really good guy...hell of a tailback too."

"Look, Mike, we're just gonna grab a booth out in the back room and sit for a while." And then I turned to Cil. "You want something to drink?"

"Vodka and tonic," she said squeezing my hand. It wasn't until then I realized she was even holding it. "I'll have a Bud," I added. "Can you bring 'em out back?"

"Sure, sure. You two go ahead, I'll bring 'em right out."

The back room was twice the size of the bar area with most of the space taken up by the dance floor. Large wooden booths formed the perimeter, which over the years, had been marred with carvings of names and initials of former patrons. Mike had talked about replacing them but locals objected, insisting that the carved names were now historical archives and needed to be maintained for posterity. Each booth had its own miniature version of the large jukebox. The smaller duplicates allowed booth patrons to spend money without having to walk the extra few steps to the box. The far end of the dance floor had a bandstand that was filled with a set of drums, some speakers and a few microphones.

After sliding into a booth, we sat in an awkward silence and I unconsciously began rearranging items in the condiment holder until Mike arrived with our drinks.

"You guys want something to eat? The grill's not on but I could rustle you up some sandwiches. Got plenty of cold cuts and stuff."

I looked at Cil and she shook her head no. "I guess we're good with these for now," I said motioning to our drinks.

He stood for a few seconds without me realizing he was expecting some payment. With everything going on, I hadn't even given that a thought until he remedied the situation. "Why don't I run you guys a tab, in case you want a second round?"

Once he left, conversation came in short spurts as the two of us sat with our private thoughts. Mike had neglected to bring me a glass and, needing something to do with my hands, I began peeling the Budweiser label off the bottle with my thumbnail.

"You called me Cil earlier. I'm not Silly anymore?"

"I guess you're a little too grown up now to be Silly," I told her.

"Too grown to be called Silly perhaps, but I can still act silly when the mood strikes me."

"Yeah, semantics I guess. I just figured Cil kind of fit you better now."

As I continued to peck at the Bud label, she flipped through the metal pages of the jukebox in our booth.

"Do you have any change?"

I fished out what change I had in my pocket and slid it across the top of the table. When she reached for one of the quarters, her fingers crossed over the back of my hand. Although the touch was almost unnoticeable, it sent a vibration through me. I studied the slenderness of her fingers as she inserted the quarter into the machine and pushed a couple of buttons.

"What do you like?" she asked me. Without hesitating, I reached over and pushed J-7, a syrupy version of Boots Randolph playing "I Really Don't Want to Know" on the sax—a song I'd played often when I was home for a weekend and sat at the bar shooting the breeze with Mike. Something about a soothing sax always got my attention. While she searched for the third selection the quarter allowed, Skeeter Davis started singing "End Of The World." She pushed the buttons for the final selection and we returned to talk of college life.

"So what else is going on in the great city of Burlington? Anything serious happening up there? What's the social scene like?" I was hoping my question would be taken as a matter of interest in her welfare more than my actual prying, while I tried to get some information regarding her social calendar.

"Oh, you know, it's college. Nobody really dates...mostly the bar scene...kids getting plastered on weekends...I'm not really into that. I do see one guy kinda regularly. I met him during orientation...upper classman...a nice guy."

For whatever reason, hearing the words 'seeing some guy kinda regularly' shot an arrow through me and gave me a gnawing feeling in my gut. To disguise my thoughts, I took a long swig of my beer. Is this serious, I wondered, is she sleeping with this guy? But, I realized I had no business asking her. I certainly had no claim on this woman other than perhaps her welfare.

Boots's sax number came flowing out of the juke box and I thought what an appropriate title I'd picked for a song because I guess I really didn't want to know.

"Are you taking Dusty's place now?" she asked interrupting my thought.

"Dusty's place?"

"Yeah. He was always checking up on me. You know, big brother, protector from all evil. Are you my new big brother?" There was no longer the earlier edginess to her voice as she asked the question. I wondered if she was fishing—perhaps open to the idea of getting together again. It was difficult to discern whether it was for companionship or, as she said, a big brother. Before I could answer, Boots finished playing his sax and The Duprees began singing "You Belong To Me."

"Dance with me?" she asked. My expression in response to her question evidently provoked an explanation.

"It's Dusty's idea," she said. "When I was done in the dumps one day, he came into my room and handed me a record. He told me whenever I was feeling bad, to play it and dance my blues away. So I put it on and did just that. So now, whenever I'm down I go into my room and dance."

"What was the record?"

"Elvis Presley singing 'Blue Suede Shoes' and I did dance my ass off. God, I wore that record out," she laughed. "Still works, too!" she added. "C'mon," she said as she slid out of the booth giving me an encouraging tug and extending her hand. "I mean, this isn't 'Blue Suede Shoes' but I could do with a slow one tonight."

Although we were the only two on the dance floor, I instinctively guided her to the center. When she turned toward me, I raised my left arm but she pushed it down and put both her arms around my neck. I offered no resistance and my arms fell and encircled her waist. It was a waist so tiny I felt I could probably wrap my arms around her twice. The feeling of her closeness combined with the light scent of her perfume told me I needed to see more of her, regardless of the role I would be playing.

As The Duprees sang about seeing pyramids along the Nile, we danced with our own thoughts and I continued to wonder how the freckled faced tree climber I had known my entire life had simply disappeared. As the song progressed, our dancing slowed to an eventual halt, but we remained on the dance floor and she nestled herself closer. Her fingertips tightened and dug into my shoulders. It was near the end of the song when her body began to shake. As her fingers continued to tighten, she trembled uncontrollably and gave way to a quiet sobbing. Somehow, she found the strength to hold me even tighter and I have to believe that it was at that moment, holding each other in the middle of Sully's dance floor, that we each found our own thoughts and shared our love and tears over the loss of Dusty.

We stood motionless until the song ended. "We should go," she said looking up at me. "Take me home."

The ride to the Barnes's house was silent for the first few blocks. "Sorry, I guess I wasn't a very good dance partner."

"You did just fine," I told her. "Maybe we can try it again some other time. On a happier occasion," I added and wondered if she got the meaning of my statement.

"I guess it finally hit me."

"Yeah, well, then I guess it finally hit both of us."

I walked her to the door and she leaned up and gave me a sisterly kiss on the cheek. "Thanks for the drink, and the good company." Her hand fell to her side and once again brushed against mine. I remembered an old saying my father told me. 'Once an accident, twice a coincidence, three times a habit.' I was hoping the coincidence of her touch would become a habit.

● ◎ ● ● ●

FRIDAY MORNING I DROVE over to Billing's Appliance Store for a second visit to Jules. When I entered, Mr. Billings was with a customer and gave me a friendly wave. Surmising why I was there, he motioned to the back room with his thumb. When I entered the storage area, I found Jules on his back, sprawled out on the floor with his head stuck inside the back end of a washing machine. He had become fully invested in the store. He repaired and delivered machines around the city and his friendly manner made him popular with the locals, which brought about an increase in the store's business. Invariably, anyone looking for a used appliance would be talked into the upgrade of a new one with Jules's cool logic and guarantee that he would take care of them if any future repairs were necessary. Mr. Billings was quick to jump on Jules's capabilities and the two had formed a positive working relationship. The owner was a man who had always been fair and felt all his customers should be treated in an ethical manner and Jules was the employee he needed.

I continued to stare at his huge figure on the floor. He was surrounded by an assortment of wrenches.

"So, does it have a heartbeat?" I asked him.

"It will when I get done with this surgery," he answered recognizing my voice. "Let me get this last nut on before I come up for air. It's a bitch getting in and out of this contraption and I'm about done."

When he stood, he gave me a crushing hug and then stepped back and became very serious. "So, did you go over to the funeral parlor last night?"

"Yeah."

"I'm goin' over tonight. I thought last night was for family. This whole thing's fucked up. He wasn't even on duty, for Christ sake." As he talked he opened the door of a small refrigerator and took out a can of Coke. He raised it high in the air as a gesture to offer me one. I waved him off and he pulled the tab on the top and took a long swallow.

"Dusty's dad called me after I talked with you," I explained. "Told me to feel free to come with the family. I should've called you to let you know."

"No big deal. It makes sense. You guys were always closer than the rest of us. Probably as close as Al and me."

"Yeah, how's he doin' anyway?"

"Ah, you know Al, probably drivin' his sergeant crazy with questions. I'm still a bit pissed at him for enlisting. Had to go play soldier, ya know? Get the real toys to play with, know what I mean?"

"He'll do all right," I assured Jules. "Listen, I just stopped in to say hello, I know you're workin'. As long as you're going to the funeral home later, I'll drop by again tonight and meet you over there. I meant to talk more with Dusty's father last night anyway. Didn't really get the chance." My statement was partially true. I realized after I'd left that I hadn't really offered any help to the family. My second motive for meeting up with Jules would be the opportunity to see Cil again. As I was leaving, Jules called after me. "Hey!"

"Yeah?"

"You hear anything from Jamie?"

"Nothing," I told him. "I've got a number for him in Boston. I tried it once yesterday but didn't get any answer. Prob'bly out on some caper," I laughed.

"You think something happened to him?"

"Hey, you know Jamie. He's usually the one doin' the happening. Maybe I'll try him again when I get home but...well, you know...have mixed feelings about that."

That evening, the two of us sat in the funeral parlor and reminisced about mischievous deeds we'd been involved in with Dusty. While we talked, I watched Cil's every move as she stood with her parents and greeted friends and relatives...the monarch that had captured all my attention and now lingered in my thoughts.

On Saturday, I stood at the gravesite and she stood between her father and me. When possible, I stole glances. Even that day, in the worst of environments, she captured my heart. It's hard to describe my feelings of that day. My heart torn between the grief from the loss of my best friend to the soaring of the feelings I had for his sister.

My eyes remained on her, looking away only when necessary to avoid any perceived rudeness by others. Myrna, whose name I finally knew for certain, stood across from me. She had been most gracious the night before, offering her condolences to the family. Knowing how close Dusty and I were, she made a special effort to tell me how sorry she was for my loss. She had the perfect amount of sorrow. Enough to let everyone know she cared, not enough to lead any of us to believe she felt there was any long-term future included in their relationship. They had been companions and lovers, simple as that.

In addition to friends and relatives, a few of our old classmates attended to offer their respects. Jules stood alone and looked rather naked without Al at his side. The contingent of Waterton police officers stood in full dress uniform, and one of the cops who normally walked a beat played a rendition of taps that sent everyone's emotions spiraling.

I attended the gathering at the Barnes's home following the interment. Jules stopped by for a brief visit and then left to assist Mr. Billings at the store. As he was leaving he brushed by me. "No Jamie?" he asked.

"No Jamie," I confirmed.

Cil and I balanced plates of food on our laps as we sat and talked. This time, conversation came easier. Our awkwardness, or at least mine, was beginning to fade.

"I'd like to go up to Dusty's room for a minute. You know...old times. Do you think it would be okay?"

"I'm sure it would. You go on up. I'll stay here and play hostess for awhile."

Dusty had his own apartment across town but his room was as I remembered it. I stood and stared at his dresser. A small box sat on top and, as it had no cover, the contents were visible. It seemed the items inside had been tossed in haphazardly. It contained his wallet along with a separate photo ID card. Beneath them I could see his watch, along with his Waterton High

School ring. Most obvious was his police badge, resting in a leather sheath. I then realized I was staring at his personal effects, which had evidently been picked up or delivered to his parent's house and then placed in his room. It was an uncomfortable realization.

My eyes shifted to the mirror over his dresser and I studied the picture he had wedged into its frame. I had seen it many times over the years but it never meant as much as it did on that day. It was our sixth-grade class photo on which he had drawn a red circle around his head along with the heads of Al and Jamie, and me. In the back row he had pasted a picture of Jules's head over the top of another student. Along the bottom of the frame, he had taped a piece of paper that read, 'The Five-Cent Gang.' I took a second glance into the box and noticed part of his key ring protruding from beneath his wallet. It was the flattened penny that caught my eye and I picked up the keys and held them in my hand. Knowing Dusty was carrying the penny with him every day as a remembrance of our capers caused the return of the lump in my throat I had fought down at the funeral parlor. My own recollection of the day we all placed them on the train track was interrupted when a familiar voice from the doorway broke my concentration.

"You guys sure spent a lot of time up here in this room," Mr. Barnes said fondly. "I'd sure hate to guess what you two were up to in those days."

"Yeah, we had some times. That's for sure," I said turning to face him.

"Funny ya know," he said, as the ice in his drink clinked against the side of the glass. "In all the years I've been on the job, never once have I drawn my weapon. Now here's my son, on the force for just a couple of years and when he's not even on duty, strolls into a grocery store and some two-bit, trigger-happy asshole shoots him dead. Maybe if he hadn't been in uniform..." his voice trailed off in thought before he continued. "Just goin' in to get a paper or something. I don't know, maybe a candy bar or a soda. Doesn't much matter I guess."

I stood in silence, not really knowing what to say. Not really knowing if Mr. Barnes was finished with his thoughts. "Ya know," he started again. "If there's anything up here of his you might like to have, feel free."

I looked around, not really thinking that I needed anything to remind me of my best friend. The memories we made would always be with me. "I would like to keep his badge, though," his father said. "I'll do something with it, have it framed or something. His mother seems to feel that's a bit morbid but she doesn't think like a cop, ya know? It needs to be in a place of honor."

As he said that, I looked at my hand and realized I was still holding Dusty's key chain with the flattened penny. "Maybe this," I said pointing to the penny. "Looks like he always kept it with him. He must've had it when, well, ya know, it was in the box here with his badge. Kinda like to put it with mine if that doesn't sound too corny."

"Ah yes, the old Five-Cent Gang," Mr. Barnes said smiling. "I'm sure Dusty would be honored to have you look after it. Besides, I never had the privilege of being a member of that elite group. And to answer your question, I don't think it's corny at all," he responded. The ice clinked in his glass once again as he turned and descended the stairs.

I removed the penny from the key ring and then twisted off the key to his safe deposit box. We each held the second key to the other's box but I saw no need for anyone else to find his and ask questions. Its shape alone was indicative of what it would open. I was now the sole proprietor of Uncle Ray and Aunt Ethel and, with only four of us remaining, the thought scared me. It was time the money found its way to the remaining nephews.

Chapter Three

The day after Dusty's funeral I drove Cil to the Greyhound terminal. It meant delaying my own departure for Cortland but I wanted to see her off. When she boarded, she leaned up and gave me the second kiss on the cheek in as many days. It was another sisterly kiss—the kind she would've given Dusty. Is that what I'd become I wondered. Her replacement brother? It wasn't the role I wanted to play right now.

I hated to admit that I used the death of my best friend as an excuse to avoid a day of classes but, in essence, that's what I did. I tried to deny that fact when I remained at my parents' on Monday.

Most of the day was spent looking through my old photo albums. I called Jules and made arrangements to meet him after work. I suggested Sully's but he successfully lobbied for the beehive.

I walked across the street with expectations of nostalgia but when I got to our old meeting place things were surprisingly different. The big table we had marred with our initials and insignias along with a stick figure drawing Al made of two soldiers dueling it out with machine guns was gone. Jules had also removed the infamous word 'B-O-O-K' from the wall where Jamie had painted the F word and, to save embarrassment to his mother, Jules turned it into a more appropriate word.

It was obvious why Jules had wanted to meet there. The entire basement area, which had hosted so many of our meetings, was renovated to imitate a second living room. The walls were covered with stained v-matched boards that gave the space new warmth. Large areas had pictures; a few were photos of The Five-Cent Gang, while others depicted his mother standing with him and Al. The cement floor was painted and covered with colorful throw rugs to which Jules had added a full-sized couch and an overstuffed chair. A coffee table sat between them. A bookshelf against a far wall displayed a small library and was topped with a stereo receiver and an eight-track player with a stack of eight tracks beside it.

I viewed the area with a look of awe when I entered and Jules stood and walked to a corner of the room where he opened a set of louvered doors to reveal the hidden washer and dryer. Unlike the set he had purchased many years ago, they were new and, he assured me the clatter and groaning of the old ones were no longer a disturbance.

"Nice, huh?" he asked me.

"Absolutely cherry," I told him. "Your mother must like these babies."

"Yeah, well, check this out," as he said the words he moved to another corner of the room. "The piece d' resistance," he said with the worse French accent I ever heard.

I stared at a new refrigerator. He opened the door and took out two Budweisers. "Managing an appliance store has its advantages," he said, grabbing an opener from the top of the fridge.

"Yeah. Looks like things are goin' okay for you with this gig."

We sat down and talk immediately turned to Dusty's death and he filled me in on what he knew. I said nothing of the conversation I'd had with Mr. Barnes about specific details and for the first of several beers we consoled each other. The discussion then turned to Al.

"So, what have you heard from the old boy?"

"Ah, you know Al. Doesn't say much anymore. Wrote from boot camp; told the powers to be he wanted to go to Viet Nam. Would've probably been shipped over there anyway but, you know, when you ask for that kind of trouble, the big boys are more than happy to oblige. Writes an occasional letter to me or Mom but hell, I don't know what's goin' on in his head."

"He's probably buggin' the hell out of his sergeant with all his questions," I laughed.

"I don't know what happened, man. He was just never the same after all that shit went down with the fat man. I mean, he always talked big...wanted to shoot guns and stuff, but when you and Dusty sent the fat man over the cliff...and then that Wenzel guy got shot..."

Jules's voice trailed off as he stared at the floor before he continued. "It was like he felt we were *all* responsible for killing those guys, no matter what I told him."

As Jules talked, I reflected on the locker-room conversation Dusty and I were privy to in high school. We were getting dressed one day and Al joined us when he came out of the shower. He stood in front of me with his towel wrapped around his waist and just stared.

"What?" I asked him. He continued staring and then exhaled a long breath out of puffy cheeks. It was the kind of exhale that always seemed to preclude bad news.

He sat down on the bench and used a second towel to dry his hair. After a few vigorous strokes, he stopped and pulled the towel off and gave me an odd look.

"Ever told anybody?" he asked.

I looked at Dusty who stopped midway in pulling on his sock. He returned my look of surprise.

"Told anybody what?" I knew full well what he meant but I guess I needed to hear the rest of the question.

"You know, about the whole bridge thing...and the fat man."

"No." I told him. "Neither one of us has. Why, have you told someone? I mean you haven't said anything right?"

"No, no I haven't. It's just that...you know...it's not that easy for me. I mean, you two are together all the time but I'm usually stuck somewhere alone. After Jamie moved to Boston and Jules started playin' football and then went to work at the store. Christ, I don't even see him anymore. It's like I'm alone with this big secret and I'm stuck with it."

"Look, any time you want to talk with us it's cool, man. Just hold it together." I told him.

"Yeah, he's right." Dusty chimed in. "I know we only have gym together but we can meet other times. We can talk. Like Auggie says, just hold it together. Try and forget it."

Al wasn't reassured enough with our responses and continued. "What do you think the statute of limitations is for what we did? I think it's seven years or something."

With that question, Dusty took over. "Statute of limitations!" he screamed.

I looked around the locker room hoping no one else was in there to hear Dusty's yell. A couple of showers were running, but no one was in our area and I motioned to Dusty indicating he needed to keep it down. He lowered his volume, but continued addressing Al. "There ain't no statute of limitations on that caper, man. We didn't actually break any laws. I mean, we didn't hold up some bank downtown. We took money from the bad guys," he reminded Al. He then continued as he slowly and deliberately individualized each word. "We don't ever talk about it to anyone else," he reminded him. "Remember the two rules we all agreed on? We don't talk about it and we don't spend it. So we continue with those rules and not talk about it and since the money disappeared, we obviously *can't* spend it."

Al played with the towel he was holding as his shoulders slumped a bit forward in a sign of resignation. "Yeah. Okay. I'll keep it together. One for all, all for one, right?"

"Yeah, right," Dusty confirmed. With the issue seemingly closed, Dusty and I left the locker room confident that Al wouldn't mention anything to anyone.

"Should we tell him?" Dusty's voice was calm when he asked me the question.

"What? Tell him we've got the money?"

"Yeah."

"No, we stick to the plan. Everybody will get their share but you and I have to set the time and place." I told him.

What Jules described in the beehive that day about Al's behavior was similar to the comments made in the locker room. That was the first time Dusty and I realized how the incident had actually affected Al. It was no surprise that Jules, who lived in the same house, hadn't noticed much of a difference in his brother's behavior until recently. I thought it best to avoid mentioning the locker room and tried to diminish the troubles Al was having.

"Yeah, I guess all of us changed in one way or another. Me and Dusty had many conversations about that day. When Al got separated from us in junior high we never really saw much of him other than weekends. Then he got into a new group of friends."

"I'm not sure how good those guys were for him. Some of 'em seemed a little screwed up to me."

Not having gone to Jules's house to add to my depression, I changed the subject. "So, you and your mom are doin' okay? Everything's good?"

"Yeah. Mom's good, and work's okay. Mr. Billings spends less and less time at the store. He's pretty much out of the picture 'cause of his health. Bad ticker, so I manage the store for him. I'd like to buy him out someday if I could swing it. I've got some ideas I'd like to put into action but he just says they're a young man's dreams ya know? He's not really interested in doing anything different at this point.

For example, I've got access to washers and dryers at cost—sometimes below cost. If the timing is right, I can get industrial-sized machines the same way. He's got an entire storage area next to the store that we could fill with coin-operated babies and run a Laundromat. There's only a couple in town now and they're terrible. Half the machines don't work and the places are filthy. He could turn a pretty penny if he'd let me go ahead with something like that."

I thought for a moment about Ray and Ethel. "How much do you figure you'd need?"

"It wouldn't really take all that much. I've been around long enough, and so has he, that we could probably get a loan from the bank. He just doesn't want to do it at his age. Says he'll be retiring soon. Told me to wait 'til he dies and then I can buy him out. Other than that, yeah, things are goin' pretty good. Good job...got me a good woman...a few cold beers in the fridge...life is good."

"Speakin' of a good woman, did you get a chance to talk to Cil in the last two days?"

"Didn't talk much but I did see her. She sure turned out to be a looker. I didn't even know it was her when I first saw her."

Not knowing how my next comment would be taken, I approached it slowly. "Yeah, well, I may have a little problem there."

"What kind of a problem?"

"I guess you could say that I'm more attracted to her than I probably should be."

"What? You and Dusty's sister? C'mon man...whaddaya doin' here?"

"Yeah, I know what you're sayin' but there's somethin' there I don't wanna let go of. At least from my end."

"And her end?"

"Well, we went out for a drink the other night and when I drove her home I got a sisterly type kiss," I told him. It wasn't the conversation I'd had in mind when I decided to visit him.

"I don't know, man, that's dangerous territory you're treading on...a friend's sister? You better watch your ass on that move."

Without the supportive responses I needed, I changed the subject once again before I left and we shared another beer over talk of Tittle and the Giants. The discussion continued with hopes of the upcoming season as we walked out to the driveway.

Before crossing the street to go home, it was Jules who changed the subject. "Listen," he said grabbing my arm. "If your goal with Silly is just to see if you can get into bed with her then I'd advise you to drop the idea. You're too close to it all right now and that includes Dusty's parents. But if you really think you two could get a good thing goin' here then ..." he hesitated, "then okay, go for it. But take it slow, man. Keep in touch with her, but take it slow. Maybe you should let her play it out first and see what she wants to do."

Once again, Jules came through with his bits of wisdom. On the drive to Cortland the following morning, my mind was filled with two thoughts. What to do about Cil, and should I tell Jules he had the money to buy out Mr. Billings whenever he was ready. A phone call wasn't the best way to do it but Thanksgiving was right around the corner. It would be better to sit in the beehive with a cold one and tell him the whole story.

* * * * *

I GOT TO CAMPUS in time for my one o'clock, which was followed by the occupation of my Tuesday afternoon barstool at Higby's.

After tipping a few, the emotion of the week caught me by surprise. With thoughts of the past few days still lingering, coupled with the drive, I drove to my apartment. I had rarely thought about Dusty when I was at school but now the thought of his absence tore at my guts. I collapsed on my bed and slept through dinner and on and off for most of the evening. It was almost midnight when Cil called.

"Were you sleeping?"

"No, not really," I lied. "Are you okay?"

"I'm okay, I just needed to talk," she told me, and some small talk got underway. Descriptions of weird people on her bus trip back to school...a guy snoring in the back...getting in late...blowing off Monday's classes. When she finished, I followed suit and confessed that I'd remained home Monday and just got back for my Tuesday class. While we talked, my mind drifted. What about us? I thought. What about our future together? These thoughts were kept alive with her occasional laugh or the mention of our dance or the trickle of enjoyment in her voice. Was she toying with me? Was this her revenge for my neglect during her adolescent crush on me? Did the girl who Dusty once said wanted to marry me now have the upper hand? And were the occasional comments about going to the library to work with some guy made to throw me into a tailspin of jealousy?

So why hadn't she called him, I wondered. Should I hope she got at least one of my signals that I wanted to see more of her? The conversation eventually rolled around to the upcoming Thanksgiving holiday.

"Maybe we should get together for a drink when we're home," I offered. The thought of either one of us having Thanksgiving dinner at the other's house seemed out of place in our current situation, unless we were seeing each other. The thought of a drink together seemed to make more sense.

"Yeah, we could do that if you want to."

If I want to, I thought. Her noncommittal response was less than reassuring. "We could go to Sully's again. Maybe see some of the old gang."

"I don't know. Sully's is more your old gang than mine. Maybe we could find a quiet bar in Troy or something."

The term quiet bar was an encouraging sign and I saw no reason to debate it. "Yeah, that sounds good. We'll find something."

The following evening the phone rang and, assuming it was Cil, my spirits were immediately lifted.

When I answered, however, it was Jules, and his tone was clearly distressed.

"It's Al," he told me with a choked voice. "I just got a call. He got hurt bad. They told me he lost one leg and a good part of the other."

I was still in a partial sleep from the late hour and had trouble finding a response.

"Anyway, the guy who called told me it was a mine. It wasn't even Al who triggered it. Some guy he was on patrol with. It killed the other guy but Al got a good part of the shrapnel. They told me he was airlifted to a field hospital in Nha Trang, wherever the hell that is. They said they'd keep me informed of his condition. You know, a shitload of details still to come but I thought you'd want to know."

"Jeezus Jules, I'm really sorry to hear that. How's your mother in all this?"

"Aw, you know, she's pretty freaked out about it. She's seen plenty of this stuff in the ER but she's been cryin' since we got the call. She's tryin' to hold it together."

"You want me to drive back to Waterton?"

"No, there's nothin' you can do here. I'll take care of Mom and I can keep you posted on what's going on with Al. I'm thinking it will be a while before he gets to our area. I just wanted you to know. I'll keep you posted," he repeated again.

The next morning I called Cil to fill her in. It wasn't that she knew Al that well as much as an excuse to talk to her. Surprisingly, she was more upset than I expected and we talked at length.

At the end of the week, I received a second call from Jules. The update I'd been promised was far from what I expected. Al's injuries were either worse than initially described to Jules, or the military was not forthcoming with the whole story.

"Your brother died during the night," the officer on the phone had said. "I was told the severity of his wounds and the loss of blood were just too much for his body to withstand," he continued. The conversation then concluded, as he expressed his deepest sympathies to the family and told Jules he would follow up with details regarding Al's body being shipped home and any military arrangements the family wanted to make.

It was another week and a half before I made the trip to Waterton for Thanksgiving break. I would certainly see Cil and now Jules was on my list of must-see visits. Al's death made bad timing for a discussion regarding Aunt Ethel and Uncle Ray, but, with Dusty gone, I had to get my own life in order. It was time to have a serious talk with Jules and, even more worrisome, it was time to find Jamie.

Chapter Four

The week of Thanksgiving was a blur. Wednesday's classes were canceled for the holiday and, seeing no reason to attend only two classes on Tuesday—one of which I had only attended three times since the semester started—I left early that morning and arrived home in time for lunch.

The first portion of the afternoon was spent at the bank transferring three-fifths of the money into my old Waterton High School gym bag and a briefcase I'd commandeered from my father's study. My plan was to give Jules the shares for him and Al on Wednesday, spend Thursday and Friday with Cil, attempt to locate and square things with Jamie on Saturday, drive back to spend time with Cil on Sunday, and return to school on Monday.

Like most plans, things didn't run smoothly. It was as if I was reliving one of our infamous capers. Before leaving school Jules called to let me know the red tape had been cleared and Al's body was being flown into Albany on Saturday. His request for me to assist him with the follow-up arrangements was not something I could deny nor did I want to mention anything about the money over the phone. I spent most of Tuesday's drive mentally prioritizing and rearranging the five days that lay ahead.

I had no difficulty getting the money and Tuesday night I divided it into three large brown paper bags that advertised the Waterton IGA.

Before meeting with Jules on Wednesday, I called Jamie's number again. This time I got through and it was Jamie's mother who answered the phone, surprised that it was an old friend from Waterton. After giving me a brief résumé regarding his attendance at Boston College, she gave me two phone numbers. The first was for his dorm, which I was told, should be a call of last resort. The second number was for the office of the parish church. His mother said that was the better number to call. If he wasn't there, they would at least take a message and get it to him. He was the coach of, as she put it, some basketball team or something and the parish office was connected to the team.

When I called, a priest named Father Thomas answered and confirmed that Jamie was coaching some of the boys in the parish but wasn't around. He mentioned Jamie had a practice scheduled for Friday if that was any help.

"Do you know what time the practice is?" I asked.

"Ten o'clock," the priest told me and then added that practices usually ran an hour and a half or so, in case I wanted to see him. His tone hinted it wouldn't be a good idea to interrupt the practice but, at my request, he agreed to give Jamie the message that I would be driving over to see him on Friday morning...either before or after the scheduled practice.

When I arrived at Jules's Wednesday morning, I realized the scenario for discussing Ray and Ethel couldn't be worse. The front door was wide open and I entered without bothering to knock. My entry went unnoticed to Jules's mother who was on the phone. Two men were making trips from the parked van in front of the house to the living room where they deposited vases of flowers with no method to their placement. The scent of the room caused me to reflect on the funeral home where Dusty's service had been only a few weeks before. I heard a stirring in the kitchen and went in to find Jules breaking eggs into a frying pan. He stopped and gave me a bear hug. "I'm just making some breakfast. You want something to eat?"

"No, I'm good. I'll take a cup of coffee though," I told him, pointing to the pot on the counter. Before I could begin my prepared speech, Jules began to review the plan for Saturday.

"Mom wants it over and done with as quick as possible," he began with no actual starting point to his explanation. "Al's body is going right from the airport to the county coroner's office. I guess the coroner has to make sure Al's dead." His statement held a note of irritation with the red tape he was facing. "Mom said just the two of us would go over to have a final viewing, although if you want to go you're certainly welcome."

I said nothing and he continued.

"Anyway, from there, the body is going straight to the crematorium and in a day or two we can pick up the ashes. Mom wants to keep them here in the house. She's setting up pictures and memorabilia for a memorial service here on Saturday afternoon. A few friends, but mostly just relatives."

"What time do you want me over here?" I asked with as much sincerity as I could muster, hoping my presence wouldn't be required until the service. As much as I wanted to help Jules, I had a full agenda for the remainder of the week and wanted to stay on schedule. I tried to keep in mind that his grief was as deep now as mine for Dusty.

"The plane is supposed to come into Albany between ten and ten-thirty. It's a military aircraft so that's as close an estimate as I could get. That's not a problem for you is it? I mean, I don't need any help or anything, I just thought you'd like to be involved and it would be nice to have a friend along," he paused and when I didn't answer added, "I know Al would appreciate it. All the arrangements for the transport from Albany to Waterton have been set up. You and I will just follow along behind."

"I think it'll work out," I told him. "I have to go out of town tomorrow but I should be back in plenty of time."

My plan to spend Friday with Cil had already been changed to Saturday and now I'd be spending a good portion of the day with Jules.

"Where do you have to go Friday? You're not going back to school, are you?"

"No. Actually, that's what I wanted to talk to you about today." I glanced toward the living room where Jules's mother was now off the phone. I could hear her instructing the delivery guys on where to put the flowers. "Maybe we should go to the beehive?"

Once downstairs, Jules with his eggs and me with my coffee, I took a deep breath. I figured the easiest way to break the news was to give Jules my schedule. "Tomorrow, I'll be having dinner with the folks. You know, the usual stuff. Then, on Friday morning I'll be heading over to Boston." I took another deep breath before continuing. "I'm going to see Jamie."

"No shit. You know where he is?" Jules's voice was filled more with surprise and acceptance of the idea than I'd expected.

"Well, I've narrowed it down and left a message I was coming over to meet with him."

"So what's up with you seein' him all of a sudden?"

"Well, that's the thing you see. That's the other reason I'm here. You remember the day when all hell broke loose because the old steam engine with all the money in it went missing?"

"Yeah. We were all pissed as hell but hey, nobody blamed you."

"Well a couple of years ago, Dusty and I found the money. Actually, we found the old train it was in and the bags were still in there." Jules had finished half his eggs at that point and was about to take another forkful. He stopped midway to his mouth and just stared at me.

"What are you talkin' about?"

"You remember Mr. Faulk from the train yard...the old guy I always used to hang out with? Well, when he died, I found out it was him who had the old steam engine and he left it to me in his will."

Jules continued to sit and stare as I went on with the story that ended with Ray and Ethel. "I know you're probably really pissed about me not telling you, but..."

Jules raised a hand signaling me to stop talking. For a few moments, he said nothing. He sat and studied the floor as if in deep thought before he spoke. "No...no, I'm not pissed." As he spoke, it was obvious that he was trying to digest the entire scenario. "You guys probably did the best thing for all of us. If you told us about the money when you found it, we'd probably all be in jail now—or maybe even dead." The sentences came out slowly as he continued to absorb the information and I exhaled a long-awaited sigh of relief.

"Well it's time to divvy up," I told him. "Frankly I'm tired of holdin' on to the money and now with Dusty gone, I don't have anyone to talk with about it."

"How much? I mean how much did we get?"

This time I looked him straight in the eye. I remembered how Dusty had toyed with me at the pool and how he strung out the answer. This part of my rehearsed plan was playing out the way I'd hoped. "First of all, there were only a few stacks of money that were fives and tens. Most of what we got turned out to be fifties and hundreds."

"No shit! Well that's good. So how much was it?"

"It came out to a little under six-hundred-fifty thousand," I told him nonchalantly. "And obviously, you get Al's share as well. It's always been a five-way split. Dusty and I were in immediate agreement on that, even Jamie gets a share which is why I'm driving to Boston. I want this money split over and done with."

"So, what was the math on that? What's the six hundred and, whatever you said, come out to on the five-way split?"

It was the question I'd hope he would ask and I remained perfectly calm with my answer. "Actually, the six-hundred and fifty thousand amount is after the split."

I could tell by Jules's expression that he wasn't grasping what I was saying. "That's the amount for each of us, man. And you get that times two with Al's share. You're a millionaire, boy!"

Jules said nothing for several seconds and I remained silent to let him think about his new riches.

"I can't believe you guys had the smarts or the patience to not say anything to us or spend any of it."

"Believe me, it was tempting. Many times we needed stuff and considered dipping into it. Which brings me to another point, and that's how to spend it."

"Yeah, well I know how I'm gonna spend it!"

"No, listen. That's exactly what I'm talkin' about. You just can't go out and start buyin' stuff. I'm sure, in time, you can figure a plan to get things you want, but I've had years to think this thing through. We can't start running around buying cars and yachts and stuff, but there are ways we can pull it off if we're careful. Actually, before the money went missing, spending it too fast was one of the things we were worried about with Al. You even mentioned it."

"Yeah, I remember. So what do you mean? Careful how?"

For the next twenty minutes I reviewed my own plan for the spending process. "You want to buy a new car, you buy it on time," I started. "You always said that some day you'd like to buy your mother a nicer house. So you do, but you buy it on time. You go to a bank, take out a loan, make a mortgage payment every month." I then changed gears to the plan he had discussed with me more than once.

"How about your idea of buying out Mr. Billings's appliance store and setting up that Laundromat next door? You can do that now. But even though you have the money, you still go to the bank, present your plan and get a loan."

"But that's like really not having the money," he argued.

"Not really. The beauty of it is you never have to worry about making any payments on anything. You'll have the comfort of knowing that no matter what happens with the business, the money is always there. That, in itself, is a big worry off your mind. And anything you can buy and pay for with cash, you do. You have to realize you've got an entire lifetime to spend a million bucks and sprinkle it on anything you want as long as you're careful. You want a new car? You get every option the dealership has to offer. Nobody seein' you driving around knows you've got all the extras. Once a week you go out to dinner to some fancy restaurant in Albany or Troy. You pay cash and leave a good tip, but not so good as to be remembered. Every week you take a couple of hundreds to a bank and change 'em into twenties. Every so often you run up to Saratoga and spend an afternoon playin' the ponies. When you get back you casually mention you had a pretty good day or made a few hundred on a long shot."

As I talked, Jules paid close attention. Of the three of us left, he was the one who I trusted most to carry through and not be reckless. Over the years I had come to learn it was Jules who had the most common sense of any of us.

"You see that stereo sittin' over there?" I asked, pointing to his eight-track player on the bookshelf. "Who's gonna know if you go to the best stereo place around and pick up the top of the line system with monster speakers? And, of course, you pay cash. And if someone visits and sees it and compliments you on it, you of course acknowledge it but also mention it cost an arm and a leg and you had to eat beans for two months to swing the deal."

As I continued, Jules gave slow appreciative nods of his head. "Like I said, you've got a whole lifetime to spend it."

"What about Dusty's share?"

"He and I talked about that. He knew being a cop, even in Waterton, had its risks. He told me if anything ever happened to him, I was to somehow get the money to Silly. Likewise, if I happened to get run over or something, he'd find some way to have my parents benefit. Neither of us ever expected anything would actually happen to the other...at least not this early in life."

"And Jamie?"

"I guess I'll find out Friday. I'll fill you in Saturday when I get back."

"I don't know if I could get away from here with all this stuff going on with Al, but I may be able to go with you and share the driving."

The sharing of the driving seemed to be an afterthought. I assumed that seeing Jamie and finding out what he was currently up to was the more tempting idea.

"Thanks," I told him. "I appreciate the offer, but seeing Jamie is something I've got to do alone. None of us really parted on the best of terms with him and I'm not sure where his head is at. Besides, you've got a full plate right here. Anyway, I've gotta get back to the house, so why don't you walk me out."

Before leaving, I talked briefly about Al with Jules's mother and then Jules and I walked across the street where I had locked two of the three IGA bags in the trunk of my car.

When I handed him the two bags he opened one and peeked inside.

"Wow, this is unbelievable. Nice touch on the IGA bags. I don't think this whole thing about being rich has sunk in yet."

"Just remember what I said about the spending. I don't have any idea where the hunt for this loot stands with the bad guys. I'm figuring it's been long enough that we're okay as long as we're careful, but guys like the ones we took from don't forget, and I'll bet they're still lookin'."

● ● ● ● ●

THANKSGIVING DINNER WAS TYPICAL although that year I had a new alliance in Jules. Since arriving home, I'd been on the go and, other than seeing Cil that evening, I knew my next chance to see her wasn't until Sunday, when I would hopefully take her to the bus terminal. It was a ride that would undoubtedly end in another sisterly goodbye kiss.

After dinner, I settled in with my father to watch some football. It was the first time in history the NFL televised four games on Thanksgiving. My father sat right next to the TV so he could switch back and forth between channels. With a belly full of turkey, I dozed through fragments of the two early games with an occasional wakening from my father's rantings at the officials whose calls he disagreed with.

Between the rants, he cheered on the Rams as they ran roughshod over the Lions and in the later game sent shouts of disgust as the Raiders doubled the points scored by Kansas City.

The evening that followed promised a good match-up between the Cowboys and the Cardinals, but I saw very little of it. I picked up Cil around seven-thirty and we went to a small lounge in Troy, as she had suggested. Since it was much quieter than Sully's, it gave me the opportunity I needed to explain my absence on Friday. I felt a bit guilty about lying to her but she believed that I spent the day in the Albany library researching a paper for school. The true events of the day had been quite different.

Chapter Five

I had no idea what to expect when I pulled onto Commonwealth Avenue in search of St. Mary's church. Everything I was about to learn regarding Jamie since he left Waterton would be news. I had never been a follower of college basketball and had no idea he was making waves, albeit small waves, with his play at Boston College. I wasn't even aware he was attending BC, although it wasn't a fact that surprised me. Simply stated, he was coaching, as his mother had said, some basketball team or something. That part made sense. He'd always been good at playing ball, and to be picking up some extra money coaching a church team was logical although, knowing Jamie, I figured he was probably working an angle.

The paper containing the scribbled directions I'd written had fallen between the passenger seat and the door leaving me to battle the Saturday morning traffic with no idea where I was headed. After hailing a man walking in the visitor's area of St. Elisabeth's Hospital in Brighton, I was directed to turn and take the opposite direction if I wanted to find St. Mary's.

It was located on a side street and parking was easy. Not trusting the big city, I tucked the IGA bag under my arm and approached what looked like a custodian who was sweeping leaves from the walkway in front of the church.

"You don't happen to know a guy named Jamie McGuire, by any chance, do you? Supposed to be working here today—with the basketball team. I'm supposed to meet him here."

"Coach McGuire?" he corrected. "Sure I know him. Your best bet is to go right in through the church here. Take a right to the stairway and at the foot of the stairs follow the hallway around to the gym." The man then looked at his watch. "He's probably done with practice by now, but you might catch him if he's expecting you."

The weight of the door was deceptive and my first pull had to be repeated. Inside, the fragrance of incense was immediate and, for some reason, I recalled the very first conversation Jamie and I had, which had been overheard by the eavesdropping ears of Susan Murphy, causing her to condemn me for talking about incest.

The choir was rehearsing and I heard the conductor instruct them on what bar they would begin with this time around and what she wanted to hear. A lone figure sat in a pew halfway between my position and the front of the church and, even after the passing of many years, I recognized Jamie's profile.

The choir returned to its singing, which allowed me to walk down the aisle unheard and I stopped just shy of where Jamie was seated. He was dressed in shorts and an old sweatshirt from which the sleeves had been cut. He sat holding a basketball in his lap as he glued his attention to the choir. I took the few steps needed into the pew and sat beside him. He continued to look straight ahead and never moved a muscle. "How you been, man?" he said, and as he did so he turned and flashed a big smile and extended his hand.

"All right," I said returning his greeting and shook his hand.

"They're good, aren't they?" It was more of a statement than a question as he nodded toward the choir.

"Yeah, they sound really great."

"The piece they're singing is Thomas Tallis's "Spem In Alium." It's a piece rarely performed any more. If you're not careful, it may bring you to tears."

The two of us sat and listened as the choir sang Tallis's piece with as much beauty and reverence as I had ever heard from any choir. The echo provided by the huge cathedral defined and amplified each note's tone and clarity as the voices resonated throughout the church. It was a good ten minutes before the choir finished and awaited the director's critique. It was then that Jamie, who had not stirred throughout the performance, turned to me a second time.

"C'mon," he instructed. "We can go downstairs and talk. I venture we have some catching up to do."

His office was off the gymnasium. It was cluttered with an odd variety of sneakers, a mismatch of team uniforms, and miscellaneous sports equipment. After a bit of small talk, he spoke of his coaching successes and his current status at Boston College. He wasn't a starter, but was seeing a considerable amount of playing time. Unlike the days of our youth, his releasing of the facts was more reluctant than boastful and it was obvious he had undergone a serious transformation since moving to Boston. Included in the updates in our lives was talk of the deaths of both Dusty and Al, neither of which he was aware.

"I'm really sorry to hear about Dusty. I know you two were really close." Following a brief hesitation adding, "You two outvoted me on more than one occasion," and then he dispensed a genuine laugh at the thought. He asked how Jules was and, as the conversation progressed, I felt like I was talking to someone I'd just met and was struck by the irony of how time had changed all of us. Jules had become a responsible appliance store manager, Al had become a cynic, Silly blossomed into an angel, and now Jamie, the master of illegal capers, was a sincere and responsible person.

"I didn't make the trip over here just to fill you in on the old gang," I started. "I've got a little something here I brought for you." As I made the statement, I motioned to the IGA bag I had set on a small table under the window.

"You drove all the way over here to bring me groceries? I'm flattered."

"Take a look inside," I told him.

He opened the bag and stared at the contents and then turned with his arms outstretched. "What's this? I mean, what's goin' on here?"

I went through the same explanation I had given Jules. As I spoke of finding the Baldwin and the details leading up to my trip to Boston, he sat and listened with a strange quietness about him. There was no air of excitement, almost as if he had expected the news of his newfound wealth.

When I began to suggest ways to spend the money, he raised a hand and interrupted. "I can't take any of that money," he told me. "I mean, I don't know how much you've got in that bag there but really, I can't take it."

"What are you talkin' about, you can't take it? We all earned it, man. There's over six-hundred thousand dollars in that bag. It's yours!"

"I'm not just working here as a coach. St. Mary's and the parish priest here have become a second family to me. That choir you heard? I came in one day and they were rehearsing so I sat and listened for a few minutes. I'm not sure exactly what happened but something inside me changed. I mean, you hear all this talk about getting the calling and so forth, and I'm not saying that happened but working with the kids here, and Father Mac—well something's definitely changed inside me. So much so that, when I graduate from BC, I've been talking with Father Mac about entering the seminary. I'm sure you're thinking there's some kind of poetic justice in that somewhere."

I opened my mouth to respond but he raised his hand to silence me. "I know, I know what you're thinking but that's not me anymore. Father Mac and I, a priest I'd like you to meet by the way, have discussed the idea at length. I've got a whole new life now and not just coaching here. I've expanded the league and got other parishes involved. That raises the number of kids we can keep off the streets. I just don't have any *need* for the money, not to mention it being an ill-conceived gain, although it would probably put the final exclamation point in our fund-raising drive for the new gym," he added, as if having second thoughts. "Anyway, I appreciate the offer and the drive all the way over here, and it's great seeing you, but I guess you and Jules can split my share and be a little bit richer."

I sat for a moment and thought. "Then maybe I need to make a confession to you."

"I can't hear confessions," he told me. "I'm a long way from being a priest...not to mention, you're not even Catholic!"

"Okay then, a friend-to-friend confession—one Five-Cent Gang member to another. That's something you would honor."

"What exactly am I honoring? I'd be more worried about that syndicate boss than me," he continued.

"He's dead."

"That guy Provinzini died?"

"Yeah, not too long ago. Kinda puts us in the clear. Jules and I think he was the last one to still be giving orders about finding the money. It happened under his watch so…"

"Yeah, well, your secret's safe with me, with or without a confession.

"Maybe I'll come back when you're a full-fledged priest just to make sure."

"Not really necessary," Jamie laughed. "But you're always welcome to come back and visit. Maybe you should think about coming over to our side now anyway. Seems like you've already got the confession thing down pretty good."

With Jamie accepting my status of wealth, he agreed to let me buy him lunch. While he showered and changed I took the initiative to seek out and introduce myself to Father Mac. It turned out he was visiting another parish that morning so I made my exit and waited in the car.

In a nearby diner, the two of us sat in a booth and reminisced about the old days. Our continuous laughter and outbursts drew stares from other patrons as specific moments of early capers were relived— memories of Miss Beezel and Big Tony and Candy Melons.

He opted to walk back to the church, and expressed his disappointment that Father Mac had been out and hoped that I would someday have the opportunity to meet him.

"I'll tell you what," I told him. "If you go through with this priest thing, I'll drive over for the final vows ceremony, or whatever it is you do when you become a priest. I'll even bring Jules with me."

"I'll hold you to that," he told me and shook my hand. As he turned and walked toward the parish office, he stopped, looked back, and reached inside his shirt. He pulled out the flattened penny. "It always brings me luck," he yelled, holding it up toward his chin. He then tucked it back in and gave me a thumbs-up sign. "The Five-Cent Gang," he called out and then turned and headed toward the church.

● ● ● ● ●

THE CONFRONTATION I HAD dreaded was over and it had turned out to be a most enjoyable reunion. If I didn't see Jamie again, I knew I'd at least keep track of his capers in the Big East Conference.

When he returned to Father Mac's office, he found the priest had returned and was standing behind his desk. He held a small slip of paper in his hands. As necessity dictated, he peered through glasses that sat on the far tip of his nose as he read. Jamie became flushed and the heat rose to his face when he spotted the IGA bag on the desk. Father Mac looked at Jamie, then into the bag and then returned his gaze to Jamie.

"I found this bag on my desk when I returned from St. Francis earlier. It's full of money, had this note inside." He lifted the paper in the air and held it at arms length to focus before reading it aloud. 'The enclosed donation is for your new gymnasium. It should make things pie easy.' I assume whoever wrote it meant easy as pie. What do you think?"

"I don't know," Jamie responded. "I guess I've heard pie easy used on occasion."

Father Mac seemed somewhat surprised by Jamie's response. He peered into the bag a second time. "Looks like a lot of money in here...and the note's unsigned. Whoever left it might be right. This may be enough to finish the gym. Any idea who might have been so generous?"

Jamie thought for a moment before responding. He thought of his promise and The Five-Cent Gang and chose his words very carefully.

"Can't say that I do," he said.

Although the strange appearance of the donation by an anonymous donor was often mentioned, Jamie was never again questioned about it.

Chapter Six

The drive home was pleasant. The sun warmed the inside of the car and the radio DJ played a great selection of tunes. My visit with Jamie had gone well, and I would soon be seeing Cil. I was feeling great inside and once on the Mass Pike, I stopped at the first service area outside of Boston and called Jules. He picked up the phone after three rings and I recognized his voice.

"He's found God!" I yelled into the phone. "Jamie's found God!" And then I laughed out loud and hung up.

Chapter Seven

Jules choked through the eulogy, which contained several long pauses as he collected himself. When time was offered for others to include anecdotes of their life with Al, several people shared precious and often humorous moments. I was the last to speak and used my time to share an abbreviated version of our childhood raid on a public place. Not knowing if we were still wanted by the military, I omitted the use of the word arsenal along with many other details of incrimination. Mrs. Daly sat in a matronly way at the beginning of the service but eventually succumbed to tears. As Jules concluded his comments, her tears turned to outright sobbing which seemed to bring a touch of finality to the grim afternoon.

When the service ended, I took Cil home. She had come down with a cold and sore throat, which canceled the plans we'd made for that night. The remainder of the day was spent at the Daly house to assist Jules and his mother.

I drove Cil to the Albany bus terminal on Sunday and during the drive we agreed to get together during the Christmas break, although I wasn't quite sure of the definition of the term 'get together'. It somehow didn't have the ring of 'dating'.

In the weeks between Thanksgiving and Christmas, the two of us ran up a higher than normal phone bill. Once we got home I spent a lot of time at the Barnes' residence and my familiarity seemed agreeable to Dusty's parents. Whether or not they knew I had designs on their daughter never surfaced. Cil and I went to the Christmas Eve church service and as we walked from the church to the car, a light snow fell. The flakes floated and sparkled as they landed silently on her hair and shoulders. If I had any doubts about my feelings for her, they were erased that night. She clung to my arm as we walked and, although it seemed we were still just friends, much of the coyness she exhibited weeks before had disappeared.

On New Year's Eve, we went to Sully's and shared a table with Jules and Gloria, the girlfriend to whom he had recently proposed. The engagement ring seemed appropriate for a man of his limited means. When the opportunity presented itself, he quietly mentioned to Cil how he'd probably be paying for the ring the rest of his life, but Gloria was worth it. Cil thought the comment was romantic and I felt it was an excellent choice of words.

The four of us discussed the upcoming new year and what we might do to make it a great one. In addition to Jules and Gloria sharing their marriage plans, Jules announced that he planned to get a loan and purchase the store from Mr. Billings.

Before Cil and I could get our own ideas out, the band drowned out any chance of conversation with "Gimme Some Lovin'", a rocking Rascals tune, and Cil dragged me to the dance floor. When the song ended, the lead singer used his stage advantage to begin the countdown to midnight. Cil seemed to ignore him as she put her arms around my neck and tiptoed up to reach me. "What Jules said about our expectation...I'm hoping my new year includes a great romance," she whispered.

The lead singer finished the countdown but before he actually got to zero, Cil and I were locked in an embrace and caught up in a magical New Year's Eve kiss...and it was not a kiss that a sister would give her brother.

● ◉ ● ◉ ●

THE NEW YEAR DID, in fact, present Cil with a whirlwind romance. If we weren't on the phone, we were out with friends or pursuing other amorous interludes. The night before our vacation ended, we went to dinner and I was anxious to find out if she knew more about our childhood escapades than she was telling. As we sat waiting for our meals, she glanced down at the gin and tonic between her hands and rolled it back and forth as if it were an upright rolling pin. "Kinda nice to be able to drink legally," she said staring at the glass.

"Yeah, I forgot, the drinking age in Vermont is twenty-one."

"Well, it's twenty-one but there's plenty to drink if you know where to go...and with some of the students, grass is the big thing now." She hesitated before adding, "and there's always the ferry of ill repute."

"Ferry of ill repute?"

"It's what everybody calls the ferry that runs from Burlington to New York, where eighteen will get you drunk. The only trick to the ferry is to stay sober enough to remember not to miss the last boat back. I know plenty who've slept on the dock in a drunken stupor."

"So, do you take the ferry of ill repute?"

"Once in a while. I think I drank more in high school than I do now."

"High school?"

"Yeah, Al's brother Jules took care of us on that."

"What—are you tellin' me he used to get you guys booze?"

"No. He and some other guy you and Dusty used to hang around with...what was his name?"

"You mean Jamie?"

"Yeah, Jamie. That's the guy. The five of you...the infamous Five-Cent Gang," she laughed. She touched my hand as she did so and it was a touch I was now accustomed to. Cil seemed to have a way with giving me just the right caress at just the right time in just the right place.

"How do you know about The Five-Cent Gang?"

"Are you kidding?" she laughed again. "There wasn't much you guys did that I didn't know about. I was the one who taught you and Dusty how to pick up the extension without getting caught, remember? You seem to forget I was the original Nancy Drew girl. I could always tell when you guys were up to something. Plus Dusty was never a very good liar. Probably why he made a good cop—or would have." The addition of the last words caused a momentary shared silence.

"You were telling me about Jules." I said, trying to resuscitate the conversation.

"Oh yeah. Well anyway, in high school, Jules and that Jamie guy used to make fake IDs and sell 'em to kids who were underage. Photos and everything...then they would sneak into the library and seal them in plastic with Mrs. Getty's laminating machine. They were pretty close to perfect. I guess they made a good penny on them too. I mean, that guy Jamie always had some kind of a scam going on."

I brought her up to speed on Jamie's new lifestyle and spewed out bits of conversation to be polite, but my mind was still focused on just how much she might know about The Five-Cent Gang. Did she know anything about the D&H bridge caper or the safe deposit boxes? "Did Dusty ever tell you any stories about your Aunt Ethel and Uncle Ray?"

"What kind of stories?"

"Oh, nothing," I said. "I was just looking at your drink there and remembered Ethel used to like vodka but she couldn't hold her liquor so your Uncle Ray gave her drinks at parties and got her all giggly. Then she'd get up and dance for everybody. Dusty told me about it and you holding that drink made me think about it."

"Nope," she said. "Never heard that one," and her voice had an odd tone that continued to leave doubts about how much she actually knew. I realized if our relationship continued, I would, at some point, have to tell her something about it. It was 'the when' and the 'how much' I wasn't sure about.

On Sunday, I made the customary drive to the Greyhound terminal. Later in the day my own drive to Cortland was done in high spirits. We were both disappointed about not seeing each other until spring break, but we agreed on scheduled phone calls.

My uncertainty about what Cil knew or didn't know presented the final loose end—that magical last piece to the puzzle. The remainder of the money remained in my safe deposit box and I knew Dusty's request to give his share to Cil, would be tricky.

"Just dribble the money out to her in small amounts, so she won't realize it," he had told me. "Tell her you hit a long shot at the track," he laughed.

Neither of those scenarios would actually be believable and we both realized it at the time. We also assumed nothing would happen to either one of us. But it had happened—and now I was in a corner trying to punch my way out.

"I never got to buy her that bike," he complained. "That stupid green bike she always mooned over. So, if anything happens to me, maybe you can get her the car she begged my father to get her when she went away to school. The Mustang—and make it green—better yet, a green convertible. Yeah, she'd like a convertible." They were words that now echoed in my mind and I heard them all the way to the dealership.

* * * * *

DURING A LONG WEEKEND in February, I made the drive to see Aunt Ethel and took out enough money to cover the Mustang.

"I don't have a green convertible," the dealer in Cortland confessed. "I could get one here if you want to pay the transport cost. I checked around and there's one in Rochester but I'd have to have it delivered here."

The delivery coincided with the spring thaw and I told Cil I would drive to Burlington to pick her up in lieu of her taking the bus home.

"I want to see your new place," I told her, trying to provide a rational explanation for an illogical drive. My plan was to drive the Mustang and surprise her with its presentation as a token of Dusty's love and affection. She and her roommate had moved off campus and were renting a small farmhouse on the outskirts of the city. After all my lecturing to Jules about being cautious in spending the money, I was the first to break the rule. I had my story ready and I felt it would be an easier sell in Burlington rather than explaining to her parents.

Her roommate left before my arrival and I pulled the Mustang into the yard and parked it under a large maple tree. It seemed to be the perfect setting as the late afternoon sunlight streamed through its branches and danced around the chrome. It was the racing green she had wanted and I had stopped to put the top down just before getting to the house. I hadn't reached the porch steps when she came out the front door and screamed at the sight of the car.

"Oh my God," she yelled. "I'm so jealous. That's the car I always wanted. I begged my father to get it for me for graduation. How did you ever swing it? I thought you were struggling along with student loans."

"It's a little gift from your brother," I told her.

"From Dusty? What do you mean?"

I realized my statement still hadn't registered that the car was for her. "It's yours," I said, holding up the keys.

"What do you mean it's mine?"

"I couldn't really say anything before today. It's been a surprise a long time in coming. Actually, it's Dusty's surprise. He put a little money away every week when he started working on the force. He told me he wanted to get it for you...said when you went to college you wanted it. He just didn't have enough saved then. He kept the money in a little box in his room...told me if anything happened to him to make sure you got it." She seemed to be buying the story, so I continued. "Remember when I went to his room after the funeral? I took the money out of the box. It just happened that I had to wait on getting the right car. That took a little doing." As I told my tale, she circled the car with an appreciative eye.

"I figured if I drove it here, you could drive it to Waterton tomorrow."

"Tomorrow?" she asked with a raised eyebrow. "I thought we were driving back today."

"Well, it's kind of late in the day and I figured with your roommate gone, it'd be a shame to waste an evening alone. She is gone, right?"

"Very gone," she said smiling. "But I have to drive it. Let me change and we can go out to eat. There's not much food in the house anyway."

We took the Mustang to Henry's Diner, a favorite eating place frequented by the UVM students. Cil proved to be a natural behind the wheel and she insisted on leaving the top down, despite the coolness of early spring. The smile never left her face and watching her enjoyment of the moment gave me great pleasure. With classes ended, only a few townspeople occupied Henry's and we slid into a booth that offered some privacy. It was somewhere between bites of her burger, that she started to question the car. I believe she was too excited during my initial explanation to have any rational thoughts about Dusty's gift.

"I know you said Dusty was putting money aside to buy the car for me but, you know, I don't think he worked long enough to put that much away. You didn't add to it, did you?"

"No, I'd like to say I did, but it was all Dusty. He probably started saving even before the job. We used to make a fair amount just on work around the neighborhood."

"You never made *that* much. We're talking about a car here. You're not trying to hide something from me, are you? I mean he wasn't on the take or anything. Isn't that what they call it when a cop looks the other way on things. Because I would never believe anything like that."

"Of course he wasn't on the take. You know better than that. It was his money and he wanted to spend it on you. You remember that green bike you always wanted? He was going to get that for you back in the sixth grade. He just couldn't make enough to pull it off. I guess I could return the car and get the bike for you now if you think it's too much. He probably figured the car would be a better idea. He knew you wanted the Mustang. Just be happy with it and leave it at that."

The whole story was close enough to being the truth that I felt it was time for full disclosure. We finished our burgers in silence and I waited until we sat over a dish of sherbet to summon up the needed courage.

"Truth of the matter is, Dusty and I happened to come into some extra money a while back."

"You and Dusty?"

"Yeah, well, me and Dusty and the rest of us. You know, Jules and Al and Jamie."

"What do you mean, you came into some money. You gonna tell me you guys robbed a bank?"

"Fact of the matter is, we did come into some money illegally, but it was a long time ago. We were kids for chrissake—back in sixth grade."

"And you're telling me that Dusty was mixed up with it? I mean, what are you talkin' about, came into what money?"

"There was this guy—he was kinda like a bag man. He ran money from The Pit. You remember the owner? A guy named Eddie? Anyway, Eddie used to make book outta that place and, well, it's a long story but we came up with a lame-brained plan to rob the guy that made the rounds and picked up the money."

Cil stopped short of putting a spoonful of sherbet into her mouth. "And?"

"And I guess things got a little out of hand. We got in a bit over our heads. Anyway, we robbed the guy all right but, as it turned out, he was making a run with a lot more money than we thought and, well, to make a long story short, Dusty and I sat on a big pile of money for a long time."

The spoon was now empty and she pointed it at me and spoke as if she was a DA and I was on the witness stand. "Well, if Eddie was a bookmaker, didn't the guys he worked for ask a few questions?"

"That's just it. We sat on it because the money belonged to some syndicate guys."

"Oh jeezus, well, you've got to give it back. You can't take money from those types of people." She said it as if returning the money was like returning a shirt with the wrong neck size. "They'll hunt you down."

"It's a little late for that." I told her, and I continued to fill her in on some of the details and the part we each played. I explained my role in getting the money to the beehive, including my escape from the fat man, but omitted my encounter with the hobo.

She sat and listened while I gave her the bits of information I felt she could handle. I made no mention of the confrontation Dusty and I had with the fat man that sent him spiraling over the cliff. I continued with talk of the Baldwin—its disappearance and its six-year absence, then reappearing with the money still wedged in the bootlegger's hole.

"So you're telling me you guys stole money when you were in the sixth grade and none of you spent any of it or ever got caught?"

"That's what I'm telling you and don't forget, it went missing for six years. The fact is, Dusty wasn't even in favor of stealing the money in the first place. He voted against the plan, but in The Five-Cent Gang, majority ruled."

"Gee, how democratic for a bunch of sixth graders. How did you vote?" As she asked the question she unconsciously took a spoonful of sherbet.

"I voted with Dusty but the outcome was predetermined, if you know what I mean. The other three were all for it."

"And that's the money you used to buy the car."

The tone of her question told me she wasn't comfortable with the thought of owning a car that was purchased with stolen money.

"No, that's not what I'm telling you. Dusty *did* save the money for the car and he was going to give it to you at the end of the school year." I lied. "I was his back-up plan and had strict instructions on making sure you got it if anything ever happened to him. We figured nothing would...I mean, there hasn't been a cop killed in Waterton in a million years."

She sat and poked at the sherbet in her dish, which had turned into a soft mound of sludge.

"Anyway, Dusty and I agreed that if anything happened to either one of us, the other would do right by the money. I'd see that you got his share and he was to do the same for me and make sure that somehow my parents got mine. The car has nothing to do with it," I lied again.

"I need to think," she said, pushing her dish away. "And I need to get out of here."

●　●　●　●　●

THE RIDE HOME WAS quiet. I drove and Cil stared out the windshield. She said nothing until we got out of the city and onto the back road that led to the farmhouse.

"So this car was bought with Dusty's money," she said, breaking the silence.

"Yes, and I'll see you get his share of the other money."

"I don't want it. Give it away or keep it yourself, I don't care. I don't want to be involved. I don't even want to know how much…or anything else about it…or talk about it again."

I suffered through another mile of silence, but it felt good to know she finally had all the facts. Looking back, I should've let her digest everything for a week or two but I've never had the best sense of timing.

Her tone seemed to have changed from disbelief to ambivalence and, seeing an opening, I blundered into a hornet's nest with the misconstrued thought that a humorous approach might work best. "So, now that you know I'm fat with cash, maybe you'll consider marrying me." I mistakenly made the statement as nonchalant as possible and unfortunately, that was exactly the way she took it.

"Marry you! If I did marry you that would be the only reason," she mocked back. "It certainly wouldn't be for your charm or good looks."

I assumed her response was intended to be humorous but I wasn't sure and the comment put me off my stride. I'd made a mistake in thinking she would jump at the offer. To try and regain some of my dignity, I made a remark about the lack of traffic, which, considering we were on an isolated dirt road in the middle of farm country, put me in a deeper hole.

At the farmhouse we opened a bottle of wine and by the time we crawled into bed, the story of the money seemed to have been put on the back burner—I never did get an answer to my bungled proposal.

I awoke first and relaxed as the morning sun streamed through the cracks in the Venetian blinds. The bed sheet covered only the bottom half of Cil's body and I studied her nakedness that radiated in the soft rays of daylight. She was lying on her side facing me and I placed my finger on her shoulder and gently moved it down her arm, then to her side and finally to her waist where it rose to follow her hip. It was the hip tracing that brought a murmur and a smile and she nestled her face into my neck and then kissed my shoulder. It was quite some time before I finally got up and made breakfast.

● ❀ ● ❀ ●

WE CHATTED OVER COFFEE and made an omelet with leftovers in the fridge. We ate and enjoyed some small talk in the country kitchen.

When the car was packed, I tossed her the key ring to which I had added Dusty's penny. She stared at it for a moment.

"Dusty's?" she asked me.

"Yeah, I guess you're officially a member of the gang now." I told her.

The early morning love-making seemed to have taken the edge off both of us and the ride home was rich with conversation and laughter. There was no mention of The Five-Cent Gang or the fat man or syndicate money.

Cil's parents bought the story of Dusty's unique savings plan and Mr. Barnes seemed to be more concerned about her safety behind the wheel than figuring out where the money came from. Mrs. Barnes was just thrilled that her daughter had the car she had hoped for at graduation and beamed with happy thoughts of Dusty and what a good a brother he was to have done that for Cilla.

Once we returned to school, our contact returned to telephone calls. It had been two weeks since my awkward seeking of Cil's true feelings for me and I followed up with a second bumbling attempt. After a bit of school talk regarding classes that evolved into plans for summer, I gave the proposal pitch a second time.

"So, I never got an answer to the question I asked you in the car a couple of weeks ago."

"Question? What question was that?"

"You know, about whether or not you'd marry me. I mean, now that you know I've got money," This time I did the laughing as the words came out.

"Jeezus, is that really a proposal? I mean, are you really asking me to marry you?"

I took a deep breath. "Yeah, I guess I am."

"You guess you are?" she questioned. "Good!" she yelled.

"Good?" I echoed, not understanding how the word good could possibly hold a tone of such anger.

"Yes, good!" she said again. "Do you remember the day when I was in third grade and some guys in my class were bothering me? It was the day I was on my way home from the baseball field and there were some guys who wouldn't let me pass. They were holding the handlebars of my bike and going through my bag. You and Dusty came along and you told them to get lost or you'd knock their blocks off and they all ran away?"

"No, I can't say that I do," I confessed.

"Well that was the day that I fell in love with you," she yelled. "Why didn't you ask me to marry you then?" she demanded to know.

My mind was in a tailspin as she relayed the incidents of a day I'd long forgotten and I struggled for a response to a ridiculous question. "Well, maybe because I didn't think a marriage between a third grader and a fifth grader would work out that well," I laughed.

"You think it's funny? You think it's funny now? Well let me tell you something August Northrup...if you think you're ever going to get me to marry you it's certainly not going to be over the phone...and you better plan on getting down on one knee to ask...and when you do, you better have some very romantically convincing words in your proposal." It was the last thing she said before she slammed down the phone.

Epilogue

It's been more than twenty years since I made that infamous proposal and, in the passing of those years, there has been much contemplation regarding our fateful day on the bridge. When The Five-Cent Gang decided to rob the fat man, the amount of money in the satchel, although significant, was never expected. The fact that we took more than three million dollars from the mob became a bit unnerving. Yes, we had planned to steal some money, but the thought of taking money from the syndicate coupled with the deaths of two men was never part of the caper.

Now—after living with years of fear and uncertainty—those are things that continue to haunt me. To shoulder such a burden since the age of twelve has been difficult and that peculiar bond, although it held us together, also became an unspoken wedge in our friendships. The D&H Bridge caper put us on another level of consciousness—a level from which we never really recovered. Now, after more than three decades, the recollection seems to hold both an imbalance of conscience as well as a social quandary.

Dusty, my best friend and the first to leave us, was such an honest cop he may have been a deterrent to our wealth when it came to explaining and spending it. But I know he'd be happy with the knowledge that Silly has her Mustang and is loved, watched over, and well cared for.

Our leader, Jamie, who meticulously planned the capers we carried out so blunderfully, was a guy who knew few boundaries. Those thoughts bring forth a smile now. His efforts ironically rewarded him with a new parish gym that provides a diversion for the youths he works with and keeps them out of capers of their own. He and I have remained in touch over the years, but the day he left the diner—the day he turned and flashed his flattened penny—was the last time I ever saw him.

Although the overwhelming resurgence in his religious beliefs remains, he never did become a priest. He did, however, build a parish basketball dynasty that spread throughout the city and continues to grow and serve hundreds of youths each year. Like me, he got married shortly after graduation and, when he's not keeping kids off street corners, he is a dedicated husband and father.

I still think about Al and try to focus on the early days rather than the days following the changes within him. All he ever wanted was enough money to purchase his shopping list of guns. It was unfortunate that, over the years, his lingering guilt was ever-present before weapons of war ended his life. I sometimes believe he found a certain peace in the jungles of Viet Nam—perhaps the answer he needed. If he were still alive, he would certainly be asking Jules and me questions about finding the money and what would we buy and when are we going to buy it and are we going to take any trips and... .

And, of course, there was the disposition of the steam engine. The Baldwin has taken its proud position in the New York State Railroad Museum. It is listed as a donation from Benjamin Faulk. A picture of him pulling the cord to trigger the precious sound of the train's wailing sits beside it—the wail of harmonious dissonance as he would say. The Bill of Sale boasting the one-dollar price he paid sits next to his picture and the curator tells visitors the story of the railroad men and their smuggling of bootlegged liquor from Canada.

In my years of reflection, I have often wondered just how much Mr. Faulk knew about The Five-Cent Gang and my connection with the fat man on that fateful day in the yard. Did he ever find the money in the hole? Did he find it and leave it, knowing I was somehow involved and would see it to its rightful conclusion? Had he welded the rumors and the truth together and forged his own scenario? It would've been just like him to never mention a word of it and at times I was guilt-stricken, believing my old friend would think less of me for possibly being involved in a crime.

In the end it was only Jules and me who reaped any monetary reward. Jules continues to make good on our agreement regarding the spending of the money. He sought and received approval for a business loan and not only bought Mr. Billings's appliance store, but over the years added four Laundromats in Waterton and has plans to add a few more. It turned out to be the perfect business. No one ever knows how many quarters are taken from the machines each week and no one can calculate or dispute his claimed income. He employs students now—students who take care of the cleaning of his Laundromats and deliveries of his appliances—students who, at the end of the week, are paid in cash. The same type of payments he makes to his gardener, his housekeeper, and the local mechanic.

He gives his wife Gloria cash for groceries and frequently treats her to nights out at fine restaurants. His mother has a beautiful home that is nearby, smaller and more manageable than the house he grew up in.

The mortgage is paid by Jules and when I see him around town, I always ask, in the presence of others, how things are going.

"Oh," he says as rehearsed. "You know, I'm gettin' by...tryin' to make ends meet."

The difference for Jules and me—the thing that helps us along—is the knowledge that regardless of how the world is going with employment, the rising cost of living, or the turmoil of Dow Jones, we take comfort in knowing we can always pay our way. The two of us share a secret that provides us with a life of financial security.

But there is always that other presence—that underlying fear that the two of us never discuss despite the passing of so many years. It's the lingering question only we can answer. Was it worth it?

It varies for me. It's a day-to-day thing. Yesterday I stood in my living room and watched my two daughters, ages seven and nine, who will grow out of their childhood and hopefully someday, enter college— a cost I will finance, like other parents, with educational loans. I'll happily repay them with interest. But that was yesterday, while I watched the two of them playing outside. It was a warm summer day and they were spraying each other with the garden hose as they washed their bikes. Our older daughter, Hattie, has a bright green one. Her mother picked it out for her on her ninth birthday.

But today was a different type of day. In the early morning hour, as I was being chased by the fat man, it was Hattie who stole into the bedroom to surprise me. She was dressed in her white cotton nightie with a neck-
line edged with tiny bows of blue ribbon and under the watchful eye of her mother, she walked ever so carefully toward me as I slept.

I was having a difficult time moving my legs in my effort to escape from the fat man. Hattie drew nearer, balancing my surprise cup of coffee on its saucer. Her bare feet tiptoed across the room and her eyes never left the rim of the cup as she came nearer. She became irritated if a bit of coffee sloshed over the cup's edge and spilled into the saucer because she wanted her surprise to be perfect.

It was, perhaps, the hot August sweat dripping from the fat man originating from the heat of the coffee, or perhaps the touch of her hand that startled me back to reality—back from the cliff's edge, that suddenly awakened me, and made me to jump up and knock the cup from her little hands.

I awoke just in time to see the expression on her cherub-like face transform from angelic to horrified. My scream, initiated by the hot coffee drenching my chest and dripping its way to the bed sheets, frightened her into retreat. The dream wasn't new but the witnessing of my nightmare by my daughter caused her to withdraw. Her turning and running to her mother for protection, was a revelation of sorts.

It's that kind of day—that kind of occasional dream that prompts me to question whether or not it was all worth it? The reality of the money versus the bad dreams that go with it.

Because the nightmares are less frequent now but occasionally... I still see the face of the fat man.

* * * * *

Acknowledgements

My thanks to the Friday morning writers' group who I refer to as Brogan's Brigade. (John, Bill, Beth, Caroline, Linda, Barbara, Brendan, and Dan.) Through their insight and encouragement, the kids in *The Five-Cent Gang* grew from childhood to adulthood.

An additional thanks to members Steve, Mary, Susan, and Lisa for their endurance in reading through drafts.

And a special thanks to my editor, Susan Landry, who checks my speling and grammor and makes me look gud.

Back cover photos reproduced by permission:

The Alright Boys:

From the collection of the late John Bignell
through The Library Time Machine
Kensington Central Library
in the Royal Burrough of Kensington
and Chelsea in The United Kingdom

(http://rbkclocalstudies.wordpress.com)

Baseball Boys:

(www.baseballplayamerica.com)

I have always felt poorly for anyone who has never heard the lonely wail of a distant train as it rumbles through the black of night.

—Benjamin Faulk

15574076R00261

Made in the USA
Middletown, DE
13 November 2014